Keep up with the latest news!
Text TBRS to 22828

D1713424

Bankroll Squad: The Beginning

one

Kyla eyed Malcolm's dark skinned, muscular arms as he held the steering wheel at the red light.

Errrrrrck!,The lime green Lamborghini Gallardo went from zero to sixty when the light turned green; then slowed down to 53 to avoid a collision. It then switched from the left lane to the right lane, passed two vehicles and sped up to 72 mph in a matter of seconds.

"Malcolm, why do you always drive like a mad man when I get in the car?"

Malcolm swerved the wheels slightly to the right to avoid the potential damage from a pothole, and then straightened the steering wheel. He slowed the $200,000 vehicle down so that he could safely make it on to the expressway.

"Kyla, don't start with me. I was driving like this before you got in my car."

"Oh, stop flexin'. You know you just tryna get home to your white bitch!"

Malcolm immediately broke his speed and shifted to the emergency lane. He slowed to a halt, took a deep breath, then reached over and grabbed Kyla's throat with his right hand and said, "I'm sick of you talking about my wife all the time Kyla. I'm sick of it!"

Kyla fought back for a few seconds, but from experience she knew that he was strong enough to have his way, no matter what it was that she did. Malcolm let go of her neck upon seeing a police car ride past him on the way to combat crime. She wheezed briefly, then tried to breathe in as much oxygen as possible as fast as possible. Sobbing, she leaned downward and covered her face with her hands.

Malcolm maneuvered the Lamborghini back onto the expressway, occasionally glancing at Kyla. "I'm sorry Ky. It's just that. .. you know how I get when—"

"Malcolm! Stop apologizing to me. No amount of apologies in the world can justify everything that you've put me through and continue putting me through, you heartless bastard! You left me for a white woman!"

"Ky, why is it always about race with you?"

"Because you left me!"

"Well, if I'm so damn heartless, why do you still deal with me? Why are you wit' me right now?"

Kyla was in tears. Malcolm hated when Kyla started crying because he already knew that he was wrong for what he'd done. He'd hurt her beyond repair. He'd made her a criminal. He'd destroyed her innocence, her dreams, and their engagement. He knew that she loved him. It had been two years since he'd left her and she still did everything he asked her to do. She still had not moved on; he was the first and last lover she'd had.

He reached over and tried to caress her shoulder, but upon contact she jumped. She is scared of me, Malcolm thought to himself. He

6

reached out to hold her hand with his free hand and she reluctantly allowed him to do so. After a few moments, he again placed his hand on her shoulder and attempted to caress her. This time she allowed it; she had let her guard down. Malcolm just felt right to her; he was her comforter.

"I love you Malcolm."

Malcolm glanced in Kyla's direction and noticed that she was gazing at him intensely. He regarded her for a moment. Kyla was gorgeous. She was of black and Puerto Rican descent, had long, curly hair and perfect bronze skin. She was 5'5" and weighed 128 pounds. Kyla was everything that anyone could ask for from a woman. At times, though, her negative traits overrode her positive traits. She could be cool one minute, and the next minute she could be a jealous, crazed maniac. The moment that she felt insecure about something, no matter how minute, she never let go of the subject; and most of the time, those moments led to violence.

$$S\sim S\sim S\sim S\sim S$$

Two years ago, Malcolm's best friend Catfish had been planning a proposal to his girlfriend, Tricia. He had shelled out

$50,000 on a splendid 5 carat diamond engagement ring. Catfish couldn't make it to the jewelry store to pick up the custom ring when it was done because he was in Miami on official business. It was completed December 19th and he wouldn't be back in town until the 21st. The jewelry store, however, would be closing for the holidays starting on the 20th. So, Catfish called and left a brief message on Malcolm's home answering machine. The message said: "The ring is finished. Pick it up, Mal. Or, if you want, you can send somebody. J.K.

knows. Holla."

At the time, Malcolm was sleeping and Kyla didn't want to disturb him so she took it upon herself to retrieve the ring. When she arrived at the store, J.K., the owner, was not present. Instead the salesperson gave her the ring gift-wrapped and said, "You must be Tricia. You are a lucky girl." Kyla gave the salesperson a forced smile and left the jewelry store with a rage building up. She climbed into her new Range Rover and called Malcolm right away. She didn't even take the time to ask legitimate questions before she started firing off her rampant accusations.

"Malcolm! You bastard, you dirty snake in the grass, you sick trick—"

"Hey man, what the hell is wrong with you?" Malcolm interrupted.

At the time, Kyla's temper had flared up like a campfire and could not be controlled. "You mothball son of a bitch! Who the hell is Tricia?"

Malcolm sighed. "Is this another one of your pathetic accusations, Kyla? If so, then you—" The phone clicked off on the other end. "Hello? Kyla? Son of a bitch!"

And that was the last time Malcolm heard from Kyla for at least a month and a half. Forty-five days later, when she finally realized who Tricia was, Malcolm had moved on. Kyla tried desperately to reconcile and reconnect with Malcolm, but to no avail. After she remained persistent about it for close to three weeks, Malcolm told her that the only way she could be with him was to become a part of the Bankroll Squad. Eager to show him that she loved him, she ditched medical school and hung onto his every word and command. Even after he married someone else, she remained the Bonnie to his Clyde. After a while, she soon became fascinated with the squad's lifestyle and even got tattoos to show her loyalty. On her right breast, the tattoo read 'Bankroll' and her left breast had the word 'Squad'.

Although Malcolm was the leader of the Squad, Kyla quickly became the most prized member. Partly because of her ability to go to Colombia and negotiate prices for bulk kilo shipments of pure cocaine. On one deal in particular, she'd negotiated a price of $6,000 per kilo and sold all 1,000 kilos for $14,000 a piece before Malcolm even knew she had them to begin with. He sent her on a private jet with 6 million in cash and she came back with 14 million dollars. She was also coveted because of the 100 girl international and cross country prostitution ring that she controlled. She came up with the idea and worked out all the kinks, including recruiting 100 girls; then she'd tested it without Malcolm's knowledge. After a week of "testing", she brought the idea to Malcolm along with about $500,000 in pure profit.

The girls made between $1,500 and $3,000 a day. A piece. She brought Malcolm about $800 per girl per day. With that addition, it made the Bankroll Squad the number nine ranked crime ring in the country. Before the addition of prostitution, the Squad wasn't even in the top 10.

$~$~$~$~$

"You passed the exit, Malcolm! Damn baby, something must be on your mind."

Malcolm sharply snatched his hand away from Kyla's shoulder and placed it on the 200 grand steering wheel. Kyla reached over and started pulling down Malcolm's zipper.

"Ky, what are you doing? Tryna' make me wreck?"

She knew Malcolm never wore boxers or underwear and wrapped her hand around his suddenly erect shaft.

"Stop Ky."

Kyla pulled it out his pants and went down on him.

"Move Ky; I mean it. Stop!"

Kyla sucked, and then made a catlike purring noise.

"What if I don't wanna stop?"

As she went down again, Malcolm suddenly exited off the expressway.

"Ky, get out. Now."

The car came to a screeching halt. Kyla sat up looking confused and disappointed. She looked around the area.

"Where the hell am I, Malcolm?"

Malcolm unlocked her door and picked up his iPhone.

"Who you callin'? Why you actin' so funny?" She tapped her fingers against her knee as she waited for his response.

Malcolm ignored her and spoke into his phone. "Catfish? Yeah, this Malcolm, man. Aye, I'm right outside of your condo and I need you to take Ky to get her truck. Huh? Nawl, she called me and asked me to pick her up from the mall earlier; she had taken a cab there but I think she was really just setting me up. She's in one of her little moods, Cat.

A'ight. Peace."

Kyla was bouncing her knee up and down nervously, her hands in her lap clasped together.

"Is that how it is, Boss?"

Malcolm rolled his eyes and replied, "Kyla Brent, you know I'm married! I don't know why you're in denial."

Kyla sighed loudly. "So what if I'm in denial? I love you Malcolm. I'm not just here because of money like your damn trophy wife! She doesn't even do anything for you. Why can't you see this, damnit! I don't need Catfish to take me anywhere."

She climbed out of the Lamborghini and proceeded to walk. Malcolm pulled off staring at Kyla on the rearview camera display. She was giving him the deluxe middle finger. He gave the machine gas and it almost ripped the pavement apart. Zero to sixty in the duration of a sneeze, a "bless you," and a "thanks".

$~$~$~$~$

Malcolm arrived at his lavish estate about twenty-five minutes later. To even gain entrance onto the premises he had to scan his thumbprint and index finger at the primary control center. After making it past that gate, he had another gate that was operated by actual people. Actually, they were trained snipers converted to bodyguards.

"Good evening, Mr. Powers."

Malcolm Powers simply waved and kept moving forward. The Lambo moved swiftly down the two mile paved driveway en route to his mansion. It was mid- spring and the pine trees lining the pathway

11

were a rich shade of green and gave the pathway a mystic effect due to the shade. The Powers' mansion, equipped with some 27 rooms, had an indoor pool and studio. Malcolm was so avid of a car collector, that instead of building a garage to house the vehicles, he had an underground closed quarter's parking lot. He pulled up to his home and cursed for having to wait on his butler to come out and park the car. He blew the horn and watched as the door to the mansion opened up and his butler, a nervous acting bookworm, ran out so that he could park the vehicle.

"Jeffrey, I've told you over and over to keep alert and pay attention to what's going on around here. You didn't see me coming with all of this surveillance posted?"

Jeffrey wiped the sweat off his face with a white handkerchief. "I'm sorry Mr. Powers. I was helping to move your library from the right wing to the left wing as you requested sir. I may park your car now, sir."

Malcolm exited the vehicle and went into his home.

two

Jennifer was 5'9" and weighed 122 pounds. She had glowing white skin, deep dimples, voluptuous breasts, long brunette/blond hair, and no job. Not only was she absent of an occupation, but she was also absent of a hustle. She was without goals, but was filled to the rim with constant requests for material items. Malcolm was first attracted to her because of her beauty. He'd launched his Crispy Frisbee potato chip linc around the time that Kyla had left him, and needed a model for his debut TV commercial for the brand. He'd launched the brand in five states and planned to expand to at least 25 states if the brand proved successful regionally on the small market. He'd held open call auditions, but found women more suitable to be in music videos than a potato chip commercial. He had originally planned for Kyla to be the face of the brand, but her sudden disappearance sent him on a sudden search.

One morning Malcolm was leaving the Galleria mall in Houston, TX; while opening the door to his baby blue Bentley, he exchanged flirtatious looks with a beautiful white lady headed to her black BMW 650 convertible. She had on a plaid Versace skirt and had long brunette hair with golden blond streaks. She had Versace bags in her hand and she gave off the aura of a celebrity actress. That day they exchanged numbers and that night they went out to have dinner.

He found out that she wasn't a celebrity, but nevertheless fell in love with her personality. It was the first time that he had ever met a woman who was just as fashion savvy as he was. She expressed her love and desire to live the good life openly; something that Kyla expressed no interest in whatsoever. Jennifer knew all about cars, rims, clothes, upscale clubs, restaurants and even private hotels.

She never knew that Malcolm did anything illegal, she just took his word that he was a successful entrepreneur. Jennifer trusted Malcolm and did what was asked of her. Catfish had even noticed that Malcolm was in a happier mood with Jennifer than with Kyla. Jenny always tried to cook breakfast and dinner at home when they weren't eating out and always put a smile on Malcolm's face when he was in the worst of moods. She cleaned, trusted and entertained as if it was the end of the world if it didn't happen. Whenever the two of them went shopping or attended any place together, onlookers gawked at the couple in amazement and envy. Black women were sick to their stomachs upon watching them go out on the town and be carefree and happy. White men simply turned their heads in disgust and hoped that the image would soon fade from their memory.

On the contrary, black men and white women simply wished that they could live so elegantly; if just for a day. In the beginning, it didn't matter that Jenny had no job; it just mattered that she had his heart. He asked her how she'd gotten her car and how she was surviving and she expressed that her father had passed away and left her with $250,000 in insurance money. She asked him if he needed some investment money for his potato chip brand and Malcolm thought the gesture to be cute. He smiled at her, politely declined, and dropped down to one knee. That was one of her happiest moments. She accepted the engagement and they were married four months later.

$~$~$~$~$

"Jen, what the fuck is wrong with you? You look like shit and smell like a liquor barrel. What the hell?" Malcolm asked after walking through the door.

Jennifer's face was red, from both anger and exhaustion. Malcolm knew that the look on her face meant trouble.

"Malcolm," she screamed.

"You lied to me!" She slung a Vodka bottle in his direction and missed.

The bottle shattered against the marble floor. Another bottle came at him; it was half full of liquor. He tried to catch it so that it wouldn't fall but it slipped out of his grasp and shattered, spilling Vodka on his shoes and his creased khakis.

"Jen… Jen, get a hold of yourself!" he exclaimed.

He went toward her, arms outstretched in an effort to hold and comfort her, no matter what the reason was that she was in distress.

"Don't come anywhere near me Malcolm! You lied!"

Damn, this is the second distraught woman in one day, Malcolm thought.

"What did I lie about baby? What's wrong? Talk to me please."

Stumbling, she walked promptly into the kitchen and made her way to the sink where raw chicken lay. Without speaking, she continued coating the chicken in flour. But something was wrong with the scenario. One of his business briefcases was open on the counter. Damn, he thought, she found my cellar. Malcolm kept a hidden

15

underground cellar underneath the library that was formally on the right wing of the mansion. There were a few rare wines there, but the main purpose of it was to keep what he called "fallback"; extra kilos in case a shipment went horribly wrong or in case of a drought. Since he now dealt directly with Colombia via airplane, a drought would only happen if Hell froze over.

"Jen, is that my shit?" he asked.

Jennifer started laughing hysterically; like a crazed maniac almost.

"What shit, Malcolm? Huh? What is it Malcolm? Cocaine?"

Malcolm just glared at her and she thought his anger was amusing.

"Oh… looky, looky; you're mad now! Hahaha! You're mad? You put my life in jeopardy and you got the right to be mad?"

Jennifer dumped a zip lock bag of cocaine into the sink, turned on the tap and let the water wash it away. Malcolm grabbed her by the waist, picked her up and attempted to take her out of the kitchen; but she kicked everything in reach, forcing him to let her go since she was kicking coke-filled zip lock bags to the floor as well. She turned and faced him, tears rolling down her face and madness building up in his.

"I hate you Malcolm!" She swung at him but he grabbed her arms and jammed her up against the wall. In a dangerous voice, Malcolm spoke sternly and precisely.

"You hate me? You live a life of luxury with no job and you hate me?"

Jennifer was crying. "You're hurting me Malcolm."

"Fuck that, Jen. Listen to me! You drive Bentleys, wear million dollar jewelry, and live in a multi-million dollar mansion and you have the nerve to complain about how the money was made? You must be out of your rabbit ass mind!"

A tear rolled down Jennifer's face and her body was trembling. "Let go of me Malcolm. Now!" she shrieked.

Malcolm let go of her and watched as she walked out of the kitchen in slow motion. She was hurt; damn near on the verge of going into shock. Malcolm approached her and put his arms around her, stopping her in place. She stopped and closed her eyes in an attempt to control her crying. She felt Malcolm's warm breath caress the back of her neck, sending erotic shudders down her spine.

"Baby," Malcolm whispered in her ear now, in a soothing voice,

"You know that I love you Jen; you know that. I've loved you since day one and I'll continue to love you until the day that the love that I give you is not returned."

When Jennifer turned around to face him, Malcolm saw that her whole face was wet with tears. Seeing how much hurt he had placed upon her hurt him. He kissed her on the lips.

"I'm sorry Jennifer, but this is who I am; and either you're going to accept me or reject me."

Malcolm turned away from her and went to change his clothes. Jen followed him into the bedroom. "Malcolm, where are you going?"

Malcolm finished changing his clothes without replying.

Jen was furious at his silence. "Malcolm!"

Without speaking, Malcolm walked out of the bedroom and went to retrieve the keys to his baby blue Bentley.

"Malcolm, you don't even have the fuckin' courtesy to answer your wife's question?" Jennifer was in a rage.

Malcolm kept ignoring her for a few more moments, then he glared at his wife with one of the most menacing looks that he could possibly put together.

"Jennifer, I'm giving you some time to think about what I said. You're going to have to accept me —"

Jennifer cut him off before he could finish and finished his statement for him. "Or reject you! I heard you the first time you said it

Malcolm. What do you think I am? Some type of deaf tramp or something?"

Malcolm walked out the house. Jen followed behind him; she was beyond furious.

"Where the flying fuck are you headed, Malcolm?"

Malcolm tossed the keys to Jeffrey so that he could bring his vehicle around for him. He turned and faced Jen one last time before leaving.

"Don't ask me a question and interrupt me when I'm giving you an answer and then turn right back around and ask me the same damn thing again. I'm going to the Power Building; I have a couple of things on my schedule that I need to attend to. Afterwards, I'm going to check out this nightclub that this guy is trying to sell. If I think it's worth it, then I'll buy it. In the meantime, you need to take a nap; sleep off some of the alcohol that you've consumed today. Then, when you wake up, think about what I said."

Jen stood still with her arms crossed as she watched her husband climb into the convertible Bentley. He let the top down and searched for his Young Jeezy "Trap or Die" CD. He found it and inserted it into the CD deck.

"Jen, put the rest of my shit back where you got it from."

He reached his hand out so that she could put her hand in his; she did, then he violently pulled her against the car so that he could enforce the tone of his next statement.

"And Jennifer! Make sure that Jeffrey doesn't start running his mouth about what he's seen. Your little outrageous outburst could be my downfall! Don't let it happen. Is that understood?"

"Yes Malcolm."

Then he released her hand and turned the volume up in the car. He pulled off, leaving Jennifer standing in the same spot with her arms crossed again, pouting. Even after he drove out of the gate and past security, and even after she could no longer see her husband's vehicle anymore, she could still hear the sound system in the distance.

I'm the realest nigga' in it/ You already know/ Got trap of the year/4 times in a row…

$~$~$~$~$

Catfish was the head of Bankroll Squad's Special Victims Unit. The SVU had been specifically developed for the people who either refused to pay their debts to any member of the Bankroll Squad or for people who owed money and decided to run and hide instead of paying their

19

bills. Catfish was 6'4", 270 pounds, and presented a most intimidating presence to all violators. He kept a.45 Magnum with a silencer on it that he used efficiently and effectively. He had a brand new Cadillac Escalade with custom paint, rims and a custom interior; but he had to be reminded by Malcolm to drive the SUV. Catfish could care less about being flashy because he was so dedicated to his job. Even though Malcolm paid Catfish a million dollars a month, Catfish still continued to ride around in his black van. It was his signature. Whenever Catfish had to pull out that.45 and use it, the body always went inside that back seat of the van until he could go burn and dispose of the body properly.

Today's Special Victim was a guy named Waller. Waller just didn't know how to keep his mouth shut. Catfish had heard from a friend of his that Waller was down at the pool hall a couple nights ago bragging that the Bankroll Squad had fronted him 10 kilos of cocaine and only wanted $15,000 each for them. This angered Catfish because Waller was running his damn mouth for unnecessary reasons and making the Squad hot. Catfish had to stop this before it got back around to Malcolm; because if it got back around to Malcolm without the situation already handled, he would be thoroughly pissed. He would also think that Catfish was slipping on his job.

$~$~$~$~$

"Get in the van Kyla," Catfish said from his van.

Kyla stared straight ahead and kept walking up the sidewalk. It was a pretty spring evening and she had every intention to take a walk to the hotel four blocks away and catch a cab to her house. But it was Catfish…

"Kyla, get in the muthafuckin' van. Now!" Kyla glared into the van.

"Stop fuckin' cussing me, you idiot! I don't need a damn ride; I'm fine."

Catfish slammed on the brakes, threw the gear into park and jumped out the van. As soon as his feet touched the ground, she swiftly walked to the passenger side door.

"Stop playing, Cat. I don't want no problems; I'm gettin' in!"

They both had to be at the Power Building in three hours and Kyla wanted to go to her house and get a couple hours of sleep since she had been up all night.

"Cat, drop me off at my house if you don't mind," she said.

"I'm on my way to go do something," he replied.

"Yeah I know. I assume you're on your way to my house to drop me off so that I can get some rest," she retorted.

"No, this is urgent. If I'm forced to drop you off anywhere that you can rest, it'll be the ocean." There was silence for a few moments.

"Catfish, I'm really sleepy and I'd appreciate it if you would just..."

Kyla's voice trailed off when she saw Catfish pull his blue gun case from underneath his seat. She knew that Catfish was nothing to play with even though they had developed a sisterly-brotherly type bond. Sure Catfish joked around with her a lot, but he rarely smiled; so it was hard to tell when he was serious or not.

"What's so damn urgent that you can't take me to the house?" she asked.

Without answering her question, he slowly merged off to a side street. The street had a vacant warehouse on it with a fence around it; the fence had a "No Trespassing" sign on it. There was a residential home located diagonally across the street from the warehouse and there was a U-turn area at the end of the street. Catfish speed dialed a number with his cell phone as he slowed to a crawl near the entrance of the warehouse parking lot. Prince Tron was on the other line.

"4530 Wekin Street, right?" Catfish asked.

"Yeah, how far away are you Catfish?"

"Shit, I'm already here man. Where the hell am I gon' park my van at?" Catfish replied.

"Damn Cat; you drove that big muthafucka? Hurry up and park it behind the warehouse before you start looking suspicious."

"A'ight Tron. Where you at?"

"I'll meet you there in about 10 minutes; stay put Cat."

"A'ight Tron. One."

"One."

Prince Tron was in control of accounts and balances and kept a long standing direct relationship with Catfish. He was the man who looked into his computer at the end of the week and reported the overdue accounts to Catfish. He was also adept at finding the location of the overdue account holders, regardless of where they were hiding. And since he was good at finding people, Catfish had requested information on the whereabouts of Waller. 4530 Wekin Street was the address of Waller's baby mother's house, and according to Prince Tron, no one was home at this hour except for Waller. Catfish pulled his van around the back of the warehouse and parked it. He pulled his .45 out of the gun case with the silencer already assembled, along with the infrared beam. He quickly explained the situation to Kyla, who immediately understood why he hadn't taken her straight to her house. Tron pulled up beside Catfish in his Porsche truck, shut off the engine and climbed out.

"Kyla, stay put in this van. If we get any visitors before we come out, call my cell phone."

"Okay Cat, I'll do that. Leave the keys so that I can listen to the radio."

Catfish left her the keys, got out and greeted Tron. Tron had a custom made crown medallion hanging around his neck that had every bit of $100,000 worth of diamonds encrusted on it. And for some reason, even when he went with Catfish to do dirty work, he always kept his crown on. No matter how bloody the situation got, that chain stayed on his neck. Catfish had on his usual attire; black t-shirt and black jeans. Black gloves and black shoes. Black gun, black bag, black diamond watch. A person could take one look at Catfish and instantly be reminded that they would one day die. Tron and Catfish crossed the street and knocked on Waller's door. Catfish kept knocking and Tron kept ringing the doorbell.

Knock, knock, knock, ring, ring. Then the sound of footsteps approaching.

Then a voice. "Who is it?"

It was Waller indeed on the other side of the door.

"Cat and Tron!" Catfish said in his deep, husky voice.

Waller opened the door smiling.

"What's up, my niggaz? Y'all come on in."

Prince Tron and Catfish walked into Waller's house, scoping out the scene just in case there were surprises. Waller suddenly looked puzzled.

"How did y'all know I was here or that I even stayed on this street?"

Silence from Catfish; Prince Tron asked Waller a question.

"Waller, is anybody else here with you?"

"Naw Tron, why you ask me that?" he replied.

"Because I got something that I wanna show you. It's some private shit Wally."

Waller was starting to look suspicious now; his forehead wrinkled up and his eyes started darting back and forth from Catfish to Prince Tron. The telephone rang and he jumped; startled. He turned in the direction of the ringing phone; when he turned back around there was a sawed-off shotgun in his face, sponsored by Prince Tron. Also there was a red shaded light in his eyes. He wiped his eye and realized that it was an infrared beam from a .45 magnum.

"Wh-wh-what did I do?" he stammered.

Waller was shaking and was on the verge of tears.

"Pl-pl-please don't kill me. I have a child to raise. Please!" he pleaded.

Catfish hit him on the side of the head with the butt of the pistol. Waller collapsed and fell through the living room coffee table.

"Tie him up Tron, and give him a shot to keep him out for a few hours."

Prince Tron tied him up and gave him a 6 hour knockout serum while Catfish pulled a small case out of his black Kenneth Cole bag.

"Cat, what the hell is you doing, man?"

Catfish glared at Tron as if he had lost his mind for questioning him. Cat opened up the small case and pulled out a needle with thread running through it. Wasting no time, he proceeded to thread Waller's mouth shut.

$~$~$~$~$

Every section leader of the Bankroll Squad was in attendance for the meeting at the Power Building. Kyla, of Negotiations and Special Services, Catfish of Special Victims Unit, Prince Tron of Accounts and Balances, Brink of Aerial Transportation, Marco the Associate Director, Pam of Contamination Control, and their leader, their boss, the brain to the body; Malcolm Powers.

three

Malcolm had graduated from Georgia State University, after majoring in psychology and minoring in business management. He'd started hustling in order to pay for his expensive education and had had every intention of leaving the "game" alone and getting a top-notch job once he graduated; but after he graduated, he realized that his dream job of becoming a psychologist would never be able to match the salary he was making by hustling. And he was only hustling part-time. By his calculations and with his connect, he figured that he could become a millionaire in 12 months maximum.

Along his path to millions, other people with the same drive and motivation reached out to him for assistance. He couldn't turn away everyone that approached him and still expect to continue maintaining the kind of business he was involved in, which at the time was coke and weed; so he put his ego aside and recruited a very small group of thoroughbreds to roll with him. To keep everybody happy, he kept everybody paid. To keep everybody paid meant that more money was required. He decided that the best way to maximize a group's earning potential was to first get organized, and only after organization, would expansion follow. If everybody knew which role they played, then there would be fewer questions down the line. And fewer questions meant less talking; thus less talking meant more thinking.

Taking a cue from his business management courses, he knew that a business or organization, no matter how big or small needed an identity; to have an identity, a name was required. So, he named his organization The Bankroll Squad. After making his first million, he soon realized that taking control of a group of hustlers to get paid and then leaving them behind would be detrimental to his health. He had assumed a responsibility as a leader and there would be no easy, quick exit, no matter where he'd graduated from. So he set about organizing The Bankroll Squad, and assigned creative job titles to his employees.

Brink, of Aerial Transportation, was simply the pilot that flew their private jets to pick up whatever was required, no matter where it was located. Marco, the Associate Director simply made sure that all of the "workers", or associates were fulfilling the supply and demand in the streets for coke, weed, ecstasy, LSD, heroin and crack. Pam, of contamination control took all of the dirty money and made it clean. She made it appear that all of the proceeds were derived from legitimate sources and also invested a lot of the money into gold bullions, which are 1 ounce bars of gold. She also placed millions of dollars into offshore accounts in the Cayman Islands.

$~$~$~$~$

They sat in the conference room at a polished oak table. Malcolm Powers was walking back and forth slowly, with his hands behind his back. He had asked a question and hadn't heard the answer that he'd wanted to hear. He decided to ask it again; just maybe Catfish had heard the damn question wrong. He glared at Catfish and tried again.

"Catfish. I received word that a guy named Waller was out in public blabbering on about us fronting him 10 kilos of coke. Have you heard about this?"

27

Catfish shifted in his seat nervously. He could feel his deodorant giving up as sweat rolled down his arms.

"Yes," he answered.

Malcolm stood in place, staring Catfish down.

"When do you plan on handling the situation since you've already heard about it?"

Catfish glanced at Tron for help, but Tron was paying no attention to Catfish. Tron was staring at the floor.

"I've already handled it, Boss. I handled it today."

"Oh yeah? You handled it today? Did you kill him?"

Catfish stared at the floor.

"No, I didn't because —"

"Well, how the hell did you handle it if you didn't kill him?" Malcolm interrupted and asked.

Tron's heartbeat sped up while listening to Catfish explain what happened. He thought for sure Cat was about to implicate him in the threading, and he knew that Malcolm strongly disapproved of torture. His motto was "either they get lectured or deaded" and he stressed this to the Squad because in the streets the shoe could always be on the other foot.

"I went over to his house and I knocked him out. Then I... I... I threaded his mouth shut."

"What?!"Malcolm exclaimed.

Malcolm walked to the water fountain and filled his cup up. He drank half of it, then he slung the rest of the water across the room. Then he kicked the shit out of an aluminum trash can. The trash can skidded briefly, then flipped until it hit the wall. It made a mark on the white, clean wall.

"Fuck," Malcolm yelled.

"You sewed a human being's mouth shut... What the fuck? Do you think that it's impossible to just cut the fuckin' thread?"

"Naw, I know it can be cut; I just —"

"Do I pay you a million a month to be an amateur? No I don't. I pay you for professionalism, Catfish; and ever since I've known you, you have always been the best problem solver in existence... Do you know why I'm so pissed off at you Catfish?"

Catfish looked at Malcolm confidently.

"Yeah Boss, you didn't want me to turn a nigga's mouth into a dishrag."

There were light snickers around the table. Kyla found it amusing that she had fallen asleep in the van while Tron and Cat were sewing a real live person's mouth shut.

"Catfish, I care about you nigga. But I don't approve of that stunt you pulled because there is no doubt about the fact that that nigga Waller is going to try to retaliate. The streets' code is humiliation equals retaliation!"

"Boss, I seriously doubt that Waller will ever try any one of us."

"Let's just hope so Cat."

Malcolm went to his desk and pulled out a manila folder. He started reading silently for a moment then sat the folder down onto the table and looked at Pam. Pam had on a Christian Dior skirt, a skin tight white shirt was wearing red lipstick and red and white stilettos. Pam was gorgeous. So, gorgeous, in fact, that Kyla swore up and down that Malcolm had hired her based solely on her looks. This assumption was only partly true. Pam also did a good job of making it seem like Malcolm's potato chip line was doing phenomenal sales. Granted, it was selling, but just not the way Pam made it look. Every now and then though, like today, Malcolm would have questions about particular decisions that Pam had executed. Pam stared back at Malcolm with beautiful hazel eyes that could hypnotize a hypnotist if he stared into them long enough.

"Pam, baby," Malcolm's vocal tone mellowed down to an almost seductive octave.

"My beautiful Pam. How are you feeling?" he asked.

Pam smiled blushingly and fluttered her eyes. Kyla thought she was generic and always putting on a show.

"I'm doing absolutely terrific, Daddy. How are —" Kyla cut her off.

"Bitch, quit muthafuckin' flexin' before I beat that ass!"

"You didn't beat that white girl's ass for taking your man," Pam retorted.

Kyla jumped up and tried to lunge at Pam, but Catfish grabbed her and held her back. Malcolm slammed his fist on the table, startling everybody at the meeting.

"Calm the fuck down!" He was talking loud now.

"Pam, what the hell are these two transactions with 250x beside them? Explain."

At first Pam had a puzzled look on her face, and then she realized exactly what he was referring to.

"Oh yeah. Those were donations. By donating money, it cuts down on how much money you'll have to pay around tax time, Malcolm."

Malcolm reached and picked the manila folder back up. He glanced at it again.

"So... Pam, what organizations did you donate the money to?"

She looked at him with confidence.

"I donated it to R.U.C., Relief for Underprivileged Children and I made a donation to Barack Obama's presidential campaign."

"Oh okay, that's cool. All you donated was $250 to both of them?"

Pam squinted her eyes up. A few wrinkles appeared on her forehead before she responded.

"No, not $250... I donated $250,000. Apiece."

"You did what?!" Malcolm exclaimed.

Pam's once seductive look had melted into the look of a scorned puppy; her face drooped and her mouth shaped in the form of a cartoon

31

sad face.

"Malcolm, you told me that you trusted my judgment and direction, so why are you negatively charged up right now? You snapped on Catfish, then you snapped on me for no reason whatsoever. I would never misuse you or misplace any of your money, Malcolm. Think about it, baby. This is Pamela Jones. I have nothing but respect for you, everything that you do, and everything that you stand for. I will die before I dishonor the Squad and I would resign from my job if I didn't feel that my decisions were going to be adequate."

A tear rolled across her beautiful skin as she spoke, and as the words decorated the atmosphere, Malcolm knew she was speaking the absolute truth. The words sank in like the Titanic; and Malcolm realized at that very moment that he was taking out the woes and frustrations from his marriage out on the Squad. He had never been as inconsistent as much as he had been at that meeting. He walked to where Pam was sitting, and wiped a tear from her cheek with a kiss. He was comforting her for his outbursts, but in actuality, he was the one that needed comforting. He took his manila folder and placed it back into the filing cabinet. He dismissed the meeting and grabbed the keys to his Bentley. Everybody got up from the table to leave as well, and they watched as Malcolm headed out of the conference room in a hurry.

"Malcolm," Marco screamed.

Malcolm stopped in the doorway and turned around.

"Yeah, Marco?"

"What time are we going to Club Splash tonight? Or are we still going?"

Malcolm had almost forgotten about the club.

"Oh yeah, we'll hit the club about a half hour after midnight. Thanks for reminding me; I'll see y'all tonight."

"A'ight," the men said in unison.

Kyla smiled weakly, then she started towards the door.

"Malcolm, I don't know if I'm coming, being that I'm sleepy; and I have a couple of things that I need to attend to. But I might... I'm not sure yet."

Pam, who always wanted to outdo Kyla in an attempt to keep Malcolm's favor, decided to try to one-up her. When Kyla started getting close to the door where Malcolm was, she spoke loud and clear, interrupting any potential moment that could have developed between Kyla and Malcolm.

"I'm sleepy too, but I'm about to go finish working on bill consolidations for everybody; then I have to in-process yesterday's proceeds that I received today. And when I finish that, I have to check the earnings report of Crispy Frisbee and see if it needs any alterations. And then... I'll be at the club."

She rolled her eyes at Kyla and walked past her. Then she walked past Malcolm, who caught a whiff of her

Cool Water for women perfume. After she got past him, she knew his eyes would be glued to her ass. She was bow-legged and her ass jiggled with every step that she took. Malcolm stared at it. He swallowed as he thought to himself, "Damn, that ass is perfect. It's shaped like a heart!"

33

$~$~$~$~$

The Wolf was broke, dead broke and was in desperate need of a come up. He sat at the gas station in his girlfriend's beat up Dodge Neon. The car was in such bad shape that whenever it was refueled, it had to sit still and cool off for about 15 minutes before the engine would start without catching fire. He was miserable, but he wasn't alone; the Cowards were with him. Sure they had names, but Wolf called them The Cowards. Cowards shoot out of fear; and more times than not, a coward would kill you quicker than a gangsta would. A gangsta would have morals, principles, rules, and guidelines; but a coward would have fingers full of fear. Fingers full of fear, coupled with guns full of bullets led to morgues full of bodies. They liked to act like they killed because they were cold, hard, and heartless; when in all actuality they killed because they were scared and softer than tomato sauce. They were all broke, the Wolf and the Cowards.

It's a lot of money in this city, the Wolf thought, *we should have no problem getting some of it.* He lit his last Newport, and the Cowards reached for it as soon as he took his first puff. He exhaled, and smiled to himself because he thought how funny it would be to change their name from The Cowards to The Clowns. He ignored the fact that they were reaching for his cigarette, and took another puff.

"Pay attention!" he barked at the Cowards.

They were supposed to be scouring the scenery in search of a come-up. So far, they had spotted a gray BMW 330 that they'd intended to take free of charge; but when they walked up to the vehicle to ask the white woman for "directions", they noticed that there was a 6 year old child in the backseat. They did have a tad bit of a conscience; and within that, they had a rule. They didn't rob or kill when children were present. They had also spotted a limousine, but the tints were too dark and there could have been a bodyguard present. They would be no match for a trained bodyguard; after all, they were cowards. They had spotted a black Mercedes Benz 550, free for the taking, but the police were in the area.

The Wolf was out of cigarettes and was running out of patience. He glanced at his watch and took a deep breath. *I'll have to try again later, I guess,* Wolf thought to himself. He figured that he should at least move on to another gas station before the manager started getting suspicious and called the police on them. They were all riding dirty; convicted felons with firearms. They drove away. Maybe about ten minutes later, they were at Prime Stop, the last gas station downtown before the 25 north and 25 south expressway exits appeared. *Everybody stops here... I'll give it an hour,* the Wolf thought to himself as he parked away from the security cameras. *There are 30 gas pumps at this huge store,* the Wolf quickly noticed. *I'm bound to hit a lick soon.*

$~$~$~$~$

Kyla Brent was leaving the Power Building in her candy pink Range Rover and was lost in her thoughts. Pam had just hit her where it hurt the most back in the conference room. There were dozens of unanswered questions unwilling to remain unanswered. She knew exactly what she needed. She needed closure. She needed to know why. Why... and how... How could Malcolm go and marry a fuckin' white bitch? How does he live with himself knowing that he went completely against the grain? Is he doing this for get back? Did he marry her out of spite? Kyla knew she had faults; a bad temper... a stubborn attitude sometimes, but the love was always there. She had always and would always love Malcolm.

Why can't he see that? She thought to herself as her eyes flooded with tears. She wiped them off her face as she drove through traffic. She knew she looked like a superstar in her Range Rover, and she knew she looked like a supermodel when she wasn't in it. But no matter how good she looked, it never helped how she felt. She felt empty, betrayed and hurt. Her soul was hurting and there was nothing that she could do to comfort it. She was about 4 cars behind Malcolm, and about to get on 25 south so that she could go home when she saw him pull into the Prime Stop gas station. At first, she was going to continue going on about her business, but she needed to talk to Malcolm. It was almost as if she was possessed, the way she yearned for Malcolm's touch... Malcolm's love... Malcolm's kiss. She wanted him and she didn't care how long it took; she knew one day that she would be back in his arms where she was supposed to be.

four

Malcolm tried to park as close to the entrance of the Prime Stop as possible. Shit, he wasn't driving a Chrysler 300; he was driving the real deal. He couldn't just park it anywhere. A Toyota Camry backed out of a parking space on the left side of the store entrance, and zoomed on about its business. Malcolm pulled right into the empty parking space listening to 50 Cent's "I Get Money/Money I Got". All eyes were on him as usual. He relished this type of attention and recognition. It's what he hustled for, what he wished for and what he lived for. He knew that if his day was fucked up, him riding in his most prized possession could cheer him up when nothing else could.

A series of horns blew back on the highway, as the vehicles started to exit to get on the 25 south expressway. He turned around to see if he could make out who it was, and realized that it was Pam, Catfish, Brink, Marco and Prince Tron headed back to their respective homes. He turned the engine off, opened the door and placed the keys in his pocket after stepping out. Little kids were pointing at him and his car screaming, "Look Mommy! Look! Wowwww!" Another vehicle pulled up alongside him on his right side. He glanced up and saw Kyla's big Kool-Aid smile. He rolled his eyes, shut the door, and started walking towards the store entrance. Kyla rolled down her window and spoke out of desperation.

"Malcolm, can we talk for a minute?"

He reached the store entrance, opened the door, and spoke in an irritated tone,

"Wait till I come out!"

He went in the store searching for some Tylenol and orange juice to give to his wife when he got to his estate. He figured that she would be suffering from a hangover pretty soon. Kyla exhaled and laid back in her seat waiting on Malcolm to come out of the store.

$~$~$~$~$

One of the Cowards saw it. His eyes got huge and his breathing sped up. It was a drop top Bentley. Free of charge. The Wolf saw it too. They showed the other Coward and he immediately put one in the chamber and got out of the Neon. The Wolf started to tell him to wait, but what the hell, he had already started walking across the parking lot towards the Bentley.

When Malcolm came out of the store, Kyla rolled her window down again.

"Malcolm?"

He held up a finger.

"Hold up a second," he arrogantly remarked as he went and sat in his car.

Then he rolled his window down the same way that she had hers.

"Yes Kyla?" he shouted.

Kyla looked at him lovingly.

"Why can't we get back together Malcolm? We belong together. I just —"

In the middle of her sentence, Malcolm started backing his car up, about to leave. His logic was that Kyla had left him once, so she would do it again. That's why he'd never given her another chance.

"Malcolm!" she screamed as loud as she could.

"Please, Malcolm talk to me!"

He ignored her. *She knows I'm married,* Malcolm thought to himself as he continued to back the Bentley out of the parking lot. Looking in his rear view, he realized that there was a line of vehicles behind him trying to exit the parking lot to get back on the highway. The car at the front of the line seemed to be waiting on the next red light in order for it to pull out into the road. Malcolm exhaled and pulled back up into his parking slot until he could get enough room to back his car out and go. Kyla was still sitting there staring at him. He pushed a button and the roof of the Bentley evaporated. Every man was giving him thumbs up and every woman was giving him the eye. Occasionally, someone would ask him, "How much?" Nonchalantly, he would reply, "200 thou." "Damn!" would be the typical response.

One of the Cowards was approaching him from the driver's side of the car, looking as if he was dazzled and impressed and had a series of questions that he wanted to ask the owner of the vehicle. He had on blue jeans and a white polo shirt and the gun was in his right hand; his right hand was behind his back. Kyla saw him, but he paid no attention to her, since he was smiling and attempting to make eye contact with Malcolm. Malcolm saw him approaching and thought,

"Damn, another car question. He's probably gonna ask me if I
39

wanna sell it or some other weird shit."

Malcolm glanced away as the Coward approached.

Kyla had a bad feeling in her stomach; she could sense that something was wrong. Then she realized what it was; she couldn't see the guy's right hand... and when she did see it, he had laid the barrel on the side of Malcolm's head. Malcolm froze. He couldn't believe it. One of the most horrible feelings that a human being could ever feel crawled through his body. It weakened his bladder, but he was too strong and too gangsta to piss on his self. He wasn't scared of dying, he just didn't want to. He was as mad as he could possibly get. Red hot. He couldn't believe that he had relaxed so much that he had failed to pay attention to his surroundings. He was mad at himself. This was an internal failure. A failure between brain and eye to communicate with each other. Had he not failed to pay attention, a fuckin' gun would not be resting on the side of his head.

"Take the watch, those rings, and that chain off and throw it in the passenger seat!" the Coward barked at Malcolm.

Malcolm started relieving himself of his jewelry.

"Hurry the fuck up!" the Coward screamed.

Damn, Malcolm thought, this is really happening to me. If only he knew... I could make a phone call and have his whole face removed from his head. This idiot doesn't know who the fuck I am.

Kyla ducked down in the seat of her truck so she could pull her.380 from the compartment under the seat. She grabbed it; it was loaded. The Wolf saw her duck down in the seat and started driving over to help out. He could tell that the Coward was paying no attention to the girl in the pink truck. What a costly mistake he could be making.

The Wolf and the other Cowards were about 20 feet away when they saw Kyla put the gun in the air and point it at the robber. The Coward in the Wolf's car panicked, and without warning, he pulled the 12 gauge shotgun from the backseat, and pointed it at Kyla's truck aimlessly.

BOOM! Glass shattered, people started screaming, car alarms went off from a few parked cars, and blood splattered against the cream white seats of Kyla's Range Rover. Kyla was hit. Buckshots burned through her body as she tried to focus on what had just taken place. She was in pain. Her body went into rapid convulsions, and then the horn sounded. And sounded. And sounded. Kyla had passed out on the steering wheel, face down, the Range Rover horn screaming out for her.

The other Coward smacked Malcolm with the butt of the gun; knocking him out cold. He pulled Malcolm out of the Bentley and jumped into the driver's seat. The Wolf smiled. For the first time, the Cowards had done something perfect; well... almost perfect. If it wasn't for the body, it would have been a brilliant job. But a damn good job of Coward 2 for saving Coward 1's life. Coward 1 sped off in the Bentley; the Wolf and Coward 2 followed. Fuck it, the Wolf thought once they hit 25 north, the job was fuckin' perfect. The vanity plate on the Bentley read: IM PAID. The Wolf smiled again.

$~$~$~$~$

Jennifer Powers plopped down on the butter soft sofa in the great room. All sorts of thoughts were running through her head. After Malcolm left to go to the Power Building for a meeting, she had taken a zip lock bag filled with cocaine, poured a small mound of it onto an ESSENCE magazine... and tried it. She did it the same way she saw it get done in the movies.

She snorted it once and thought that maybe she had done it wrong. She started to panic because she couldn't feel her face.

"Oh my God, I hope I'm not allergic or something. OhmyGod, ohmyGod, ohmyGod!" she said in a rush.

Her chest felt like she was standing in the club directly in front of the speaker. House music. *No, yes, ohmyGod, ohmyGod, what's happening to me?* Jennifer thought to herself. Her nose burned... then went numb. Her tongue tasted bitter. She rubbed her hand across her face to make sure it was still there. It was. She pinched it hard and then jumped from the sofa. She looked around the room frantically; she thought she heard someone talking. It was someone talking. She quickly poured the mound from the magazine into her purse, and threw the zip lock bag into the purse as well. She brushed off her nose so that no residue showed. She ran to a mirror; her nose was red. She took make-up from her purse and quickly coated her nose. She went back and sat down. Her left foot was tapping against the floor at the same pace as her heart beat. She put her hand to her chest; yes, it was still beating at a rapid pace.

She listened... the people in the house were still talking. It sounded like they were in the next room. She ran and grabbed the biggest knife she had out of the kitchen. It had a soft, black, flexi-grip handle. The blade was a whole chicken's worst nightmare. She ran back into the great room, knife in hand, purse on arm. It was dark outside, so she was a bit scared since it sounded like complete strangers were in the house.

"Malcolm, is that you?" No response.

"Jeffrey! Is that you? Who are you talking to?"

No response, but the damn voices continued. I don't understand how anyone could get past all of our security and end up in the house. It must be Malcolm... and he must have company. She thought to herself, even though none of the voices sounded like his. She decided to go find out what the hell was going on. She jumped up and ran towards the voices that she was hearing. Then she saw them; it was the intruders... it was the television. Jennifer was high.

$~$~$~$~$

The get-together at Club Splash that night was canceled. Pam, Brink and Malcolm were at Sinai Memorial hospital in full support of Kyla. Catfish, Prince Tron and Marco were out hunting. They took the surveillance footage from the Prime Stop by posing as FBI agents. They told the manager that they were in a hurry and left them a phony business card. The real police officers were searching the crime scene for clues and, or witnesses. The ambulance had already come and gone when Catfish came out with the footage. After studying the footage, Marco stated that he knew one of the guys. The driver. He lived on the east side and they call him "Cat," or "Bird," or "Wolf"; it was one of those three animals. Then they started the animal hunt. They were on a mission like no other. A member of the Bankroll Squad was on her death bed, and the leader had been robbed. Retaliation was mandatory. If the streets caught wind of the Prime Stop incident, there's no telling what would happen next. Everybody would be plotting. We have to make some examples, reasoned Catfish. They were all in the van dressed in all black.

Prince Tron even left his chain at home for this. The artillery they had was dangerous and illegal enough to get them all federal life sentences. Rocket launchers, grenade throwers, car bombs, and Uzis. They had their ears to the streets and were following up every possible lead on the Animal's whereabouts. At one of the bars, when Catfish went in to ask questions about the Animal, the bartender told him that she hadn't heard anything about a stolen Bentley or a shooting. Then, after Catfish displayed a photo printout of the getaway driver, the bartender recognized him

"Ohhh, I know him. That's Wolf," she said.

"Wolf, you say? Tell me about him, if you don't mind."

The bartender glared at him for a moment.

"Well, actually I do mind; I'm working here. If you're not going to tip me then you need to keep it moving so that the people that do tip me can sit down and tip comfortably."

She walked away and went to a customer. Catfish pulled a $50 bill out and waved it at her in order to get her attention. She saw it but continued serving the other customers. He looked at the long string of drinkers that were ahead of him and decided that he didn't have much time to just be sitting around waiting on her to serve them all. So, he reached in his pocket, pulled out a fistful of $100 dollar bills and held them in the air. The bartender wasted no time in pouring Grey Goose for her current customer and hurriedly made her way back to Catfish. She was grinning; so was he.

"I figured that I could get some type of attention if I went about it like that," he said.

"Don't be so sure of yourself. I just came to tell you to put your money back in your pocket. I'll get to you when I get to you," she retorted.

With that, she smiled seductively and went to service another customer. If she wasn't so pretty, Catfish would have pulled a pistol out on her. He went outside to tell Tron and Marco to give him a little more time, because he might have a good lead. As soon as he told them that, they started reaching for their guns.

"Wait a minute," Catfish directed.

"It's just a girl. A bartender actually. I don't need any help. Y'all just give me a few minutes!" he continued.

"Man, fuck that!" Marco exclaimed.

"Anybody that has a lead on these bastards gotta come with us. Now!" Marco tucked the gun under his waistband and tried to get out the van.

"Wait muthafucka!" Catfish was getting irritated.

Sometimes it seemed as though Marco thought he was in charge.

"You don't think that I can get information out of a bitch?" Catfish asked.

"Not if you thread the bitch's lips together, you ass-hole!" Marco retorted.

"Fuck you Marco!"

Sensing that the situation was getting entirely out of control, Prince Tron intermediated.

"Stay focused!" Tron shouted.

45

"Catfish, you're the leader of this shit, so you know what's best! Marco, this is not your specialty, so let this nigga do what he does best!"

He looked at Catfish with eyes of trust. "Do your thing man; we gonna follow your lead regardless of what Marco says. We're doing this for Kyla. We're doing this for Malcolm, for the Squad, for respect and principles. We're down for whatever!"

Catfish gave Tron a nod and walked back in the bar. Marco laid back in his seat. He exhaled.

$~$~$~$~$

Sinai Memorial Hospital smelled like Lysol and death. It was gloomy and ice cold. The emergency room had a variety of different types of patients. One guy had endured a stroke at a gay porn theater. Another guy was suffering from internal bleeding; he had been hit by a car while trying to run across three lanes on a freeway to save a dog. It didn't work. A construction worker had fallen off of a house and couldn't feel anything on his body. These were Kyla Brent's new neighbors. She was in a coma. Buckshot had been removed from her chest, shoulder, arm and there were even a couple in her neck. When her truck window shattered from the 12- gauge blast, a small piece of glass flew back and scarred the right side of her face. There was white gauze taped from the side of her eye down to the bottom of her cheek. The doctor told Malcolm that she probably wasn't going to make it.

He asked, "Probably isn't? So there is a chance, right?"

The doctor answered, "No, more than likely she will not make it. Don't get your hopes up." But she was fighting. She hadn't let go yet. Malcolm, Brink and Pam were in the waiting room in a prayer circle.

They knew that there was only one person who could deliver her, and He would do so if it was His will. Pam was crying. Brink was crying. Malcolm was going crazy. If there would have been a gun around, he would have killed himself. Malcolm fell to his knees with his hands clasped together. Please Lord, please bring Kyla through this. He sat down and covered his face with his hands out of shame. Pam and Brink came to his side to comfort him. Pam put her hand on Malcolm's shoulder reassuringly.

"It's going to be okay Malcolm. We all love Kyla. I know we argue all the time, but nevertheless, she's just like family to me. You know God always has a plan for everyone and everything. Don't worry."

"Don't worry?" Malcolm asked.

"You're telling me not to worry about Kyla, my ex-fiancé, who damn near gave her life trying to help me tonight? This woman adored me and I treated her like shit. And now I'm about to lose her!"

Malcolm's eyes were wet and he was completely shaken up from the incident. In his mind, he kept replaying the scene. The robber's instructions, then BOOM! He was knocked out afterwards, so he'd had no clue that Kyla had been shot until he saw her slumped over on the horn of the steering wheel. She had lost huge amounts of blood. Her fragile body had suffered from the effects of a 12-gauge blast. *Why didn't they just shoot me too?* He thought to himself. At that very moment, he felt like the worst person in the world. He thought of all the horrible things that he had made Kyla endure and how no matter what he put her through, she still loved him completely. She loved him for who he was, not what he possessed. Not for what he did for a living, but for the characteristics that he was composed of. Unconditional love that never wavered regardless of the conditions.

47

Malcolm thought of the good times that they'd shared. All of the times before the misunderstanding. She was the type of woman who was fascinated by the simplest of activities. Fishing. Cooking. His wife couldn't cook a rat in a house fire, but he was attracted to the fact that she tried every day and night. He thought back to the time when him and Kyla graduated from college. She was headed to medical school and always had him factored into every single one of her plans. He'd had other plans, ones that required him to put aside everything that he had worked for. In her desire to make Malcolm happy, and against his and her family's wishes, she'd thrown her plans into the exact same bucket as Malcolm; and tried to follow his new, fast- paced plan for success. She'd followed it faithfully. Now she was on her death bed.

"Excuse me. Umm, Mr. Powers?" The doctor interrupted Malcolm's train of thought.

"Yes, Doc?" he answered, expecting to hear the most horrible news that he had ever heard in his life.

"Let me speak with you privately sir." He got off the floor and walked up to the doctor.

"We're all family. Whatever you need to say to me, you can say to all of us."

The doctor adjusted his glasses and flipped a couple of pages through the notes on his clipboard.

"Okay, well... She lost a lot of blood. The impact of the buckshot threw her body into immediate shock, which in turn, caused her to faint. After passing out, the blood loss was so severe that it caused her to flat line. Twice. Both times we were able to bring her back, but she's in a vegetative state. She's being kept alive via life support. I advise you to pull the plug —"

"What?! Why are you out here telling me to pull a fuckin' plug instead of replenishing her blood? If she dies, I swear to GOD that —"

"Well, sir, Dr. Henry has already found her a match and is giving her a blood transfusion as we speak. However, if she does recover, she'll more than likely be partially brain dead and bound to a wheel chair."

"A wheelchair?! She didn't have any spinal injuries … what the fuck are you talking about, MAN?"

Pam rubbed Malcolm's shoulder in an attempt to calm him down, but he jerked away and scowled at her as if she was an enemy.

"Mr. Powers, please try to relax a minute so that I can explain the situation. One of the buck shot pellets that we removed from her neck severely injured one of her spinal nerves. It doesn't look hopeless, but when added to the rest of her injuries, it doesn't look promising. I'm sorry that I couldn't deliver you any better news, but I wanted to be truthful. You understand?"

Malcolm's shoulders slumped down. "Yes Doc..."

"I'm also sorry that I suggested for you to pull the plug. I didn't know if you would be able to handle the financial aspect of it. That machine is very expensive, but if you can pay, we'll leave her on it as long as you can pay for it."

Typical... he thinks I can't afford it, Malcolm thought.

"Doc, how long do you think she'd need to stay on life support until she becomes conscious?"

The doctor rubbed his chin briefly and his forehead wrinkled as he appeared to be lost in thought.

"Well," the doctor said, "there are different situations and results for every individual. There are some people who awaken after 2 months, or even pass away after 2 months or even less time than that. However, there are situations, though extremely rare, in which a person stays on life support in a coma for 7 or 8 years and one day... wake up." Malcolm pondered this for a second.

"Pam, cut this hospital a check for $2,000,000. That should cover at least two years, right Doc?"

The doctor's eyes seemed to bulge out of his head like a cartoon characters'.

"Uh... certainly Mr. Powers."

The doctor looked as if he had lost his train of thought for a minute. Then his whole demeanor changed.

"Mr. Powers, I assure you that me and my staff will do everything in our ability, and use every medical procedure available to bring Ms. Brent back."

"Thank you Doc. I appreciate it. Can she have a visitor now?"

The doctor wanted to say no, but realizing that he was speaking to a very rich man, he catered to his interests.

"Ummm... sure, but just one visitor for right now; actually... give us another hour or two to finish up and then you can visit her. Okay?"

Malcolm nodded his head at the doctor and sprawled out in one of the seats in the waiting room. Brink, unusually silent, went and sat right beside him. The doctor brought them out some pills to calm them down; and after taking the pills, they went to sleep. Pam stayed awake thinking to herself, *I can take her position without any problems now. And since Kyla won't be following Malcolm around all day and night, I should be able to finally make my move. His wife is no match for me... besides, he don't love that bitch anyway.*

five

The Wolf and the Cowards had that Bentley broken down to the smallest denominator. A.S.A.P. After taking it, it had become unrecognizable and untrackable within 35 minutes. Jelly, the man who was the owner of the North Side Chop Shop, offered them $80,000 for everything at first, and the Cowards were happy; but the Wolf said no. Actually, he said, "hell no." He demanded at least $100,000 for the vehicle parts and engine. Jelly said $80,000 was his final offer. The Wolf took it. Then they showed Jelly the jewelry. He said $40,000 after inspecting the diamonds and checking to see if it was real platinum; and again, the Wolf said no. "$80,000," the Wolf demanded.

"Fuck your jewelry!" Jelly exclaimed nonchalantly.

The Cowards were getting frustrated at the Wolf for messing up sure money by trying to be a negotiator. Desperately, Coward 1 said, "Okay, forty thousand dollars is fine. We'll take it."

Jelly looked directly into Cowards 1's eyes. "I said... fuck your jewelry!"

Shit, Coward 2 thought to himself, *Wolf just fucked us out of forty thousand dollars by trying to be greedy. Fuck!* When they left the chop shop, Wolf acknowledged that he had overstepped his boundaries with Jelly. Instead of him getting his usual 50%, he decided that he would take $20,000 and let the Cowards take $30,000 apiece. They happily agreed, and all negative thoughts left the Cowards' minds. They turned the radio up in the Dodge Neon and sang along with the music. They were all in festive moods. Wolf put on the stolen watch, Coward 2 put on the stolen chain. We're ballin' now, Coward 1 thought to himself as he rubbed his hand across the stack of money that belonged to him.

$~$~$~$~$

Jennifer had been calling Malcolm's cell phone for about four hours now. Every single phone call went straight to his voice mail. At first she thought that maybe he had been arrested, but after calling the jails, that concept was never confirmed. He has never done this before, Jennifer thought to herself. He's cheating on me. That bastard! Around this time of night, Jennifer would usually be asleep, but the cocaine had other plans. She was fully energized and there was no chance of her going to bed anytime soon.

She went and took a bubble bath, dried off, then took a stroll into their walk-in closet. Inside the closet was a computer that kept inventory of every outfit available. All you had to do was type in the particular occasion, and a picture of every outfit that was either new or clean appeared on the monitor. Jennifer typed in "club, dress". She didn't like what she saw when she hit enter, so she typed in "club, skirt". Jennifer hadn't been to a club in three years, but if Malcolm was cheating, then so be it.

A short, black Prada skirt appeared on the monitor; along with the section where it was located. She clicked the "accessory" feature and a patent leather pair of black high heels appeared on the computer monitor. The heels had straps designed to wrap around her legs and stop at the bottom of her thighs. Since Malcolm had started fucking Jennifer, her ass had spread about four inches. She had went from 34C-24-32 to

53

Bankroll Squad Trilogy

34C-24-36. Her ass was phat! At least, that's what she heard whenever she went to the grocery store or the mall to go clothes shopping. Guys always swarmed around her, and every time it happened, she always made sure that they understood the fact that she was married.

She'd never cheated on her husband, not even once. But tonight, two could play at that game. Besides, he hadn't given her any dick in two months now. If you turned a woman into a freak, you must service that freak. Otherwise, that freak will attempt to get service elsewhere. Jennifer got dressed and went to stand in front of the full-sized mirror. She turned to the side and admired her "apple bottom" pushing out the limits of the skirt. There was a split going down the middle of the front and the middle of the back. No bra or panties tonight. She grabbed about $500 and went to go wake Jeffrey up. Jeffrey was stunned but he did not comment. She asked him to go bring out her BMW.

"The old one?" he asked.

"The old one," she confirmed.

He went to retrieve it and she went to the mirror and started applying lip gloss and a light coat of make-up. She stuck her fingernail in her purse to dig out more cocaine. She snorted it and felt a rush surge through her body; she felt good. She got in the car and turned the radio up loud, listening to Trina's "The Baddest Bitch".

$~$~$~$~$

Catfish was trying to get more information from the bartender.

"I'll pay you $1,000 to show me where the Wolf stays," he said.

"I don't want your money. I'll show you where he stays for free, and

54

then I'll show you where I stay," she said.

Catfish was slightly irritated because it wasn't the right time to be flirting; but at the same time, the bartender was nice. Plus, she said that she was going to show him where the Wolf lived, so his job was still getting done.

"What's your name? Or should I just call you Ms. Bar-tender?"

"No, you should not. You should call me in an hour when my shift is over with."

She smiled at him and held out her hand; her other hand was on her hip. Catfish didn't know what she wanted. He assumed that she wanted money, so he tried to put some in her hand. She looked insulted.

"Baby, you don't do a good job listening, do you? I told you that I didn't want your money. Gimme your phone so that I can program my number into it."

He pulled out his phone; it was an iPhone just like Malcolm's. He handed it to her.

"It's hard to listen when I'm always giving orders," Catfish said.

"Oh... so you're a boss. That's what's up. My name is Tracy... but everybody calls me Wet."

Catfish's eyes seemed to enlarge after she made her last statement. He glanced down at her waist. It was tight, slim, flat and exposed. He glanced at her shorts. They could almost pass for a pair of bikinis. He saw her pussy print and started thinking about what he could do with a woman like that.

"Ahem..." Wet cleared her throat and handed him his cell phone back.

"Don't forget to call me in one hour."

Catfish nodded and turned to leave before Wet called out.

"Damn, I can't catch your name?"

He stopped. *Damn, where is my mind at?*

"My name's Catfish." He smirked at her and left out of the bar.

Catfish? Wet thought. I knew that was that nigga. Muthafucka!

$~$~$~$~$

Seeing Kyla with tubes, needles, tanks, monitors and machines going into her body made Malcolm cry. His heart hurt. He owed this woman his life, and if she ever recovered, he vowed to give it to her twice over. Maybe even three times over, depending on how many kids that she wanted. I hope she still feels the same way about me when she recovers, Malcolm thought. He took his left hand and rubbed it across the left side of her face. There was no wound on that side of it. It was beautiful; smooth and bronze.

She appeared to be sleeping, but Malcolm knew this wasn't true. He knelt down beside her bed and said a prayer for him and for her.

"Lord, I know that I've made some mistakes in life. Sins. Some sins unintentional and Lord, you know that I've even made some intentional sins. Lord, I wanna ask for forgiveness for everything that I've ever done that went against God's will. With a clean slate, Lord, I wanna ask you to deliver Kyla out of this coma. Forgive her for all the sins that she's committed. Please help her Lord, and please help me to have her. In Jesus Christ's name, I pray. Amen."

"Amen," came three voices in unison from behind him. He stood up and turned around. It was the doctor, Pam and Brink.

"I'm sorry Mr. Powers, but there are a couple of tests that we have to run on Ms. Brent. Why don't you go home tonight and get some sleep? It's been a very long day for all of you. Just visit her tomorrow, whatever time that is convenient for you and your friends. She's in good hands; and in the event of a miracle or an emergency, someone from the hospital will contact you." The doctor offered his hand to Malcolm.

"Wait," Malcolm said.

He turned to Kyla again, wiped the tears from his eyes, and gave her a kiss on her left cheek. He turned, shook the doctor's hand and Malcolm, Brink and Pam left the hospital. Malcolm had arrived at the hospital via ambulance, but when he heard Pam pulling out her keys, he knew that she had driven her vehicle instead of Brink driving his. He didn't know what vehicle she'd brought out until she pushed a button and a raspberry colored Aston Martin roared to life. They all got inside; Malcolm in the passenger seat, Brink in the back. Pam started to turn the music up, but Malcolm told her to turn it off, because there was an important issue that needed to be discussed. She turned it off.

"Okay Pam, I need you to take over where Kyla left off. Brink is your pilot, as he was Kyla's when she was able to... be mobile. You will be making flights to Colombia as well as to the countries where the prostitution operations continue to thrive. Brink will teach you everything that you need to know about Kyla's position. I think you can

57

handle it."

Pam was stunned and excited simultaneously. She stuttered at first, "You-you-you... You really think I can?"

"Hell yeah you can!" Malcolm exclaimed.

"Well, drop me off at my house so that I can get some sleep. We got business to handle tomorrow evening," Brink said.

At that, Pam put the car into gear and drove off. Malcolm had turned his cell phone off when he'd went in to see Kyla. It was the only thing that the robber hadn't taken from him. He turned it on. There were three unheard voice messages and three unread text messages. The first text message said: ANSWER YOUR PHONE! It came from Jennifer, his wife. The second text message said: I KNOW UR CHEATING. I HOPE IT'S WORTH IT. 2 CAN PLAY @ THAT GAME! That message pissed him off. He deleted it and checked the next text message. By this time, they had arrived at Brink's residence.

"Bye Boss. Pam, be ready tomorrow night at 7 p.m. We fly out at midnight, but it's going to take at least five hours to go over the rules. Okay?"

"Okay," Pam said with a smile on her face. "Bye Brink."

"See you tomorrow, Pam."

He shut the door and went into his house as the Aston Martin sped off into the night. Malcolm had a furious look on his face, so Pam didn't say anything at first. She thought that she had done something wrong. Malcolm laid back and stared out the window of Pam's car thinking about what the third text message said: DON'T BOTHER TO

COME HOME 2 NITE. I KNOW I WON'T BOTHER.

$~$~$~$~$

The Wolf dropped Coward 1 and 2 off at their residence, then he went home and jumped in the bed. Coward 2 was drifting off to sleep when Coward 1 asked him if he could borrow the stolen chain.

"Take it," Coward 2 mumbled.

Coward 1 was about to hit Club Lynx, one of the biggest and hottest clubs in the city. It was about fifteen minutes after midnight, so he had at least two hours and 45 minutes before the club closed. Flaunting his newly earned wealth, he rented a limo for eight hours on short notice, by calling Exotic Rentals, a company he'd found in the Yellow Pages. The limo was elegant, the receptionist explained.

"It comes with champagne, a highly skilled driver —"

"Okay, just hurry and send it," the Coward exclaimed, cutting the receptionist off mid-sentence.

He took a shower and got dressed. As he was spraying cologne on, the limo arrived. He put the chain on and grabbed a small bag full of X-pills. There were about 15 pills in the bag; they were very potent. It was all he would need to get some ass tonight. He did it all the time. He got in the back of the stretch limo and instantly felt like a celebrity. He had about $10,000 in cash on him and he was ready to have a good time. He hadn't had a good time in months.

"Where to?" the driver asked.

"To Club Lynx, sir."

The driver tipped his hat at Coward 1 and said, "As you wish."

The driver had a very formal, British accent. He gave the limo gas and they were on their way. They arrived at the club at about 1 a.m. The line to enter the club stretched down the block and curved around the corner. The women were beautiful. High heels or stilettos were on almost every pair of feet. The women wearing flats were leaving the club and had their high heels in their hands. There weren't many women leaving the club though. Coward 1 searched the line of women looking for a potential one night stand. There was a beautiful girl who looked like Halle Berry in the line, but she was in the front and he knew that he would have a better chance getting a girl out of the back of the line. When his limo got to the extremely short VIP line, he told the driver to loop around one time. Halfway through the loop, he told the driver to slow down by the end of the line so that he could pick up his "friend". The driver slowed down to a snail's crawled as Coward 1 searched the end of the line. Then he saw her. She was exactly what he wanted. She looked like a star. He felt like a star. It made perfect sense.

$~$~$~$~$

Damn, I hope that's not Malcolm in that limousine, Jennifer thought as she fidgeted in line. The limousine stopped. Fuck! It is him! Jennifer got so nervous when the door opened that she almost pulled her heels off and ran to a security guard. Instead, she tried to turn and slip around the corner unnoticed. It didn't work.

"Hey, where you going gorgeous?" the voice said. It was not Malcolm's voice. This voice was gentle, almost musical. She turned around to see the face. The face was smiling. She smiled back.

"I was going to leave because the line is just way too long. Why?"

"Because I thought maybe you'd wanna go in VIP with a star," the Coward explained.

Jennifer looked at his necklace. She knew it was expensive because Malcolm had the same type of cross pendant, and he had shelled out $120,000 for it. A real star, Jennifer thought.

"What's your name?" she asked excitedly.

"Everybody calls me Ward 1. What's yours?"

"You can call me Jen; and yes, I'd be delighted to go in the club with you."

The Coward extended his arm. She wrapped her arm around it and went with him back to the limousine. Jennifer was so excited that she could barely control her emotions and statements. Her inner groupie was starting to leak out.

"What do you do Ward?" she asked him.

"I'm a rapper, plus I just did a new movie with Will Smith."

Wow, she thought to herself. *Now I can leave Malcolm and still live the good life.*

The Coward had thoughts of his own. I'm fucking her tonight, no doubt about it. Jen reached in her purse with her pinky and dug out some cocaine.

"Do you mind?" she asked. "It's a new habit but it makes me feel good as hell."

The Coward glanced at the white substance and shook his head.

"Go ahead, but I have something that will make you feel ten times better than coke."

She thumped the coke back into her purse and stared at the celebrity with eyes of wonder.

"What could top that?" She was curious.

The Coward grabbed a champagne glass and poured some orange juice into it. He did not add liquor, wine, champagne or beer. He reached in his pouch and handed her a blue pill with a dolphin inscribed on it.

"Ward, what is this?" she asked while putting it up to her nose to smell it.

"It's beautiful. The greatest feeling ever. It's an ecstasy pill," he replied.

"An ecstasy pill, huh... it's not going to have me going crazy or living in the streets trying to collect cans and sell them for another pill, is it?"

The Coward laughed at her naivety. But cut his laugh short when he noticed that she was serious.

"No Jen, an X-pill won't have you selling cans. That's crack." He got a giggle out of his statement.

She put the pill in her mouth and swallowed it. It's a wrap, the Coward thought. The driver dropped them off in the VIP area of the club. The Coward leaned back in the car to whisper something to the driver.

"Give us an hour and 20 minutes, max. Pick us up from the same spot."

The driver nodded his head. He understood. Jennifer and the Coward went in. It was on and poppin'.

six

Catfish walked to his van with a smile on his face. He was suddenly confronted with the possibility that he could find Wolf and solve that problem on the same night. Malcolm would be elated. He would be rewarded. The Squad's reputation would strengthen. He couldn't wait! Tron woke up when he heard the door to the van open. His gun was in his hand awkwardly as he focused on the face and put the gun back down.

"Damn Cat, you was in there forever my nigga. What's the word?"

Catfish hoisted his body up until he was settled in the driver's seat of the van. He smirked at Tron and laid back in his seat, exhaling.

"Shit, I told y'all I could handle my job!" Catfish exclaimed enthusiastically.

"I got a bitch that's about to get off in about an hour and she gon' show us where that fucking nigga Wolf stay at."

Tron grinned at Catfish's arrogance and nodded his head in approval.

"Hell yeah, that's what the fuck I'm talkin' about," Tron expressed.

He looked over at Marco, who had a straight face on display. He was expressionless, emotionless, just ready to handle business. He was tired of waiting. Tired of riding around in a van when he had major business that he needed to attend to.

"Fuck this," Marco stated.

He grabbed the sawed off shotgun and threw it into his Louis Vuitton sports duffel bag. He slid on a basketball wrist band and matching head band so that he could exude the image of a basketball player having a late scrimmage. Catfish had anger darting out of his eyes as he gave Marco a menacing look.

"Where you think you goin' Marc?" Catfish bellowed.

"Nigga I'm 'bout to go get something to drink. I ain't 'bout to sit here for another hour."

Catfish and Tron exchanged glances. Catfish rolled his eyes, then he slammed his arm against the door, startling Marco.

"Nigga, everything is already set up; so DON'T fuck nothing up. I'm warning you!"

Marco looked at Catfish and mumbled something inaudible as he moved Catfish's arm and hopped out the van. What's wrong with that nigga? Catfish thought as he watched Marco enter the bar.

$~$~$~$~$

The bar smelled like a big ashtray to Marco. As soon as he entered, he wrinkled his nose up in an effort to minimize the smell of second hand cigarette smoke. There were four pool tables, all of them fully occupied. He went to the bar, but stood at an angle so that he could still look out of the small window that faced the parking lot. He wouldn't let the police roll up on that van if he could help it. That would be an instant federal case. Weapons of mass destruction. Marco put some

65

money into the jukebox as R. Kelly's "12 Play" album boomed out of the speakers. A few women put their drinks down and got up to exhibit some of their drunken dance moves. *It looks horrible,* Marco thought as he fanned cigarette smoke away from him. *The nerve of this bitch... to walk up this close to me blowing cigarette smoke.* She was smiling at him; he was frowning at her. She caught the hint, frowned back, and walked away.

About thirty minutes or so passed before the bartender saw him and started making her way to him. Before she could make it over to Marco, her cell phone rang. She had about a zero percent surprise factor, as Marco listened to T-Pain's "Bartender" play as her cell phone ring tone. She answered the phone and turned her back in order to have a private conversation. Marco checked his watch and listened as the R. Kelly song faded out. The lower the volume on the song got, the more of the bartender's phone conversation he could hear. He really wasn't trying to hear it, but listened absentmindedly; not focusing on the dialogue between the bartender and the caller. Then he heard something that struck a nerve. He could barely make out the complete statements since there was so much noise in the bar. Women giggling, men whooping, and the constant sound of billiards clacking against each other on the pool tables.

All he could make out was, "Catfish... van... yeah..."

Marco moved so that he could get closer to her. He could hear a little bit better now.

"You said you was 15 minutes away? Okay baby, be careful; you know that nigga Catfish is crazy. If you want me to, I'll seduce him and kill the bastard myself... Oh, okay then. I'ma fall back. I love you."

Marco turned and stared at a game going on at one of the pool tables so he wouldn't seem so suspicious. He was shocked at what he had just heard the bartender speak into the phone, but he couldn't let it show on his face. He kept his cool. He drummed his fingers against the clear plastic counter top and jumped, startled, when the bartender came up to him. She smelled like baby powder and had an enchanting smile.

"Would you like something to drink, sir?"

Thinking at a frantic pace, he devised a plan.

"Sure baby... just pour me some Hennessey."

"On the rocks?"

"Hell no... just straight Hen."

She smiled and went to pour his drink. Marc stepped back so that he could survey the parking lot for any new vehicles arriving. He didn't see any. The bartender approached him with his drink in her hand, still smiling.

"That'll be $3.50, sir."

Marco reached into his pocket and retrieved a $10 bill. He handed it to her. As soon as her hand touched the money, Marco grabbed her arm and pulled her across the counter top, knocking over glasses in the process. She let out a scream, and Marco jammed the $10 bill into her mouth, causing her to gag. Then he slapped her across her face and told her to shut the fuck up. He grabbed a handful of her hair with his left hand and grabbed his duffle bag with his right hand. He started to turn and leave when the owner spotted the calamity and yelled out,

"Hey buddy! Let that woman go or I'm calling the police! Tracy, baby don't worry!"

The owner grabbed the business phone as if Marco was really going to sit there and watch him call the police. Marco grabbed the sawed-off out of the bag and heard people start screaming,

"Watch out, he's got a gun!"

The owner looked shaken when he saw the men and women that were at the pool tables duck down onto the floor. Marco raised the sawed-off shotgun in the air and aimed it at the owner.

"Nooooo —"

KA-BOOM! His head split open like a piñata as blood and skull fragments splattered across the Patron and Seagram's Gin bottles. The women in the bar started screaming; Tracy started trembling. Marco aimed the shotgun around for a minute just in case someone wanted to jump up and play superhero. No one moved.

He looked out of the window and saw Catfish and Prince Tron getting out of the van carrying AK- 47s. He dragged the bartender like a rag doll as she cried out in pain and fear.

"Please don't hurt me. I didn't do anything," she whined to Marco.

Marco smacked her across the head for spitting out the $10 bill and mashed her face against the dirty tile floor, instructing her to put it back in her mouth. She was crying hysterically and shaking so bad that he was sure that she was about to pass out. Catfish barged in with Prince Tron right behind him. When the bar attendants saw the size of the guns that they were carrying, they sounded like a group of kids gasping all at once. A couple of guys were down on the floor in prayer.

Catfish damn near pissed his pants when he saw what was unfolding. "Nigga! What the fuck is going on in here?" Catfish was careful not to say Marco's real name in front of all of those witnesses.

"Chill dude! This bitch was tryna set you up!" Marco expressed, forehead wrinkled up and eyes full of rage.

Tracy shook her head; frantically denying the accusation. Catfish looked up and saw blood splattered from the counter top to the section where the drinks were sitting. He walked over to get a better look and saw a man with half of his brain missing.

"Holy shit," Catfish said as he jumped at the sight of the body.

"That's not what we came for man... damn!"

"Shit, he was talking about calling the police on me nigga!"

Catfish looked around the room at all the potential witnesses and had the right mind to blow everybody's brains out to take extra precaution. Instead, he had a better idea. He told Prince Tron and Marco to take Tracy, toss her into the van and wait for him. He grabbed the duffle bag from Marco and watched them as they carried the bartender to the van. Then he proceeded to go to work.

seven

"What's wrong, Daddy?"

Pam's voice sounds so sympathetic, so concerned... soothing...
erotic, Malcolm thought, as the Aston Martin whipped through the
night like a shooting star. He thought about all that had happened that
day. The fight with Kyla, the fight with Jennifer, the uncharacteristic
behavior that he'd exhibited in front of his squad. He thought about the
12-gauge blast that should have been for him, but instead had Kyla
lying in a coma strapped to advanced equipment. His emotions were
unreadable, even to his self. He looked at his iPhone again, thinking
about the text messages that were manufactured by his wife. The
coldness of it. The reality of it. He stared at Pam as she maneuvered the
steering wheel as if she was a professional driver. She smiled at him. A
warm, sexy, confident smile that seemed to comfort him; if only but
temporarily.

"Nothing's wrong Pam. I'm just lost in thought, that's all," Malcolm
lied.

Well, half-lied since the other half was true. Pam shot Malcolm a
knowing look as she slowed down, approaching the intersection. The
light was red, but that only gave her the green light to continue flirting.
She had to flirt indirectly and gradually build up to the direct requests
that she wanted to ask.

"You wanna hang out at my house for a while?" She regretted asking that question as soon as it left her mouth.

Silence. The type of silence that makes one nervous and uncomfortable. Malcolm heard her question but he was at a loss for words. He wanted to believe that none of the horrid events had taken place at all. He knew what he wanted, but his body and soul knew what he needed. He needed to be comforted. He needed to be loved. He needed his wife to apologize, for her to send a text message saying that she was at home. After the long, lingering silence, he finally gathered up enough complete thoughts to make a statement.

"Yeah, Pam. We can hang out."

Whoa, Pam thought. *Pam and Malcolm, hell yeah.* Pam intended to take full advantage of the opportunity at hand. She had her man and she wasn't letting go.

Catching her by surprise, Malcolm reached over and started caressing her right thigh. *Damn,* she thought as she felt her juices roll from her pussy to her pussy lips. He got exactly what I need, she said to herself as she reached over and grabbed his left thigh. Out of the corner of her eye, she saw Malcolm pull off his wedding ring and put it in his pocket. Her hand moved to the inside of his thigh where she felt a thick, long, rock hard dick laying against it. She jerked her hand back to the wheel; she had almost run off of the road. Malcolm smiled. She was slightly embarrassed. She saw a sign that said that her exit was only 5 miles away. Almost there. She smiled.

$\$\sim\$\sim\$\sim\$\sim\$$

When they entered the club, the DJ was playing rap music. Some Lil Wayne, Rick Ross, and Young Jeezy. After about 30 minutes, everything switched to reggae. This was Coward 1's cue. He knew she couldn't dance, and he knew that the pill had kicked in. He grabbed Jennifer's arm and led her on to the dance floor. As soon as he touched her arm, she felt goose bumps pop up on her body. Her two major goose bumps were sticking out through the front of her outfit. She noticed her nipples protruding and realized that there was nothing that she could do to hide them. She was too embarrassed to let the Coward see her like that, so once they made it to the dance floor, she turned around and started grinding her ass against the Coward.

The Coward instantly got an erection and Jennifer noticed it immediately. His manhood wasn't as big as Malcolm's, but it was hard and exciting her more and more. It seemed like the more she grinded against it, the wetter she got. After about two minutes, a trickle of cum rolled from her pussy down to the inside of her thigh, and then down to the inside of her calf muscle. When the Coward noticed this, he leaned forward and put his warm tongue behind her ear and circled his tongue from the back of her ear to the front of it. A tremor ran through Jennifer's body when he did that, and her pussy only got wetter. The Coward kissed her ear, then his lips went down the side of her neck, where he kissed her passionately. A sexual rush had run through Jennifer, and Coward 1 was caught completely off guard when she reached back and wrapped her hand around his crotch. The other club attendees were dancing and having fun, but the Coward and Jennifer were taking it beyond the extreme on the dance floor.

After about seven minutes of the dance floor foreplay, Jennifer became self- conscious because she realized that there were a lot of club patrons staring at them. The Coward was oblivious to the attention, seemingly caught up in his own little world, until Jennifer pulled him out of it and led him to the bathroom. Jennifer was horny. The Coward was horny. They had both taken X-pills, two bodies powerless to the effects of the Blue Dolphin.

Jennifer looked into the women's restroom and noticed that there were too many women putting on make-up and standing around conversing. She turned and looked at the Coward, then shook her head solemnly, letting him know that the women's bathroom was a complete "NO."

Determined, the Coward took charge. He grabbed her by the arm and led her to the men's restroom. He knew that the men's bathroom would be empty, with all the ass out there on the dance floor; so it was no surprise when the only dude that was in the bathroom made his way past Coward 1 en route to the dance floor. He led Jennifer to a stall and locked the door. The Coward pulled her skirt up, revealing a shaved and perfectly pink pussy.

"Ward, do you have protection?"

Knowing that he had no protection at all, he French kissed her while circling his middle finger around her clitoris. Her kisses became more aggressive until he broke from the kiss and started sucking on her right nipple. In her mind she was thinking about telling him to get a condom, but the stimulation proved to be too intense for her to try to mumble those words again. Unable to withstand the teasing any longer, she reached down and started unfastening his pants, then she wrapped her hand around his wood. She was staring at Ward, waiting on him to make the next move. He wasted no time. He turned her around and bent her over, sliding a finger in her pussy to test her readiness. When he pulled his finger out, it was covered in cream. She is soaking wet. He wiped her pussy cream around his dick and slid it through the opening of her warm pussy. He then pulled back, parted her pussy lips, and slid his manhood in as far as it would go. He stroked and stroked, his dick sliding against her vaginal walls, bringing her to orgasm again and again.

She was panting, breathing uncontrollably when she managed to whisper the words, " let me get on top." He pulled out and sat down on the toilet, dick still covered in pussy cum. Jennifer was high off of cocaine and ecstasy and the Coward had never had a woman on that combination of drugs before. She climbed on his dick and threw her pussy up and down on it frantically. She slammed against his dick until it hurt him, and when he moaned out of painful pleasure, she went even harder. After a few more strokes, the Coward cried out,

"I'm coming," to which she replied, "Oh baby, me too! I'm coming!" The bathroom stall sounded like a porno movie as the Coward pumped semen into Jennifer, while she simultaneously released a stream of cum around his dick. As soon as they came, it seemed as though she was ready to fuck again.

"Wait a minute," the Coward exclaimed, out of breath. "You wanna go get a hotel room instead of fucking in the bathroom of a club?"

"Yeah Ward, let's go."

Jennifer was having the time of her life. *I'm having sex with a real celebrity*, kept running through her mind as they both climbed back into the limousine.

"To the Hilton," the Coward directed the chauffeur.

"Downtown?"

"Yeah, the Hilton Downtown."

The chauffeur obliged and drove off, headed to the hotel. Jennifer cuddled up next to the Coward, fondling with his penis. The limo hit a deep pothole and Jennifer's purse fell off the seat, causing the contents to spill to the floor.

When the Coward saw how much cocaine she had in her purse, his eyes bulged out like a cartoon characters'. Instantly devising the next scheme for him, Coward 2, and the Wolf, he decided to ask a few questions first.

"Jen, how much did you pay for that blow?"

"Blow?"

"Yeah, the white shit that was in your purse?"

"Ohhh, the cocaine."

The Coward looked at her as if she had lost her mind. "Yea Jen... the coke... the blow."

She giggled at herself for not catching on to the slang when he first spoke it. After all... it was only last week when she was actually watching a movie on HBO that was entitled "Blow," and it was about cocaine.

"Well, I didn't actually pay for it."

She unzipped his pants, pulling his erect penis out. Slumping down in his seat, the Coward tried to stay focused on his series of questions.

"How did you get it if you didn't pay for it?"

She giggled again thinking about how the truth was about to sound once she spoke it aloud. "I just took it."

"You took it from a drug dealer? As in you stole it?"

She pondered the question for a brief moment before answering.

"Well... yeah... I stole it."

"And what are you going to do if he finds out you stole it?"

"He would never find out; trust me Ward." The Coward looked at her suspiciously.

"How can you be so sure that he won't find out?" She didn't particularly enjoy being questioned over and over and a look of frustration invaded her facial features.

"Because he has a room full of it. It's wall to wall, over 100 feet long, and comes up to my knees," she snapped.

The Coward noticed that he was irritating her with his inquisitions and leaned over to start kissing her. Noticing that both of their mouths were dry as sandpaper, he grabbed two bottles of bottled water. She drank half of hers, then she leaned down and wrapped her lips around his dick. She sucked him until they arrived at the Hilton. The whole time that he was getting his blow job, the Coward just kept thinking to himself, *I'm 'bout to be rich!*

eight

Catfish was in total control of the situation at hand. "Everybody get in a single file line and shut the fuck up! If any one of y'all muthafuckas fail to cooperate accordingly, or try some ol' funny ass shit, I will blow your brains out of the very head that holds it!"

The men and women lined up even quicker than he could finish his statement. They had already saw what had happened to the owner, and they could only imagine what would happen to the bartender.

"I'm walking by with an open bag. Each of you need to drop your driver's license into the bag. Don't worry about not having a license because in three days I will personally bring everyone's license back to their homes, provided that none of you go to the authorities!"

While collecting IDs, he ran across a knucklehead. Catfish saw the guy drop the ID on the floor and cover it with his boot before he was even approached.

"ID in the bag, shit stain!"

"Sir, I do not have an ID."

Catfish was amused at how the guy could tell a lie directly in the face of an imminent threat.

"You have no type of ID at all?" Catfish asked him.

"No. I —"

BLAT-BLAT-BLAT-BLAT-BLAT-BLAT!

"They'll be able to ID you with your dental records then," Catfish told him.

He collected the rest of the ID's with no problem, then he picked up the two bodies from the bar and took them to the van. Into the seat they went. Tracy's mouth was gagged shut with duct tape and a $10 bill, so her words were indecipherable. She was trembling like it was ten degrees below zero. She was thoroughly frightened and mad at herself for even being a part of this situation, when it initially had nothing to do with her. Catfish backhand smacked her across the face so hard that the entire van started rocking side to side.

"Stop speaking bitch!" Catfish screamed at her.

Then he ripped the duct tape off her mouth.

"Speak bitch!"

Tracy was so frightened and confused that she didn't know whether to speak or shut up. She knew another slap was about to come across her face, so as soon as Catfish made the slightest movement, she flinched like a scared child who knew that he had done something terribly wrong and greatly upset his parents.

"Wh-wh-wh... what do you want from me?"

"I suggest we just blow her shit off!" Marco exclaimed, still clutching the sawed-off shotgun.

"Nooo, please don't hurt me, I —"

Catfish cut off all her whining with a back hand slap that had such a profound impact that it made her flip to the floor cartwheel style, and that was from a sitting position. Catfish picked her up off of the floor and slammed her against the seat.

"Who you workin' wit'?" Catfish hollered at her in a deafening decibel.

Shaking, she finally managed to whisper out the answer to his question.

"I'm not... working with anyone; it's just... my baby's dad told me to keep an ear to the streets and to alert him if I ever heard anything about the name Catfish."

Catfish gave her a confused look.

"Who the fuck is yo' baby's daddy?"

"Sw-sw-sweetback Fatty..."

"SWEETBACK FATTY?" they all yelled in surprised unison.

They all knew that Sweetback Fatty was the head of the Organized General Committee, which dealt strictly with hit man work. Marco and Prince Tron shook their heads in disgust as they thought about what Sweetback would do to them once he found out that they had abducted his baby's mama. No one wanted to piss off Sweetback. Starting the van, Catfish picked up his cell phone to call Malcolm, but put it back down because he knew that Malcolm had been under a lot of stress in the past 24 hours. Thinking about what had happened to Malcolm and Kyla earlier gave him a sudden rage of fury.

79

"Arrgghh!" Catfish screamed as he slammed his heavy fist against the dashboard, resetting the clock in the process.

"Tracy," Catfish started, staring at her in his rearview mirror, "What the hell does Sweetback want me set up for? I thought we were on good terms."

"His little brother told him that you hurt him for no reason, messed his mouth up to the point that drinking water makes him scream out in anguish from the pain."

"What? Who the fuck is his little brother?"

"A guy named Waller."

When she said that, everyone put their hands to their foreheads. They knew that fucking with Sweetback's gang was bad for your health. He'd once blew up a whole gymnasium full of kids and adults, just to get one person who had a price on his head.

"Tron, why didn't you tell me that Waller was Sweetback's brother?"

"Catfish, I had no possible way of knowing that type of information. Man, you know how secretive Sweetback operates in these streets."

Catfish drove in silence, contemplating his next move and occasionally shaking his head in disgust of the situation.

$~$~$~$~$

Pam's mother was red-boned, her grandmother being a young black paralegal who, back in her day, had been seduced by a young white attorney. As soon as the lawyer found out that he had impregnated his

Negro paralegal, he paid her $200,000 to get as far out of town as possible, preferably to another country. She left the state and had Pam's mother at a hospital in Dallas, Texas.

Pam's mother was the envy of all women dark and light in high school and college, and was the object of desire for all men, dark and light. She'd dated a caramel-complexioned guy whom everyone thought was definitely going to the NFL. He was the top college quarterback in the country as a sophomore, but fell victim to a career ending injury in his junior year. Her mom fell in love with the guy even more since they then had more time to spend together and more time to develop their relationship. After they graduated, they got married and Pamela Jones was born. A yellow girl with hazel eyes, the perfect body, and long shiny black hair; guys had been after her since she was in the 6th grade. She was raised in a good home, by great parents, and had a strong set of values instilled in her.

As a high school freshman, just like her mother, she was the envy of girls and the desire of boys. She was so beautiful that even her female teachers were jealous of her, and they often gave her a hard time. Her first love was a player, a cheater and a complete liar. Her mom used to always warn her about dating seniors when she was only a freshman, but she was under the impression that she could have whomever she wanted. When the guy took her virginity and left her heart broken, she used all of her anger and fury as fuel. That harsh taste of the real life let her know that everything wasn't peaches and pears. She learned how to be cold at times, calculating and manipulative; seductive and aggressive. She would get what she wanted and keep it. She would let no one get in her way when she wanted something; and she definitely wanted something.

$~$~$~$~$

"Good morning Malcolm! I made you some breakfast... I'll go get it. Don't move."

Before he could reply, Pam was gone to the kitchen to retrieve the breakfast that she had cooked.

After arriving at Pam's house the night before, they drank some champagne and fell asleep watching a movie. Malcolm was distraught over everything that had unfolded, so emotionally, he was extremely vulnerable. Although they flirted heavily, they never took it all the way to a complete sexual level. Although Pam really wanted him, she knew that the best way to capture her man was psychologically, not sexually. She cuddled up next to him, constantly reassuring him that everything was going to be absolutely fine. After a while, she opened up to him about her relationship problems. She told him that it was very difficult to get a real man because every man that she encountered was always intimidated both by her beauty and possessions.

She knew that the only way to get a man to open up, was to open up first. And it worked. After venting over some of her relationship woes, Malcolm felt compelled to make an attempt to relate to her. He told her about the argument that he and Jennifer had. He also told her about the text messages that she had sent him. He expressed how he felt about Kyla, and Pam said that her feelings for Kyla were mutual; that she also loved Kyla. Pam knew that Malcolm's heart was fragile due to all it had just endured, so she had to handle it delicately.

Malcolm looked around Pam's plush bedroom, admiring the decor and the original interior design. The carpet was about five inches thick, and was the color of a chinchilla coat. Her carpet looked like it cost the same amount as a hard-top Bentley. The blanket was chinchilla, and the mattress on the bed actually contoured to every curve on his body and it did the same thing on her side without disturbing his. Malcolm was impressed with her place and was delighted when she told him that he could stay as long as he wanted to. It wasn't really about the house, it was more about the home.

Malcolm knew, as well as Pam, that he could go buy another house before lunch time and be in it before dinner, but Malcolm also knew that life was too short and too valuable to spend alone. Granted, he still loved his wife but what good was that if love don't love you back, he reasoned. Besides, the love that Kyla had just exhibited made him realize the difference between telling someone you love them and showing someone you love them. Kyla had shown her love by sacrificing the most important thing that she would ever own... her life.

Pam walked into the bedroom wearing a red and gold silk kimono carrying a plate of pancakes, bacon, sausage, and eggs. In her other hand was a bowl of Captain Crunch.

"That's my favorite cereal, Pam; how did you know I liked Captain Crunch?" Pam smiled, as she sat his plate and bowl of cereal on the lamp stand.

"Because you told me years ago, and when you told me, I remembered planning out this very exact breakfast for you if ever provided the opportunity. So... lo and behold."

She turned to go back into the kitchen to get her breakfast, the sunlight highlighting her golden skin tone, as if to underline her beauty in order for the world to see it. When they got through eating, she laid back cuddled up in Malcolm's arms. He checked his iPhone and saw that he had missed 24 calls from Catfish throughout the night. *None from Jennifer,* he thought to himself. He thought of Kyla laying in the

Emergency Room of the hospital in a coma and promptly broke away from Pam and got dressed.

"Pam, I'm on my way to the hospital. I'll be there for a couple of hours. How about I call you around lunchtime, so maybe we can meet up?"

"That'll be perfect for me because I still have a little work to do; and if I finish in time, I'd planned on going to the mall to pick up a few things. Take my Aston Martin; I'll just drive my Benz today," she said as she tossed him the keys.

Malcolm kissed her on the cheek and left her house, looking for the nearest Flower and Gift shop so that he could get Kyla something nice while she was in the hospital. He was going to nurture her spirit back to good health, because he knew that the spirit would, eventually, nurture the body. And once her body was nurtured back to health, he was going to nurture their relationship until it was completely repaired.

nine

As soon as Coward 1 and Jennifer had arrived at the hotel the previous night, Coward 1 realized that he had bit off more than he could possibly chew. After two hours of sex, he was thoroughly exhausted, but Jennifer was still full of energy. When he realized that he wasn't going to be able to keep up with her drug induced sexual marathon, he decided to snort some of the cocaine that she was sniffing. He had done coke before, but it wasn't his drug of preference because it was so difficult for him to come down off of the high.

He preferred the almighty X-pill over everything. Until he tried Jen's coke. He snorted half of a line and immediately stopped because he thought that a drug this powerful must be either one of two things; either mixed with something else or just completely PURE. It burned his nose as if he had just snorted rubbing alcohol, but that small side effect was nothing compared to the immense high that he was experiencing. He did the rest of the line, and after a few minutes they took more X-pills. They had marathon sex all night.

They took a nap at 7 a.m.; and at 9:30 a.m., they were both laying in the hotel bed staring at the ceiling wide-eyed. Reality had set in on both of them. Jennifer Powers' reality was that she was now a slut... a groupie... something that she had never been, because she had done something she'd never done. She'd cheated. She had officially violated the sacred sanctity of her marriage. Malcolm's words ran through her body like a laxative.

I loved you since day one, and I'll continue to love you until the day that the love that I give you is not returned.

She lay there, knowing that yesterday was the day that she didn't return her husband's love. After sending him all those text messages, he'd tried to call her once, and she sent that call directly to voice mail. He sent her a text message that she didn't even read. She looked at the sender and quickly replied: FUCK U.

She got out of the bed and went to get her purse. She turned on her cell phone and viewed the text that she didn't read. Her legs wobbled when she read the message. It said: DO U LUV UR HUSBAND? A deep sense of regret flushed her heart as she slowly walked into the bath room to take a shower. She regretted going out, she regretted cheating, she regretted doing drugs. She had turned her life into a nightmare. She turned on the water and got into the shower.

Coward 1's reality was that he was a nothing. He was not a rich actor; hell, he was a robber. He shot people out of fear, and robbed people out of greed. He was worthless to society, but he felt good because he didn't slave for anyone. He made his own way and he aspired to be rich like his Uncle Brandon. His uncle had encountered a similar situation back in his day. He'd run upon a beautiful girl that the top drug dealer in the city trusted. The dealer paid her to rent upscale homes in the suburbs so that he could stash large amounts of cocaine in them.

Uncle Brandon won the girl's heart and the girl told him about everything. He convinced her to get him a key to the house and then they would be able to move to Paris in about a week and be filthy rich, never having to look back again or worry about a thing. This appealed to the woman greatly, who had two small kids, and didn't want to continue having the stash house rented in her name once she saw the amount of drugs it held. She gave Uncle Brandon a key and his squad of goons retrieved 300 kilos. *100 feet long,* the Coward thought as he lay down plotting. *That's a lot of cocaine. Now I gotta get her to take me to it.*

$~$~$~$~$

Although there is no concrete proof, there are variations of accounts of what a person goes through when they're in a coma. Some of the people that have made it out of comas claim that they were unaware of their existence for that time period. Some people say that they were asleep; and when they came out of their comas, it seemed like only one night had passed. Kyla dreamed. The doctors didn't expect her to make it through 24 hours, but she was still alive. It seemed as if her body was repairing itself without the need of a physician. Love was keeping her alive.

$~$~$~$~$

Four and a half years ago, Kyla was working part-time at Pizza Hut as a delivery person. She was about to graduate college and the extra money helped out with various small expenses. She and Malcolm had been dating for two years already. She knew he hustled, but since he was never flashy, she thought nothing of it. Besides, he would have his diploma soon and then he would be able to start his career. One evening she had to deliver a large pepperoni pizza and 2 liter Sprite to a nearby Hampton Inn. When she arrived at the specified room with the delivery, the door was wide open with R&B songs were playing from a small boom box. She knocked on the door as hard as she could, but soon realized that her knocking would not be heard over the sound of the music. She took it upon herself to walk into the room. After taking about four steps, she was able to see around the wall that separated the kitchen from the bedroom. The room had a double bed, and smelled of an exotic strawberry-themed fragrance. On one bed was what looked to be a million dollars in cash, and on the other bed was her man, Malcolm. Malcolm had a huge grin on his face, and Kyla had her poker face on.

"Malcolm, what are you doing? Why is all of that money on that bed?"

Malcolm got off of his bed and went to embrace Kyla. "Baby, you don't ever have to work again. Money is no option. You can quit your Pizza Hut job now if you like."

Kyla broke free from Malcolm's warm embrace and stared at him. "Malcolm, I don't want money. I want a life... I wanna be a doctor one day—"

"But Kyla, I'm telling you that you don't have to do anything, just be my woman. You don't have to worry—"

"Malcolm, you have a listening problem. I want to be a doctor. I want to be able to help people. I don't want to get caught up in the illusion of a free ticket because nothing's free. Everything has a price.

"Everything."

"Including you?" Malcolm said, smirking.

"No! Because first of all, I'm not a thing, I'm a person! I can't believe—"

Malcolm cut her off with a delicate kiss on the lips.

"Malcolm, we're about to graduate college; we don't need this dirty money. We—"

He kissed her again.

"Malcolm..."

He kissed her on her neck, then sucked on one spot which caused a passion mark to show up on her light skin.

"I love you Kyla."

"Ooooh baby, I love you too... but that doesn't change —"

"Ssshhh. Relax baby. I'm your man, your protector, and your lover. I promise you that nothing's going to happen to you as long as we're together."

Malcolm took the pizza out of her hands and laid it on the dresser. He turned back towards her, and noticed that she was trembling. It had only been two weeks since Malcolm had taken her virginity, and they had not had sex again. Malcolm didn't believe in making sex the focal point of a relationship. Besides, every time he got close to Kyla and kissed or touched her intimately, she always started shaking. She trembled out of a mixture of nervousness and eagerness. Malcolm fell in love with her easily. For a woman whom every man wanted to be with, she had every right to be arrogant, conceited, and self-absorbed. Especially when that type of output was expected from her. People that thought she was arrogant couldn't have been more wrong if they'd said that two plus two equaled seven. Kyla was the ultimate defiance of the stereotype.

"Baby, try not to be nervous... relax Kyla... I got you baby," Malcolm whispered into her ear.

Then he softly exhaled a warm, moist stream of air into her ear. Kyla shivered, a soft feminine moan escaping her throat. Malcolm laid her down on the bed and pulled her shirt up so that he could kiss her navel. As soon as his warm, wet tongue made contact with her stomach, she gasped harshly. Her breathing pattern sped up twofold, and her petite hands grabbed the side of his head in a feeble attempt to stop him from torturing her.

"Mal... ahhh... ooohh... you know I'm working right now..."

Malcolm's tongue trailed from her navel to her hip bone.

"I'm working too, Kyla."

He started sucking on her left hip bone, causing a shudder to run straight through her entire body. She could barely take all of his tongue massaging, which was evident in all of her shaking and fidgeting. He pulled her jogging pants and panties down at the same time, pulling them completely off of her body. Instantly, he went from sucking her hip and waist area to twirling his tongue in circles on the inside of her right thigh. She had never had a man's tongue anywhere close to the area that Malcolm was terrorizing.

He slowly slid his tongue from the bottom of her right thigh, all the way up to her right pussy lip, then he licked it once like it was an ice cream cone. She squirmed, trying to get away from Malcolm's grasp, but she couldn't pry herself away as Malcolm licked her left pussy lip. She jerked and twisted while simultaneously moaning and screaming from the foreign pleasure of receiving oral sex. Malcolm gripped her ass to hold her in place, then his lips softly wrapped around her clit, causing her to sweat from the pleasure. Then he flicked his tongue gently across her clit over and over until she let go of an orgasm so big that estrogen combined with adrenaline; and gave her enough supernatural strength to throw Malcolm off of her.

She didn't even realize what she had done, nor did she realize what had just happened to her. When Malcolm looked at her again, she was laying sideways with her legs shut and her thumb in her mouth. She had her eyes closed and she seemed to be mumbling some incoherent dialect to herself. When he took her virginity; she'd done the same exact thing afterwards. He knew that she would be sleep soon so he went into the bathroom to wash the female juices off of his face while she fell asleep. He needed her to be asleep in order for him to carry out the next part of his plan.

$~$~$~$~$

Even though Kyla was dreaming, Malcolm had no way of knowing that she was lying there thinking pleasant thoughts. The doctor had told him that she was doing much better, but he couldn't tell. He just kept replaying the scene in his head over and over as though he could mentally change the outcome and Kyla would be awake and flirting with him. After about an hour and a half, Malcolm started wondering about what Kyla would say if she knew that he was not handling business. He knew then that it was time. He said a prayer for her and kissed her on the lips. Then he left the room with business on his mind. It was time to handle it.

$~$~$~$~$

Catfish was sitting in the waiting room when he saw Malcolm walking down the hallway. After not being able to reach him on his cell, at home, or at The Power Building, he called Pam. She told him that he would be there visiting Kyla, so Catfish rushed over as soon as possible.

"Malcolm. Hello my brother. How's Kyla?"

"Aww man Cat, she's fucked up real bad. A coma is not a place for a woman like that. You know?"

"Yeah man, I feel you... Hey, you know I been calling you all night? I got a serious fuckin' problem Malcolm."

"What kind of problem?"

"Come out to the van so that I can show you."

Despite it being a beautiful spring morning, Malcolm's day quickly turned sour when he saw the bloody faced woman duct taped in the van.

"Is this The Wolf?"

"No... this is Sweetback Fatty's child's mother." Malcolm looked at Catfish like he had vomit on his face.

"What the fuck is wrong with you, you imbecile?"

"Man, I been tryna tell you what happened all night... listen..."

After Catfish told Malcolm what happened, Malcolm pulled out his cell phone.

"Who you calling yo'?" Malcolm ignored Catfish.

"Heeey, whassup Sweetback? What's poppin'?" Catfish stared at Malcolm intensely, trying to figure out what he was up to. He knew that

Malcolm had a serious level of respect for the man, but he didn't know how serious.

"Yeah man... my right hand man made a mistake last night..."

Catfish could hear the man's boisterous voice even though the speakerphone option wasn't on.

"You got-damned right yo' folks made a mistake last night!" Sweetback was enraged, his voice sounding hoarse, yet psychopathic.

"I'ma make your whole squad pay for that!" Malcolm took a deep breath and walked away from Catfish to talk to Sweetback privately.

"Aye Sweetback... don't do it like that. It was a mistake. We're better than that. Where do you want me to drop your girl off at?"

Despite Malcolm utilizing his psychological skills and remaining calm amidst a crisis, it had no effect on the cold-blooded killer.

"Nigga, you can have that bitch; prepare for war, you soft-ass nigga!" With that, Sweetback and Malcolm both hung up their phones concurrently.

When Malcolm turned around, the look of dread sparkled in his eyes; Catfish eyed him suspiciously.

"What did he say Mal? Drop her off?"

Malcolm looked Catfish in the eye and spoke what he hadn't had to speak in over eighteen months.

"Let's prepare for war."

93

"A war with Sweetback?" Catfish asked in a lifeless manner.

"Not only with Sweetback, and not only with the Wolf, but a war with everyone in the city. It's time to remind people who runs shit around these parts."

Catfish smirked at him slyly. He had great difficulty suppressing his smile because he knew. He knew that the young, hungry Malcolm was back in full effect.

$~$~$~$~$

Marco was fuming. He'd wasted half of his night with Catfish, trying to help him out only to come home to gargantuan sized problems. Every soldier that reported to him said that they were out. They needed coke. Fast! It usually wouldn't be a problem, but that was because Kyla would work her magic. But with no Kyla... no magic. Marco knew that there was a big chance that the Dynasty Cartel could take over easily if they stayed out of product long enough, and he wasn't having that. He hit speed dial 1 and called Malcolm.

"Hey bro... we out... completely."

There was a pregnant silence as Malcolm measured the effects of his next statement.

"Okay... I'm sending contamination control this evening to fix things..." Silence again.

"Man, you know that shit's not gon' work Malcolm..."

"Fuck, it has to work right now! Besides, we got bigger problems... Sweetback declared war!"

The pitch of Malcolm's voice was eerie. It reminded Marco of the times when Malcolm used to go handle shit with Catfish, instead of just sending him solo or sending him with Prince Tron.

"Damn... a war? It's gonna be another war going on in the streets if the Dynasty Cartel confiscates our turf, our street and mid-level soldiers, and our clientele. Nigga... we need product!"

Malcolm sighed into the phone.

"Marco, I said I was sending Contamination Control. Everything's about to be back on track."

Marco shook his head as if Malcolm had lost all comprehension.

"Mal, they are not going to do business with someone new and you know it."

"Homeboy calm down, I got this... trust me. If worse comes to worse, then I have a reserve that should last us about long enough to find a new connect. But we'll take this one step at a time."

"Okay then, you're the leader... just keep me posted so I'll know what to tell these young hungry niggas."

"One."

Ten

Pam was dressed to impress. She had on a skin tight black and red mini shirt with some closed toe black and red heels. Her hair was dark and silky; not to mention laser beam straight. It made her look as if she had walked straight off of the cover of a magazine. Her nails were French-tipped, her skin was glowing, and she had applied a light coat of lip gloss which truly transformed her into a supermodel. Malcolm had called her and told her to meet him at the IHOP for lunch so that they could discuss some urgent matters. Pam was already there when Malcolm arrived. He didn't even know if she was early or if he was late because he was so stressed out. He gave her a hug when he reached their table and couldn't resist getting an erection when he wrapped his arms around her body. Her body was so tight and petite that he couldn't help but to imagine himself toting her around her bedroom on his dick. Malcolm noticed that Pam wasn't in a hurry to break away from the hug and politely took it upon himself to pull away. As he sat down, she couldn't help but to smile as her eyes wandered from his bulging crotch to his handsome face.

"You look beautiful, as always Pam," Malcolm said, truly meaning every word.

"You look good too, Daddy."

There was an uncomfortable silence lingering in the air as they both thought about what happened the last time she'd called him "Daddy". Kyla had been outraged and ready to fight her at The Power Building on that fateful day. Malcolm cleared his throat.

"Pam, I was going to wait before I sent you and Brink to see Franco Roberto, but Marco told me that we're completely out of cocaine. I trust you to make the deal go through just as smoothly as Kyla would have. The only issue existing is the one that Marco raised."

Pam glared at Malcolm defensively.

"What did that bastard have to say about me this time?" Pam said, rolling her eyes at no one in particular.

"Nothing major... he only stated that Franco Roberto wasn't going to do business with someone new. I just want you to prove him wrong," Malcolm said to her while staring in a different direction.

Pam reached out and tilted Malcolm's chin towards her so that she could make eye contact.

"Anything that Kyla can do, I can do too. I won't let you down Daddy," Pam spoke in a seductive tone.

Malcolm kissed her on the back of her hand, and then dismissed the waiter in irritation. He glanced out the window and saw Catfish pull up in his Escalade.

"Pam, I want you to be careful because a war has been declared against us and I don't know when or where the first strike will come, nor do I know who it will come against. I left you some weaponry in your Aston Martin. Brink is in the Escalade with Catfish. He's going to drive it to your house since he also has to go over some do's and don'ts of the negotiations game."

Pam nodded her head, all the while thinking, *What have I gotten myself into... a war?*

"Pam... try your best not to let me down baby."

Even though she was nervous inside, she still managed to display her most confident smile.

"I won't let you down, Daddy."

"Okay, good. I'm about to ride with Catfish and see if I can have this war shit settled by the time you return from your trip. Be careful Pam."

"Noooo," she said with concern in her voice, "you be careful Daddy."

He smiled at her and exited the restaurant. She didn't know whether to have a solo lunch, or leave the place like Malcolm did.

$~$~$~$~$

The last time that Catfish was involved with a street war, he tried to send his wife clear across the country so that she could go stay with her sister until the mayhem died down. Instead, Tricia's home girl convinced her that she could just stay with her and just say that she was in Boston. This time was no different from either angle. He told her to pack it up and she asked him why. He told her not to question his authority and she acted like she was mad. He paid for her a plane ticket and she went straight to her girlfriend's house.

"Not again Tricia. What's wrong with Catfish? Hasn't he made enough money so that he can get outta this shit? You know if you play with fire, you might get burned!" Tricia's girlfriend, Bonnie, said as she fired up a blunt.

The weed was so strong, that when she exhaled, a wheezing sound stirred from within her lungs as if she had the flu.

"Damn! Tricia, where the fuck you be getting this weed from girl?" Bonnie managed to choke out before passing it to Tricia.

"Shit, Catfish and Malcolm nem be flying to Egypt to get this shit," Tricia said before almost choking on the second hand smoke.

"Egypt? Niggas smoke weed in muthafuckin' Egypt? Got damn."

Both women started laughing at Bonnie's silly joke, but both women secretively wondered if niggas really did smoke weed in Egypt. Tricia got up and walked into the kitchen. After looking into the refrigerator, she went back and sat down on the sofa.

"Damn Bonnie, what you got in this house to snack on?"

"Man, my food stamps ain't came yet girl." Tricia eyed her with a teasing look on her face and said, "Damn, B, you just as ghetto as I don't know what."

Bonnie giggled, then shook her head at Tricia's remark, although it was true. No doubt about it, Bonnie... was ghetto as hell.

"Shit, I ain't got it like you Trish... you wanna go to the grocery store?"

Tricia already knew that question was coming. She was beginning to think that Bonnie only invited her over so that she could buy the groceries, and Bonnie could just sell the food stamps. Nevertheless,

Bonnie was her home girl and she had no problem with that. Besides, Bonnie was always there when Tricia needed her.

"Yeah B, let's run to the grocery store... wit' yo' trifling ass."

Bonnie started laughing and went off to retrieve her keys. Bonnie's car was an ashy black, 1996 Nissan Maxima. She had possessed the same vehicle for numerous years. When Tricia got in the car, she couldn't get away from noticing the similarities between Bonnie's apartment and her Nissan. They both could use a thorough cleaning, and both smelled of cheap weed masked with an even cheaper cherry incense.

"Damn B," Tricia said after observing the empty McDonald's bags covering the floor of her car, "you need to clean up yo' car, girl."

"Yeah Trish... I know right? It's just that I haven't been motivated to do nothing lately. I need to find me a man... I'm gettin' so sick of using my Lil Pocket Rocket that it's a shame."

"B, that's too much info."

Both women started laughing. Bonnie inserted the keys and turned the ignition, but the car wouldn't crank.

"Damn! You see what I mean Trish? I don't know shit about cars... I'm sick of being lonely."

Bonnie got out and pulled up her car hood, more in an effort to signify that she needed help, because she definitely had no clue as to what the hell she was staring at. After a few minutes, a guy pulled up in a Ford pick-up truck. He got out of his truck wearing a Jiffy Lube jacket and a concerned look on his face.

"Hey, what's the matter?" the guy asked in a concerned manner.

Bonnie instantly started flirting as she told the man about her vehicle not being able to start. He grabbed his toolbox from off the back of his truck and made his way back to the car.

"Hey Miss Lady, turn the ignition so that I can try to fix it for you."

"Okay," she said delightedly as she hurried back to get behind the wheel, "I hope you can fix everything." She smiled at Tricia, who smiled back at her girlfriend's inside joke.

"Okay, hold it... now turn it... hold it... try it again... okay stop."

The man fidgeted in his tool box until he found the tool he was looking for. Then he walked around to the driver's side and motioned for Bonnie to roll down her window.

"Hey, ain't yo' name Bonnie or something like that?" The man asked while smiling.

Surprised, and caught completely off guard, Bonnie stared at the man, trying to see if she knew him from somewhere. She couldn't recall.

"That's my name. Where do I know you from?" she asked inquisitively.

The man started to laugh, and then his face turned serious.

"You don't know me from a can of worms!"

He then laid the stainless steel Glock on the side of her head and despite the women screaming, and despite the "Please! You can have everything!" plea from Bonnie, he still blew her brains clear across to the passenger side window. The woman's lifeless body slumped over sideways as blood rushed from her head onto Tricia's trembling hands. The gunshot itself sounded like four 15-inch subwoofers being powered by four 3,000 watt amps all hitting simultaneously. The car was the speaker box. It was good music for Sweetback Fatty, who was sitting inside the Ford pickup truck behind the tinted windows.

Another one of Sweetback's men jumped out and helped carry an already traumatized Tricia into the truck. She was shaking and convulsing so hard, they thought that she was going to shatter. They gagged and hog-tied her, then they drove off. Sweetback had struck, and he was only warming up.

$~$~$~$~$

The Dynasty Cartel was the most powerful organization in the city before The Bankroll Squad emerged. At one time they were pumping coke, crack, weed, and heroin on almost every street corner and project housing unit in the city. They had even infiltrated the suburbs by setting up trap houses in some of the most upscale communities inside and on the outskirts of the city. Those days, Malcolm's newly formed crew simply wanted the South side, leaving The Dynasty Cartel with the North, East, and West sides of the city. Out of courtesy, Malcolm set up a meeting with Rally, who was the leader of the cartel.

At the meeting, Malcolm made his case, and by the end of the meeting, Malcolm's request for control of the South side was denied. He politely shook Rally's hand, then he exited the meeting. That same night Malcolm made a decision that would propel the Bankroll Squad from ambitious hustlers to the ultimate bosses. Malcolm, Catfish, Marco, Prince Tron, and Veronica all went on a rampage. It was mayhem in the city. They successfully took out entire blocks and neighborhoods that were being run by the Dynasty Cartel. They shot up trap houses and used the street sweepers to clean up the corners where the work was being served.

Rally was pissed when he heard that all of his soldiers were getting knocked off the map, so he immediately sent a message to Malcolm to let him know that him and his Squad could have the south side. But by the time he could deliver that message to Malcolm, the Bankroll Squad was already running the whole city. They had run the Dynasty Cartel off of all major corners within the time span of four hours. Just like that, they went from asking for the south side to setting up shop on every side; leaving the Dynasty Cartel powerless. The Bankroll Squad's reign went from local to global in under four months. Malcolm had weight and break-downs selling in his city, but had Marco strategically place small teams in every other major city in the U.S. that strictly sold weight.

Rally was seething with anger because of what had turned out to be a huge disaster for the Dynasty Cartel's reputation and for their income. But there was nothing that he could do about it without placing his entire fortune at stake. He would have to re-recruit and spend money to go to war with a group of young, wild ass niggas who had nothing to lose. It wasn't as if he didn't have enough money to handle it; it was just the opposite. He had too much money to handle it. He didn't want to risk catching a case and not being able to enjoy the fruits of his labor; or somebody in the Cartel catching a murder case and telling on the whole Cartel. Rally just couldn't see the war being an intelligent response during the time. Besides, he figured that all those young niggas lacked the wisdom that the dope game required in order to have longevity. He estimated that they would all have Federal convictions within a year's time frame. His estimation was wrong. The only person

103

to catch a case in the Bankroll Squad was Veronica; and she only had about a year left on her manslaughter conviction.

During the first year of the Bankroll Squad's reign, Rally just sat back and watched. He didn't need the money, and he was planning on taking an extended vacation anyway. But during the year that he prayed for their downfall, he saw them floss, stunt and ball like no other. He saw them do things with their money that hadn't been possible for him to even think about during his first year hustling. They threw parades for the city, had food drives every month, celebrity-hosted parties every week, and did donuts in Bentleys.

When Malcolm started the potato chip business, Rally nearly lost his mind. The Bankroll Squad's lifestyle had become so attractive, that almost half of the Dynasty Cartel's remaining soldiers were begging to be a part of their squad. That was the last straw for Rally, who had no intentions on having his Cartel dissolve completely. However, there was nothing that he could do to prevent that from happening. Malcolm paid his soldiers double what Rally paid his, and since Rally was aging, it also made his Cartel less appealing. Rally was suffering from jealousy until one day he came up with an ingenious idea. He had to send multiple buyers to the Bankroll Squad; he had all of them request a different product from them, just to see if the idea would work. And it did work. It turned out that they had almost every other drug except for meth.

On a hail mary attempt, he tried to flood the city and state with the drug. And the users bought it. He was back in the game, but not the game that he loved the most: cocaine. His Mexican connect berated him as if he was beyond incompetent for letting a young group of niggas take over the coke game. The part that hurt the Mexican the most was that he had tried to supply the Bankroll Squad at $12,000 per kilo;

provided that they buy at least 100 at a time, and Malcolm declined his offer. Then Malcolm had the audacity to try to sell him his coke at $9,000 a kilo. The Mexican was baffled, and when he told Rally, he too was baffled. Rally stepped back into the shadows, while continuing to peddle his meth. He stepped back because of two reasons that he always believed in: one was that every dog had its day, and two was that all things must come to an end. The day he had waited for, for so long had finally arrived. The run had come to an end.

eleven

Rally was sitting in the game room of his mansion massaging his temples when Diaz, his right hand man, barged into the room.

"Hey Ral, guess what?"

Rally gave Diaz a dumbfounded expression before covering his face with his hands and shaking his head.

"I'm in no mood for guessing games Diaz."

Rally then leaned back on his leather couch and stared at Diaz weary-eyed. Knowing Diaz, he would probably force him to guess before he told him what the deal was.

"What D? You saved a whole bunch of money on your car insurance by —"

"No silly," Diaz said, cutting him off.

"I got a surprise visitor for you with some surprising information. Information that I guarantee will make you a very, very happy man!"

"Diaz," Rally said with a hint of heavy fatigue in his voice, "I'm not sure that any visitor can surprise me. When you get to be my age, my man, the feeling that most people identify with as surprise starts to register in your brain as irritation."

Diaz's forehead wrinkled up, then he shook his head at Rally's foolish philosophy. He walked out of the room, then a tall, lanky guy entered the room. The man looked in both directions, as if he was crossing a street with heavy traffic. He made his way up to Rally and kept looking around as if he was paranoid. Rally recognized the man instantly; he had known him since he was still in Huggies. It was his little brother, Dexter.

"Hey bro —"

"Don't hey bro me after you betrayed your own flesh and blood by working for that damned Bankroll Squad! You sell out!" Rally snapped at him.

"Ral, I begged you to give me a job in the Dynasty Cartel and you told me no! I wasn't good enough to work for you? I needed money man, and my joining them was an attempt to get paid. It was a decision that any young hustler would have made. Even you, my brother," Dexter shot back.

"I'm not your brother!" Rally snarled at Dexter.

"Ral, we will always be brothers. We are two men, blood and flesh of the same, and products of the same source."

Dexter extended his hand to Rally, who finally let his arrogance subside long enough to accept his brother's hand.

"Dexter, I didn't give you a job because I didn't want you to be a part of this world. A world of living above the law and above your means and doing any and everything possible to get to the top. And even at the top, you're still at the bottom. And we'll always be, because this is the underworld. I wanted so much more for my little brother,"

107

Rally said with sadness in his voice and concern in his eyes.

"I understand what you're telling me Rally, but look at how successful I've become. The game is in my blood."

The door opened and Rally's personal servant brought in two champagne glasses and a bottle of Ace Of Spades. He poured both men a glass and left the room without speaking a word. Rally took a sip from his glass, then stood up and walked to his window. His brother sat for a couple of minutes, and after finishing his glass he soon joined Rally at the window.

"There is no way for me to deny the fact that the game is in your blood. You've made a serious name for yourself in the streets, but when are you going to graduate to being a boss?"

The words sank in as Dexter imagined himself owning a sprawling estate like his big brother Rally.

"Rally, that's why I came to you today. I've been putting in major work for the Bankroll Squad by following directions from a guy named Marco. As long as I've been risking my life and freedom for the squad, I have yet to meet Malcolm or even get a promotion. I came to you to let you know that I'm ready. I've proven myself Rally. Make me a boss."

Rally met Dexter's gaze briefly, then turned away.

"Dexter," Rally said while rubbing his chin, "your clientele and specialty is cocaine, am I correct?"

"Yeah, cocaine and crack. Why?"

"Because I don't deal coke! I deal meth! You and your little group owns the coke game, so how could I possibly make you a boss?"

"Well, I came to let you know that if we make a move now, the coke game will belong to the Dynasty Cartel, and things will be back to how they're supposed to be."

Rally frowned at Dexter suspiciously.

"Dexter, do you owe them some money or something? Keep it real with me please. What's going on, little bro?"

Dexter smiled at Rally's outlandish assumptions.

"No Rally, I don't have any type of personal vendetta or anything; it's just that... I tried to re-up last night and Marco didn't answer the phone. Thcn I finally get a hold of him this morning and he gathers the nerve to tell me that he's out. So at first I think he's yanking my card, right? But nah man, everybody in the streets is buzzing about this shit 'cause it's the first time they ever went dry. Right now, I got 100 niggas that are willing to switch sides if you can get the work. Our clientele are lining up as we speak, waiting on your reply Rally."

Rally looked at Dexter in astonishment.

"Dexter, don't you realize that you're standing here begging for a war? All 100 of your little friends could end up in the morgue, don't you see?"

Dexter shot Rally an icy glare.

"You think that we don't already know this Rally? We're all grown men; just put me in charge and I promise that failure is not an option. I'm ready for war!"

Rally admired the spark in Dexter's voice, but wondered if his little brother could perform under pressure in the most critical situations of a full-fledged street war.

"Diaz! Come here!" Rally shouted through the intercom microphone.

It only took a few seconds for Diaz to arrive in the room.

"Dexter, you know Diaz has been my best friend since forever, right?"

Dexter looked at Diaz, then at Rally and nodded his head.

"Okay then Dexter; now kill him."

Diaz looked like a deer standing in the headlights of a speeding truck as Dexter pulled out a .44 with lighting speed and pointed it at Diaz's chest. Before Rally was afforded the opportunity to yell, "wait," Dexter pulled the trigger. WHAM! The bullet penetrated Diaz's shirt and knocked him off of his feet and across the couch. Before Diaz could move again, Dexter had jumped over the couch after him with a Glock 40 in his other hand and slammed the barrel against Diaz's hairline.

"Dexter!" Rally screamed ferociously. "That's enough! Good job. And Diaz better be thankful I made him wear his bullet proof vest!"

Rally walked around the couch and gave Diaz a hand so that he could get up.

"Diaz, call up the Mexican and tell him we need 600 kilos within the next three hours. We're back in business."

Rally embraced Dexter warmly.

"Welcome home kid. And before I forget; hey Diaz… never let people come into my house with a weapon on them again."

Diaz nodded and walked off, still clutching his sore chest in agony.

$~$~$~$~$

Catfish and Malcolm took Tracy to the Bankroll Squad's main trap house, which was located a couple of miles south from the downtown Greyhound station. The house had been nicknamed "Trapquarters" by Marco since it made the most money of all twelve houses. The house was headed by a young lieutenant named Luther, who carried an AK and looked like he hadn't showered in days. Marco had stopped by earlier and explained that there would be more cocaine later on in the evening, and told him for now, to push the heroin, X, and weed.

Luther called him back two hours later and told him that their clients wanted crack, and the traffic was the slowest he had ever seen since he'd started working there. Marco passed the message along to Malcolm, and also told him that every employee at Trapquarters was getting antsy about the situation. Malcolm decided that since they didn't have anything to do, they could just watch Tracy for him. Catfish knew, as well as Malcolm, that those young niggas would end up fucking the shit out of her against her will.

When Malcolm, Catfish, and Tracy went inside the house, there were a series of fiends knocking on the door. They thought that Trapquarters had re-upped its coke supply. When Luther told a few of them "no," it seemed as if they disappeared into thin air. Before Malcolm could explain the situation to Luther, his cell phone rang. When he glanced at the caller ID and saw Sweetback Fatty's name blinking, he knew that he had to take the call. He hit the speakerphone option and it seemed like volts of electricity ran through Catfish's body when he heard his wife on the phone screaming his name for help. Then the screaming stopped and Sweetback's voice came crisply through the speaker.

"In this particular war, the theme is chess and the city is our chessboard. Catfish, it is only fair that if you take my queen off the board, then I find it imperative that I remove your queen from the board. I do this shit for a living, so there's no possible way for you to checkmate me in three moves. On the contrary, you have no idea what kind of shit your whole squad is in. I will prevail from your mistakes and you will collapse under my pressure. Now I advise you to move. You are in check!"

The window in the traphouse shattered and everyone hit the floor as bullets flew throughout the house. Malcolm looked out of the broken glass and saw an old model Monte Carlo speeding up the block.

"Cat, let's go!"

Malcolm and Catfish were running towards the door when they heard Luther tell a guy named Mike to watch Tracy and keep the house intact. All three of them jumped in the Escalade and sped off.

"Fuuuuuuuuucccckk!" Catfish screamed as he bent around the corner speeding after the vehicle.

He slammed his clip in his .45 and screamed out again as the thought of his wife being kidnapped ran through his mind.

"I'ma kill that bastard! That's my word Malcolm; I promise! Sweetback is as good as dead!" Catfish said, but seeing that he wasn't going to catch up with the Monte Carlo, he decided to bust a left and drive to the heart of the ghetto.

He was headed to Sweetback's soul food restaurant. Under normal circumstances, Malcolm would have objected to attacking a place that held so many innocent bystanders, but today was not a normal day. As soon as they got within eye sight of the eatery, Catfish rolled all the windows down, and Luther hung out the back window with a loaded AK and let loose. Malcolm stuck his machine gun out of his window and let loose; Luther and Malcolm shot up the restaurant, shattering all the glass and causing everyone to duck for cover. Malcolm aimed his .45 at the big, bright neon sign that said "SWEET'S" and put a hole in every letter, causing the sign to come crashing against the cement. As Catfish sped from the scene, Malcolm's phone lit up again. It was Jennifer. He hit connect, but he couldn't hear her over Catfish's ranting.

"Cat... Catfish! Hold the volume down for one second; let me take this call. Whassup Jennifer Powers?! What the fuck is wrong with you?" Malcolm screamed into the phone.

"Fuck is wrong with me? The fuck is wrong with you? Out all fucking evening yesterday with your little whore? Is that what happened? Is that why you had your phone turned off?" Jennifer shot back with an attitude.

"No Jen... I was at the hospital with Kyla. She —"

"For what? Is that bitch pregnant? Fuck this; it's over with me and you, Malcolm!"

There was a silence on the phone as both of them registered the effects of that statement.

"Jen, you got the nerve to divorce me over some petty shit like that?"

113

"Malcolm, this is far from petty. Our relationship has been going downhill for the past three months," Jennifer said while starting to cry,

"I know you dream about that Kyla chick, because I hear you calling her name in the middle of the night. I know it's her you want. Your mind says Jennifer, but your heart and soul screams her name!"

Jennifer's voice was trembling so bad that she could barely finish.

"I've already packed up and moved out Malcolm. Good luck. Criminal."

They got back around to Trapquarters and dropped Luther off. They told him that they would take Tracy with them; Malcolm had a strategy that he was about to implement. Luther escorted her back to the Escalade and dapped up Catfish and Malcolm.

"Aye Luther," Malcolm said, "Program my cell number into your phone; I'm proud of you, young nigga. I want you to call my phone direct if you have any problems. Also, in a few hours, the coke will be here; so hold tight and tell everyone else to do the same."

This meant a lot to the young guy, for the big man himself to reassure him that he was doing a good job. He took Malcolm's number and went back into Trapquarters with his head held high. Before Catfish could pull off, Malcolm got into the backseat of the Escalade with Tracy. He took the duct tape from over her mouth and untied her wrists. Her eyes were bloodshot red and the rope was so tight that her wrists were bruised. Malcolm felt sorry that she had to be a prisoner of war, and felt even worse for Catfish. Catfish's other half was in the same exact predicament. He simply hoped and prayed that she would remain okay until they got a chance to rescue her.

"Will you p-p-p... please... just kill me?" Tracy asked Malcolm in a hoarse voice.

Malcolm stared at the woman, who happened to be very attractive.

"No, I will not kill you Tracy. You've done nothing to harm me. I just wanted to know if you were hungry."

When he showed concern and common courtesy, her eyes lit up like Christmas lights.

"Yes! Please sir; I am both hungry and thirsty. Please sir!" she pleaded, almost on the verge of begging.

Malcolm placed his hand on the back of her hand gently, and looked into her eyes. Her windows to the soul revealed both fear and surprise.

"Everything's going to be fine Tracy. Just relax. I know this is a very difficult situation for you. I apologize for the inconvenience. And... from now on, don't call me sir, call me Malcolm."

Catfish shot a glance at Malcolm in the rear view mirror and shook his head. He knew that Malcolm could play mind games like no other.

twelve

Franco Roberto would not accept a substitute for Kyla. He had lived in the United States for five years before the FBI indicted him. The charges were heavy and his penalty was more than likely going to be life in federal prison. His extremely high paid team of lawyers were able to get him a million dollar bond. Before trial, they tried to get him to settle for a 30 year plea deal. He told them to let him think about it and he would get back to them later. At midnight, right before the deadline for him to choose between the plea deal and the trial, he became a United States fugitive. He went back to Colombia and only trusted a select few people. Pam was certainly not one of them.

As soon as he saw her and Brink on his security monitor, he immediately thought that she was a spineless gold digger. He felt like if the FBI pressured her enough, she would definitely lead them directly to his whereabouts. He decided that the best thing for him to do was to never let her see him. He'd only do business with either Kyla or Malcolm, but he had long since stopped Malcolm from taking those trips. Franco figured that the feds would waste no time investigating a black man who took frequent flights to Colombia, but wouldn't press so hard on a low-key Puerto Rican who could pass for Colombian. But this chick... this woman... she was absolutely too flashy.

She drew way too much attention to herself for this line of work. Pam stood at the gate, impatiently twirling her hair around her finger.

She buzzed the intercom alert for the tenth time. Finally, a voice came through the speakerphone.

"May I help you?" The voice spoke, in broken English.

Pam then cleared her throat, and tried to sound as professional as possible. The whiteness in her genes was more than obvious in her vocal accent.

"Yes, Malcolm sent me to see Franco Roberto..." she trailed off.

Silence decorated the atmosphere. Pam hit the buzzer three more times before the broken English speared its way through the speakers again.

"Are you Kyla?" the voice said.

"No, I'm Pam. I'm a part of the Bankroll —"

The voice then cut her off. "I'm sorry. I know nothing about a bank roll, and furthermore, there is no Franco anybody residing at this residence."

Brink then rolled his eyes because he'd been taking this same trip for years and hearing that same voice forever.

"Come on man; she's good people," Brink added in.

"Is this the fuckin' pilot speaking to me? Listen close knucklehead... take your saddity looking broad and go back where you came from. I don't even like sugar substitute, much less a Kyla substitute. Be gone!"

The intercom beeped off and Pam was about to buzz it again but Brink stopped her arm in mid-air. A look of frustration and defeat eclipsed her face and her skin was red. She scowled at Brink with eyes that could kill.

"Brink, you know I gotta make this work! Malcolm told me not to let him down!"

She started wrestling with Brink's grip, trying her best to free her arms, but to no avail. Brink went ahead and put her in a bear hug so that she couldn't move.

"Pam, listen! It's not going to work, so we need to leave before we get ourselves killed out here. Look around, don't you see what's on the roof?"

When Pam looked at the roof, all of her determination leaked out of her and was replaced by a mixture of anger and terror. Anger because she felt like everyone favored Kyla over her. As if Kyla was a fuckin' queen or something. Terror because gunmen were aiming at them from all angles, just waiting on them to try something funny. Finally defeated, they returned to their friend's house where they had landed the jet.

"Brink, why can't Malcolm just give that loser a call and tell him that I'm substituting for Kyla?" Pam asked.

"Malcolm and Franco never talk on the phone; it's way too risky for the both of them. I'm sure that Malcolm will understand the situation, so try not to stress over it too much."

"But I wanted to prove myself to him! I wanted him to know that I could be the Bonnie to his Clyde!"

Brink realized that he was no longer hearing determination in her voice. He was listening to emotions. Emotions left room for mistakes. He shook his head and went to go refuel the jet.

$~$~$~$~$

Sweetback was far from pleased when he found out that Malcolm and Catfish had shot up his restaurant. His eatery was not only his hangout spot; it was also his pride and joy. He had saved quite a bit of money up from his hitman work in order to build a legal establishment that his son could be proud of one day. His heart fell to the ground when he saw his soul food restaurant shot up and reduced damn near to debris. He'd been unable to secure any type of insurance on the place simply because it was located in a drug infested area. It was located in the heart of the ghetto, but the food was so good that it attracted business from all over the city. Now it was gone. The only good thing about it was that none of the customers got hurt. That, he was very thankful for.

The police arrived at the scene while he was calculating the damages. Bone, Sweetback's right hand man, peeped the cops and pulled off in the Ford 1500 while Sweetback handled his business. He wanted to stick around, but he couldn't because he still had Tricia held hostage in the vehicle. Plus the truck was loaded with guns. He certainly wasn't trying to go out like that. When the police finished up with their questioning of Sweetback, Sweetback called Bone and told him to come back around and pick him up.

"What they talkin' 'bout Sweet?" Sweetback sighed and looked into the extended cab at his potential kidnapping charge.

"Man, them crackers talkin' about they're going to position two police officers outside of my house for the next ten days! I told them

119

that it wasn't needed but they insisted because they think that this shooting was an attempt on my life. Maaann... Bone, we're going to have to end this bullshit with Malcolm and them. I can't afford to have the police watching me while I'm keeping this bitch hostage. Besides... when me you, and Waller rode by Trapquarters, Waller didn't fire one single shot. You were driving, so that's explainable, but Waller... it was his fuckin' idea and he just sat in the back watching me shoot. Sometimes I don't believe that he's really my little brother when he does shit like that. The man had his mouth sewed shut because he couldn't keep it closed, and here we are fighting a war and risking our lives and possessions for him. He's a grown man now. It's time for him to man-up. I'm going to have to let him fend for his self."

Tricia was happy to hear that they were going to let her go, but she was haunted by the fact that these two heartless men had killed her best friend in front of her. They'd literally blown her brains out of her skull and were acting like if they let her go, everything would be okay. Fuck that, she thought. She would avenge her friends' death by any means. She sat in the extended cab, gagged and bound, thinking about how she was going to pull it off.

$~$~$~$~$

Malcolm took Tracy to his private quarters, and fed her a healthy sized T-Bone steak, eggs, toast, and orange juice. He apologized again for the situation, and she told him not to worry about it. She was amazed at the size of his house and shocked by his hospitality. She didn't even get this type of treatment in a real relationship. When she finished eating, he asked her if she would like something additional to eat. After she declined, he went into his bathroom to fill up the Jacuzzi for her to have a nice relaxing time after all she'd been through. The Jacuzzi had been purchased in China and had a state of the art, oscillating water distribution system. The water spun around and back around, giving whomever was in it a satisfying body massage without the need of a masseuse. Tracy got into the contraption and was on the brink of an orgasm within two minutes. It was feeling too good to her at first, so she climbed out and started drying the water off her body.

However, she didn't want to leave out of the bathroom hot and horny and have no way of fixing her dilemma. She threw the towel onto the floor and climbed back into the tub. The water twisted and tickled against her nipples, vagina, and clitoris simultaneously, pushing her deeper and deeper into the valleys of ecstasy. Her pussy started contracting and convulsing involuntarily as an orgasm rippled through her body, causing her to moan and squirm in the exotic Jacuzzi. After the first orgasm, another one immediately proceeded to develop afterwards. She came again, and afterwards she jumped out of the tub and grabbed the towel. Her knees were wobbling and her body was weak, but her pussy was soaking wet.

Malcolm had given her a gray sports bra and some gray cotton boy shorts that fit her voluptuous body like biking shorts. The attire had come out of Jennifer's closet and had never been worn. Jen's ass was 36 inches around, but Tracy's was 38 inches. Tracy came out of the bathroom and sat on the waterbed. When Malcolm entered the room, she had her legs spread, rubbing lotion onto her skin. He saw that, but he couldn't avoid spotting the huge wet spot in her vaginal area. Her pussy cream was leaking through her panties.

"I'm sorry," Malcolm said, as he turned to exit the room.

"Wait," Tracy's voice called out, "it's okay; I need your help anyway..."

A look of surprise framed Malcolm's facial features as he stood still without moving. She held up the bottle of Lubriderm lotion.

"Can you rub this onto my back please?"

Malcolm hesitated for a minute, and just kept staring at her. Finally he broke out of the trance and made his way over to the bed. He grabbed the lotion bottle and she turned over and laid on her stomach. When Malcolm saw her beautiful body from the rear, his dick immediately got rock hard. He pulled up her sports bra and she grabbed it and pulled it all the way off. He kept staring at her wet pussy print as he massaged her lower back in a circular motion. When he heard her moan in ecstasy, he felt like he had to try her.

He tugged at the band of the extra tight boy shorts and she lifted her waist up so that he could pull them all the way off. He unbuckled his belt and slid down his Donald Trump slacks. Malcolm was sporting a revolutionary erection and was positioning his manhood at a downward angle so that he could enter. He planned to take his time, but Tracy had other plans. She reached behind her and wrapped her petite hands around Malcolm's thick manhood. She was amazed at how thick it was and became nervous when she stroked her hand down its length. It was longer and thicker than any dick she'd ever taken, but as wet as her pussy was, she knew she would be able to take it. Malcolm moved her hand out of the way and placed his thick piece of meat at her wet, warm entrance. He parted her pussy lips with his left hand and slid half of his shaft inside of her with his right hand.

"Ooooohhh," she moaned as she fell face forward to the pillow, running away from his dick.

As soon as she hit the bed, Malcolm straddled her by sitting on the back of her upper thighs. His dick was already dripping wet from her pussy cream, so he used it as an additional lubricant and slid his dick all the way inside of her. Her fingernails dug into the sheet and her teeth sank into the pillow. Her pussy was sloppy wet as Malcolm continued to slide in and out. Every time she tried to squirm away, he would go harder into her. His long, thick strokes were causing her to scream out into the pillow. Although the sounds were muffled, they were still audible throughout the room.

"Ah-ah-ah-ah-ah-oooh-ah-ah-ah-shit-ah-ahdamnah-ah-ah- this dick is gooood-ah-ah-ah."

The only other sound was her pussy farting as she came all over his thick dick. The farting noises were constantly happening every time he slid his dick all the way back into her sloppy wet pussy. Pussy cream had splattered out of her as he fucked her and had created a big, dark wet circle underneath her on the champagne colored sheets. After she came for the fourth time, Malcolm pulled out of her convulsing body and went to go wash off. As she lay there thinking, she knew that that dick was all she would want for a long time to come.

thirteen

Sweetback and Bone dropped Tricia off at the car wash and gave her $150 for cab fare and something to eat. They called Malcolm and explained their standpoint on the whole Waller situation and informed them that they didn't want to take it any further than it had already gone. Catfish was anxious to go pick up his wife, but Malcolm was wary that it might be a setup and didn't want to go for the "Okie dokie." However, when Tricia called Catfish's cell phone from the pay phone booth and all she could do was cry for the first few minutes, Catfish jumped to his feet and said that he would go get his wife with or without Malcolm. Malcolm felt his pain, and told him to give him a couple minutes to call for back up.

He called Prince Tron, Luther, and Marco, and all three arrived within the span of twenty minutes. Malcolm's plan was to drop Tracy off at the same location that they were picking up Tricia. They all hopped into the Escalade; all five of them were carrying firearms with military strength scopes and ammo to go with each gun. When they approached the car wash, they saw that there were no vehicles there. They checked their surroundings, and when it looked like it was fine, they pulled the SUV into the car wash parking lot. Before they could even stop good, Tricia came running from the side of the building towards the SUV. At first it scared the men, who had pointed AK's and M-16s at the female who seemingly came out of nowhere.

Catfish hollered at everyone, "put the guns down!"

Malcolm dropped the AK when he saw the familiar face, and everyone else followed his lead. Catfish unlocked the door and Tricia jumped into the truck, crying frantically.

"They... they... they... killed her! Catfish, they killed her! Malcolm, Catfish, they —!"

"Tricia, calm down a second. Tell us what happened. Who killed who? "Malcolm inquired.

A look of horror was displayed on Tricia's face as she stared straight ahead without responding.

"Tricia!" Catfish screamed.

Still no response. Tracy, recognizing the symptoms of traumatization, slapped her across the face, surprising everyone. Tricia instantly snapped out of her trance and slapped Tracy right back across her face. Everyone in the SUV started smirking despite the seriousness of the situation.

"The people who kidnapped me, killed my best friend, Bonnie!"

Catfish was beginning to get irritated. "How the fuck did Bonnie get in this shit?"

Tricia dropped her head down because she knew that she had disobeyed her man.

"I... was at her house and they —"

"What the fuck were you doing at Bonnie's house when you were supposed to be in Boston?!" Catfish blared at his wife.

"I was sick of having to leave my home, my city just because of these games that y'all are playing in the street! I'm sick of this shit Catfish. I can't keep living like this."

The SUV got quiet as Tricia started back crying. Malcolm opened his door and got out without saying a word. He shut the door and got on his cell phone. After about five minutes, he climbed back into the truck.

"Tracy, I told Sweetback that I was going to drop you off here so that he could pick you up and he said, "Fuck that broad," and hung up on me. What's the deal with you two?"

"Fuck that nigga! He care about his child, but he don't give a damn if I die or live. He hates me!" Tracy said.

Malcolm checked his watch and saw that it was about time for Brink and Pam to check in.

"Well hey... look... I'll personally take you to wherever it is that you're trying to go in a couple of hours if you can wait, because right now I have something very, very, important that I need to tend to."

Tracy was more than happy as she thought about the possibility that she would be able to spend more time with Malcolm.

"I can wait. I'm ready when you're ready."

Catfish started the vehicle and started to head back towards Malcolm's estate when he remembered something.

"Say Tracy, didn't you say you knew who the Wolf was?"

All eyes turned towards her.

"Ah... yeah... why?"

"Do you know where he stays?"

"Of course I do; it's only about ten minutes from here." Catfish glanced at Malcolm, and Malcolm nodded his head, letting Catfish know he was on the same accord.

"Okay... show us where he stays at."

After Tracy showed them where the Wolf stayed at, the Squad decided that they would handle him later and let Malcolm handle his business. Like Malcolm, everyone else was anticipating Pam's return, and hoping that she would return with good news. They headed back to Malcolm's estate and waited on them.

$~~~~~~~~~~~~~~~~~~~~~~~~$ *S~S~S~S~S*

Pam was a failure. When she told Malcolm the news, it hit him like an anvil and he felt sick to his stomach. His face displayed a look of disgust and his mind was gently approaching panic mode. Marco was raising hell, talking about how the Dynasty Cartel was going to lock the city down. Luther was speechless; he had never been in such a situation in his life. He was used to the Bankroll Squad's coke coming like clockwork, 24/7. Catfish just twiddled his thumbs because that wasn't his line of work anyway. He was still pissed off about the Kyla situation, and even more so now that they knew where the Wolf stayed and he was still breathing. Prince Tron was also pissed, but what could he do but what his leader ordered him to. Brink tried to take up for Pam.

"Malcolm, this girl tried her hardest man."

"Fuck that Brink. Her hardest was definitely not hard enough," Malcolm said while getting up off of the couch.

He walked over to Pam, who was standing up with her head down and her hands behind her back.

"I'm sorry Malcolm... he just wouldn't give me a chance," Pam said somberly, as she raised her head up to his chest, still avoiding eye contact.

Her self-esteem was shot. She really wanted to prove that she could do whatever Kyla could do but she had not been very successful.

"I wouldn't give anybody a chance if they were dressed like you're dressed. You don't look like you went to conduct a drug deal; you look like you went to set a muthafucka up and have him killed."

If those same words had been spoken by anyone else, they would have had no effect on her; but when Malcolm spoke those words to her, she could feel the hurt and pain deep down in her soul. She was embarrassed and didn't enjoy being made a fool of by the very man that she wanted.

"Malcolm, no one told me what the damn dress code was supposed to be!"

"Ohhh, so you figured that you would just dress like a slut and that would be fine?"

"I didn't dress like a slut, Malcolm. I dressed with taste; something your honky wife doesn't have and Kyla will never have!"

"What?! Get a taste of my front door, then get a taste of the highway before you get a taste of blood in your mouth!"

"Malcolm!" Brink and Catfish shouted at him in unison.

"Bro, you know it's not Pam's fault. I say we fix the root of the problem... The Wolf," Catfish blurted.

"Naw Cat," Malcolm said.

"Actually this is Pam's fault. It's her fault because she's a jealous and conniving bitch who always wants to try to outdo Kyla in some form or fashion," he continued.

When Pam heard him say that, a single tear rolled down her face and she finally looked Malcolm in the eyes. She wanted to search his gaze to see if he actually meant the words that he was speaking to her, or if he was speaking out of frustration and anger. She stared into one of the coldest gazes that she had ever seen Malcolm form, and was immediately at a loss for words. To her it felt like her heart had short circuited and her life had vanished right before her very eyes.

"Malcolm... I've never told you this... but I have always loved you. That's why I tried to outdo Kyla all the time. I wanted your attention. I wanted you to love me in return." Pam wiped her eyes and took a deep breath. "Just telling you the truth about how I feel makes me feel a whole lot better. Now... I just wanna ask you one thing Malcolm. Why wouldn't you love me?"

Malcolm had a confused look on his face. "Pamela, first of all, this is the first time that you've ever revealed your feelings to me. I couldn't read your mind. Second, how could I love a woman who is scared to be herself? If a woman is scared to be herself, then I'm scared of who she really is."

Pam stood there for a moment, letting the words sink in while finally

129

coming to grips with reality. The reality was that Malcolm did not love her, nor would he love her anytime soon.

"You know what Malcolm? You're absolutely correct about your assessment of me. I'm really not being myself. Here I am with a college degree and I'm still risking my life and my freedom by playing these silly games in the streets. I could have ended up like Kyla... a beautiful woman with a college degree who may never make it out of the hospital. It was fun in the beginning, the lure and attractiveness of large sums of money coming at breakneck speeds; but now I walk... I will no longer risk my life for the Bankroll Squad again. I'm rich, as we all are, so I don't see the point in continuing this lifestyle."

Pam kissed Malcolm on his cheek, turned and walked out of the mansion, leaving everyone's jaws hanging on the floor. Everybody knew that Malcolm had overreacted; as he tended to do a lot of at times. Pam walked out of the organization. She was finished.

$~$~$~$~$

Dexter had 590 kilos of coke left. He had been successful in putting The Dynasty Cartel in control of only one of the Bankroll Squad's trap houses. The leaders of the other trap houses declined the offer, saying that they would just wait it out a while. The house that he'd put the Dynasty Cartel in control of wasn't that difficult of a task since it was actually the same house that Marco had put him in control of for the Bankroll Squad. Rally gave Dexter a small crew and told him that he had thirty days to show him that he deserved to be a boss. Dexter accepted the stipulations, but he had butterflies in his stomach because he had never been in such a powerful position before in his life. He definitely didn't wanna let Rally down, but he just wished that he could have as much faith in his own self as Rally had in him.

130

Diaz and Rally were at the estate sitting back watching the two strippers that they had hired play in the pool. Diaz always went to the strip clubs and recruited the best of the best. He always paid them $2,000 a piece to spend the whole day with them, but Diaz, nor Rally ever paid them any attention unless they wanted to have sex.

"They look like dolphins," Diaz said as he watched the naked girls swim from one end to another.

"Well shit... you certainly treat them like damn dolphins," Rally remarked.

"How so?"

"It certainly doesn't take a genius to answer that question Diaz. All you do is feed them little pieces of fish and let them play in the water!"

Both men started laughing at the wisecrack. The men got silent as they watched the women climb out of the pool, water glistening off of their bronze and brownish skin tones. The short girl's pussy was so fat that they could see it hanging almost 30 feet away. Diaz felt himself getting an erection and decided to quickly change the subject before he ended up locked in a bedroom for the rest of the evening when there was still business that needed to be handled.

"Rally. You think your little brother can get off of all of that coke? It's damn near... what... a life or death responsibility; am I correct?"

Silence from Rally as he twisted the top off of his bottled water and downed two pills.

"Diaz, if a man can't move 600 kilos in a drought, he don't deserve to live. Kin or no kin. It'll take about a week before people start

131

realizing that Dynasty runs the city again, so until then, let the dealers stay in denial. Once they spend everything but their re-up money waiting on the Bankroll Squad to make it out of their drought, they'll have no choice but to switch sides. This is not about loyalty, this is about business. If, in one week, we haven't gained control of Trapquarters... then we'll buy the house across the street to trap out of and let the hustlers in Trapquarters know that we mean business."

"That's a helluva stunt boss. I like that shit."

"Diaz, I don't need a co-signer; my credit is A-1!"

Rally then stood up, tossed the empty bottle of

Viagra onto his seat, and jumped into the pool to be with the girls. SPLASH! The girls started giggling and then jumped back into the pool after him. They were a part of the Bankroll Squad under Kyla's prostitution ring. They hadn't heard from Kyla in almost two days, and her cell phone was going straight to voice mail. So, at first they decided that they would wait until she finally felt like calling. But this was urgent. They had heard way too much juicy information in the past seven hours to keep waiting on Kyla to call. The girls knew what they had to do now. They had to contact Malcolm.

fourteen

Kyla was still in the hospital dreaming. Dreaming about that life altering day when Malcolm licked her to sleep. No one had ever satisfied her, in any way, to the capacity that Malcolm had satisfied her. The doctors figured that she wouldn't be in a coma that much longer the way her vital signs were improving. It was still not clear if she would be able to talk or walk or even if she would be able to speak coherent sentences when, and if, she regained consciousness.

$~$~$~$~$

When she awoke in the Hampton Inn, the music had stopped playing and all the lights were off except for the glow from the television. She smiled when she realized that she had gone to sleep cuddled up next to Malcolm. Her mind wandered off as she started replaying the sexual torture that Malcolm had administered to her that evening. As she got up to go use the bathroom, she noticed two things... two potential problems. One, was that she had not returned to work. The red Pizza Hut heating bag was just sitting on the table beside the keys to the store's delivery vehicle. Her boss must be blazing hot by now. She was surprised that he hadn't called the police yet. Two, was that she had a ten page project that was supposed to be due in two days. She had told Malcolm earlier that day that she had quite a bit of research that she needed to double check before she made her edits and drafted her final copy.

She made it up in her mind that she would confront him about this after she came out of the bathroom. However, on her path to the bathroom was one of the most absurd things that she had ever encountered. It was a path of roses. Not even on TV had she ever seen a path of roses leading to the bathroom. It just didn't seem as though it made good sense to form something so pretty and delicate to lead to the place where humans go to take a dump. She wanted to question Malcolm about the purpose of the flowers, but she figured that she would let him get a few more minutes of sleep since he was sleeping like a baby. She used the bathroom and stood at the sink rubbing soap on her hands before noticing the bright red tomato paste on the mirror. On second thought, maybe it was lipstick. After reading the words, she knew that it was time to wake him up.

"Malcolm!" Kyla screamed out.

This was his cue... he knew that she would wake him up. He knew her like the back of his hand. Malcolm entered the bathroom and saw Kyla staring at the words in the mirror with a confused look on her face.

"Malcolm, what is this about?"

Malcolm stood behind her and wrapped his arms around her petite waist. He kissed her on the neck and whispered in her ear.

"Kyla, it's actually not that complicated. I asked you to marry me by writing it in the mirror so that you could look yourself in the eyes and give me the answer I deserve. I've already went through the delightful trouble of buying you a $40,000 engagement ring, so I hope you don't turn me down."

Kyla could barely get her thoughts together. She was very emotional, and the prospect of marriage almost made her pass out from excitement.

"Malcolm, you don't even know what size ring I wear. How—?"

"Kyla, I know you like the back of my hand... the very least you could do is know the back of your own hand."

Kyla realized that Malcolm was literally speaking as she held her perfectly manicured hand up to the light, revealing a staggering six carat diamond solitaire mounted onto a platinum setting. Kyla let out what sounded like a hybrid of a scream and a squeal then turned around and gave Malcolm a passionate kiss on the lips.

"Yes Malcolm! Yes! I will marry you! Without a shadow of a doubt, baby!"

Malcolm picked her up and swirled her around one time. He was the happiest that he had ever been in his life. He had found a million dollar cocaine connect named Franco Roberto; and he had secured a wife on the same day.

$~$~$~$~$

Marco had been waiting for the perfect time to ask, and it occurred to him that there would be no greater opportunity than the present.

"Malcolm, you said that you had some extra coke put away, right?"

Luther's eyes widened as he listened to the bosses conversation.

"Yeah, I do," Malcolm replied nonchalantly.

Marco got up and started walking towards the stairs.

"Where is it? The attic?

Malcolm stared at Marco as he stood at the bottom of the stairs awaiting a reply.

"Malcolm, you did tell me that if Pam's situation didn't work out, we would use the reserve until we could find a new connect."

Malcolm knew that the only reason that he had initially made such a ridiculous promise, was that he thought for certain that Franco would have no problem dealing with Pam. Now he was forced to eat his words.

"Yeah... you're right Marco. Follow me."

The two men started walking down the long, expensive, state of the art hallway. The ceilings were decorated in gold chandeliers and the walls held over two million dollars' worth of paintings and security monitors. They walked past a bag of trash that was obviously in the wrong place; as the very sight of it made Malcolm grimace. He always let Jeffrey have the weekend off, but he made a mental note to make him work over time when he came back to work. Malcolm and Marco got into the elevator and Malcolm pressed G for ground floor. After the elevator stopped, the door opened automatically, revealing a stunning collection of exotic and foreign cars.

"Damn," Marco exclaimed, "you doing some major shit over in this piece."

Malcolm ignored him and pressed the G button again. The flat screen security monitor that was mounted on the elevator wall immediately went blank; and then a virtual keypad covered the screen. He knew that Jen must have hit the G button again by mistake and then effectively guessed the pass code. The pass code was easy to guess for Jennifer because he used the same pass code everywhere, from the ATM machines to internet passwords. When the elevator door opened again, he almost passed out from what he saw. The cellar was empty. He had been cleaned completely out, left not even with an 8 ball of coke to his name.

"Fuccckkk!" Malcolm exclaimed as he grabbed a bottle of wine and slung it across the room.

The glass shattered, and the sound of it echoed off of the walls in the empty storage. Malcolm and Marco exchanged worried glances and stood in place for a while, motionless. Marco didn't even have to ask. The scene spoke for itself. Malcolm and Marco then took the elevator to the security room. Malcolm walked up to the central computer and hit a few buttons. He was checking for the last ten minutes of recorded movement in the cellar. The computer searched its archives for a few seconds and finally produced a file. He hit the play option and the video clip instantly filled him with anger and rage. The guy who'd robbed him was wearing his chain and fucking Jennifer doggy style while one guy looked on. At first he thought she was being raped, but when he fast forwarded the clip to about four minutes, he saw Jen laughing and hugging on the robber. Then another guy emerged out of the background with another four kilos in his hands. Marco looked at the screen hard. The guy holding the coke looked vaguely familiar. Then it hit him.

"Malcolm... I know who that is," Marco exclaimed.

"Who is it?"

"That's the fuckin' Wolf!"

137

They had just hit Malcolm for 17 million dollars in untouched cocaine.

$~$~$~$~$

There was nothing left to discuss. Malcolm, Catfish, Prince Tron, Luther, and Marco were waiting outside of the Wolf's house. When the Wolf arrived, he was driving a new Lincoln Navigator with paper tags. He had Coward 2 with him. They left the vehicle running and hurried into the house. Malcolm and Catfish were at the front door moments later; Marco, Luther, and Prince Tron were at the back door. Catfish kicked the front door, but The Wolf must have saw them outside and locked the door. The door was dead bolted. Malcolm and Catfish took out their.44's and shot the door off its hinges. When it was barely hanging on to the frame, Catfish took his heavy foot and kicked off what was left of the door.

Malcolm stepped into the house right after Catfish, and frantically searched the living room. There was no one in sight. Marco, Tron, and Luther had specific instructions from Malcolm to just wait at the back door, and if the Wolf tried to slip out, kill him and that clown with him. But when Marco heard gunshots, he grew extremely impatient. Not knowing who was doing the shooting or who was receiving the bullets, he kicked in the back door, despite Malcolm's instructions. The back door led directly into the kitchen where the Wolf and Coward 2 were trying to hide underneath the dining table.

Marco pulled back the pump on his Mossberg shotgun and let off a shot that turned the wood table to firewood chips. But he hit no one, and by the time he could aim the gun again, hollow point bullets opened up both sides of his stomach. He dropped the gun and clutched his sides, which felt like a bed of fire ants had crawled inside of him and bit him on the inside of his skin. He looked down at the blood that had turned his hands into fire hydrant colored paintbrushes and felt his legs start to give.

The Wolf seized his opportunity and ran at Marco with a professional strength wooded baseball bat. Whack! Marco died on impact, as the bat broke his skull and the velocity from the baseball bat sent the broken piece of skull straight through his brain like an ice pick.

Catfish peeped around the corner and saw Marco on the floor with the whole top left portion of his head smashed in. He threw the.44 down and grabbed the flamethrower out of his bag. Whooosh! The flame enveloped The Wolf completely. He screamed out from the excruciating pain of being burned alive. The Wolf staggered back and dropped the baseball bat on the floor.

"Aaaaargh!" the Wolf screamed as he fell towards Coward 2.

It never failed. Coward 2 was scared as hell and didn't know what else to do, so he closed his eyes and started shooting. He emptied the whole clip and hit nobody.

Malcolm ran over to him with his.44 in hand and kicked him in the nose. Blood started gushing out of the Coward's nose as he started screaming,

"I'm sorry! I'm sorry! I'm sorryyyyy!" All the bitch flowed out of him when he ran out of bullets.

"Where the fuck is my shit at?"

"I-I-I know I made a mistake..." The Coward stammered.

"You got-damned right you made a mistake; coming up in my

139

muthafuckin' house and stealing my muthafuckin' work! Where the —"

"But we didn't steal it," Coward 2 blurted out of desperation, "that white girl gave it to my homeboy!

"They're down at the Hilton hotel with it right now!"

Images flashed through Malcolm's mind of Jennifer getting fucked in his own house by another man. Images of Kyla slumped over on the steering wheel of her Range Rover, bleeding to death. Images of the elevator door opening and revealing an empty cellar. Marco was dead, his wife had betrayed him, and Kyla was in the hospital. Malcolm was against using torture techniques; after all, he had just got on Catfish's case about sewing Waller's mouth shut when they were back at the Power Building, but this was different. The man in front of him had caused him so much pain, that the only way to pay him back was to torture him. Malcolm grabbed the baseball bat and slammed it down on his right shin, causing it to snap. WHACK! Across his knee cap. WHACK! Across his shoulder blade.

Coward 2 screamed out in pain. He had never in his life been in as much pain as he was in now. Catfish stood back and watched Malcolm finally unleashed all of his pent up aggression. WHACK! Arm. WHACK! Scrotum. WHACK! Ankles. WHACK! Elbows. It was officially the ass beating of the century. Malcolm had snapped. After a few more swings, Malcolm sat down in a chair right in front of Coward 2 and watched him suffer. Watching him scream, squeal, and squirm because of the intense pain made Malcolm feel better. It was like therapy.

Luther and Prince Tron had walked in halfway through the beating and were standing beside Catfish. They had never seen Malcolm lash out like that, ever. After about 15 minutes of watching Coward 2 squirm and grimace from the pain, Malcolm finally noticed his surroundings. He was in a zone and didn't even realize that the rest of his crew were watching him torture the Coward. The Coward had begged for Malcolm to take his life 260 times — he'd counted — since the beating had ended. He didn't want to suffer any longer and was unable to move a limb. Malcolm noticed that it was getting dark outside and went ahead and granted him his wish. He stuck the.44 barrel in his mouth and blew his tongue out the back of his neck. Then, just to be on the safe side, he blew his brains out of both the right and left sides of his head.

"Two down, two to go," Malcolm remarked.

"Two?" Catfish said curiously. "I thought it was only one to go."

Malcolm glanced at The Wolf's scorched body and shook his head.

"Naw, Cat... Jennifer must die too! If you hang with dogs, then of course you must get treated like dogs."

Luther just listened intently; hanging on to every word and quote that Malcolm spoke like it was the gospel. He wanted to be the top dog one day, just like Malcolm.

$~$~$~$~$

Malcolm had called the Hilton's front desk and asked to be connected to Jennifer Power's room. Eight times. After the eighth time, he waited about fifteen minutes before he decided to call back. When he called, the receptionist recognized his voice from all of the repeat calls.

"Hey sir. Are you the one calling for Powers?"

"Yes I am. Jennifer Powers."

"Okay, let me send someone up to the room to see whether someone is in there. Please hold."

"Sure."

Malcolm was put on hold for about five minutes, only to have the receptionist come back on the line with bad news.

"Sir? Are you holding for someone?"

"Yeah, I'm holding for Powers?"

"Oh okay, well, there is no one in the room at the current moment. Would you like to leave a message? I can make sure she receives it whenever she arrives."

"No, but thanks," Malcolm spoke as he hung up the phone.

Catfish had been driving around in circles waiting on Malcolm to tell him to go kick the door in. He didn't give a damn that Jennifer was his wife. He would kill that bitch with no remorse. All violators, male and female, must pay the fee for violating. Catfish suddenly made a U-turn in the middle of the street.

"Damn Cat, what you doing?" Malcolm asked.

"We 'bout to go post up at the hotel and wait, if she's not there by now!"

They drove up to the Hilton and backed the Escalade into a parking slot at an angle so that they could retain a clear view of the front entrance. After waiting for over an hour, Jennifer's BMW sped through the parking lot. Everybody in the Escalade picked up shotguns and AK'S, preparing for a straight slaughter. Catfish opened his door, but before his left foot could touch the ground, he pulled it back in and slammed the door.

Every door that had initially opened when they saw Jennifer's car, closed immediately after Malcolm, Luther, and Prince Tron caught a glimpse of what Catfish saw. Jennifer was being trailed by three police cars; each car's lights were flashing, illuminating the dark night life. Malcolm wanted to help out. To reach out... as she was still his wife, regardless of the sheisty shit she had pulled. Then the images flashed through his mind again. Her getting fucked by another man. Then the thought that she could possibly have kilos of cocaine in the car.

"Let's get the fuck on. Catfish. We'll handle this shit another time," Malcolm spoke, as calmly as he could.

"I was thinking the same thing Mal. We got one too many guns in this vehicle and I don't want to have to kill a cop tonight!"

Damn I'm slipping, Malcolm thought. I forgot all about the consequences of getting caught with all this shit.

Catfish started the vehicle and slipped his way out of the parking lot. Malcolm looked back to see what the cops were doing. Confused and stunned, he sighed. Jennifer looked horrible. Her hair was a frizzy disaster, and her eyes were bugged out. She looked like she had just seen a ghost and her outfit was dirty.

Luther was observant, absorbing and analyzing the entire situation at hand. He knew that look all too well. It was the same permanent paranoid look that his cocaine abusing customers kept on their face. Malcolm noticed it too. He sat back in his seat gathering his thoughts.

All the drama that had unfolded as of late had threw him off of his square. It was time to live again.

"Aye y'all, let's go get dressed up. We'll hit Club Supreme first, then, after a couple of hours there, we'll hit the Red Carpet strip club."

Prince Tron and Luther's mood lightened up a little bit, but Catfish's mood stayed the same. Catfish had known Malcolm would say that. After all, they had just lost Marco, and instead of sulking over his death, they were going to celebrate his life. Plus, Malcolm always treated the clubs like his press conference to the streets. He answered all questions, regardless of if it was positive, negative, critical or sarcastic. He also used it to show the streets that the Bankroll Squad was unfazed amidst a crisis. And... just like the rap stars and music executives do, he used the clubs for photo opportunities. As every club attendee knew, the Bankroll Squad always bought out the bars, and always made it rain. Say cheese!

fifteen

" I put on for my city/ On, on for my city/ I put ooooooooooonnn," The Young Jeezy song blasted through the huge club speakers.

This song ignited the Squad's swagger, and made them feel that it was okay to put on. So they put on... in a major way. All eyes had already been on them when they first entered Club Supreme, but now, they were the absolute center of attention. All the lights in the club had dimmed except for the spotlight that shined on the Bankroll Squad as they stood on the top tier balcony, over the dance floor. Their wardrobes were immaculate. A couple of lower level ballers knew that all of their clothing had to have been custom made because they had never seen any of the apparel in any of the upscale clothing stores. The jewelry that they were sporting was so bright that it looked blurry. Ears, necks, and wrists were sparkling so strong that everybody swore that their diamonds were moving; as if the jewels had miniature lives and business that they needed to get handled.

"I Put Onnnnnnnn," the DJ played the chorus one last time and then let the instrumental play without the vocals.

The DJ screamed into the mic over the instrumental, then he stopped the instrumental.

"Wait, wait, wait! I don't think y'all understood me when I said that these niggas were about to make it rain! Show some respect to the

145

biggest ballers in the city and some of the biggest in the state! The Bankroll Squad!"

"I Put Onnnnnnnnn."

As the song started back playing, Malcolm started emptying a duffle bag filled with one dollar bills out over the dance floor. Both women and men dropped to the floor, frantically scraping up as many of the dollar bills as they could. Malcolm smiled at the sight of literally throwing away $25,000 like it was a candy wrapper. The spotlight was so addictive to Malcolm, that as soon as he made it rain in memory of Marco — Marco used to say that he made $25,000 a minute, so what's spending a minute on a watch — he bought out the bar in memory of Pam. All the females wished that they could catch one of the members of the Bankroll Squad and all of the guys wished that they could have it like they had it.

When the valet pulled the Lamborghini up to the door, all the women went crazy trying to give Malcolm and Catfish their cell and home numbers, but the club's security worked diligently to protect their biggest customers from the harassment.

Luther was soaking it all up. He knew that if he stayed down, his dedication wouldn't become overlooked and Malcolm would possibly reward him by giving him Marco's job. Luther rode with Prince Tron as they trailed Malcolm's Lambo on the way to the Red Carpet. Catfish rode with Malcolm, but he was paranoid as hell sitting in the expensive car with him. He held on to an Uzi and looked all around him at the traffic lights and stop signs, thoroughly prepared to let any robber, jack-boy, or nemesis have it.

$~$~$~$~$

As Malcolm drove to the strip club, he couldn't help but to think about what Pam had said to him earlier. It made sense... they were all rich so why were they still hustling? It certainly wasn't the money; he had plenty of that... $170 million in cash, $12.5 million in stocks and bonds, and an extremely lucrative potato chip company that had just expanded its products from Plain and BBQ, to Salt and Vinegar and Sour Cream and Onion. The property alone that he owned was worth millions. Maybe it was time to quit. Kyla had told him a long time ago that the money meant nothing to her. She was happy just spending time with him, but Malcolm wanted to spend more than time. He was born in the ghetto and had never been afforded the opportunity to splurge, but that could no longer be used as an excuse. He had been given his opportunity 70 plus times over and he was still using his old excuse.

When they arrived at the Red Carpet, they headed straight to the VIP section. Malcolm waved off the strippers and the waitress.

"Give us a couple of minutes please," Malcolm told them with a forced smile.

He wanted to have an emergency meeting. He had called Brink's home and cell number, but it was going directly to the voice mail. That was highly unusual for someone of Brink's importance to not answer his phones. He's probably at the hospital with Kyla, Malcolm thought. The manager, seeing that it was Malcolm, personally brought a bucket of Cristal over to the table. He knew what Malcolm wanted, since he had been doing the same thing every month for the past year and a half.

"Thanks," Malcolm said as his crew each grabbed a bottle of Cristal.

Luther smiled because this was an absolute dream for him. He felt like he had already been promoted.

147

"As you all know, we lost a good man today... what made me initially put Marco in command was his heart. And I don't mean heart as in love, but heart as in he would take your head off if you fucked with something you had no business fuckin' with. He didn't take shit from no one and he was smart as hell. I called this meeting to let y'all know that his death took a lot out of me. I wish he would have followed my directions and just stayed at the back door, but I guess if you give directions for a living, then it's pretty hard to follow them." He paused for a minute and let his last words sink in.

"I'm letting y'all know right now... that I'll be leaving —" Just as he was about to complete his sentence, two strippers came up to Malcolm firing questions left and right.

"Where's Kyla at?" one stripper asked.

"Why won't she answer the phone? We got the money we owe from last week," the other stripper said.

Prince Tron had a bewildered look on his face and Luther didn't know what the hell was going on. Prince Tron had never been introduced to any of the prostitutes because Malcolm knew that he would trick off compulsively, which would start rumors amongst the gold diggers that the leaders of the Bankroll Squad were just a group of tricks. He didn't want Prince Tron to set that type of precedent and have to dodge every gold digger in the city every time he exited his car. So he'd never introduced him. Until now...

"Tron, Luther, this is Sunshine and Rain... they work for Kyla, therefore they are an extension of the Bankroll Squad; of course, Catfish... you already know this."

The girls smiled at the men seductively. Sunshine had golden skin and long black silky hair. She was 5'7" and weighed 125 pounds. Prince Tron guessed her measurements to be around 36-21-36. She had tattoos on her breasts that were almost identical to the tattoos that Kyla had. The right breast had "Bank" on it and her left breast had a picture of a roll of money. Her tattoo was colored green and had a black outline. Rain was dark-skinned and short. She was 5'2" and weighed about 136 pounds. *She gotta have the fattest ass in the city,* Prince Tron thought. Luther wasn't even thinking anymore, all he could manage to do was stare.

"Y'all go ahead and sit down," Malcolm spoke while fanning away two more strippers that were on the verge of approaching them.

The other chicks walked off with an attitude.

"Hatin' ass bitches," Rain muttered to Sunshine, who nodded her head in agreement with her girlfriend.

"Kyla is in the hospital," Malcolm said to Sunshine, whose face immediately turned red.

Rain put her hand over her mouth and her forehead wrinkled up when she heard those horrible words. Kyla was like a sister to them.

"What happened?" Sunshine asked, concern evident in her voice.

Malcolm looked over at Catfish, who was shaking his head as if to answer Malcolm's silent question of whether or not he should tell them.

"I don't want to ruin you girls' night by discussing the situation. It's really not the time nor place for it, but I'll tell you what... call me tomorrow evening and we'll meet up so that I can fill you in."

The girls nodded their heads, but remained silent. Just the mere
149

thought of Kyla being in the hospital had the girls feeling down and depressed.

Suddenly, Sunshine spoke.

"Oh yeah... um... we was tricking with Rally and Diaz earlier today... and we heard some stuff we thought you might need to know."

"Rally? As in The Dynasty Cartel Rally?" Malcolm asked.

"Yeah... him."

"Well? What did you hear?"

"Ummm... what's his name? Umm... Rain what was old boy's name?"

"Who? You talking about Dexter?"

"Yeah! That's his name! They bought a lot of coke and put Dexter in charge of moving it. They said something about the Bankroll Squad was out of cocaine and they were going to reclaim the city within the next week."

Luther couldn't control his silence after hearing such a preposterous statement.

"Dexter?" Malcolm looked at Prince Tron for help.

"Oh yeah... Dexter works for us, Malcolm. He runs Trap Eight over by the Wilmert Projects," Prince Tron said while stroking his goatee.

Malcolm was so hands off with his workers that he had no idea who Marco had hired.

"He doesn't work for y'all anymore," Rain spoke in her softest voice. "He switched sides; along with everybody else in Trap Eight. They were also talking about taking over Trapquarters by choice or by force. If Trapquarters don't get down with the Dynasty Cartel, they said they would just operate from directly across the street."

Catfish smirked at the thought of Dexter betraying the squad.

"If it ain't one problem it's a muthafuckin' 'nother," Malcolm said aloud in an exhausted tone.

"It seems like ever since the situation unfolded with Kyla, everything just went fuckin' haywire. Ladies, I appreciate the loyalty and honesty that you two continue to display, and I want you two to know that your efforts are definitely appreciated. Don't forget to call me tomorrow evening okay?"

The girls smiled and nodded their heads at Malcolm.

"Now excuse us ladies. We would have stayed longer and had a little fun, but there are a couple of things that we need to get handled."

Malcolm went and paid the manager, then they left out of the Red Carpet.

sixteen

Traffic at Trap Eight had been booming all day and had not broken its speed deep into the wee hours of the morning. The fiends were literally lined up and were from all over the city awaiting the almighty high. Business was beautiful for the Dynasty Cartel, and Dexter couldn't wait to tell Rally how much Trap Eight had made in one day. It was looking like the 80's again. Until the van showed up.

The van sat in front of Trap Eight and waited until the line died down a little. Then the passenger side window of the van rolled down, where Catfish was sitting. He pointed the machine gun at the house and held the trigger. *Tat-tat- tat- tat-tat-tattat- tat-tat-tat-tat-tat-tat-tat-tat-tat-tat-tat- tat-tat-tat-tat-tat-tattat-tat-tat-tat-tat-tat-tat-tat-tat-tat-tat-tat-tat-tat-tat-tat-tat-tat-tat-tat-tat-tat-tat-tat-tat-tat.*

He didn't give a fuck who he hit and he didn't give a shit what Malcolm's orders were. He was doing the only damn thing that he was good at. He was handling shit his way. After they'd left the Red Carpet strip club a few hours earlier, Malcolm conducted a meeting which basically said for everybody to go to the house and rest and they would strike first thing in the morning. Everybody did as they were told simply because it was their leader that was giving the orders. They all wanted to exhibit a display of loyalty. Except for Catfish. Catfish felt like Malcolm was speaking from a stand- point affected by depression instead of setting his emotions aside and speaking like a commander.

His wife, Tricia, had begged him to let her drive the van for him but he'd declined her offer. He managed to convince Prince Tron that Malcolm was confused and that he needed to drive the van for Catfish. After Catfish let out fifty shots, him and Prince Tron came back 10 minutes later and let off fifty more shots. He ended up knocking off six fiends and fourteen workers.

The morning news had declared it to be a drug war. Catfish heard about it on the radio. Malcolm was asleep.

$~$~$~$~$

Dexter was at the car wash when he got the call. He wasn't mad when he heard the news, he was scared as hell. He had built a solid reputation when he was with the Bankroll Squad, but it was all small stuff. After receiving the call from one of the workers at Trap Eight that survived Catfish's attack, he kicked the female crack head out of his Dodge Challenger while she was in the middle of her blowjob.

"Can I still get a dime?"

Dexter ignored her, slammed the passenger side door, and sped off. He wasn't carrying a gun on him because he was a known drug dealer and a convicted felon who constantly got harassed and humiliated by the local law enforcement. They wanted to nab him bad, because they knew he was in deep. Dexter turned on the air conditioning and turned his sound system up almost to the maximum so that he could try to stay alert behind the steering wheel.

"I don't like it if it don't bling bling, and to hell with the price nigga, money ain't a thang." The song by Jay-Z and Jermaine Dupri was coming through the speakers.

When he reached a stoplight on his way to his stash spot, he took the opportunity to take that CD out because it didn't reflect the mood that he was in. He put the CD aside, and in its place, he inserted a Tupac mix CD. The first song blared out of his sound system: "It's either my life or your life/ and I'ma bomb first." Dexter bobbed his head to the song while waiting at the red light. The whole time that he was sitting there fumbling with the CDs, he never noticed the black van on his left with the door wide open.

Catfish jumped out of the van and ran towards Dexter with a pistol gripped Mossberg pump shotgun with a cooling system on the front aimed directly at Dexter's head. *Boom!* The shot split his head open like a watermelon dropped onto the pavement. The only thing that Dexter saw was the front end of a hole before the shot turned his cream white interior to cranberry sauce. Catfish jumped back into the van and Prince Tron hit the gas.

$~$~$~$~$

Tracy had made herself at home and was granted the opportunity to stay overnight in Malcolm's guest room. That morning, she went and woke Malcolm up at 10 a.m. She had on a Louis Vuitton bathrobe that belonged to Jennifer. Even sporting a bathrobe, Malcolm noticed that she was very easy on the eyes. It had been a while since he had actually had sex with a dark skinned woman, and it was definitely a wonderful experience. Tracy had a shape that made men's mouths water. At 4'11 and 129 pounds, she was stacked! Full lips, full breasts, slim waist, long, black, curly hair, and a bubble butt made her a helluva catch. At one point, Sweetback had been in love with her and took her everywhere he went;., but when she started working as a bartender he started keeping his distance. He was too jealous of a man to let a woman belonging to him work in such a flirtatious environment. He argued against it for weeks, but she kept insisting that she continue because she was tired of sitting around in the house all day and night, doing nothing. Sweetback got mad, and kicked her out. She had been on her own for several years now, but always tried to maintain a cordial friendship with her child's father.

"Malcolm, I just wanted to thank you so much for being a gentleman. I've always been attracted to you, but I didn't even know if you would like me because —"

The house phone started ringing and interrupted her in the middle of her statement.

"Excuse me for a second Tracy," Malcolm said as he got up and answered the home phone.

What he heard brought a flabbergasted look to his face. "This is a collect call from the Potson County Detention Center from: "Jennifer Powers." For rate information, press one. To accept, press two. For inmate call blocking, press —"

Malcolm pressed two and immediately heard noise in the background.

"Hello?" he said.

"Hello," a female voiced answered.

"Jennifer? What the fuck are you doing in jail?"

Malcolm shouted into the phone. Tracy left out of the room to respect his privacy. "I'm so sorry Mal! I fucked up big time! I never should have —"

155

"Not on the phone, Jen. This call is being recorded!" he cut her off and said.

"Sorry..."

"Jen, what are you locked up for? Tell me your charges," Malcolm said as he laid down across the bed.

He laid on his stomach and closed his eyes when he heard Jennifer start to cry on the phone.

"He tricked me Malcolm! He took my anger that was directed at you, and used it against me."

"What are your charges Jennifer?"

"Hhhhhh," Jen exhaled a deep breath into the phone and said, "Possession of crack cocaine." Jen started crying hysterically.

Ignoring her cries, Malcolm continued to prod deeper despite the fact that he could barely believe his ears.

"Jen... now you're trying to sell crack? What the fuck has gotten into you?"

"Malcolm, I wasn't trying to sell nothing..." she replied and trailed off.

This caught Malcolm completely off guard.

"What...? What's...? Jen...?" Malcolm stuttered over his words trying to figure out what to ask.

"He made me smoke it Malcolm!" Tears ran down Jennifer's face as she sobbed into the phone.

"FUCK!" Malcolm screamed as he jumped out of the bed.

"You're smoking rock?" Malcolm couldn't believe what he was hearing.

"Malcolm! He tricked me. I swear!"

The sound of the agony in Jennifer's voice, combined with the complications in his life, almost brought tears to his eyes. He had always heard the phrase, "what goes around, comes around," but he never knew when or how it would come. He'd made his fortune by constantly and consistently pumping drugs into the lives of out of control abusers. The same vice that he'd utilized to build his fortune with, had come back and destroyed his life. His heart sank as he stood there thinking about what his wife had just told him. Never would he have imagined that a wife of his would ever have stooped so low. And despite all of the transgressions that she had committed against him, he still possessed an everlasting love for her.

"You have... one minute, remaining." The operator's recording split through the silence of Malcolm, and interrupted the crying of Jennifer on the telephone.

"Jennifer, don't cry... I'm about to come downtown and bail you out."

Jennifer's tears of sadness immediately turned to tears of happiness. She hadn't initially believed that Malcolm would even accept the collect call, much less bail her out.

"Thank you so much, Mal!"

"Jen... where are my things?"

"That dude got it. He got my car too! He's downtown at the —"

"Thank you for using PCS communications."

The fifteen minute phone call had come to an end, but it didn't matter because he already knew where the guy was at. He was just verifying it through her. Malcolm threw the house phone across the room, where it shattered against the wall.

"Shit!" he muttered.

Life never ceased to amaze him.

Seventeen

After calling Brink and still getting no answer, Malcolm called Catfish using his cell phone. After he explained the situation, Catfish made his way over there driving the Escalade. The plan was to pay the Coward a visit, then they would ride to the city jail and bond out Jennifer. They rode past both of Malcolm's security checkpoints and reached the end of the driveway. There was a medium flow of traffic and as soon as he could get a break, Catfish was going to pull out and get into the right lane so that he could head left towards the downtown exits. Suddenly, a car slammed into the front left side of Catfish's Escalade. The impact shook up Catfish and Malcolm and by the time the Escalade stopped rocking from the crash, they were surrounded by FBI. ATF agents had guns drawn and were yelling as they approached the vehicle.

"Hands up! Hands up! Get your fuckin' hands up!"

Malcolm and Catfish complied.

"Keep your hands up and step out of the fuckin' vehicle!"

They did as they were told.

"Lie face down and put your hands behind your back!"

As soon as they touched the ground, they were bombarded by agents

159

and cops carrying guns and handcuffs. *The Feds?* Malcolm thought, as he was read his rights and placed into a police car. Catfish was placed in a separate vehicle. For a moment, Malcolm stared at Catfish with cold, demented and suspicious eyes as if to say "you set me up?" But when he saw the look in Catfish's eyes, he recognized the familiar look of innocence that he often displayed. Catfish felt bad for the murders he'd committed against Malcolm's orders and prayed that Malcolm wouldn't have to take a murder rap for some shit that he didn't even know had taken place. Malcolm asked an agent what he was being charged with and he told him that he would find out later. He shifted uncomfortably in the police car and sat there being the only thing that he could be: patient.

$~$~$~$~$

"Conspiracy for international drug trafficking, 30 years to life. Unlawful possession of unregistered firearms, two to ten years, and unlawful possession of an automatic assault rifle… damn Malcolm... what the fuck were you thinking? Money Laundering... Racketeering and RICO charges..." his lawyer trailed off.

"Man Bill," Malcolm said as he placed his hands across his eyes and shook his head, "throughout the years, I've paid you close to $1.3 million dollars in retainer fees. Will you fight for me honestly and fairly for that amount?"

"Of course I will," his lawyer, Bill Green, said.

"What is Catfish charged with?"

The lawyer flipped through some papers, and adjusted his glasses in the process. "Catrell Smith has been charged with everything that you're being charged with, Mr. Powers. It's clear that they are applying a divide and conquer strategy in an attempt to pressure Catrell into rolling over on you."

Malcolm took a deep breath and closed his eyes for a moment. His heart was pounding as he visualized spending the remainder of his 25 year old life rotting away in the government's prison system. His soul bled from a deep emotional puncture. Hope was leaking out of the wound. Life was dripping away. In its place, failure and hurt were substituting.

"Bill, I've been locked up for three days now.

Can you get me a bond?"

"It's highly unlikely that you'll be granted a bond. Your other co-defendant, Bradley Finks has been locked up for four days. He lost his bond hearing yesterday. You're scheduled to go in front of the judge tomorrow, but even if you were granted a bond, how would you make it?"

Malcolm's forehead was wrinkled up as he frowned at Bill Green.

"What the fuck?! What is Brink charged with? And what do you mean by how would I make bond! I'm RICH!"

Bill opened up another manila folder and studied the contents.

"Bradley is only being charged with the conspiracy count which, as I said earlier, carries a 30 year mandatory minimum sentence. And as far as you being rich... Your assets have been seized under the forfeiture provision and accounts have been frozen."

Malcolm's eyes got wide upon hearing the news and small beads of sweat began forming on his forehead and face.

161

"Look Bill, I got at least $25 million remaining in an offshore account in the Cayman Islands. I need you to contact my friend, Pamela Jones, and let her know what happened. Tell her that I have a bond hearing tomorrow, and I need her there."

Bill took his glasses off and laid them on top of the table. He sat the folder down beside his glasses and stared directly into Malcolm's eyes.

"You still don't get it, do you Malcolm? There is no reason to call her, Malcolm... she has already planned to come to your bond hearing. She'll be sitting directly beside the prosecutor."

"What?" Malcolm asked. "Why would she be sitting beside the prosecutor?"

"Shit Malcolm, that's where the special agents sit!" his lawyer said in exasperation.

$~$~$~$~$

Even after four months of being detained, Malcolm still had not gotten over the fact that Pam was an undercover federal agent. She was the only evidence on the conspiracy charge, but he knew that she would be heavily protected by the FBI until after the trial, so it would only get him in deeper shit if he had her eliminated. Luther and Prince Tron kept at least $5,000 on his books, and visited him every other week. One week they visited Catfish, then the next week they visited Malcolm. Although he always made store, and always had a visitor, nothing could stop Malcolm from stressing out. He began to find himself emotionally dependent on Tracy. She accepted all of his calls, and visited him faithfully. He had received only one letter from Jennifer. And it said:

I DID 3 MONTHS IN JAIL. I'M ON PROBATION NOW!

THANKS 4 NOTHING! LET'S GET THIS DIVORCE OVER WITH. CAN I MAIL YOU THE DIVORCE PAPERS? - JENNIFER.

Since the beginning of his incarceration up until the fourth month, he had lost a total of 40 pounds. The food they served was complete garbage. A rat would prefer a bowl of rat poison over the so-called food that the jail served. He spoke to Catfish and Brink when they were allowed to go on the rec yard. All three had been offered different types of deals. They'd offered Catfish 3 years if he testified against Malcolm, and he declined. Brink had been offered one year if he turned on Malcolm and Franco Roberto. He declined. Malcolm had been offered a 3 year plea deal, if he led them to Franco Roberto. He also declined. They all had high powered attorneys and were prepared to endure whatever the government threw at them. They'd known the consequences of their actions the first day that they'd gotten involved. It was their morals and principles that gave the government a hard time. They couldn't get anyone to mutter a word!

$~$~$~$~$

"Aye man, if y'all beat this shit... I wanna be down with y'all. The Bankroll Squad! Channel 13 said you was bringing in $19 million a month! Is that true?" Malcolm's cellmate asked him.

Malcolm laughed, ignoring the question like usual.

"Mail call!" The stubby guard said as he stood by the nearest table with mail in his hands.

"Powers!"

Malcolm walked to the table and retrieved his mail, which consisted of a new XXL magazine, KING magazine and three letters.

163

"Aye, let me get that book when you finished!"

"Let me get it after him!"

There had been ten requests by the time Malcolm made it back to his cell. He put the magazines down and looked to see who the letters were from. The first was from Jennifer. He didn't even open it because he knew it was the divorce papers. The second one was from Tracy, and when he saw the hearts that she had drawn on the envelope, he smiled. The last letter blew his mind. His heart beat sped up to almost double the speed when he saw who the letter was from. He ripped the envelope open and read the letter:

Dear Malcolm,

I love you so much! I've been out of the hospital for three months now. At first, I was temporarily paralyzed and I didn't know what to do. I was lost. The doctor told me what happened to me and I didn't even care. I just kept asking him where Malcolm Powers was. He said that he hadn't seen you in over a month, so I thought that you had given up on me. I called your cell and house phones constantly... with the help of the nurses. After I came out of the coma, the doctor told me that I would never walk again and initially, I was going to give up and let that be that. Then, one day I got a visit from Prince Tron, who told me everything. When I heard the news, I was desperate to walk again. I had to. I asked for Tron to enroll me into a rehabilitation center, which he did. In there, I worked harder than I ever worked in my life. I can now stand tall and look into the mirror with no assistance. But now when I look at myself, instead of being weak, I see strength! I can walk, run, and function as if nothing happened, but something did happen.

Something monumental happened. You showed me that you loved me by putting me on life support when the doctor said that I was dead. A check for $2 million on a "dead" person? And now I'm alive.

I feel the pain that you're going through while being held with no bond. And they're alleging that you sent "Special Agent Jones" overseas to retrieve cocaine? Ha, what a backstabbing bitch. A 30 year charge? I promise that it's not going to stick. I'm coming to see you this weekend; from this point on, I wanna be known as Mrs. Powers, and I promise to never disrespect your last name. How do you feel about it being me and you? Because when I was paralyzed, that was the only thing that I

COULD feel....

Your Wife,

Kyla Powers

P.S. I'm handling all of your "problems" in the streets. One down, a few to go. Watch the news.

Bankroll Squad 2: Kyla's Revenge

Keep up with the latest news!
Text TBRS to 22828

CHAPTER 1

Heavy pains streaked through Kyla's body as she stood in front of the mirror, shivering. She wasn't shivering because of the temperature; she was trembling out of anger. Someone had just tried to *murder* her, had pulled the trigger on a shotgun and tried to send her to her death bed, but she would not be denied. By the grace of God, she had managed to fight her way off of a life support machine and out of a coma. She thought back to the day of the attempt, to the day that changed her life forever.

$~$~$~$~$

She had been trying to talk to the love of her life, the leader of the Bankroll Squad, Malcolm, when she spotted a stranger sneaking up behind him with something in his hand. By the time she grabbed *her* pistol to try to help Malcolm, someone else had come up behind *her* and unloaded a shotgun shell into her body.

The memory of it haunted her. The buck shots had felt like a pot of boiling hot grits crawling inside of her skin, and that was the last thing that she remembered.

$~$~$~$~$

Next, she remembered waking up in a hospital and feeling weaker than she had ever felt in her life. She remembered the nurse causing a big commotion, talking about, "Hey! She's awake! Dr. Henry! Dr.

Emory!"

She remembered thinking, *Why wouldn't I be awake? How long have I been out?* When she tried to say what she was thinking, the only thing that came out of her mouth was "uuuwwuuw."

Why do I sound like this? Why can't I talk?

"Uuuuwuuuuu! Uuuuuuuuwwuu!"

These seemed to be the only sounds that she was able to make. She tried to force herself to get up, but she soon realized that she was unable to move any of her limbs. Quickly, she glanced down to see what was restricting her from moving and saw nothing.

"Uuuuuuwwuuuu!"

Why can't I talk? Got damnit! What the fuck is wrong with me? She wondered while the doctors and nurses stood around her bed in awe. They were staring at her like she was some sort of science experiment, and she was stared back at them intensely with various questions in her eyes.

Why the fuck am I surrounded by white people? What have they done with my voice?

She took her tongue and swirled it around her mouth and panicked. Something was definitely wrong. She took her tongue and skimmed it across the surface of her upper lip. *What the fu...*

"Uuuuuuuuuuu!"

Her lip was disfigured. It felt like someone had taken a pair of scissors and disconnected the left side of her lip from the right side.

169

Horror and panic surged through her body, and she passed out immediately.

$~$~$~$~$

When she woke up again, there was a strange black dude sitting beside her bed with a concerned look on his face.

"Kyla, are you alright?" he asked.

His voice seemed familiar, and his face contained tiny tidbits of resemblance, but she still couldn't quite figure out... *Wait... Prince Tron?*

"Kyla, I know you're wondering why I'm wearing this disguise," he whispered, "but a lot has happened in the last few months since you've been in a coma."

Coma? Months? She tried to speak again, but was only able to force out sounds that *resembled* words.

"Moooonnnsss? Coooomwa?"

Tron shook his head. "Don't worry, Kyla. I'm taking you to a plastic surgeon tomorrow to get your lip fixed, but I gotta get you out of here immediately! I think the FBI have indicted me. They went by my mother's house and told her that there's a federal warrant out for my arrest."

$~$~$~$~$

That was over four months ago. Tron had taken her out of Sinai Memorial and signed her into a private hospital under a false name. She had stayed there for a month after undergoing reconstructive lip surgery. At the end of that month, her words were starting to make sense again, and, once again, Tron came and got her.

He was moving real low-key, and it was the first time that she'd ever seen him not rocking his expensive jewelry. When she tried to find out what was going on with the rest of the squad, he insisted that she get better before he told her the situation.

After months of intensive therapy, expensive medicine, and aggressive treatments, she was slowly returning to her old form. She understood that she would never be one hundred percent again, but, as long as she lived, she made a personal vow to address every issue and handle every hater that she possibly could.

Because she was a loyal woman, her only understanding of life was "Bankroll Squad or Die." Her college education was nothing when compared to the degree that she had in loyalty. On her last day at the rehabilitation center, she had jogged at a slow pace on the treadmill while wondering why none of the members of the Bankroll Squad had visited her in all of those months.

She set it in her mind, that day, that she was going to leave the rehab center and find out what was going on, whether Prince Tron allowed it to happen or not.

$~$~$~$~$

She had just downed a glass of milk by the time Prince Tron showed up to the facility. The way she was staring at him when he arrived, Prince Tron knew that it was time for her to find out what was going on with the squad, so he told her.

He said everything that she needed to know in one long, run-on sentence.

"Cat, Mal, and Brink are facing thirty from the feds because Pam is an undercover agent and she set us all up and Jennifer ran off with the dude that robbed Malcolm that day."

Tron took a deep breath and shook his head before continuing.

"Malcolm's assets have been seized, and there is no income flowing in whatsoever. We've been out of cocaine for so long that the Dynasty Cartel has taken over completely. Pam, or should I say Special Agent Pamela, put us all in a headlock financially. That bitch was in charge of handling every single dollar we made, and she was an undercover cop!"

Kyla stared at Prince Tron silently and showed no emotion. Sure, she was angry, but she had just risen from her death bed and been granted another chance, and nothing would have made her angrier than lying in her death bed.

Abruptly, she stood up from the table and accidentally knocked over her glass of milk. The glass rolled off of the table and shattered against the floor. When it shattered, she didn't flinch, didn't even avert her eyes to the floor to survey the damage. It seemed as if she didn't care that she had been so careless.

She stared into Prince Tron's eyes, and, immediately, something about him registered with her. It was something that she had never seen in any of the members of the Bankroll Squad, and she despised it with a passion: fear.

She gauged that Tron was afraid to go to jail, could see that he had become the type of dude who would probably turn into a star witness if the pressure came down on him too hard. Choosing her words carefully,

172

she decided to get as much information as she possibly could.

"So... you're broke?"

Prince Tron exhaled and nodded his head solemnly.

"I spent my last dollars putting you in this center, Kyla. I don't have anything else left. That was it."

Kyla shook her head but didn't say anything. She had gone silent on purpose because she had a feeling where that conversation was heading.

"Kyla, the only other person in the squad with some major money stacked up is you. You got the international prostitution ring jumping and all. Why don't you tell me where the money is, so I can go get it?"

Something had changed in Kyla since she'd been shot; it showed on her face and was highlighted by the way she spoke. She was never going to let another person deceive, trick, or blind side her ever again, and she could tell that Prince Tron was trying to do all of the above. She was furious, but she wasn't going to let it show.

"Just take me home today, and I'll get you some money, Tron."

Tron glanced around nervously before he responded.

"There is a forfeiture provision on your house, as well, Kyla. The feds have seized it because it was in Malcolm's name. You had Malcolm buy it in his name because he owned a legal business, right?"

Kyla stared at him without saying a word. To her, it was obvious that Prince Tron was working with the FBI and trying to set her up. That was the main reason that she had knocked that glass to the floor and shattered it. As soon as it broke, fear appeared in Tron's eyes. It was

173

showing because he was wired up, and the feds were listening in on the conversation somewhere nearby.

The sound of breaking glass would have been cause enough for the FBI to barge in and rescue him if he hadn't have been able to show that he still had control of the situation. The whole time Kyla had known Prince Tron, she had always looked at him like he was a brother, but, on that day, it was like talking to a complete stranger. Tron had become a traitor with the cruelest of intentions. A traitor so low that he had helped her to recover from her death bed, just so he could try to put her behind bars in order to save his own ass. The thought of it made her sad, but no tears would come. The treachery in Prince Tron's heart made her angry, but her appearance remained peaceful and serene.

The old Kyla hadn't been through what the new Kyla had endured. The new Kyla was a survivor, a goddess, one of the most powerful women in America. Six months ago, she hadn't recognized the value that she possessed, but, on that day, she could clearly see the diamond encrusted insulation of her heart.

She could see that the whole Bankroll Squad's fate depended on the decisions she made from that moment forward. She decided that she would never let them down. She cleared her throat and squeezed Prince Tron's hands.

"Okay, Tron. I got you, baby. Just let me get some rest tonight, and we'll handle everything first thing in the morning."

Prince Tron was disappointed, but he tried his best to mask it, so it wasn't so apparent.

"So, it's no way at all you could do it this evening, Kyla?" He was lightly applying pressure to the situation, but she could see directly through his deception.

"No, Tron. I'm feeling a little tired right now... just a little weak... but let me rest tonight, and you can pick me up at six in the morning. Is that cool?"

The feds had promised to place Prince Tron in the witness protection program if he could get Kyla to tell him where her money was stashed. He would, also, have to testify against Malcolm, Catfish, Kyla, and Brink if they decided to go to trial. If he didn't work with the police, they had threatened to indict him under the same charges as the other members. Plus, they were going to add a murder charge to it.

He knew that he was taking a coward's way out, but there was nothing in his DNA that would allow him to just lay down and take thirty years or better. He sat at the table across from Kyla and reflected on all of the good moments they had shared together, but, in the blink of an eye, none of those moments mattered to him.

The only thing that mattered to him was his freedom, and he was going to go to forbidden extremes to get it. He averted his eyes from Kyla's and stared at the floor. Because of what he was in the process of doing, he couldn't even summon the strength to hold his head up high like he once had.

"Okay, Kyla," he finally said. "You get your rest tonight, and I'll pick you up in the morning. That's fine."

Kyla forced a smile in response, but he couldn't tell if the smile was genuine or not. He smiled back at her as he stood up. He held his arms open, and Kyla soaked into his embrace. They hugged, and, during the hug, Kyla felt sorry for Prince Tron. She didn't feel sorry for his situation. She felt sorry for him because he had dared to try to betray her during one of the worst times of her life.

"Thank you, Tron. Thank you for understanding."

Tron smirked at her and shook his head. "Don't thank me... thank *you*. Without your help, I wouldn't be able to make anything happen, Kyla. I really am happy that you're doing better. You're the sister I never had."

He kissed her on the cheek, smiled one more time, and turned to walk to the door. He opened it and turned back around to face her.

"Kyla... Malcolm, Cat, Brink, and me... we're going to beat all of these charges, you know? It's inevitable. Our defense team is too good."

There were many questions that laid on the tip of Kyla's tongue, but she asked none. She simply nodded her head. Tron looked like he was going to add something else to his statement, but didn't. Instead, he sighed, as if exhausted.

"Good night, Kyla."

Again, Kyla nodded.

$~$~$~$~$

As soon as Prince Tron stepped into the elevator, Agent Monroe grabbed him and slammed him against a wall. He reached under Tron's shirt, snatched the wire off of his chest, and mashed it against the side of his face.

"Owww! What is wrong with you, man? She said tomorrow morning! Just be patient and—"

The agent punched him in the mouth.

"You don't tell me to be patient, snitch! You think this shit is a game? Do you think we're going to keep wasting manpower on this bullshit? We're about to yank your cooperation agreement and send you off somewhere, so you can jack off for the next thirty years!"

Prince Tron grimaced at that thought.

"No! Please give me until tomorrow morning! Just a few more hours, and I'll be able to lead you to over ten million dollars in illegal cash! Please!"

Agent Monroe raised his fist, prepared to hit him again, but his partner grabbed his arm. Agent Malinda Watts was thinking about the huge promotion that they would both get when they brought in $10 million to their supervisor. They would both be given a bonus of one million dollars apiece and would more than likely be front runners for the employee of the year award. And all at the same time, she would be helping put away that group of law breaking scumbags that called themselves the Bankroll Squad.

"Let him make it, Monroe. We can wait until six A.M. for this."

Monroe looked at her and scowled. For some officers, the good cop-bad cop act was just a game, but Monroe and Malinda Watts had been playing the game for so long that it had become real life.

"I oughta break his jaw and lock him up until tomorrow morning! If you don't deliver that money to us tomorrow morning, we'll personally see to it that your name is changed from Tron to Tranisha for the next thirty years! Are you ready for that, boy?"

Defiantly, Tron glared at him.

"My name will never be Tranisha! My manhood will *never* be compromised. No matter what! I'm a grown—"

"Oh, yeah? Is that what you thought, boy?" The agent was furious that a snitch had developed enough nerve to challenge him. "We'll see how much of a grown man you are when the prisoners find out that you set up the whole Bankroll Squad!"

Prince Tron jumped as if being hit by a stun gun.

"But I didn't do that! Pam did that!"

Beads of sweat, suddenly, appeared on his forehead. Agent Monroe laughed hysterically.

"Yeah, but that's not what your paperwork is going to say. We're going to work you over real good, snitch!"

At that moment, the elevator door opened, and a white man with blond hair stood there, startled and unsure of what to do next. He didn't have to wonder for long.

"The elevator is occupied! Take the stairs, ass wipe!"

The man hurriedly turned and went back the way he had come. When the door closed, Agent Monroe relaxed a little and said, "Fine. We'll just see you in the morning. And don't even think about trying to run. We have more people watching you than the royal wedding, snitch!"

$~$~$~$~$

At the rehab center, Kyla was not been able to leave the premises until Dr. Paschel cleared her. On that night, she finally realized what it actually meant to be "cleared", so she knew that she had to immediately find a way to exit the facility. A couple of hours after Tron left, she was standing in the vending room when the door opened suddenly. It was her personal trainer Zaglin.

Bingo! She thought as she started to implement the pieces to her plan.

"Kyla, what did I tell you about stuffing your body with junk food? Either you put real food in, or nothing at all. It's important that you get healthy, and it's my job to make sure that it happens."

Zaglin was a total health freak, but he, also, had a crush on Kyla. He had attempted to go against facility policy many nights before when he offered to take her out to dinner and sneak her back in. That night, it was exactly what she needed.

"Ha! You caught me again, Zag, but I'm so hungry!"

Zaglin stepped towards her and smiled.

"This time, I'm not asking you. I'm *telling* you. Take my card key for the elevator and hit the G button for the garage. My car is the orange Honda Accord. Wait for me there while I clock out. I'm going to get a duplicate card key made and join you in about ten minutes... I'll just tell them that I misplaced my original."

Kyla looked at him skeptically.

"Awww! Come on, Kyla. Don't do that. I just wanna show you a good time and treat you how you're supposed to be treated."

179

Kyla blushed and shook her head.

"I can't go out to dinner looking like this... And look at my hair... it hasn't been done in months! Besides, what if someone sees me standing outside of your car? I don't think it will work, Zaglin. I'm sorry."

Kyla had turned away from him as if to leave, but he stopped her in her tracks.

"Kyla," he spoke softly, almost whispering. "Wait a second... we don't have to go to a restaurant to have dinner... I mean, I'm a pretty good cook... That is, if you don't object to eating at my humble residence."

Kyla stood there with her hands on her hips as if she was considering his offer, while, in all actuality, she had already had her mind made up about what she was going to do.

"That's fine, but I don't want any issues with your girlfriend, Zaglin. Please don't thrust me into a physical confrontation."

He quickly responded, "I don't have a girlfriend, Kyla! I have too much respect for you to ever do you like that."

Kyla saw sincerity in Zaglin's eyes, but it didn't matter whether he was for real or not; she was just trying to get the hell on. She glanced at the wall clock and saw that it was almost midnight. She had about six hours to make a serious move.

Zaglin saw that she seemed to be worried about something, but he had gotten too close to finally spending some time alone with her for her to back out at that moment.

"Don't worry about the time, Kyla. Don't worry about anything whatsoever! I promise to cover all the bases and assume responsibility for tonight, but I'm going to need you to trust me just a little bit. Do you trust me?"

She didn't respond immediately, just flashed the brightest and most feminine smile that she could muster up. To him, Kyla was as innocent and naive as a young college freshman. He couldn't possibly begin to imagine that she was a major player in one of the most dangerous gangs in the world.

"But, Zag... What do I do if someone spots me standing outside of your car? What could I possibly say to the administrators if that happens?"

"First, tell me that you trust me, Kyla."

"Okay. I trust you, Zaglin."

He didn't know if she was for real or not, but he was so excited that it didn't even matter.

"Well, I trust you, too, Kyla." He tossed the keys to his Honda Accord to her. "Just wait inside the car. The tints are pretty dark, so no one will be able to see you sitting there. I'll be down in a few minutes."

$~$~$~$~$

The roads were empty as Kyla raced through the city in Zaglin's Honda Accord. She knew that he was probably pissed off that she had stolen his car, but she really didn't care because she knew that he would *never* get a chance to see her again. She had serious business that she needed to handle, but she was unable to because she didn't even know the real story. She needed to talk to people that she trusted, people that had already shown her that they could be loyal to her without excuses and on a consistent basis.

The Honda was a world away from the pink Range Rover that she was accustomed to pushing, but she didn't feel that a time of war was a time to stunt anyway. Besides, as soon as she reached her destination, no one was ever going to see that orange Honda ever again.

As she made her way into the city limits, it came to her in a rush. She knew exactly who she could trust with her life, so she made her way to them.

CHAPTER 2

For Malcolm, this was the first time that he had ever been arrested for any reason whatsoever, and it was hell. It was everything that he wasn't. It was loud and obnoxious, while he was a tacit intellectual. They were followers and petty thieves, and he was a boss and a world-class baller. The other inmates seemed to be almost enjoying themselves.

They had heavy rotations of spades players, people slamming dominos against the solid table surfaces, and people shouting while cheering on a UFC fight as it aired on television. There were a few inmates reading books or magazines, but they were usually white inmates.

Occupying a back corner of the unit was a small workout group. They were doing push-ups and sit-ups, had been doing the same workouts for a whole year now, and still hadn't gained any muscle because there simply wasn't enough food for them to gain any weight. Even if they ate every meal that the jail served, cleaning the trays in their entirety, they would still be on a perpetual diet.

Malcolm wasn't interested in any of the games, wasn't interested in doing any push-ups, and certainly wasn't interested in watching a UFC fight. He was in his cell, brainstorming up a way out of prison, when Tomy Rarez appeared in the doorway and said, "Hey! Catfish wants you to come to the door."

"Alright. Thanks, Tomy."

The "door" was located in the back of the unit and stayed locked at all times. Had it been unlocked, the inmates in Unit 1 would have been able to just walk into Unit 2 with no problems. That would have caused serious conflict if there were co-defendants testifying against each other. However, there was a small crack in the side of the door that allowed the inmates in Unit 1 to talk to the inmates in Unit 2.

When Malcolm came out of his cell, the other inmates quieted down several notches. They all knew the type of money that the Bankroll Squad handled and were all desperately hoping to become the latest member of the organization. As Malcolm made his way to the door, the group of guys that were working out respectfully dispersed to another section of the unit.

They didn't want Malcolm to think that they were trying to eavesdrop on his conversation. Everyone, except for Marbro.

Marbro hated Malcolm and despised the level of respect that he received from the other inmates. If it had been up to him, he would have tried to get the Bankroll Squad buried in the floor of the ocean.

He continued doing his push-ups even though Malcolm was trying to have a private conversation. The other inmates stared on in amusement as Marbro kept working out, barely twelve inches away from where Malcolm was talking.

"Aye, Catfish... this me..."

Catfish's deep voice was muffled, but Malcolm could still make out what he was saying.

"Yo, Malcolm! Did Prince Tron come to visit you today?"

After hearing the question, a look of surprise appeared on Malcolm's face. "No! I haven't seen Tron in three weeks. I thought he had been visiting you and Brink these last few weeks."

"Nah, I talked to Brink earlier, and he hasn't seen him in over a month and a half. And I haven't seen him in over a month. I tried to call his phone yesterday and today, but it's been going to voicemail."

"Oh, yeah?" Malcolm said. "That's strange... I hope everything is okay out there. I think Luther is just getting back in town, so I'll have him check on the situation."

"Back in town? What did Luther leave for?"

Malcolm started to speak, but noticed that Marbro wasn't even doing push-ups anymore. He was just eavesdropping without even trying to disguise it.

"Hold on, Cat... Aye, my man... could you give me a little privacy?"

Marbro looked up at Malcolm and acted as if he didn't exist. Then, he stared off into nothingness like whatever Malcolm had said was a joke. Malcolm started to speak again, but was interrupted by Marbro.

"Nah. I ain't about to stop what I'm doing to kiss your ass. I got as much right to this space as you do."

Not seeing a solid point to argue, Malcolm nodded his head. Then, he leaned back to the crack of the door.

185

"I'll have to holla at you tomorrow, Cat. One."

As Malcolm turned to leave, Marbro, out of the blue, went off on a verbal assault.

"That's what I thought, sucka-ass nigga! You better walk off! Boy, I will gut you like a fish!"

Malcolm turned and faced him, confused at how Marbro's attitude had become so aggressive. He noticed that Marbro had a glint of shiny metal in his left hand and decided that he most definitely needed to receive an attitude adjustment, but he was going to wait until later to give it to him.

"I'm sorry, Marbro. I won't interrupt your workout ever again."

"That's good for you, boy! You just don't know how close I was to stabbing the daylights out of your punk ass! Bitch!"

"Why would you stab me, Marbro?"

Marbro noticed that he had attracted a small crowd and was trying to make the most out of his performance.

"Because you don't deserve to live! That's why! So, watch your back because, next time, you won't be so lucky!"

Malcolm simply nodded his head and walked back into his cell. A few of the inmates, who didn't know the history of the Bankroll Squad, giggled and snickered at Malcolm. He knew that it wouldn't have been wise to try to fight. Marbro was 6'6" tall, 240 pounds and holding a shank in his hand, so Malcolm laid in his bunk and waited on lockdown time.

$~$~$~$~$

Each cell held two men and had electric locks on them that popped open at five in the morning. Even after the doors opened, no one bothered to actually get out of their bunk beds until around 5:30 when their breakfast came. On that particular morning, Malcolm had gotten up at 5 A.M. on the dot. After retrieving his bowl and spoon, he headed to the microwave.

Every morning, Malcolm ate a bowl of oatmeal mixed with honey, although not usually that early. He put it in the microwave and stood there, allowing his breakfast to bubble and boil. He let it overcook. Then, he used a t-shirt as an oven mitt and carefully removed his bowl from the microwave.

Next, he walked straight into Marbro's cell and poured the blazing hot mixture onto his face and walked out.

"Arrrghgghhh! Ahhhhh! Arrgghhhhh! Argghhhh!"

By the time the other inmates got up, Malcolm was back in his cell. Marbro, on the other hand, didn't realize the magnitude of the hot potion that was scalding his face off. He tried to wipe the steaming stuff off with a cold, wet bath cloth, but, every time he wiped, he tore some more of his skin off. The potion wasn't just oatmeal and honey; baby oil had, also, been added to the sizzling mixture.

The honey was ingenious because either you let it continue to scald you or you ended up tearing all of your facial skin off. Marbro had a face full of pink, exposed muscle tissue by the time he stopped trying to wipe the honey off of his face, and Malcolm didn't have any respect issues after that.

$~$~$~$~$

The three women stood in the VIP lounge of Diamond Club Cabaret in an emotional group hug. They were easily the most beautiful women in the club, and almost every man in the club wished that they could participate in that hug.

"Kyla! Me and Sunshine missed you so much! We didn't know what happened or what to think!"

All three of the women were teary faced for different reasons. Kyla, because she knew that those were *her* direct employees in the Bankroll Squad, and she didn't have to worry about them double crossing her. Rain was crying because too much had happened in the past four months, and she desperately needed Kyla's guidance to stay on track. Sunshine was crying because, even though she loved men, she had a secret crush on Kyla. Just seeing Kyla again brought out emotions that she had suppressed during her absence.

"I'm sorry that you two didn't know how to get in contact with me, but I had no control over anything until a few hours ago."

"We're just so happy that you're okay," Sunshine said as she squeezed the two women's bodies as close to hers as she could.

Kyla broke the embrace and wiped her eyes as she said, "Look... there is a lot of stuff that we need to discuss, so you two get dressed. I seriously doubt that you two will ever work in a strip club again. I got bigger jobs for you two."

$~$~$~$~$

Kyla had a house on the outskirts of Houston that no one knew about, not even Malcolm. It was the place she retreated to when life became too overwhelming for her. It was, also, where she kept the bulk of her money stashed in an underground safe. By the time she reached her house, she had heard everything that she needed to hear.

Sunshine and Rain had shared with her everything that they knew, and she, in turn, had told them about the Prince Tron incident. She pushed Rain's purple Benz to the depths of its potential because she knew that she didn't have one second to spare if she was going to bring the Bankroll Squad back to greatness, which was where it belonged.

The first thing she did, once she made it to her house, was send Malcolm a letter letting him know that she was okay and that she was handling his problems for him. She sent it from an anonymous address, and she used a false name, so it couldn't be traced back to her. She wanted to wait until he received the letter before she actually handled the first target.

For the next three days, all she did was plan.

$~$~$~$~$

Besides Sunshine and Rain, the only other member Kyla called was Luther. He told her about what happened between Sweetback Fatty and Catfish's wife, Tricia, so she told him to bring her with him. Her best friend's brains had been blown out in her presence, and Tricia felt like it was all her fault. If it was the last thing she did, Tricia wanted to even the score, and Kyla knew that she could use a woman like that on her team. The only thing more dangerous than a mad black woman was four mad black women.

They sat in the great room of Kyla's house and admired the design and the stylish decor. It was very modern, yet it had none of the typical

189

appliances or devices. There was no television, stove, or refrigerator present. If not for the expensive furniture, it would have seemed as if Kyla had just moved in that morning.

Everyone sat in silence while they waited on Kyla to come out of the back room. When she finally came back into the room, the small group of girls couldn't help but admire the beauty that Kyla still possessed, even after being hit with a shotgun shell. She wore the look of strength, determination, and power. The usually soft look that her eyes once contained had hardened. Her usually passive personality was now aggressive and demanding.

The new Kyla exerted the energy of a female version of Malcolm, and no one in the room could deny it. She stood in front of the small group in silence for a moment, as if she was at a loss for words, but she wasn't.

"Until Malcolm gets out of jail, I will be running the Bankroll Squad. The reason that I asked for this specific group of people to be assembled is because y'all are the only people that I trust. The way I see it, I paid for my position in blood. That's not to say that I'm trying to take Malcolm's position because I'm not, but what I am going to do is be that down-ass bitch while our original leader is incarcerated. And I'm going to personally see to it that our men aren't locked up for too much longer. Luther, I want you to keep running the show by moving the drugs and—"

"Ummmmm," Luther uttered, cutting her off. "Kyla, we don't got no cocaine at all to sell. We don't even have a connection to buy the drugs *from*."

Kyla smiled at him, showing all of her white teeth. "I have always been prepared for this day, Luther. Every time Malcolm sent me to get 1,000 kilos of cocaine, I would return with 1,500 kilos. The extra 500, I would stash somewhere safe. I did that for years. So, basically, what I'm telling you is that I got enough coke to last us for damn near ten months straight."

Luther's eyes nearly bulged out of his head as Kyla told him that information. Never in his life had he *ever* encountered a woman of her caliber. She was a hustler's dream woman and a boss in her own right. Luther couldn't even put any words together to reply with. He just sat there, nodding his head in astonishment.

"As for us, ladies, we're about to lay the streets on their backs and expose them for the hoes that they are. It's been far too many people disrespecting the Bankroll Squad, and I wanna see to it that this shit gets handled once and for all."

The women nodded their heads because they felt empowered by the speech that Kyla had just given.

Luther interrupted, "What do you mean 'lay the streets on their backs'? Explain please."

Kyla and the girls exchanged knowing glances. Then, after staring at him for a few seconds, she answered, "I *mean* that I have just enough artillery to make a small army base blush. And I—"

"Wait, Kyla," he interrupted again. "Why don't you leave all the dirty work for me? I could get a small crew together in no time. That way, you ladies won't have to get involved with the harshness that takes place during street wars."

Kyla held her hand up, causing him to stop mid-statement. With

191

poise and confidence, she looked Luther squarely in the eyes and spoke.

"With all due respect to the men of the squad, I just think that this empire needs a lady's touch."

Even though Luther knew that Malcolm would object to what Kyla was proposing, he, also, knew that Malcolm had never witnessed the look that Kyla wore on her face at that moment. It was a look that he had only seen on the faces of mothers who had lost their children too early. The look was a mixture of revenge, scorn, payback, and misunderstanding. While looking into all of the women's faces, he completely understood.

$~$~$~$~$

Catfish and Brink were on the recreation yard, watching a group of guys play basketball. The sun was out, but it was making no effort to fight through the cool winter day. The only reason that the inmates were out there was because they were tired of being cooped up in the dehumanizing prison cells.

"Brink... they took Malcolm to solitary confinement this morning, man."

Brink's face tightened as he asked, "What is he in the hole for?"

Catfish heard him but didn't immediately respond. He had to make sure that no snitches were in earshot.

"From what I hear, they say he permanently burned the face off of a man, but no one saw it, so I expect him to be out of there either today or tomorrow. The correctional officers are trying to get people to talk, but, if anyone says anything, I'll make sure their whole family feels it."

Brink looked straight ahead. He was visibly irritated by Malcolm being sent to the hole. After an extended silence, he turned to Catfish.

"Man, I wish somebody could make Pam's family feel it! That sloppy-ass bitch got us all facing thirty got damn years! I'll murder that bitch personally!"

Catfish noticed that Brink was talking too loud and tried to calm him.

"Aye, Brink! I forgot to tell you! Before Malcolm went to the hole, he got a letter from Kyla!"

Brink perked up immediately. Kyla and he had taken many trips together to buy cocaine, and she had always been a professional when it came to handling her business. When he heard about her getting shot, it had hurt him to his core. But, if she just wrote Malcolm a letter...

"Kyla is okay?" Brink asked ecstatically.

"Not only is she okay," Catfish smiled, "but she just told Malcolm that she is going to handle all of our problems out there. So, if she handles her business, our cases may never make it to trial."

Brink's enthusiasm faded. He went from looking ecstatic to solemn in less than five seconds.

"What's wrong, B?"

Brink shook his head as if he had no energy left in his body. "Man, Cat, I don't wanna get my hopes up, man. For our cases to not make it to trial, we would have to first eliminate Pam. And Pam is protected like the president right now. She has people watching her around the clock. Man... Kyla is just going to get herself into some serious trouble.

193

Get her address and tell her to chill."

Catfish looked at Brink sympathetically. He knew that Brink and Kyla had a pretty serious bond because of all of the business that they had done together. "Aye, B... I wish I could help you, but there is no return address, and she's *already* been handling business. In the letter she wrote, she told Malcolm to watch the news. I've been watching for the past four days, and I still haven't heard anything, so I honestly don't know right now."

A basketball hit the side of the rim hard and rolled over to where Catfish was sitting. He picked it up and threw it back onto the basketball court.

"Thanks, Catfish!" one of the players yelled.

Catfish looked at Brink and sighed, "Man, I pray that *something* happens because I would prefer not to be sitting around like this for the next thirty years, but, if I have to do it, then fuck it. I'm a grown man. Besides, when has Kyla ever given her word and not delivered?"

Brink nodded his head as he absentmindedly stared at the basketball game. "You're right, Catfish... she always keeps her word. She's like the female version of Malcolm."

$~$~$~$~$

Coward 1 had wasted no time jumping into the extravagant life. After Jennifer helped him steal $20 million worth of cocaine from her husband, he got scared and sold the whole thing for $9 million on the very next day. If he had hustled it himself, he could have stretched the coke and possibly made $40 million. Or, if he had broken it all the way down to user amounts, he could have made an unprecedented amount of money, but selling it all for $9 million seemed like the right thing to do at the time... it was just that, after only four months, he was down to $400,000. It had all seemed so "unspendable" in the beginning.

The first thing he did was spend $3 million on a house. It had a huge pool and came in a package with fifteen acres of land. Things were fine at that point, until Jennifer stepped in.

She insisted that he allow her to do the interior design of the mansion, and she spent $2 million remodeling a $3 million home. One day, Jennifer brought him a magazine article about a new sports car called a Bugatti. She told him that, if he wasn't riding like that, then he wasn't doing anything, so he went and bought one. It had a price tag of $1.5 million.

He didn't put insurance on it, and he wrecked it on the way home from the dealership.

Then, Jennifer wanted to shop nonstop. In the beginning, he hated it when she went and bought all those clothes every day. Until, one day, she brought home three new white girls. There was a red head, Julissa; a blond, Sarah; and a brunette, Maria. They were all bisexual freaks, and he took great pleasure in watching the four women have orgies every night. They had gotten permission from Jennifer to move in, but the only problem that existed was that they never allowed the Coward to have sex with them.

He was sick and tired of watching, but he knew that he couldn't do much else; he was, after all, a coward.

Coward 1 locked the bathroom door and counted his money again, just to make sure his mind wasn't playing tricks on him. Unfortunately, it wasn't.

195

He was really at $400,000 after four months. He sat on the toilet, hung his head, and tried to figure out where the other $2.1 million had gone. He knew the girls loved to shop, but $2.1 million? He closed his eyes and thought back to the wild nights of partying. The drinking, smoking, pill-popping, the cocaine... *Wait a minute!* It was the *cocaine*!

Julissa, Sarah, and Maria were like human vacuum cleaners. They sucked everything but his dick. Jennifer was their idol because they all thought that she was filthy rich beyond belief, but there was only $400,000 left!

What really pissed him off was that he had spent so much money buying *back* the cocaine that *he* had stolen, just so him and his white girls could snort it. He closed his eyes and was starting to doze off when there was a rapid tapping at the door.

"Ward! Baby! Someone is on the telephone for you!"

It was Jennifer at the door, so he rapidly tried to hide the money that he had been counting as the door opened.

"Ward, you know I have a key to the bathroom... what are you about to do with all of that money?"

Jennifer's eyes were huge and soaked with the flaws of greed.

The Coward stammered, "I-I-I was—"

"Let me and my girls go car shopping, Ward. You're a star for goodness sakes! You don't want your girlfriend to be driving an old Benz, do you?"

The Coward's eyes bulged like he was a 3-D animation.

"What do you mean *old*? You just bought the Benz three months ago!"

Jennifer sulked and looked at him with the saddest face that she could pull together. The Coward saw her looking sad and broke down.

"Alright, I tell you what, Jen... Why don't you go ahead and get those butt shots you've been talking about forever? You said you wanted a bigger butt—"

"Oh, Ward! Thank you so much!"

He didn't know how much it was going to cost, so he gave her $30,000. She started to leave the room when he stopped her.

"Jennifer! I thought you said the telephone was for me?"

Jennifer gave him a weird look. It was a look so strange that he couldn't even determine which emotion lay beneath it. It seemed as if it was a look of love, but there were some elements to it that made him feel like it was a look of hatred. Jennifer shook her head slowly, as if she pitied herself and the man she had left her husband for.

"Ward, I lied. The phone wasn't for you. I was on the phone setting an appointment to get my butt shots."

The Coward was furious. He was sick of getting handled by Jennifer all the time. "But, Jen, how did you know that I was going to—"

Ka-bam! She left, slamming the bathroom door shut in the middle of his statement.

"Tell you to get butt shots..." the Coward finished his statement to himself and hung his head in shame.

197

$~$~$~$~$

Prince Tron had installed a tracking system on Agent Monroe's vehicle. His thought was that it would come in handy one day. That day had come. Early that morning, he had received a phone call from Agent Monroe, letting him know that Kyla was nowhere to be found. She had stolen a vehicle and left the rehab center late that previous night. The strange thing about it all was that Agent Monroe wasn't even angry.

He was calm on the telephone; yet, his words still sent a strong chill through Prince Tron's body: *"Don't worry about it. You'll be indicted and arrested before breakfast. These are your last few minutes of freedom."*

Looking on his monitor, Tron saw that Agent Monroe was fifteen minutes away from his house, so he used that to his advantage. He packed a light suitcase and got the hell out of dodge. If Kyla was nowhere to be found, that meant that he would no longer be able to help the government. The only thing they wanted him for was to lead them to the money.

He knew, then, that his life in the United States was done. He needed to come up with a way to get smuggled into Mexico as soon as possible, but, first, he needed to get out of the grasp of the federal agents. He drove his Porsche truck clear across the city while occasionally checking his iPhone to see how close the agent's car was.

When he was fifty miles out of the reach of Agent Monroe, he spotted a little hole in the wall strip club called Vanessa's Cabaret. The sign on the outside said OPEN 24 HOURS, so he knew that he would, more than likely, be able to hide out in there for the rest of the day while he tried to come up with a better and more precise plan.

He found a table in the back of the club and slumped down low in the seat. He shook his head, while he watched what seemed to be the ugliest strippers in the world slide up and down the smooth metal pole.

He tipped the waitress and started his day off with a triple shot of Patrón. *Even the waitress is ugly*, he thought as he downed the drinks. Briskly, he moved on to gin. Then, he was drinking vodka.

By the time lunch came around, he was punishing a half bottle of Gentleman Jack whiskey. From the hours of 7 A.M. to 2 P.M., he had managed to get drunk beyond comprehension. The strippers were taking turns going into his pocket and relieving him of his bankroll, one twenty dollar bill at a time.

At 2:30 P.M., he tried to order another drink. "Tomita ahhhh toopa. Frankie and Neffie... Jessie... Moomboo! Moomboo! Moomboo!" The waitress politely asked the bouncer to escort him to his vehicle.

Prince Tron sat in his Porsche and dozed off until his face was laying on the horn. He woke up angry about the noise.

"I'm tryna sleep!"

Then, he laid his face back on the horn. This time, he woke up ready to fight.

"Tryna SLEEP!" he screamed at the steering wheel.

Absentmindedly, he started the engine and recklessly made his way through the city traffic. After driving for five minutes, he found a Steak 'n Shake restaurant and parked as far away from the entrance as possible. He went to sleep with the gear on the vehicle in reverse and his feet firmly pressing down on the brakes.

He was wasted.

CHAPTER 3

Tricia had been pushing her husband's old black van through the city since early that morning. Kyla was in the passenger seat. Rain sat directly behind her, and Sunshine sat at an angle, so she could keep an eye on Kyla. She loved the way Kyla looked, loved the way she smelled, the way she spoke, and the way she moved. The more time she spent around Kyla, the more her obsession grew.

If only Kyla knew how much I loved her, Sunshine thought as her eyes wandered from Kyla's hair to the sharp inward curve of her waistline. *Damn! I could just taste…* Suddenly, Kyla turned around and faced her.

"Hey! You daydreaming back there? Wake up, Sunshine. We don't have a moment to spare. We gotta lotta business to tend to."

Sunshine blinked out of her fantasy and wiped the sweat off of her hands. She had been clutching a TEC-9 for the past eight hours, and they still hadn't located any of the people that they were looking for. First on the shit list was Pam; then, there was Prince Tron, Coward 1, Jennifer, and the whole lot of individuals who had attempted to take over the Bankroll Squad's trap houses.

Instead of looking for one person at a time, they'd made the mistake of looking for everybody, just riding around hoping that they could bump into any one of the targets on the shit list. The van smelled like a variety of feminine body washes, lotions, perfumes, and deodorants. The mixture was giving Tricia a headache, so she pulled over at a McDonald's.

"Listen, Kyla. I know you know this, but I'm going to say it anyway. We can't waste time riding around aimlessly. I say we pick one specific target and go hunt them down. Otherwise, we might as well be joy riding, and—"

Tricia got quiet when she saw what Kyla was staring at. Rain and Sunshine both checked their guns to make sure that they were loaded and ready. They didn't have a clue what they were staring at. They had only seen the look on Kyla's face and sensed the sudden change in her demeanor. From that alone, they knew that someone was definitely about to die.

Tricia asked, "Who is that dude getting in that Benz, Kyla?"

Choked up, with tears running down her face, she turned to face the women in the van and tried to speak as clearly as possible.

"That's the guy that robbed Malcolm on the day that those people tried to kill me."

Silence blanketed the van as the girls surveyed the area to make sure there were no officers around. Finally, Tricia spoke hesitantly. "How can you be certain that that's the guy who robbed him? I mean, it happened so long ago."

Kyla's authority returned to her voice as she stared into Tricia's eyes. "Because he's wearing the same chain that Malcolm was wearing. It's only two of those in the world, and I got the other one."

The van lurched from the parked position and swiftly closed the distance between the van and the Benz.

"Hey! Slow down, Tricia! We don't want to scare him away. Let's just follow him to his spot and handle our business there," Kyla ordered confidently. "Put those guns away and relax. Don't allow your emotions to cause you to make terrible decisions."

Sunshine put her gun away and continued staring at the woman she loved. Every time Kyla's lips moved, it seemed to make Sunshine hornier and more obsessed with her. Tricia trailed the Benz by three car lengths through the city of Houston. They didn't know what Malcolm would want them to do about the situation, but the wrath of a woman scorned would certainly make up for the difference.

$~$~$~$~$

Jennifer's butt shots had been a success. Her ass was now forty-four inches around, and she turned heads like she had never turned them before.

At the gas station: "Aye, white chocolate!"

At the restaurant: "Damn, girl! What you doin' with all that?"

At the convenience store: "Got dammmnn! Let me take you out sometime."

She was getting more attention than she had ever received in her life. Men whistled and shouted every time she stepped out of her vehicle. The butt shots almost made her feel better than cocaine did.

What if I take the cocaine while I got my new butt shots... She suddenly had an idea, but she thought better of it. *I'll wait until later to*

203

go pick up some coke, she thought while she continued to joyride in her Mercedes. She didn't want to go by the house right then because she feared that Ward wouldn't let her leave the house after seeing how fat her ass had become.

She wanted to enjoy herself while she could, so she threw on the new Katy Perry CD and cruised while listening to her favorite artist on repeat. As she noticed the contrast between her white hands and the black steering wheel, she thought, *I need to get a tan pretty soon.* She rubbed her right breast with her free hand while she entertained the thought of getting Ward to let her get silicone implants. *I'll ask him when I get back,* she thought as she smirked to herself.

At a red light, she stopped and pulled down the sun visor mirror, so she could study her reflection. There were some men in the car next to her. The driver blew the horn at her, and they all waved. She waved back at them, and the entire group smiled at her. Behind her, more horns blew, so she turned around to wave at them, also, but they did not wave back.

They gave her the finger.

She heard a muffled voice that told her what she was doing wrong.

"Move, asshole! The fuckin' light is green, bitch!"

Quickly, she got it together and drove off. After another hour, she'd come up with her brightest idea to date. What she was about to do would make her feel like she was on top of the world for the rest of the year.

Gosh! I'm so smart! She thought as she proceeded to execute her brilliant plan.

$~$~$~$~$

Kyla became nauseous when she saw the size of the Coward's mansion.

"There's no way he's living like this off of carjacking. I simply can't believe it," Kyla said as she laid her binoculars down.

Tricia had parked the van a quarter of a mile away from the Coward's estate, so they could talk their plan out in detail. Rain and Tricia were anxious. They had both suggested that they just knock on the door and then bust in with guns drawn. Sunshine was more reserved. She emitted the soft spoken aura of a timid teenager. Although, in all actuality, she was one of the deadliest women in the world when it was required.

Tricia banged her foot against the door of the van before she spoke. "So, come on, Kyla! Let's get it done!" She had become impatient after driving the van around the city all day.

"This shit is tiring! We got a long list of shit that needs to be handled, and we're just sitting in a van, looking through some fuckin' binoculars!"

Tricia's voice was loud and aggressive as she directed all of her statements at Kyla. "Kyla! Did you hear me?"

Kyla finally, broke her focus from the Coward's mansion and stared into Tricia's face. A thought flashed through her mind. She realized that Tricia was the reason that she and Malcolm had broken up to begin with, and it left a bad taste in her mouth. Just staring into her face seemed to anger Kyla, but she knew that it wouldn't be a good idea to hurt Malcolm's best friend's wife. Instead, she checked her.

"Tricia, I swear to God… bitch, you better not ever raise your fuckin' voice at me again. I'm not gonna sit here and listen to you talk that *shit!*"

Tricia was very similar to her husband because she and Catfish were both quick-tempered and would scrap, shoot, or stab at the drop of a dime. Tricia's face squinted up as she spoke.

"If I raise my voice again, then what? That's what I thought, you weak ass bitch! I'll kick yo' ass for talking that—"

She didn't get to utter another word, because, in the blink of an eye, Sunshine had stuck her pistol into Tricia's mouth. The entire van went silent and still. Everyone was surprised. Sunshine had seemed like the sweetest girl in the vehicle, and, now, she was only one movement away from taking a person's life.

When she spoke, her voice was feminine and sweet, but her words were masculine and bitter. "Bitch! Raise your voice at Kyla again, and I'll make sure that you make it to hell sooner than you expect."

Sunshine couldn't even believe what she was doing, but she knew that she'd have to go to extremes if she planned to win Kyla's love away from Malcolm. She definitely wasn't about to let another woman talk crazy to the woman that she loved.

Tricia trembled while the cold steel barrel laid between her lips. Saliva leaked out of the corner of her lip, and a tear slid down her face and splashed against the pistol.

After a cautious moment, Kyla spoke up and said, "Sunshine, take the gun out of her mouth. Don't hurt her, baby."

Something about the way that Kyla spoke to her softened her up a little. *Man, I wish Kyla knew how I felt about her,* Sunshine thought as she removed the pistol and laid it down on the seat next to her. The pain she felt from holding onto such a secret caused tears to form in her eyes. The whole van was getting emotional for all different reasons, and Kyla knew, from watching Catfish and Malcolm, that there was no place for emotions when on the job.

"Listen, y'all. We're a team right now. The entire world is against us and our men, and I know that it's impossible to fight the whole world *and* have to fight each other at the same time. Let's get it together, ladies."

The group of women nodded their heads, and they each reached a new level of motivation. Kyla looked at Tricia and gave her a reassuring smile. "Alright, Trish. I think he's home alone... but, even if he isn't home alone, his house guests will have to die, too."

A look of relief appeared on Tricia's face as she put the van into gear.

"Okay, ladies. Here we go," Tricia stated as she pressed her foot on the gas and rocketed the van onto the Coward's property. They were not going to let him out of there alive.

$~$~$~$~$

Hustle. Hustle. Hustle. Hard. Closed mouths don't get fed on the boulevard. Luther was pushing his black on black BMW through the city with the new Ace Hood song blaring through the speakers. He couldn't believe his good fortune. For months, his money had been dwindling lower and lower, but, no matter how low his money got, his loyalty would never let him betray the Bankroll Squad.

207

Even though the leaders were locked up, he still refused to join any rival gangs. The Dynasty Cartel had offered him a lieutenant position, and he had turned them down, even though he really needed the money. And now this...

In one day, his whole life had changed drastically. Kyla had given him a 1,000 kilo cocaine shipment to *start* with. There were so many ways to sell it that he didn't know how to start. He guessed that he could make between $17 million and $100 million dollars off of it. His dream had, finally, come true. He was a boss now.

He pulled his BMW up to the gas station, so he could fill his tank up to the max. As he pulled up to pump number ten, he saw a group of people standing around a car wreck. A Porsche truck had backed into a taxi and ruined it. The cab driver was arguing with somebody, but he couldn't see who it was because of the size of the crowd. After he finished pumping his gas, he drove over to the crowd to get a better look.

When he arrived, he noticed that it was Prince Tron's Porsche, but Tron was nowhere in sight. Luther grabbed his pistol and made his way through the crowd. When he reached the cab driver, his heart stopped in his chest. The cab driver wasn't arguing with Prince Tron. He was arguing with a white man he'd never seen before.

"Where is the man who hit my taxi? I don't want you! Where is the other guy?"

The white man kept a straight face the whole time as he repeatedly said, "It was *me* who hit your taxi!"

"You lie! That man gave you lots of money and ran, but I couldn't see what car he went to! Now, tell me!"

But the white man wouldn't change his tune. "It was me who hit your taxi. I'm sorry."

Luther's heart was racing, and he couldn't take any more of the bullshit. He pointed his pistol at the white man and yelled, "Where the fuck is he?"

The white man passed gas accidentally. "Shit! He took my old Pinto! There he is, leaving right there!"

The entire crowd swiveled their heads around and caught a glimpse of an old raggedy Pinto with chipped paint fleeing the scene. Everybody was enjoying watching the drama as it unfolded, except for Luther. He was pissed that Tron had attempted to set Kyla up while she was recovering from a coma.

The white man stuttered, "I-I-I- I'm sorry. That man paid me a lot of money to say that it was me who did it. I was broke, and I—"

"Shut up!" Luther screamed at him as he ran back to his BMW. He knew that a Pinto couldn't outrun a BMW, and he was going to make sure that he ran Tron's punk ass down. On his first day as a boss, he was about to make his first boss move.

$~$~$~$~$

Her supervisor had ordered for her to stay in the small town of Wisconsin Dells, Wisconsin until the trial started, but she had snuck back into Houston, so she could visit her family. She had never gone this long without seeing her mother, and it seemed like, if she waited on the Bankroll Squad to go to trial, she would have to wait for up to two years.

There was no way that she would have been able to maintain her sanity without seeing her mother for two years, but, if her supervisor or one of the members of the Bankroll Squad found out that she was there...

Special Agent Pam Jones shivered at the thought of what would happen to her if someone discovered her. Certainly, a member of their gang would probably kill her, and, certainly, her supervisor would have her locked up for disobeying direct orders and putting one of the biggest cases of the century in jeopardy.

As soon as she arrived at the airport, strong waves of paranoia swayed her body like a sailboat in the middle of a hurricane. She felt sick to her stomach, but she knew that, if she vomited, it would only serve to attract more unwanted attention to her presence. She closed her eyes and prayed that the sickness would pass.

$~$~$~$~$

Life as a special agent was more difficult than she had ever imagined it would be. She, basically, got paid to betray people. The first few assignments were easy, but this last case not only got her a promotion and a pay raise, but also heartache and pain. Malcolm Powers was one of the few men that she knew that she could actually love forever.

When her superior briefed her for material, she constantly pleaded that she needed more time. To Pam, it would never be the right time to send the man that she loved to prison forever. She knew that she was treading a thin line between love and insanity, but there was nothing she could do except follow her heart.

One night she had almost broken the cardinal rule by sleeping with Malcolm, but nothing ever went down between them. Pam knew that she would have helped him stay free forever had that happened. She was so in love with Malcolm that she had even tried to go overseas and buy a shipment of cocaine for him. She'd put her job on the line by taking an unauthorized trip, and, when the deal didn't work out as it was supposed to, she got scolded by the man she loved.

That final argument that she'd had with Malcolm let her know that they were headed down two separate paths. He was dead set on living his life as an organized drug kingpin, and he had no intentions of turning his life around, so she felt like she had to turn his life around for him. She turned in records, taped meetings, phone conversations, and a few pictures. The only catch was that she didn't turn in the most damning evidence because she wanted to make sure that she remained the most critical element to the case.

If she had given them everything, the FBI could have convicted the Bankroll Squad without her ever having to show up. No way was she just going to hand over her blood, sweat, and tears without receiving her career promotions. But, now that she had her promotions, she wished that she could trade it all back in and have the charges on Malcolm dropped. She loved him and missed him more than words could explain.

But like her psychologist constantly had told her, "You must learn to detach your emotions when you do your job. Otherwise, you should quit. If you do not, your mental health will deteriorate."

$~$~$~$~$

Pam selected a rental car with dark tints and pushed it onto the expressway. She had a lot of things on her mind, and she knew that her mother would help her smooth everything out. She was listening to

211

Dondria through the stereo, and the sound of her voice soothed her nerves temporarily. When she saw the Airline exit approaching, she broke her speed, so she could blend in with the slower flow of traffic.

A couple of blocks up, she ran into a red light. She sat there patiently and watched the cars at the intersection take their turns at the crossing. She coughed, and a huge lump of phlegm rose out of her throat. The cool Wisconsin weather had not been nice to her. She rolled her window down and spit the green substance onto the street.

As she wiped her mouth, a beat up Pinto with the horn pressed down came speeding by her and ran the red light. *Crazy*, she thought to herself. She rolled the window up on her rental car and continued to wait on the light to turn green. When she looked to her left, she almost shit on herself. Luther was sitting in a BMW, staring at her car.

Did he see me? Damn!

Panic overtook her body, and she was about to run the red light as well, but, then, she remembered that the windows on her car were tinted, and he probably didn't know that it was her in the car, but, if he *did* know that it was her...

She grabbed her pistol and leaned back in her seat, completely prepared to accept whatever her fate would be. But, as soon as the light turned green, Luther sped off like a bat out of hell.

"Whew!" Pam said after barely escaping a disaster. She decided to take the next left turn and take an alternate route to her mother's house.

By the time she made it there, a stream of tears had flowed down her face without her even realizing it. As soon as she finished visiting her mother, she knew she would need to contact her private psychologist as soon as possible.

CHAPTER 4

Tracy didn't have a lot, but she gave all that she had to try to make Malcolm's prison stay comfortable. She sent him THINKING OF YOU Hallmark cards, wrote love letters, sent magazines, and made herself a regular weekend visitor. She spent every second with Malcolm on her mind, and it made him feel like he really had someone in his corner.

The emotional support that he got from Tracy was one of the main things that kept his morale up. The prison guards had come to know her on a first name basis, and they marveled at how she was able to just sit around and talk to a prisoner for eight hours out of a day for the whole weekend.

And not just any prisoner... She spent her weekends talking to an inmate who was facing thirty years minimum. The female guards thought that it was sweet, but they all knew that there was no future in that. Some of the male guards didn't have girlfriends, and they weren't even behind bars. This angered a few of them and caused them to hate on Malcolm out of jealousy.

They made sure to take extra long when it was time to alert him that he had a visitor. They made sure to harass his visitors more than anyone else's. They, also, made sure to shoot off slick comments, as well.

"Damn, girl! You're way too beautiful to be wasting your life waiting on some prisoner! You didn't break the law; he did. Let me take you out

sometimes!" And, *"Baby girl, this dude ain't EVER getting out of prison. It's time for someone new to come into your life. Let that someone be me."* And the funniest one Tracy had ever heard was, *"This nigga you coming to see is gay! He raped another inmate, and he might bring you home a disease when he gets home in thirty years!"*

Tracy had never brought any of those lies to Malcolm's attention because she felt like he already had enough stuff to worry about. It amazed her how the black prison guards kept trying to kick another black man while he was down. She, also, knew that none of them would have had the balls to say any of those things if Malcolm had been free.

They were the same dudes who would be driving their Fords, while marveling at the man driving the Lamborghini. In the streets, they would have looked up to him, but, in prison, they followed the white man's plan to try to dehumanize him. That Saturday's visit would be extremely different from the previous visits. She had endured all of the usual body searches and negative statements and was four hours into her visit with Malcolm when something astronomical happened at the front desk of the visiting room.

$$\$\sim\$\sim\$\sim\$\sim\$$$

"Hi! I'm here to see Malcolm Powers."

The correctional officer was playing on Twitter all day and didn't even look up from his computer.

"Excuse me... Did you hear me?"

He reluctantly looked up at the woman slowly, but, once he laid his eyes on her, he was entranced. "Damn, beautiful! What's your name?"

215

The woman smiled. She felt like she was finally making progress. "My name is Jennifer Powers."

The officer instantly got angry when he heard her last name. "You're *married* to that dude?"

Jennifer giggled shyly. "I used to be, but it's over now. I just came by to show off real quick."

The potential drama piqued the officer's interest.

"What are you trying to show off, lil mama?"

Jennifer, who now had a continuous smile on her face, slowly turned around and gave the officer a view of her backside.

"Got damnnnnnnnnn!"

"What is it, Tyrone?" another officer yelled from the back office. When he scurried out of the office, he, too, was blown away. "Holy shitttt! Who you come here to see?"

Shyly, Jennifer answered, "Malcolm Powers."

The second officer grunted in amazement. "Tyrone, take her back there ASAP."

Tyrone looked at his co-worker in confusion. "But he already has a visit—"

Tyrone's confusion slowly morphed into understanding. He smirked at what his co-worker was telling him. There would be drama unfolding right before their very eyes, and they would have front row seats.

This nigga is about to get what he deserves, Tyrone thought as he smiled at his co-worker. He pulled two blue latex gloves out of a box and started sliding them on his hands. He managed to get only one glove on before he realized that his co-worker was staring at him like he was crazy.

"Whatsa matta, Jimmie?" Tyrone asked while he thought about how good it was going to feel when he gave Jennifer her body search.

"You know whatsa fuckin' matta! Put those damn gloves away and take this lady back there, so she can see her husband!"

Damn! Tyrone thought as he looked at the roundness of Jennifer's ass. *She looks like a white Nicki Minaj. Damn!* He was devastated about not getting a chance to put his hands on her body, but he had to follow his co-worker's orders. After all, Jimmie was his brother-in-law.

$~$~$~$~$

A short, red-headed female with glowing white skin answered the front door.

"May I help you?" she asked innocently.

Kyla stood in front of her with a blank expression on her face.

"Excuse me... I said, 'Can I help you?'"

Kyla was unprepared for the Coward to have visitors at his home, but she knew that there was no turning back. "Sure, you can help me out. Is Jennifer here?"

The white girl smiled. "No, she's not here. Are you a friend of hers?"

217

Thinking quickly, Kyla answered, "Yeah, Jen is my home girl. We've known each other since we were freshman in high school."

The red head smiled at the prospect of finally meeting one of Jennifer's black friends. She'd always wanted to hang with a black girl, and it seemed like she would finally get her chance. "Wow! Well, why don't you come in? We're just sitting around the pool talking girl talk. You want to join us?"

The naivety of the white girl caught Kyla completely off guard.

"I… well... I would join you, but..."

"But what?" The white girl interjected with a huge Kool-aid smile on her face.

"Ha! Ha! Well, I have the rest of my girlfriends in the car with me, so I think I'll just come back another time."

"Oh, that's nonsense. Friends of Jennifer's are definitely friends of ours. Feel free to come in and have a drink."

Kyla was carefully playing mind games with the girl.

"I don't want to come in there and be around all of those men..."

"Well, just the owner of the house is here, but he's in the bedroom watching a porno. We don't even let him come around his own pool. He truly is a lame, so we treat him as such."

Kyla had to laugh at that.

"Okay, then," Kyla said. "If you insist that it's cool, I'm gonna go get the other girls."

The white girl smiled and nodded her head.

"When you all come in, just come to Wing G. That's where we'll be. Oh... and I didn't get your name..."

Kyla had gathered all of the information that she would need and knew that it was time to make a move.

"That's because I didn't give you my name, bitch!"

The white girl had a surprised look on her face. "Umm... I don't think I quite understand—"

"And I don't think I quite feel like explaining," Kyla said as she gave the signal for her girls to get out of the van. Kyla had been clutching her pistol during the entire conversation, but the girl didn't know it because she never would have thought that a female would have a pistol in her purse to begin with.

"You seem like you have some type of attitude problem, so I'm going to let you go. I'll just tell Jen that one of her little *black* friends came by," the red head said with attitude in her voice.

As she turned to close the door, Kyla let loose. *Wham!* The pistol didn't have a silencer on it, and the sound of the gunshot echoed throughout the entrance of the huge mansion.

All of the girls got out of the van and entered the house with their guns drawn. They made their way to Wing G, while Kyla filled them in on the pertinent details.

Going from one wing to the next, they realized that each room and each wing was soundproof, so there was really no need for a silencer anyway. When they entered Wing G, all of the girls were sitting in the

Jacuzzi and watching *Sex and the City* on a huge plasma screen television. They had champagne glasses sitting on the edge of the Jacuzzi, and they seemed to be enjoying themselves.

Their backs were turned as Kyla, Tricia, Sunshine, and Rain walked up to them with their guns drawn. Tricia, accidentally, dropped her gun, and the sound of it hitting the floor got one of the girls' attention.

"Is that you, Julissa?" she asked, but, once she turned her head, she was staring down the barrel of multiple pistols. Before she got to get another word out, all of the women let loose.

Wham! Wham! Wham! Wham! Wham! Wham!

"Okay! That's enough! That's enough," Kyla said as she watched the two white women's blood turn the entire Jacuzzi red. One girl, who had been shot in the head, was still fighting for her life. She was using every ounce of remaining strength to pull herself out of the Jacuzzi. Her arms trembled, and dark red blood poured from her skull.

She slipped once and fell into the water. Even though it was obvious that she was going to die, she didn't give up and kept trying to pull herself from the water. She managed to get her arms across the edge of the Jacuzzi, but, when she fell back for the final time, she splashed into the water backwards and sank to the bottom of the Jacuzzi, where she drowned.

Kyla pointed to the winding staircase, and the ladies took off. They couldn't run too fast because they were still stylishly clad in Louboutins and dressed in Dolce, Fendi, and Gucci. They were sacrificing their lives for the Bankroll Squad, but they would never sacrifice their style.

The Coward was sitting on his bed with the headphones on while watching a porno on his computer.

He was in a completely different world as he stroked his penis with lotion, unaware that he was surrounded by four of the coldest women in the world. He pressed a button on his computer and skipped to a different scene in the movie. He skipped the oral sex and went straight to the hardcore action.

He turned the volume up even louder as he imagined himself being a part of the scene. Rain smirked, but Sunshine and Kyla both had disgusted looks on their faces. Tricia's face was non-reactive; she was just ready to handle her business and leave. Kyla held up a finger to the girls, signaling them to be quiet and not to move. She walked up behind him with her gun in her hand and stood there, unsure of whether she should kill him fast or let him die slow.

A flood of emotions went through her body when she saw Malcolm's jewelry lying on the Coward's bed. Her mind went back to the day of the robbery, the day that she had been sent to her death bed. She couldn't control herself any longer.

The Coward had his eyes closed and was, suddenly, lying sideways on the bed, facing the girls, but he was unaware of their presence. If he had opened his eyes, he would have seen death in high heels. He was so caught up in listening to the moans of the girl in the movie that he didn't even need to see it to finish masturbating. As he got closer and closer to his climax, Kyla's pistol met him halfway.

Bam! Kyla shot him in his dick, and he, immediately, lost a ton of blood, like a woman on her period. The scream that the Coward let off sounded like the worst thing that Tricia had ever heard in her life. She looked at the Coward's dick and saw that it was hanging off of his body by a slim piece of skin.

He was clutching it and trying to save it, but it was obvious to the girls that it was done.

"Argghhh! Argghhh! Argghhh!"

The Coward went into shock as he writhed against his bed like a fish out of water. He rolled off of the bed and hit the ground, landing with a thud.

"Argghhh!" He moved his hand off of his penis to look at the damage, and the skin that was holding it to his body snapped, and his penis fell off completely.

He passed out.

The Coward never looked up to see who had shot him. He was in such a deep state of shock that the only thing that he could focus on was the hot bullet in his penis. He laid there unconscious, while Kyla stood there in tears. She was crying because of everything that the robbery had done to her life. It had changed everything about her, from her optimistic view of people to the way that she watched her surroundings.

She was a different person now. A person that she would rather have never changed into, but, since she was there, she knew that there was no turning back now. She was a killer. She had broken a lot of laws since joining the Bankroll Squad, but Malcolm had never put her in a situation where she had to kill someone. Realizing how fragile life was and how easy it was for her to take it made her see her pistol in a whole different light.

The Coward woke up and started screaming again.

Tricia spoke up, saying, "Kyla, let him live. Believe me. I think he would rather you kill him than make him live without his dick. Make him suffer for the rest of his days, Kyla. Make him see how it feels to be *robbed* of something with a pistol."

Kyla nodded her head at Tricia and wiped the tears from her face. She put her pistol back in her purse and backed away from the Coward's flailing body. Kyla took a deep breath and turned to leave with Rain and Tricia following suit.

Bam! Bam! Bam!

Sunshine put three bullets into the Coward's head, leaving his brain matter splattered on his silk sheets and his tan carpeting. Tricia was furious that Sunshine hadn't followed her advice.

"What you do that for?" Tricia asked.

Sunshine ignored her and smiled at Kyla. Kyla smiled back at her. It felt good to know that someone genuinely had her back.

"I'm not leaving him alive, so he can hunt Kyla down and try to kill her! We finish what we start! Otherwise, there is no point in doing it in the first place. It's over now."

Kyla was crying because the closure that she had been looking for had finally come. She stood in place and closed her eyes while the tears seeped through the crevices. Rain and Sunshine both embraced her.

"It's alright, Kyla. It's over now. It's all over now," Sunshine whispered as she glared at Tricia.

$~$~$~$~$

Luther had been chasing Tron's Pinto for five minutes when, suddenly, it started going slower and slower. The Pinto was rolling as if...

That muthafucka done ran out of gas! Luther thought as he drove towards the Pinto with his.357 out. Before Luther could even let a shot off, he realized that he had been tricked. He ducked as a barrage of bullets shattered the windows on his BMW and made their entrance through the luxury car's door panels.

A bullet hit him in the shoulder and another one hit him in the arm. Then, there was silence. He listened intently, trying to see if Tron was going to try to get out of his car to finish the job or not. Then, he heard exactly what he needed to hear.

The Pinto's ignition coughed as Tron turned the key, and it was clear that Tron would need a mechanic to crank that raggedy bucket back up. As soon as Luther heard the door on the Pinto slam, he rose up in his seat and let his pistol scream.

Wakka! Wakka! Wakka! Wakka! Wakka!

The kickback from the.357 caused his skinny arms to jerk back after every shot. Luther grabbed his door handle, so he could get out and shoot Tron once in the head, but he saw that he was losing too much blood, and he didn't want to pass out at the scene of a murder, so he thought better of it.

He sat upright and focused on getting back to Kyla's house, so he could figure out what to do next. He had to hurry up, though, because, if a police officer saw him driving a Benz with bullet holes in the door and shattered windows, the outcome of that might not be favorable either.

$~$~$~$~$

Malcolm had a fresh haircut and was sitting as close to Tracy as possible. It wasn't cold, but Tracy still had a thin windbreaker jacket covering her lap. The reason was so that Malcolm could play in her pussy while he whispered in her ear. After being around grown men all day, every day, a contact visit with a woman brought out the savageness in every man in the visitation room.

"Oh! Damn, Malcolm..." Tracy was imagining that it was Malcolm's dick instead of his fingers, and she shuddered as she felt him stroke against her vaginal walls. If she could, she would ride his hand, but she knew that such an act would cause too much suspicion and get them both thrown out of the visitation room.

The visits with Malcolm each week were the main things that made her life easier. Sweetback had disowned her, and she felt like she owed her life to the man who had spared her life and treated her like a lady during the strangest of situations. Malcolm had started stroking her faster, and her vaginal fluids were flowing like a faucet, leaking onto his hand.

"Damn, Malcolm! That feels good to me."

After a while, Malcolm thought he saw one of the correctional officers staring at him, so he pulled out of her and shifted in his seat. Tracy smiled at him and shook her head.

"Malcolm, what is the lawyer talking about?"

The question, immediately, brought Malcolm out of his sexual fantasy and back to reality. He shook his head and took a deep breath before he said, "They're talking about, maybe, I should think about signing the thirty year plea deal."

Tracy felt a sharp pain go through her body after his statement.

"That's the best they can do, Malcolm? Thirty years? Seriously?"

Malcolm put his arm around her neck and pulled her close to him. "Don't worry about it, Tracy. Everything is going to be fine. I'll figure this out."

He looked into her eyes and saw that they were misting up. It amazed him how Tracy had all the love in the world for him, considering the circumstances that they met under. He would have never thought, in a million years, that something like this would have happened. For her, it was a completely different experience. She was holding on to a secret that she had yet to tell Malcolm.

It wasn't that she didn't care for him, because she did, but she had another secret that was causing her to really ride it out with Malcolm. She was four and a half months pregnant with his child. She had done the best she could to be as solid a woman as she could be, but, if Malcolm went away for thirty years, it would be the second child that she would have to raise without a father figure in the household.

She didn't want Malcolm to commit to her under pressure, and she didn't want to commit herself to him when she knew that, maybe, neither of them would be able to honor the commitment. She just wanted Malcolm to be there for his child. She would be content playing the baby mama role as long as he did what Sweetback Fatty hadn't done for his child— spend time.

"Malcolm, there's something important that I wanted to talk to you about."

Malcolm sat up in his seat and gave Tracy his undivided attention.

"What is it, Tracy?"

Tracy sighed and grabbed Malcolm's hand while she spoke. "Well, I just wanted to tell you—"

"Who the fuck are you, bitch?"

Jennifer had just made it into the visitation room and was standing directly in front of Tracy with her hands on her hips.

"Bitch? Who the fuck are you calling a bitch? Bitch!"

Tracy was heated. She had never had a white girl talk to her like she was a slave, and she didn't like it one bit. Malcolm stood up.

"Jennifer, what the fuck are you doing here? Your name isn't on my visitation list!"

Jennifer grinned at him for a second and tossed her hair behind her back. "I'm your wife, muthafucka! And who are you, bitch?"

Tracy tried to lunge at her, but Malcolm held her back. By now, everyone in the visitation room had their eyes on the spectacle that was unfolding in front of them. The other inmates were amazed that a white girl had the baddest body in the entire visitation room.

"What the fuck do you want, Jennifer? I signed the got damn divorce papers. You didn't get 'em?"

"No, I didn't, but I didn't come here for that anyway!"

Malcolm took a deep breath as he stared daggers into Jennifer's eyes.

227

It was the first time that he'd seen Jennifer since all of the bad luck had started happening, and it was clear that she had completely changed. She had the look of a... dope fiend. Her face was skinnier than he remembered it, and her eyes were bloodshot red, but the rest of her body... damn!

"What the fuck are you here for? I'm on a visit, Jennifer."

Jennifer pointed her finger in Tracy's face and said, "With this bitch? She ain't got an ass like mines! She's ugly, and she will never be me! I'm the baddest bitch in the muthafuckin' room, and *she* knows it. I stepped in here and lowered that bitch's self-esteem ten notches. I'm just here to show you what you lost!"

Tracy grabbed Jennifer's hair and dragged her to the ground like she was a rag doll. "Stupid bitch! I'll show you who's the baddest bitch!"

Tracy started punching Jennifer in the eye relentlessly. Even though it lasted only a few seconds before the correctional officers came and broke it up, Tracy was able to do some damage.

"Visiting room is *closed!*" The C.O. yelled.

The other inmates were pissed that they were closing the visitation room because of a fight, but they had to admit that the fight had been damned good, though. The officers were holding Tracy and Jennifer apart, but only Tracy was still yelling.

"Let me fucking go! I need to black that bitch's other eye since she wanna be *black*! Let me at that white ho!"

Jennifer became extra quiet after witnessing Tracy's strength and didn't want any more problems. She just wanted to go back to her

228

mansion and snort some more cocaine. While they were escorting the two women out of the prison, Jennifer realized that, maybe, she had made the wrong person mad. Her brilliant plan was turning into a mistake.

$~$~$~$~$

After the correctional officers escorted the two ladies outside, they walked off. Then, they went back inside the prison and looked out of a window to see what was going to transpire next.

"Bitch, what was that shit you was talking? Huh? What was you talking, you white bitch?"

Jennifer feared for her life, so she ran to her car to grab her pocket knife. She was sitting in her car, trying to figure out how to pull the blade out, when a fist slammed into the side of her face.

"Bitch, what the fuck you pulling a knife out for? Is you trying to die, ho?"

Tracy snatched the knife out of Jennifer's hands and slammed her face against the steering wheel. Tracy, then, pulled the blade out of the knife like a professional and stabbed Jennifer in the ass.

"Is this what you care about? You having a bigger ass than me, you stupid bitch?"

She stabbed her again on the other butt cheek and, then, slapped her across her nose for the final time.

"Nooooo!" Jennifer cried as she grabbed at the stab wounds with both hands. "Why would you do that to me? Noooo!"

The stab wounds weren't deep, just light enough to puncture the skin. Tracy wasn't trying to catch a case on federal property. She just wanted to teach that white bitch a lesson.

"From here on out, bitch, I want you to stay the fuck away from Malcolm!"

Jennifer didn't respond because she was crying and trying to find her car keys.

"Bitch, do you fuckin' hear me?"

Jennifer nodded her head. "Yes, ma'am!"

She didn't want any more problems from this deranged-ass black girl that Malcolm had visiting him.

What kind of woman stabs another woman in the ass? Jennifer wondered as she searched for the keys to her Mercedes. She had just paid for those implants not too long ago, and, now, it was looking like she would have to get them done again.

Gosh, I need some cocaine! She thought as she drove off crying.

CHAPTER 5

Malcolm had been cleared of any wrong doing and was finally allowed to come out of solitary confinement. He was sitting in his cell with his head in his hands while he thought about the scenario that had just unfolded.

"You alright, young buck?" his cellmate asked him.

His cellmate was an older gentleman, who had been doing time for the past ten years. He had recently been released from prison and was back in jail on a probation violation.

"Yeah, I'm straight, Phil," Malcolm said as he held his head up and took a deep breath. "Can you believe these C.O.s let my ex-wife interrupt my visit when she wasn't even on the visitation list? I can't believe that shit, man."

Phil smiled at Malcolm, but didn't speak. He was reading a Sidney Sheldon novel while he laid back on his bunk.

"Phil," Malcolm said, "I didn't think that they could do something like that."

Phil set his paperback novel down and sat up in his bunk. He had strands of gray around his goatee and along his sideburns. His voice was raspy, and his demeanor was calm.

231

"Young buck, check this out. I know you may not believe what I'm going to say, but I'm going to say it anyways. These people can do whatever they want to do to you, and there is nothing that you can do about it. They can poison your food before they serve it to you, and what can you do about that? What if they decide to lock you in the hole for no reason? You can't escape the hole, can you? They make the rules as they go, and it's always been like that. I thought I was off the hook since I did my ten years in prison and went home, but, boy, was I wrong. I was riding in the car with my son, just enjoying my freedom, when the police pulled us over. We weren't the least bit worried. The cops told us to get out, and he asked to search the care, and my son was like 'Sure', so the officer searches the car and goes up under my seat and pulls out a fuckin' Glock 40 that I had never seen before! It wasn't mines, and it definitely wasn't my son's. So, I told the police that the gun was mines, so my son could go home. Initially, the lawyer said I would have to do fifteen years because the new charge would make me a career offender. I didn't even care at first. I was going to do the fifteen, so my son could stay free and continue living his life. I never want to see someone else go through the hardships that I went through for ten years."

Phil took a deep breath and shook his head. Then, he continued. "My lawyer came to me yesterday and told me that the ballistics came back and that the gun had been used in a string of murders. So, now, I'm facing murder charges that I didn't commit all because of a gun I had never seen before, but how can I defend that? What do I say? It wasn't mines? I'm already a felon, already done ten years in prison. So, in their eyes, I will never change. I will never be nothing. So, Malcolm... I'll tell you this once and for all. There is nothing in the world that the white man can't do to you. They've been doing it forever, but I do believe that you're starting to notice."

Malcolm sat back and watched the old man while he reflected on his words. Everything that he was saying had made a lot of sense, and the stuff that he was going through was nothing when compared to what Phil was going through. With Malcolm's charges, Malcolm knew that they had done their homework and that the charges were accurate. It was a whole new ball game with his cellmate because his celly claimed that he was innocent.

Malcolm opened his mouth to ask his cellmate something, but he was interrupted by Tomy Rarez.

"Aye, homes! They're talking about the Bankroll Squad on TV again!"

Malcolm shook his head and made his way to the general viewing area where the inmates were watching the local news. He stood there with his arms folded as he listened to the news reporter break the news.

"A member of the Bankroll Squad crime organization has been shot and killed on the block of Crosstimbers and Airline. Details are sketchy at this point, but the victim is said to have been working secretly as a confidential informant for the FBI and was going to be a key witness in the trial against Malcolm Powers and the criminal organization known as the Bankroll Squad. Names have not officially been released, but it is believed to be a guy that went by the street name of Prince Tron. A member of the street gang by the name of Kyla Brent is believed to be a person of interest in the murder. She escaped from a federal rehab facility not too long ago and is believed to be armed and dangerous. No further details are available at this time."

Malcolm's stomach turned upside down upon hearing such devastating news. He felt sick and couldn't believe that the woman that

233

he loved was getting herself into so much trouble all because of him. No matter what happened, he promised himself that, one day, he was going to make it up to her. Everything that had happened to her had basically been his fault, and he wanted to correct it.

His legs got weak as he stood there, and he finally figured that, maybe, it was time for him to lay down. Maybe, it would be best if he signed the thirty year plea deal to give the government what they'd been lusting for. Maybe, that way, Kyla would no longer be on their radar, and, perhaps, they'd even cut Brink and Catfish's time in half. He went back into his cold prison cell and weighed his options out.

Decision time was fast approaching, and he would have to decide if he would go to trial or sign a plea deal. *Damn!* He thought as he calculated how old he would be after doing a thirty year bid.

$~$~$~$~$

"Person of interest?" Kyla and Sunshine had been searching for a decent song on the radio when they heard the news report about the murder of Prince Tron.

"That's some bullshit!" Kyla said as she shook her head. She had been planning to kill Prince Tron, but she hadn't been able to find him. And they *still* pinned the murder down on her.

"Damn!" Suddenly, it came to her. "Luther..."

The girls shook their heads as Tricia spoke up and said, "Luther did exactly what he was supposed to do— waste that snitching muthafucka. That's one less person to testify against Catfish and Malcolm."

Kyla nodded her head in agreement. "You're absolutely right, Tricia.

And I would do time for Tron's murder if it helped Malcolm, Brink, and Catfish to get out of their situation. I would definitely take the murder rap for that reason."

Sunshine shook her head in disapproval, but she didn't say anything. She had seen the suspicious look on Rain's face earlier in the day when she had given Kyla a hug. She knew that Rain knew her better than any of the other girls and could probably detect it when something was funny or when she was acting strange. And, with her eyes constantly glued to Kyla, she knew she was definitely acting strange.

"I would do time for Luther for that reason, too!" Tricia said as she pushed the van through the traffic. "I love Catfish with all my soul and being, and I wish like hell that I could get him out of his stupid predicament."

Kyla brushed a strand of hair out of her eye and sat back against the comfort of the passenger seat. She watched the passing scenery in silence while Sunshine and Rain sang along with a new song by Beyoncé that had just come on the radio.

Girls! We run the world! Girls! It was her first time hearing that song, and it truly motivated her. She nodded her head to the club anthem as she thought about how accurate Beyoncé's statement was. She had a couple of ideas, so she spoke up.

"Hey! I need to speak to Malcolm some type of way. If I can speak to him, he can tell me who the witnesses are and what the evidence is against them. Beyoncé is dead accurate... We *do* run the world, and I'm sure that, if I knew the specific details, we could get them out of their situation."

Sunshine and Rain didn't respond to Kyla's comment, but it was

235

known that they would be down for whatever their leader proposed.
Tricia glanced over at Kyla when they had reached a stop sign and said,
"Kyla, I hear what you're saying, but do you think it will work? I really
want Catfish home. I miss him so much! I don't want him to have to do
all of this stupid time. I am already so lonely!"

Kyla met her glance, nodded her head, and responded, "Of course, it
will work, but we just need the details. How could the government win
a trial if they have no witnesses, no evidence, and can't find the special
agent that set up the whole case?"

When there was a break in traffic, Tricia pulled back off and, as she
hummed along with Beyoncé's new song, an idea hit her.

"Kyla, what if there are a lot of witnesses? What if it's hundreds of
people? And what if the evidence is too much?"

Kyla heard her, but didn't respond. She was lost in thought, thinking
of what the best way to handle that situation would be. They slowly
turned the van into the entrance of Kyla's estate while the question
lingered in the air. Kyla looked at everything that she had been able to
acquire in her short lifetime and knew that she cared about none of it.
The home, land, cars, the money— it had never meant anything to her,
and it certainly didn't mean anything to her at that moment.

She thought about how much she had fallen in love with Malcolm,
and she knew that the love that he had for her hadn't completely
vanished. It had to be there in him somewhere. And, if it meant that she
had to remove every obstacle standing between them in order to find
out, that was exactly what she would do. When she spoke, she sounded
innocent, but every word she uttered was cold and calculated.

"If there are a lot of witnesses, then there are going to be a lot of

SBR Publication Presents......

funerals. The city is about to be involved in a bloodbath, and I don't care if I have to take out 200 witnesses in the next two weeks; I *will* get it done. Even if I have to do it by myself, I will get it *done*. I don't care about the consequences, I only care about results. I only know how to be one thing in life, and that's *real*. I'm the realest bitch a man could ever meet in his life. I don't honor disloyalty; I honor honesty... and, when I get to a situation where I have been betrayed, then I honor the pistol."

Kyla's vicious words sent chills through every woman sitting in the vehicle. They knew that it was about to go down in a major way, and, if Kyla was so committed to putting her plan in motion, then they would certainly make sure that they had her back through it all. Killing the Coward had been easier than they thought, and, if they could do one person, then there was no limit on how many others they could do.

Sunshine was the first to speak up. "Well, the city better get ready for this bloodbath."

The other ladies nodded their heads as they pulled up to Kyla's home.

$~$~$~$~$

When the lights went out, Malcolm laid there for hours, unable to sleep. He had tried to just close his eyes and wait on sleep to approach him, but it seemed to have approached his cellmate first. He opened his eyes and stared into the darkness. At such a young age, he had managed to get an entire dream life assembled and to have the entire thing fall apart in a matter of moments.

Sure, he had made some questionable decisions, but what man hadn't made bad decisions at his age. Among the top of the bad decisions that he had made was the decision to marry Jennifer. His family hadn't even approved of it when he was getting the wedding details finalized; yet, he pressed on anyway. Even on the day of the wedding, he still had Kyla in the back of his mind.

He should have known, then, that Jennifer wasn't the one for him. He was biting off more than he could chew, but his pride wouldn't let him acknowledge his mistake. Instead, he constantly tried to keep Kyla's memories from interfering with his marriage to Jennifer. It was hard, but he had somewhat managed.

When he thought about all of the things that Jennifer had done to betray him after finding out that he sold drugs for a living, he knew, for a fact, that she had never loved him. How could she have loved him if it was that easy for her to leave? It didn't make sense to him.

He laid there and bashed his brain, trying to think of whether it was a good decision to sign the thirty year plea deal or whether there was a chance for him to win his trial. *Maybe*, he thought, *I can, at least, get less time than they are offering me.*

It was pitch dark in the cell, but a slim beam of light shined through a crack in the window, so Malcolm took the opportunity to look over some of his paperwork again. He reached under his mattress and pulled out his evidence documents. He sat up in bed and squinted his eyes, trying to see if there was anything that he had originally missed when he first read over it.

When he saw the first sentence, he stopped, already feeling defeated.

The following statements have been found to be true by special agent Pamela Jones, out of the Northern District of Georgia.

He put the paper back under his mattress, suddenly feeling tired.

I'll just read this stuff again after I wake up in the morning. Then, he thought about the name again. *Pamela Jones...*

He laid there in deep concentration and tried to remember how he had met her and brought her into the folds of the Bankroll Squad.

$~$~$~$~$

"Hey! Excuse me. I know you two may think that I'm silly or whatnot, but I just have to ask you. Can I take a picture of you two?"

Malcolm and Kyla looked at each other as if to say, "Do you know her?" Neither Malcolm nor Kyla had ever spoken to her or ever seen her on campus, but that didn't actually mean much because they barely noticed anyone on the campus. They were so into each other that they seemed to be floating and living in their own little world.

Malcolm finally spoke up and asked, "Who are you?"

The strange girl smiled bashfully and wiped her hands on her skin tight jogging pants as she said, "I'm so sorry. Where are my manners? My name is Pamela Jones, and I just think that you two are the absolute most beautiful couple that I have ever seen in my life, and I wanted to capture this moment. This will forever be my reference picture of what true love looks like."

Kyla thought nothing of it at the time. She just figured that she was like every other college student that she had encountered— a teenager who had been thrust into the preliminary stages of the real world and was trying to find an identity.

"Sure, you can take a picture of us, but under one condition," Kyla

239

found herself saying. "You have to make sure to email me a copy of the picture."

Pam grinned, showing her perfect pearly whites. "That's not an issue, just give me your email address, and I'll make sure you get one in your inbox."

$~$~$~$~$

Malcolm laid on his bunk and shook his head while he thought about how that one incident had changed his life for the worst.

He had initially thought that something was strange about Pam when she kept bringing gifts for him and Kyla, but, at some point, both he and Kyla let their guards down and just figured that she was just a nice-ass country girl who had never been anywhere in her life.

They'd embraced her as a friend and invited her to go bowling with them. They'd even invited her to dinner, and she had come along happily as the third leg of the date. They knew that, if they invited her to do anything, she would absolutely jump at the opportunity to show them how much she liked them. And, with all the gifts that she had been giving them, it made it kind of hard to not want to invite her out with them.

One of the gifts that she had given Kyla and Malcolm was a little key chain with their picture on it. Below their picture, it read: From Pam, your friend to the end! She constantly gave gifts of that caliber, and it softened them up for what would be a complete overkill in the future. After about six months of her "act", one day, she came on the campus with an entirely new role to play.

$~$~$~$~$

Malcolm saw her in the morning when she had just arrived at school, and her face was puffy. Her eyes were red, and she was wearing the same thing that she'd worn the previous day.

"What's wrong, Pam? Is everything okay with you?" he had asked her, concerned.

It would turn out to be the worst question he had ever asked in his life.

"No," Pam sobbed, while she shook her head slowly as if it was the end of the world. "I've been evicted from my apartment because I couldn't come up with the money to pay my bills. The landlord wouldn't even let me go back into the place to get my clothes. I slept in my car last night outside of a Walmart. I'm doing bad right now. I may even have to quit school."

Malcolm was hustling at that point, but he was only moving half a brick per day. He was well on his way to becoming rich, but he had no plans of just giving Pam money when she could be making some of her own. Early in life, he knew the importance of earning as opposed to receiving. If she had just received money from him, she wouldn't have appreciated it as much as she would have if she had done something for it.

"You don't have any family up here?" Malcolm asked her, suddenly feeling bad for his and Kyla's friend.

"I don't have any family at all. My father passed, and my mother... I haven't seen her in over twelve years. She left me with her sister, and my aunt has been hating my guts ever since. She says that I cramped her style when I moved in. I don't know what I'm going to do, Malcolm."

241

Malcolm thought hard, trying to figure out a way to help her get some money. He sighed as he asked, "Pam, do you know anything about investing?"

Pam seemed to come alive when he mentioned investing. "That's what I'm about to do as soon as I graduate. I plan on working as a financial advisor at a multi-billion dollar corporation. I plan on guiding them to make more money, keep the money that they already have churning to the point where their dollars bring them more dollars without them doing a thing..."

Pam went on and on about tax write offs and tax safe havens. She seemed to be very enthusiastic when it came to investing money.

"So, what if I paid you $600 per week to help me invest money? Would you need to know where the money came from?"

Pam smirked at Malcolm. "If you paid me $600 per week to do my dream job, I wouldn't care if you got the money from an eggplant."

$~$~$~$~$

It had seemed simple to Malcolm at first, until he began to get more and more comfortable around her. When his business began to boom, she still had the same job title that she'd had when he was in his beginning stages, but it had gotten to the point where he was paying her $75,000 per week to show him how to invest and hide his money.

She had always told him that he was paying her way too much money, and he always brushed her off. Now, while lying on the top bunk of a prison bed, he knew that what she had said back then was completely accurate. He *had* been paying her too much because she was getting all of her income from the federal government. She had been basing her entire career on the case against the Bankroll Squad and was, finally, about to get the win that she had been working towards.

Before he fell asleep, he thought about how triumphant the government would be if he signed a thirty year plea deal. He thought about how Pam would revel in her success, while he suffered between the walls of federal prison until he was fifty-six years of age. He knew he wouldn't be able to do it.

He would *have* to go to trial and make them prove to the world that he was guilty. They would have to spend countless man hours and plenty of government money if they were going to convict him because there was no way that he was going to sign his life away voluntarily. *Fuck that!* He thought as he dozed off to sleep.

$~$~$~$~$

Dr. Jacobs had been a doctor for ten years of his life before losing his license. He had gotten caught selling syrup prescriptions. He had been selling "scripts" as a side hustle, and, at one point, he was making more money selling those prescriptions than he was at the clinic that he worked at.

He was approaching his mid-fifties and didn't know how to do anything else in the world except be the doctor that he'd gone to school to become. So, even though he'd lost his license, that never prevented him from practicing medicine. He had plenty of repeat customers who he serviced from his lavish home. The majority were gangsters, drug dealers, pimps, robbers, and other hustlers who probably would have gone to prison if they went to a regular hospital.

From his point of view, he was doing the world a service by helping these people because they probably would have died before seeking

243

medical attention.

He had just patched up Luther after cleaning up his bullet wounds. "I stitched you up pretty good there, Luther, and I believe that you will be perfectly fine. They were only flesh wounds, and there were no bullets left inside of you, so everything looks good. If you have any pains, I'm about to give you a bottle of Tylenol 3 that you can take for that."

Luther nodded his head and smiled. "Doc, I really appreciate what you've done for me."

Dr. Jacobs shook his head and shooed him off. "Luther, I didn't do anything but help a dear friend of mine out because I know that he would do the same for me. Speaking of which, how is Malcolm holding up?"

Luther thought about the question for a second and realized that he really didn't know how Malcolm was doing. Amidst his waiting on the Bankroll Squad to beat the charges and finally come home, he had forgotten to do one of the most important things that a boss could possibly do. He had to support his people when they were down.

"I'm going to see Malcolm in the morning, doc. Anything you want me to tell him for you?"

As Dr. Jacobs washed his hands and dried them off on a towel, he said, "Sure. Tell him that I want him to get out of there and marry that beautiful mixed girl that loves him so much. What's her name?"

Luther nodded his head and said, "You're talking about Kyla. I think he should marry her, too. She's the most down chick on this planet. No joke."

Dr. Jacobs sat down on a cushioned stool and folded his hands in his lap. "I know she is, Luther. That's why he wanted to marry her in the first place."

Luther stood up and tried to stretch his arm out a little bit, but the pain prevented him from doing that. "Well, I better get going, doc."

Luther turned to leave, but he was stopped in his tracks by the doc's next comment.

"How is my partner Prince Tron doing?"

Luther turned around and looked at the doctor with a bewildered expression on his face. "Prince Tron is your partner? I didn't even know that you knew him."

"Of course, I know Tron. He's the one who helped me after I came home from prison."

There was an eerie tone to Dr. Jacob's voice, but Luther thought that, maybe, he was being overly paranoid.

"I guess he's okay. I haven't talked to him lately."

As he said the words, he noticed that the doctor had something bulging out of his white coat. After seeing it, Luther ignored it and tried to leave again. As he turned to the door, the doctor stopped him again.

"I already know the situation, young buck. Come on here and sit down, so we can wait on the police together. It's a $150,000 reward out for the arrest of Kyla Brent, but I do believe that they just might be looking for the wrong person. What do you think? Turn around and have a—"

Before the doctor could finish his words, Luther turned around and pulled the trigger on his.357. The shots knocked the doctor off of his stool, and he was dead as soon as he hit the ground. Luther knew that he only had a few minutes to get out of there before the shit hit the fan.

CHAPTER 6

Kyla stared at herself in the mirror and noticed the changes in her appearance. Before she'd had an innocent and beautiful look, but, now, it looked as if she had been through some things. The plastic surgeon had done a decent job on her lip, but it still didn't look like it had originally looked. She used to keep her hair done up, but, at that point, it hadn't been touched by her hair stylist in so long that she doubted that she would ever get it back to the form that she liked it in.

She studied her breasts, and they looked like they had lost a little of their firmness since she had been in her coma. She looked into her eyes and saw tears running down her face. She was still trying to wrap her mind around the fact that someone had tried to kill her and taken her all the way to the edges of death.

She was still trying to figure out what the purpose was for her, of all people, to keep living. *Why didn't God allow me to die?* She wiped her tears with her washcloth and went and sat inside the warm water of the Jacuzzi-style bathtub. The smell of cucumber melon body wash penetrated the room, and there was a sensor in her bathtub that dimmed the lights whenever it detected a warm body laying against it.

She laid there and relaxed, thinking about the huge task at hand and the responsibility that she had taken on. She had never wondered if it was worth it or not. Her only issue was whether she would be strong enough to pull it off. Lately, she had been feeling weak, and she seemed not to be able to hold down any foods. She knew that she wouldn't be able to go to a doctor because her face was all over the news, and she was wanted for a murder that she didn't even commit.

She closed her eyes and let the water stream massage her back.

𝓢~𝓢~𝓢~𝓢~𝓢

Sunshine, who was standing in the doorway, was in awe. Kyla hadn't seen her standing there, so Sunshine embraced the moment of her life. Her eyes wandered up and down Kyla's beautiful body with the intensity of a microscope. She studied the curves from her waist to her thighs and lusted over the two smiley faces sitting right underneath both of her ass cheeks.

Mmmm, Sunshine thought as she slipped her hands into her panties. As she watched Kyla study herself in the mirror, Sunshine pleasured herself, fantasizing that she was laying her body against Kyla's. She stroked her clitoris slowly at first, rubbing it in a circle and switching it up to rub it vertically. After a minute, she sped up and rubbed her clitoris vigorously, as if she had sprinkled itching powder on it and was trying to soothe it with her fingers.

After another minute, she felt herself about to come, and she couldn't control herself. While still looking through the crack in the door, she saw tears in Kyla's eyes, and it was as if Kyla was looking directly into Sunshine's eyes and making love to her. Sunshine couldn't take it anymore.

Mmmmm, mmmmm, mmmmm, mmmm! She moaned as she felt her vagina getting wetter and her muscles contracting. Her knees buckled as a powerful orgasm ripped through her body and almost made her scream out loud. As she watched Kyla get into her bathtub, she reached down to pick her panties and pants up. While she did this, she sensed that someone was behind her.

She turned around and saw Rain staring at her with a pathetic look on her face.

"I see you found the bathroom, Sunshine. How did that work out for you?"

$~$~$~$~$

Jennifer put some peroxide on her two small stab wounds and covered them with gauze and bandages. She was on her way to the Coward's mansion when a reporter came on the radio, talking about the Bankroll Squad.

"It is truly one of the most vicious gangs that have ever been assembled. The murders, the drug smuggling, and the prostitution allegations are lightweight charges when compared to the totality of the crimes that they have committed. The federal government has stated that they plan to upgrade the charges against the leaders of the crew to mandatory life sentences if convicted at trial. This includes the charges against the man in charge of creating the deadly gang— Malcolm Powers. Malcolm is a college graduate who used proceeds from illegal activities to start the potato chip brand entitled *Frisbee Crispy.* He is currently facing life in prison."

Jennifer shook her head after hearing the news reporter's spiel on the squad. She had married Malcolm, so she knew, for a fact, that he wasn't as bad as the news made him out to be. *But oh, well,* she thought as she continued to drive her Benz through the pothole ridden streets.

She thought about Catfish. She knew that he was a straight softie. There was no way that the Bankroll Squad had done all that they claimed that they had done. No way at all. She pulled onto the Coward's estate with a smile on her face. She was smiling because she had managed to leave Malcolm and still have the opportunity to live the good life. At first, that was her most pressing concern. She didn't even *know* of anybody who was getting money like Malcolm was, so she thought that she was going to end up broke, like all of her girlfriends.

She just *knew* that she was going to be the laughing stock of Houston. Despite the altercation with Tracy outside of the prison, everything still looked perfect to Jennifer. She had all the cocaine that she could possibly snort; she had all of her friends living with her, and she had Ward, who seemed to have even more money than Malcolm did.

If he didn't, he sure acted like he did. He showered her with money constantly and let her have her way. The freedom that Ward provided her was a luxury that she never thought she would have in this lifetime.

She pulled her Benz up into the garage and got out. When she got to the door, she immediately noticed that something was terribly wrong.

There were pistol shell casings on the ground, and the door was wide open. She looked around nervously, but didn't see anyone.

"Waaaaard! Juliiisssssssa? Are y'all here?" Jennifer shouted as she stood outside of the mansion.

She took a deep breath and walked in. After taking three steps, she almost pissed on herself when she saw Julissa's dead body. It laid awkwardly on the carpet. There was a pool of blood from where a bullet had split her head open. Jennifer immediately went into shock.

"Arrrrrghghhh! Arrggghghhh! Arrrgghhghgh!"

She ran into the house, screaming, only to see her other friends floating in the Jacuzzi.

"Arrrggghhhh! Arrrrrgghh! Hellllpppp! Hellllllllp!"

It was too much for her to take, so she ran straight to the Coward's room to ask him why he had killed her friends. *If he wanted to have sex with them that bad, he should have told her that he was beginning to get desperate,* she thought, but, when she got to his room, it was obvious that Ward wasn't the person who had committed the murders. His body was completely mutilated and looked like something fresh out of a horror movie.

Jennifer suddenly felt dizzy. She felt like her mind was there, but her body was elsewhere. The whole scenario seemed unreal to her. The room started spinning, and it seemed like she was slowly being sucked into a winding vortex. She began to panic, but quickly realized that there was a sensible solution to everything that was going on.

She ran straight to the closet and grabbed two bricks of cocaine. Then, she opened the safe and pulled out $50,000. She put it all into one of her Louis V handbags and ran straight to her car. Once she got there, she busted the seal on one of the bricks of coke and dug her pinky into it. She took a mini mound straight to her nose and vacuumed every particle from her finger.

She sat there as the drug pounded through her body and tried to figure out what to do next. She would have to go to a hotel and call 911 as soon as she got there. Shaking, she tried to insert the key into her vehicle's ignition but failed. She kept trying until, eventually, she got the key in. She started her Benz and tried to back out of the garage, but she had put the car in the wrong gear and was going forward.

She ran over two steel trash cans and grimaced as the front end of her Benz hit the wall. She gathered her senses quickly and put her car into the right gear. She, finally, backed out of the garage. An aggressive calmness embraced her as the cocaine spiraled into her blood stream. She loved the feeling of being high on cocaine. It was almost as good as *crack* to her.

I really need some crack, she thought as she spun her wheels, getting off of the Coward's property. *But I promised myself I wouldn't do it anymore. What should I do?*

She licked her finger and tasted the cocaine residue, letting the bitterness invade her taste buds. She loved everything about cocaine. The taste, the way it felt when she smoked it, the effect it had when she sniffed it, the color of it. Even the way it tasted when she put it in her fruit punch.

Thinking back on the day that she'd first found out that Malcolm sold it, she wished that she could rewind time and embrace it, instead of flipping out the way that she had. If she had known that cocaine was this good, she would have never, in her lifetime, left Malcolm. As she looked for a hotel, she wondered if it was too late to try to get Malcolm back or not.

I'll try in a couple of days. I'm still his wife. Maybe, he'll forgive me.

She felt the cocaine numbing her nose and working its way to her emotions. *Damn, this is the life.*

She had already forgotten about her problems and everything that she had done wrong to Malcolm. She was truly an addict.

"Hello?" Tracy said, after answering the phone on the second ring.

"Yeah... one of my boys said that he saw you back at that fuckin' jailhouse."

Tracy sat up in her bed, irritated by Sweetback Fatty's questioning. "Yeah, so what?"

"So what?" he bellowed. "So, you get your dumb ass kidnapped, and, the next thing you know, you done fell in love with the person! You're a fuckin' clown! Who the fuck does that type of shit?"

Tracy yawned and rolled her eyes. "Is there anything you want besides being in my muthafuckin' business?"

"Bitch, you is my business! What the fuck... Who the fuck... You know what? Bring your muthafuckin' ass home! You been on your little vacation for long enough. Now, if you don't get your dumb ass over here, I'm going to have to send my goons after your stupid ass!"

Tracy frowned and felt bile rising to the top of her throat. First, he didn't want her; now, he wanted her. That was stupid, and she was sick of going through the same shit over and over with Sweetback.

"I am home! He may have done what he did, but he still treats me better than you have *ever* treated me! There is no way in the world that I would come back and live with you!"

She slammed her phone against the wall as she laid there in her bed, seething. She was tired of being threatened by Sweetback, but it had been going on ever since they first met each other. She just wanted to live her life with the least amount of conflict as possible, and Malcolm provided that. She didn't have any delusions about being the next Mrs. Powers, but she knew that she provided the emotional support that he needed, and he provided the same support in return.

She was truly happy and didn't want to be back under the thumb of Sweetback ever again. Every since she started going to the jail to visit Malcolm, Sweetback's people had been reporting to him every single outfit that she wore and every single move that she made. His ego couldn't take the fact that his baby's mother was the best looking lady in the visitation room and that she was going to visit his enemy. He was pissed, and she could care less. She was going to continue to do her.

$~$~$~$~$

It was the afternoon of the next day, and Kyla was lying in her comfortable bed, relaxing. Despite the bright sunlight outside, her room was dark, as if it were still night time. She stretched her legs and turned to lay on her side while she stared at the phone, almost willing it to ring.

Earlier that morning, Luther had left to go visit Malcolm in jail, and she had asked him to give Malcolm her phone number, so she could talk to him. It would be the first time they had communicated since the incident, and the thought sent jitters through her body.

But what she really wanted to do was see him, to hold him, and tell him how much she loved him and cared for him, but she knew that would never work. Her face was on the news, and she was wanted by both the local and the federal authorities. She almost felt like she could never leave her hideout.

She flipped the switch on her security cameras and saw Tricia in the kitchen, cooking something. It didn't have sound to it. There were only visuals, so she couldn't figure out what type of song Tricia was singing

254

along to.

She thought about how Tricia must have been feeling, to have her husband facing enormous amounts of time, and sighed. She felt like the outcome of the entire predicament fell into her hands, whether anyone else admitted it or not. She clicked the remote, and the security screen switched to her garage. She looked at her three Range Rovers, and memories came flooding back to the day that she got shot while sitting in her pink one.

She quickly hit the button on the remote again, switching to her game room. Sunshine and Rain were standing at a pool table. They were having a deep discussion. It seemed as if Rain was scolding Sunshine for something, but Kyla couldn't be too sure about it. Rain took one of her fingers and stuck it in Sunshine's face in a disrespectful manner. Afterwards, she leaned in and hit one of the billiards into the corner pocket of the pool table.

Maybe, they're talking junk to each other about pool. Or, maybe, they're gambling, Kyla thought as she switched the monitor off. She thought about turning on a movie or listening to some music, but she knew that she wouldn't be able to concentrate on anything until she heard from either Malcolm or Luther. This was the day that she had fought through a coma to make it to, and she was anxious.

Being the leader of a vehicle as powerful as the Bankroll Squad took a lot of concentration, but she would be able to guide it easier once Malcolm explained to her how the wheel should be turned. After a couple of hours had gone by, Kyla dozed off to sleep. The tapping on her shoulder woke her up.

"Yeah?"

255

It was Sunshine, carrying a plate of food in her hand.

"Ummm, I- I...," Sunshine stuttered, trying to get her words out, and Kyla wondered why she was acting so strange all of a sudden.

"Is everything okay, Sunshine?"

Sunshine blushed and sat the plate down on the night stand beside Kyla's bed. "Yeah, ev- everything's fine. I just thought maybe you were hungry since you hadn't eaten this morning. I fixed you a plate."

Kyla smiled at Sunshine and sat up in her bed. Of all the girls in the house, Sunshine seemed like the coolest one. She seemed like the girl who genuinely had Kyla's back, while the other girls seemed as if they were obligated to have her back. Kyla still had on her pajamas, but Sunshine was dressed to kill in a skin tight mini skirt and peep-toe Louboutin pumps.

"Wow! You look good. You have a date today or something?"

Sunshine blushed again. "You really think I look good?"

Kyla shot her a strange look. "Are you really asking me that? I would ask you to sit down, but I don't want you to mess up your outfit. I—"

Sunshine cut her off, blurting out, "I'm not going to mess my outfit up if I sit down! I don't care about this. I don't got nowhere to go."

Kyla noticed the urgency in Sunshine's voice, but thought that it was due to her being nervous since she was the one who had hired her to begin with. Kyla figured that she was simply trying too hard to please her boss. She watched as Sunshine pulled off her peep toe pumps and sat on the bed beside Kyla.

256

"Dang! Your bed is super comfortable, girl."

"I know, right? I don't have a man to hold me at night, so I let my mattress do it for me."

Sunshine swallowed hard and realized that she would have to try to figure out a way to get Kyla's mind off of those no good men and open it to the possibility of them being together. After noticing the awkward silence, Kyla broke it.

"You don't have a man, Sunshine? As good as you look, you don't have anyone?"

Sunshine was stunned by the question and was unsure about how to answer it.

Do I have someone? Hell, yeah! I have someone! It's you! You're the one I wanna be with. I want to hold you at night. You're all I think about. Can't you tell? She thought, but she couldn't bring herself to it. Instead, all she said was, "No, I don't have anyone."

Kyla put her hand on Sunshine's shoulder and spoke softly to her. "Don't worry, Sunshine. Your knight in shining armor will come. You look way too beautiful to be single. In fact, if I was a lesbian, I'd—"

Then, the telephone rang, interrupting Kyla's sentence. "Excuse me, Sunshine. Give me a few minutes. I need to take this phone call in private, but thanks for bringing me something to eat, baby."

Nooooo! Sunshine's heart was screaming as she sulkily stood up and stormed out of the bedroom. She was furious because she was about to hear the words that she had been longing to hear forever, and a stupid phone call had interrupted it.

257

CHAPTER 7

Luther had taken a huge risk by going to visit Malcolm in jail that morning because he didn't know whether or not Dr. Jacobs had told the authorities who he was, but it turned out perfectly. He had been able to sit down and have a long conversation with the man he had idolized all of his life. It saddened him to see Malcolm in such a horrible situation, and he told Malcolm exactly how he felt.

But Malcolm made him brush off his emotions. He told him that there were consequences to being a boss and that they were different for each and every boss. He said that it just so happened that these were his consequences. They'd discussed the future of the Bankroll Squad, and Malcolm seemed optimistic that they would beat the charges at trial, despite the overwhelming evidence against them.

Then, they discussed Kyla. It had been obvious that Kyla was his one soft spot because he seemed to become depressed when discussing everything that she was out there doing for him. The last thing Luther had been able to do was give Kyla's phone number to him, so he could call her. As soon as he gave him the number, he cut the visit short. He was anxious to speak to the love of his life.

"I'm sorry, Luther, but I have to go make this phone call. I would be lying to your face if I said I wanted to sit here when I could be talking to Kyla right now. I'm sorry."

And Luther understood him wholeheartedly. Who could blame him? To Luther, he would never be a complete boss like Malcolm until he had a boss bitch like Kyla, but he wasn't going to force it by settling for any old chick. His chicks had to be thoroughly battle tested and still be able to stand tall like Kyla.

He sat in the car outside of the jail. He thought about his personal life for twenty minutes before he finally started the car up. He had to make it back to Kyla's headquarters ASAP because he knew that Malcolm would have given her plenty of information and instructions, and the girls would be ready to strike again.

He had to see if they would let him roll with them this time. He wanted to continue proving himself. Killing Prince Tron seemed to have earned him a few brownie points, but it hadn't gotten him the praise that he sought. He had to try harder.

$~$~$~$~$

Pam's mother's house was located in a gated community on the outskirts of Houston. To gain entrance, you had to have a member's card and be fingerprint verified. Pam had been relaxing the entire weekend and had managed to clear her mind of all of her life's stresses. Her mother had cooked a big dinner for her, and she had taken the opportunity to overindulge on some of the greatest recipes that have ever existed.

She was lying in a hammock with her sunglasses on while the breeze gently massaged her body. She had on no shoes or socks, and was wearing a string bikini as if she were on a beach somewhere. When her life became too much to bear, her mother's house had always been her sanctuary. No one knew where it was located, not even her superiors at

259

work.

That was why she almost blew her top when her mother interrupted her from the hammock's gentle support.

"Pam! I think you better leave right now!"

Pam opened her eyes and saw her mother standing there with a worried look on her face.

"Huh?"

"Leave! Your boss called my house and told me he was on his way over here. I told him you weren't here, but he insisted that he was coming to do a thorough search. He said he knew you were here and that you were disobeying direct orders."

"Mom!" Pam wailed as she jumped up from the hammock and slid into her sandals. "How in the world did he get your phone number? You sure you didn't tell them I was here, Mommy?"

Her mother frowned at her. "Pam, why would I do such a thing? I'm your mother! I would never betray you."

Pam nodded her head and gave her mother a kiss. She retrieved her keys and grabbed her laptop. She slid on her shorts and ran to her car. She had to get back to Wisconsin Dells on the first thing smoking. It was silly of her to try to disobey orders from the FBI, but she had done it many times prior to this and had never gotten caught. Why the big deal now?

She jumped into the driver's seat and proceeded to drive as far away from her mother's house as possible.

$~$~$~$~$

"Hello?"

"Hey, baby."

Malcolm's voice resonated across the sound waves, while Kyla sat on her bed, shaking. She shook from excitement and love, from dedication and loyalty. This was the man that she had always wanted. She didn't say anything for a moment. She just allowed the tears to flow from her eyes and her soul to connect with his.

"I love you, Malcolm."

"I love you, too, Kyla."

And it was the first time that she had heard him say those words to her in years. He had married Jennifer and had thrown Kyla out of the picture. She thought that she had lost the love of her life forever, until now. In between her own sniffling, she thought she heard him sniffling on his end of the phone as well, and it overjoyed her.

"Malcolm," she said in tears, "are you crying, too?"

"Ha! Ha!" Malcolm laughed, even though it was evident that he was really crying with her. "There you go, worrying about the wrong thing, Kyla."

They both laughed, and it felt just like the old days. The days when they joked with each other all day every day. The days when either one of them could say just about anything and get a laugh out of the other one. The days of their initial firestorm romance.

"Malcolm, how many minutes can you talk to me on the phone?

261

Fifteen, right?"

Malcolm laughed again. "No, baby. I called you straight through. You know they smuggle cell phones into jail."

Kyla giggled. "Still finding ways to break the law, huh?"

"Not the way I hear you're doing it these days. I didn't know you had it in you."

Kyla found herself blushing, even though no one was around to see her. "Oh, well... I learned from the best."

There was silence for a moment. Then, Kyla asked, "Malcolm, are you all right in there? What's going on with Catfish? How is Brink?"

Malcolm sighed. The stress of the situation was evident in the way that he breathed. "We're always going to be okay, Kyla. The real question is, are *you* going to be okay?"

"I'm going to be okay as soon as I know that you, Catfish, and Brink are going to be okay."

"We're going to—"

"Let's stop with the sugar coating, Malcolm. How much time are you three facing?"

Malcolm grabbed his updated list of charges and read off the new allegations against them.

"So, all three of us are facing life in prison, Kyla, but I've been thinking about signing a plea deal and taking mines on the chin, so everyone else won't have to suffer."

Kyla almost jumped through the phone as she yelled, "You will do no such thing! You make them crackers prove every single muthafuckin' charge that they laid against you. Fuck that! We don't lay down unless we're about to fuck or take a nap! You know this."

Her tone and choice of words surprised him. He knew Kyla was a strong woman, but he had never seen her in her current element.

"Kyla," he said gently. "Don't get me wrong. I'm a fighter and everything, but why fight something when all of the odds are stacked against me? I'm planning to fight them regardless, but I always find myself asking that same question, Ky."

That was what she had been longing to hear him call her. *Ky*. It was what he—and only he—called her. There had never been anyone else in her life that called her Ky, and it reminded her of all of the small things Malcolm did that made her love him.

"Malcolm, the odds are in your favor, baby. They're not against you."

Malcolm laughed, then shook his head in disbelief. "I love your optimism, Kyla, but the absolute clincher for this entire case is their special agent in charge of developing it— Pamela Jones. If someone could convince her to withdraw her charges or to stop pursuing the case, I'd have a better chance, but, for the time being, that's not going to happen. And, even if she did withdraw, they still have countless witnesses."

Kyla looked around the room. Malcolm's words had caused her to think a thousand miles a minute. "So, without Pam, there is no case, right?"

263

Malcolm's lips tightened, and he found himself unable to speak. He didn't want Kyla getting into any more trouble, and, the way she was talking, she would end up facing more time than him, Catfish, and Brink combined if she did anything to Pam.

"I didn't say that, Kyla. Without Pam, the case would be weaker, but there would still be a trial. And there's no telling what would happen at a trial against the United States of America."

Kyla's heart pounded against her rib cage as she thought about living her life without Malcolm in it. She instantly felt sick, felt like it would be the end of the world if he was taken away from her.

"Malcolm, is there any way that I can come see you?"

Malcolm immediately responded. "Hell, no! You're wanted by the feds, so you just need to stay the hell away from here. I really want you to go overseas, somewhere where the U.S. can't touch you. I need you to leave the country, Kyla."

As soon as the words left his lips, he knew that his words had fallen on deaf ears. He knew that there was no way he would possibly get Kyla to back down from trying to help him. Anger rushed across Malcolm as he thought about the way he'd been betrayed by Pam. He clenched his fists, and let the anger subside. He took a deep breath.

"I'm sorry, Kyla. I'm—"

"Can your lawyer come see you on any day of the week?"

Malcolm was perplexed by her question, but he answered, "Umm…yeah…"

"Anytime of the day?"

Malcolm tried to guess where she was going with her line of questioning but couldn't quite figure it out. "He can visit me anytime as long as it's not after nine P.M. lockdown time. We have our attorney visits in a private room with no cameras. He did come by at seven P.M. one time on a Sunday."

Kyla nodded her head as her mind went into overdrive.

"Alright then, I'll see you in a few hours, Malcolm."

"What?" He was startled. "See me? What—"

"Bye, Malcolm. See you."

"Wait, Kyla. What—"

Kyla hung the phone up before Malcolm could talk her out of what she was about to do.

$~$~$~$~$

Kyla took a shower and threw on her black and teal Alexander McQueen outfit and black and teal peep toe stilettos. She applied her M·A·C lip gloss and wrapped her hair, so she could tie it into a ponytail. She applied a few drops of her signature fragrance to her neck. She'd had it custom made when she was in Italy. It had cost her $10,000 for one bottle. Then, she checked out her reflection in her full-length mirror.

Since she was pleased with the way she looked, she went and grabbed her briefcase and went to the game room, looking for Sunshine and Rain. When she got to the game room, there was no one in there. She left there and went to the theater room. Tricia and Rain were asleep, but Sunshine was sitting there, staring into the darkness, not

265

even paying attention to the movie that was playing.

"Sunshine..." Kyla whispered, trying to get her attention without waking the others. "Sunshine..." She had to whisper her name a little bit louder in order to get her attention. Finally, she looked up with a smile on her face.

"Come here, Sunshine."

Sunshine got up and walked out of the theater room, happy that Kyla was talking to her of all people.

"Check this out. I'm about to go visit Malcolm at the jail, and I need someone to have my back in case something goes wrong. I'm going in as a lawyer, and I *need* to make it out of there. I can't let them lock me up, so I need you and the rest of the girls to roll with me. Bring those AKs, and let's roll."

Sunshine nodded her head enthusiastically while she listened to her speak. She hated that Kyla was risking her life for a dude when she could be just as happy with the woman who loved her. She wanted to tell her so badly, but she knew that it wasn't the correct timing. She would have to wait until all the trial stuff was finally over with and the government had sent Malcolm away.

"We don't need to wake the other girls, Kyla. I'm the only one you need. Let's not risk everything on one mission. I can handle the AK with no problems."

Kyla smiled at her and gave her a hug. "Thank you, Sunshine! This really means a lot to me. Let's go!"

As Kyla turned to lead the way to her car, Sunshine's heart got caught up in her throat. She was hypnotized by Kyla's curves and the smell of her body. Kyla's outfit was show stopping, and it looked so beautiful to Sunshine that she almost confessed her love to her right then.

She had not met another woman who could compare to Kyla in her entire life, and she knew that she was the only one of her kind that had ever been made. There was no way that she could let a woman that beautiful slip out of her grasp, especially when she was in that deep with her.

I'll just have to find a way to turn Kyla out.

She stared at Kyla's ass every step of the way, all the way, until they made it to the Range Rover.

$~$~$~$~$

"I need some credentials. I'm trying to visit Malcolm today!"

Malcolm's lawyer wasn't in, but his assistant was there and didn't seem the least bit shocked by what Kyla was saying. In fact, he seemed to already be prepared for the situation.

"We already have your credentials. Had them made awhile age. With the amount of money that Malcolm Powers has been paying us over the years, we've had plenty of time to think of everything that the people close to him could ever need."

Kyla was surprised as the assistant handed her a brown packet.

"Just make sure that you return it once you're finished with it, so that we can burn it."

Kyla took the packet and opened it. Inside the packet, she found an ID with her picture on it and a false name. Today, she was Spritzer Peller, one of the lead defense lawyers on the Bankroll Squad's case.

"Thank you, sir. I promise to bring it back."

$~$~$~$~$

Kyla stood in the small attorney's room with her brief case in her hand. She was too nervous to sit down, and the fake reading glasses that she had on were starting to annoy her a great deal. She took them off as she stood there and waited on them to bring Malcolm out. She loved Malcolm to death, but, if she got caught there, pulling that stunt, she would be in for a rude afternoon with the law.

Her legs were shaking, and she didn't know if it was because she was scared or if it was because she was about to be reunited with the man she loved. Suddenly, the door opened, and the correctional officer appeared.

"How long will you be, ma'am?"

Kyla glanced down nervously, then answered, "I just brought some papers for a plea deal that the government has offered him, so I won't be long. Maybe, about thirty minutes."

The correctional officer seemed to perk up at hearing the news of Malcolm signing a plea deal. "Well, if you want, I can give you forty-five minutes, ma'am."

Kyla could sense the hatred in the officer's voice, and it caused her lips to tense up. She forced a smile out. "Thank you. That will be fine."

The CO went back out the door and didn't return for another three minutes. Those three minutes gave Kyla a chance to briefly reflect on things. She thought about everything that had led to her being in one of the toughest predicaments in her life. She asked herself if it was worth it.

Of course, it was! she thought. *Anything that Malcolm wants to do, I feel he should do. What is the use of being free if you can't truly be free? Malcolm had a mansion, drove Rolls Royces and Bentleys. He had the world at his fingertips, and he wasn't selfish about it. He gave everyone around him whatever their hearts desired, and I applaud him for that. I'm going to get my man out of here. I'm going—*

Her self-motivation speech was cut short when the door opened again. Malcolm walked inside of the room. He was wearing an orange jumpsuit. His dark skin was glowing, and his hair was still perfectly groomed. Not much had changed about his appearance since the last time she had seen him, and she was grateful for that.

Her mind blanked out completely, and the only thing that she could think to do was jump into his arms. The door locked, and she heard the officer's hard bottom boots clapping against the hard tile floor on the other side of the door. When the echo of the officer's boots faded away in the distance, she couldn't control herself anymore.

She walked around the single table and stood in front of Malcolm with tears in her eyes. Malcolm shook his head in disbelief at how courageous Kyla had been under the worst of all situations. He was amazed by how beautiful she was inside and out. He looked at how delicate her features were and wished that he could hold and protect her for the rest of his life. He didn't know what he had been thinking to leave her for Jennifer, all because of a misunderstanding.

He was thankful that he had been given a second chance to make things right, but he was bitter because of the circumstances surrounding his second chance at love. He leaned down and brushed his cheek against hers. Her body smelled of an exotic strawberry citrus concoction that he had never before smelled on a woman. He couldn't take it any longer.

He kissed her.

That kiss was more powerful than any kiss he had ever had before in his life, and it took the breath out of Kyla. She accepted the first kiss with her eyes closed and stood there, motionless, as harmonious waves rippled through her body. The kiss made her so weak that she felt like she wasn't even in the room.

It was as if the first kiss had paralyzed her, but the second kiss came from *her*, and it came with a renewed passion and vigor. She didn't think it was possible for the second kiss to be stronger than the first, but she surprised him and herself.

Malcolm's hands brushed across the outline of her jaw, and he pulled her in, even closer to him.

"I love you, Kyla."

"I love you, too, Malcolm."

The kissing grew more and more frantic and urgent, as if they were both kissing each other for the first time and the last time ever simultaneously. It was extremely different than the kisses he had shared with Jennifer. These kisses were more passionate, more meaningful, more *real*.

It had been years since Kyla had had sex with anyone, and the last person she'd had sex with was Malcolm. It was only right that the next person she had sex with be that same person. She had been longing for him for so long that she often woke up in the middle of the night crying because she couldn't have him. Plenty of nights, she had been ready to murder Jennifer for being with the man she loved, but she always stopped herself because, if Malcolm was happy, she wanted him to remain that way.

But, at that very moment, in the attorney/client visitation room, there was nothing stopping her. There was nothing between them but fabric. With her petite hands, she unsnapped the buttons on his jumpsuit. He had absolutely nothing on underneath it, and that excited her even more. She grabbed his shaft and squeezed it, not believing that she had gone so many years without it in her life.

Malcolm grabbed her petite body and placed her on the cold steel table. The temperature sent a chill down Kyla's spine, and she squirmed, but all was forgotten once Malcolm slid her panties to the side and rubbed his penis against her narrow opening, getting it wetter and wetter. She moaned in ecstasy and kissed him on the neck.

Once he saw that she was wet enough, he entered her slightly, careful not to hurt her. She tensed, grabbing his neck but careful not to scratch him with her long nails.

"Please don't hurt me, Malcolm."

The words had a double meaning that they both understood.

"I will never hurt you again, Kyla. I promise."

He pulled his penis out of her and pushed back into her a little more.

271

Her petite arms wrapped around his torso in blissful frustration, and her legs wrapped around his buttocks.

He pressed in deeper.

He pulled out again, and she started shuddering, already in the midst of an orgasm, and he hadn't done much.

He pressed in all the way, penetrating her fears of loneliness and massaging her walls of fear.

His dick stroked her with power.

With assertion.

With authority and commitment.

Her legs felt too weak to keep them locked around Malcolm's waist, so she let them flail powerlessly.

Malcolm noticed this and picked her up off of the table. He picked her up and proceeded to bounce her up and down on his penis effortlessly, while she trembled and shook violently from her orgasm. She'd had two orgasms back to back and was on the verge of another one when Malcolm whispered in her ear.

"Baby, I'm about to come, so I'm gon' have to put you down."

"Come in me, Malcolm."

Malcolm was stunned. His situation and his emotions confused him.

When he and Kyla were together before, she wouldn't allow it. It shocked him that Kyla's mindset had changed so much.

"No, Kyla. I don't wanna do that... I don't know how much time I'm gonna, and, if I get you pregnant—"

"Bust that nut in me, Malcolm! You're not doing any time."

Malcolm couldn't bring himself to believe what Kyla was saying. He just stood there and held her firmly. Stood there with his penis in as deep as it could go.

"Lay down, Malcolm. Now."

It was as if he no longer had control over his body. Kyla had him hypnotized.

Malcolm laid down on the table. She got on top of him. He didn't even get a chancc to voice his opinion before Kyla started riding him frantically.

"Kyla... shit..."

"Shhhhh. Just relax, baby. Relax."

"Damn, Kyla!"

"I just want you to feel good, baby. I don't want you to stress... ahhhmmm..."

"But I already feel good, baby.... damn..."

"But I can make you feel even better..."

"Shit, Kyla! I'm coming! Got damnit!"

"Keep it down, baby... relax..."

273

"Shiiiittt," Malcolm whispered as he felt every drop of his orgasm erupt from the opening of his penis and flow into the woman that he loved.

It was clear, at that moment, that she had been the only woman he had ever loved besides his mother, and he was grateful for having a woman of her caliber.

"I love you, Kyla. I'm sorry I hurt you in the past. I apologize."

Kyla kissed his lips. "Baby, you don't have to apologize to me. I'm the one that owes you the apology. I'm sorry for overreacting over that stupid ring."

They kissed each other again and stared into each other's eyes. It was apparent to them both that they would have to do some drastic things in order to be with each other again. They weren't going to settle for a prison relationship when they didn't have to.

Kyla stood up and looked at her watch.

"He gave us forty-five minutes, and we have fifteen minutes left, baby. What do you have for me in that legal envelope?"

He snapped his jumpsuit back together and grabbed the envelope off of the table.

"These are some of the statements that have been made against me by Pamela Jones. There are also some statements from some confidential informants in here. My lawyer has the actual names *and* addresses listed. He had to verify their statements."

Kyla took the contents out of the envelope and replaced them with some generic legal papers in case the CO decided that he wanted to search Malcolm's envelope when he left the room. She didn't want to raise any suspicion. She took a deep breath and closed her eyes for a moment, savoring Malcolm's presence while she had the opportunity.

It felt good to be in love, and she never wanted to be out of it again.

"I love you, Malcolm," she said in her sultry voice, "and I'm going to make sure that I get you out of prison if it's the last thing I do."

Malcolm hugged her, pulling her body close to his. Then, he kissed her cheek.

He leaned in close to her and said, "I know you want to do a lot for me, baby, but we both know Pam is the key to everything. If you can't find her, then I'm not sure that I'll ever get out of here."

They heard the footsteps of the CO approaching the door, and they broke their embrace. Malcolm stood there as Kyla went to stand on the other side of the steel table. A look of sadness entered both of their faces. Malcolm's— because he knew that she had just gotten out of a coma, and he knew that there was going to be a lot of pressure on her.

The sadness on Kyla's face was because she knew she had a fail proof plan, but it would a suicide mission if she got caught. She knew that she couldn't tell Malcolm her plan until it was all over with. Otherwise, he wouldn't let her carry it out. The CO opened the door, carrying handcuffs and keys.

"See you in court, Mr. Powers," Kyla said with a hint of dread in her voice. She winked at the officer, and he smiled in triumph.

CHAPTER 8

Pam was coasting. She had been going ten miles over the speed limit, nonstop, on her way to the airport. She had managed to avoid getting pulled over the whole time. When she parked outside of the rental return section, she breathed a sigh of relief. All she wanted to do was return her vehicle and take her flight back to Wisconsin.

She grabbed her small bag and got out of the car. As soon as she closed her car door, an unmarked vehicle pulled up behind her with the lights flashing. *Shit!* She thought to herself as she felt the panic level in her body rise. The driver's side door on the car opened, and her boss stepped out with a frown on his face.

"What the fuck do you think you're doing, Ms. Jones?"

Pam didn't have a decent enough excuse, so she just decided to tell the truth. "I wanted to see my mom. I—"

"Your mom? You mean to tell me you're trying to ruin your got damn career and put your life and your family's lives in harm's way because you didn't have enough patience?" Her boss had walked up to her and was standing directly in her face, scolding her.

"Mr. Berlin, I'm sorry! I'm sorry! I just wanted to see my mother. I'm about to go back to Wisconsin and wait until you need me for the trial. I'll leave—"

"Oh, no, you won't!" Mr. Berlin interjected. "You get in this car right now. The trial is set to start in three weeks, and we can't afford to have you taking any more risks with your life. You'll be staying with me until the trial starts."

Pam was appalled. "You're holding me *hostage?*

"'Hostage' isn't the word for this shit, Ms. Jones. I'm holding you *prisoner*! I don't know if you got the memo or not, but earth to Pamela... This is one of the biggest got damn cases that Texas has ever seen, and we need this conviction!"

Pam hung her head down as if she was a child just learning that she was on punishment. "I won't let you down, Mr. Berlin. Just let me go back to Wisconsin. Please."

She would rather be in Wisconsin than under the watchful eyes of her stern boss. Three weeks with him sounded like a nightmare. He took a cigarette and a lighter out of his shirt pocket and lit it. He inhaled the smoke, held it, and released it.

"Pam, if I let you go back to Wisconsin, I'm going to have them lock you up as soon as you land. So, do you still want to go?"

Pam slumped her shoulders as she walked around to the passenger side of his car. She'd rather stay at Mr. Berlin's house than spend three weeks in protective custody. Mr. Berlin got into the driver's side of his car and started it up. The cancer stick was still lit, and it caused Pam to cough.

"Oh, I'm sorry. I forgot that you didn't smoke cigarettes, Pam."

She let her window down and sat back against the leather seat. "How

277

did you know where I was, Mr. Berlin?"

Her boss laughed for a second, then shook his head.

"The same reason that you're so good at what you do, Pam."

"Huh?" Pam was confused and didn't know what he was talking about.

He smiled at her and then clarified his statement. "Betrayal is in your blood, Pam. That's why you're so good at what you do. Your mother called us and told us that you were disobeying orders. She wanted us to lock you up. Can you believe that?"

What? She thought as she sat there, dumbfounded. She would have never guessed that her beloved mother would ever want to put her in such a horrible situation.

"Why would my mother do that to me?" she whispered.

Mr. Berlin didn't have any issues answering the question for her.

"Your mother has been a confidential informant for the FBI for the past fifteen years. Apparently, you didn't know that. She knew that, if she turned you in for disobeying orders, she would get a pretty hefty bonus."

Pam shook her head in disbelief as she tried to grasp the concept of her own mother betraying her. *I'm just going to leave the country as soon as this case is over,* she thought as she pressed the seat belt hook into the clasp.

$~$~$~$~$

Luther had been back in the trap and he planned on staying there for the remainder of the day. After Kyla left from visiting Malcolm, that had been the first instruction that she issued.

"I need you to keep bringing this money in for the squad, Luther. We may all have to leave the United States soon, and we'll need as much money as possible, so let's get it, baby."

And he was getting it.

When people realized that the Bankroll Squad was back in business, all other traps were put on stand-by notice. In his first hour, he'd made $70,000, and he was on hour nine already. He yawned and thought about taking a break, but he kept thinking about how much money they would miss out on if he took one. For the first time in his life, he had an unlimited supply of cocaine, as much cocaine for sale as any person wanted to buy.

He was doing business while holding an AK, and he had just made a phone call to Tricia and Rain to have them join him. He had reservations about putting women in harm's way, but Kyla had insisted that he trust family only, and they were definitely family. After ten hours of stacking cash nonstop, he was ready to lock up for the night when there was a knock at the door.

"Closed!" he shouted through the metal slot on the door.

"Luther! Let us in, boy!"

It was five in the morning, and Tricia and Rain had finally arrived. He peeped through the slot and saw the black van parked in an abandoned lot, adjacent to the trap house. He opened the door, and Tricia and Rain walked in dressed like they were headed to a fashion show. Once Rain was in, he quadruple locked the door and activated the intruder alert system.

"About time y'all finally made it! I called you two hours ago, and y'all are only fifteen minutes away. Dang!"

Rain pinched his cheek and gave him a kiss on his temple. "You woke us up at three o' clock in the morning, Luther. It took us both a minute to comprehend what you were talking about. Then, it took a little while longer for us both to get dressed. I had to raid Kyla's closet, and all I came out of there with was this cute little pink dress. None of her other stuff fit me."

Tricia rolled her eyes as if to say that the conversation meant nothing. "What do you need us for, Luther?" Tricia asked, getting down to business.

"I needed you two to come pick this money up. It's like $670,000 in cash here, and the dope boys will probably be right back over here in another hour or two to bring me more money. I'm gonna get a nap in and get right back to business."

Tricia had a frustrated look on her face. "Money? You woke us up, so we could pick up some got damn *money?* My husband is locked up, facing life in prison, and you want to talk about some got damn money? This shit is pitiful."

"Tricia," Luther spoke with an air of authority in his voice. "Malcolm told Kyla to keep stacking money, so we could all leave the country. If it wasn't for that, of course, I wouldn't be calling you to come by and get some damn money."

Tricia shook her head, irritated. "How the fuck is my husband going to leave the country when they won't even give him a bail amount? They won't let him out to do *nothing*, so how is this shit possible?"

Luther sighed and spoke in a relaxed tone. "Trust me when I tell you, Tricia... Kyla and Malcolm have come up with a great plan. It's going to work, and everything's going to go back to normal, but you have to have faith, Tricia. Don't worry."

Tricia sat down and stared at the table full of money and shook her head. "So, this is the way my husband made his living, huh?"

Luther didn't say anything, because, if she knew how Catfish had really made his living, she would shit her pants.

Catfish was a killer, an enforcer, not a drug dealer, and he earned every penny of the money that Malcolm had paid him.

Rain sat beside Tricia and stared at the money, as well. Even though she was a member of the Bankroll Squad, she had never seen that much money in her life before. She had turned tricks and slid down poles trying to make a few thousand, but $670,000?

"Damn," she whispered.

"What is it, Rain?" Luther asked as he looked into her pretty hazel eyes. "What's the problem?"

She snapped out of her daydream and noticed that Luther and Tricia were both staring at her. "It's nothing really... I just have never seen this much money in one place before. It's amazing."

Whenever there was the potential for greed within the crew, Malcolm had always curtailed it with unexpected gifts, so everything could continue to go smoothly.

281

"It is amazing, Rain, and, as soon as we get to where we're going, you'll have your own personal bank account already loaded with cash."

Tricia frowned at him, but Rain's face erupted into a glowing smile. "You really mean that?"

"Of course, I do," Luther said convincingly. "You're a part of the Bankroll Squad, aren't you?"

Rain nodded her head and laid back on the sofa. She kicked off her high heels and crossed her legs while she daydreamed about balling out of control in a foreign country. Tricia grabbed an empty duffel bag and started sliding the money off of the table and into it. Luther grabbed another bag and tapped Rain on the shoulder, breaking her out of her daydream. All three of them bagged the remainder of the money up like luggage.

$~$~$~$~$

For the rest of the week, it was the same routine. Luther was bringing in more money than he could count, and Tricia and Rain had been making countless pickups. Kyla and Sunshine had been getting up at five A.M. and coming back at eleven P.M. every day. Kyla hadn't said much about what was going on, only that she was going to fill them in on everything very soon.

On the first of the month, Tricia and Rain had to make two pickups. One was for $590,000, and the other one was for $630,000. Luther had been averaging close to $800,000 a day, but he had never actually cracked the million mark until that day. He was excited, but he controlled his excitement because he knew that there was still a lot of work that had to be done. When the girls came by to make their pickups, he instructed them to bring their weapons with them.

They came in miniskirts and carried their M-16s in their large handbags, in case anyone dared to try them. He'd told them to shoot first and ask questions last, and that went for either a common street thug or a police officer.

When Sweetback Fatty came by the trap to pay Luther a visit, his friendly demeanor threw Luther for a loop.

"What's up, boy?"

When Malcolm was out, Sweetback would have never been brave enough to come by a trap that belonged to the Bankroll Squad, so Luther found it irritating that he would now treat him with less respect.

"What do you want, Sweet?" Luther asked condescendingly.

"That's Mr. Sweet to you, son. You gotta learn to have some respect around this muthafucka, especially seeing that it's only one man manning a trap house. That's rookie shit, but I'm not here to teach you how to sell dope. I'm just here to find out where my baby mama is, and I'm certain that you know."

Luther clenched his AK tightly and scowled at Sweetback Fatty.

"Man, I don't know shit about your baby's mama. You go find that bitch your muthafuckin' self."

Sweetback smiled at him. He admired the young man's arrogance and dedication.

"You're sure right, young blood... You sure are right... But what if I made you a deal that you absolutely could *not* refuse?"

The right corner of Luther's lip tensed up as he aimed the AK-47 at

283

Sweetback Fatty.

"Listen, nigga. You ain't got nothing that I can't refuse. I should blow your muthafuckin' top off right this moment and get you out of everybody's way! Fuck you and your weak-ass deals!"

Luther was hyped up as he trained the AK on Sweetback's body. He couldn't understand why Sweetback would risk his life by coming in here without any of his goons with him anyways. This was the first time he'd ever seen him roll solo like that.

Maybe, he does have a deal worth discussing... Maybe, he's giving up control of his crew and bowing out... hmmm... Luther thought as he let the rage surpass and regained control over his temper.

"Okay. Tell me the fuckin' deal, and, if I don't like it, I'm gonna blow your muthafuckin' top the fuck off! Talk, old nigga!"

Sweetback Fatty laughed. "Here's my number. I want you to call me when you make up your mind about my proposition. The word on the street is that a bitch named Pam set y'all up. I remember seeing that bitch when she was rolling with Malcolm on multiple occasions, so I know how she looks. Now, I'm standing here telling you that if you tell me where Tracy is, I'll tell you where that bitch Pam is. Talk it over with your boss. Find out where she is if you don't know, and get back to me."

Sweetback Fatty laid the white piece of paper on the table with his number on it right beside Luther's stack of money. Without uttering another word, Sweetback turned and left.

$~$~$~$~$

For the entire week, Kyla and Sunshine had been terrorizing the city without restraint. They were making sure to leave no business unhandled. They had turned the city upside down searching for and finding witnesses against the Bankroll Squad. The first person they found was a guy named Timothy Biller. In his FBI statement report, he claimed that he had once purchased thirty kilos of cocaine directly from Malcolm for the amount of $150,000.

She knew that was a lie because Malcolm never would have directly sold drugs to anyone.

The ladies found him at ten A.M. one Sunday morning at the gas station. They didn't know who he was at first, but he gave himself away when he hit the gas and swerved out of the parking lot like a bat out of hell. Kyla was sure that the streets had alerted him, by now, that she was looking for him, and he was doing what he did best— running.

She took off right behind him, following him through the mild Sunday traffic in her purple Ranger Rover. Timothy tried to be slick and drive into a church's parking lot. He jumped out and ran inside the church, as if that was where he was headed initially. Kyla pulled her Range Rover into the parking lot and put the vehicle in park. She exhaled, closed her eyes, and asked God's forgiveness for what she was about to do.

When she opened her eyes, she saw Sunshine getting out of the truck with a grenade in her hand. "Whoa! Whoa! Sunshine!"

But Sunshine didn't hear her, she was already out of the truck and making her way up to the church. Kyla blew her horn frantically. Sunshine stood a few feet away from the church, as if looking for a window that she could throw the grenade through.

Kyla got out of the truck and ran up to her.

"Sunshine!"

Suddenly, Sunshine looked at Kyla, the look of lust evident in her eyes, visible for everyone in the world to see. Everyone could see it, except for Kyla. "Yes?"

Kyla put her hands on Sunshine's shoulders. "What are you doing, baby?"

When Kyla talked to her like that, it made Sunshine melt, made her whole thought process turn to scrambled eggs and sent shivers all the way from her spine to her toes.

"I'm trying to get him for you, Kyla."

Kyla smiled at her sidekick. It had turned out that she didn't even need the other two girls to handle their business because Sunshine had been more than willing to stand strong under pressure.

"You're trying to get him for me? With a *bomb?*" Kyla laughed aloud, but Sunshine kept a straight look on her face. She just wanted to please Kyla in every way possible. She had it set in her mind that she was willing to do anything in the world if it would finally get Kyla's mind off of Malcolm. She hated the way that Kyla smiled whenever he called her cell phone. She hated the way Kyla's face glowed after she visited Malcolm.

She hated it with a passion because she wanted to be the one who created that happiness for her. She felt like she— and she alone— knew what Kyla needed in life, and it certainly wasn't a man.

"How am I gonna handle it if I don't throw this grenade? The church is too big, and there are too many witnesses in there, Kyla."

Kyla smiled at her favorite girl again. "Just get in the driver's seat. I got this."

Kyla walked into the church and went straight up to Timothy Biller, who was trying to act like he was unaware that anyone was after him. She sat behind him on the bench and listened to the preacher. She was listening for a certain cue. Finally, she heard it.

"Let us bow our heads and let the Holy Ghost..."

She shot him in the back of the head with her 9mm with the silencer on it. Before anyone could notice, she wiped the brains off of her hand with a handkerchief and laid him down gently in his seat. She promptly exited the building.

$S{\sim}S{\sim}S{\sim}S{\sim}S$

Jennifer Powers was sitting under the bridge with her best high school friend, Ashley Jenkins. Ashley had started smoking crack since right after her high school graduation, and, many years later, she was still going strong. Whenever Jennifer wanted to get away from her hectic life, she would go and sit with Ashley under the bridge. To Jennifer, it was a leisure spot, but, to Ashley, it was where she *lived*.

In the past, whenever Jennifer visited, it seemed as if she had come by to poke fun at Ashley. Only recently had Ashley begun to take Jennifer seriously again, and that was because they had a common habit.

Ashley lit the pipe, and the smoke ran through her body like electricity. The volts from the crack rock seemed to cause every hair on her body to stand up, and she could feel the gentle tug of gravity as it pulled her skin away from her body. Jennifer sat wide-eyed, staring at Ashley as if she was going to smoke *her*. In less than ninety seconds, Ashley had busted into a drenching sweat.

It wasn't a light sweat. It looked as if she'd run a marathon in the desert with an electric blanket wrapped around her body. She had never, in her life, smoked a rock that powerful. It was one that Jennifer had made using the last remains of the pure cocaine that she had stolen from her ex-husband. Jennifer hit the pipe next. Its effect on her was similar to Ashley's, but the only difference was that she had come to think that that was how *all* crack felt.

She wasn't aware that not everyone had access to pure cocaine and that the side effects would never take her to those dangerous heights again. Jennifer felt her nipples vibrating like usual, so she pulled her shirt off.

She unfastened her bra and let it drop to the dirt.

Ashley just stared at her, wide-eyed. Jennifer's breasts looked like aliens to her. The two women sat in silence.

Jennifer stared at her left nipple as if there was something strange and unusual about it. She picked it up and tried to inspect it like she had a magnifying glass in her hand. Five minutes passed, and she had still not broken her concentration on her breasts. Ashley continued to stare at it the whole time, too.

They were sitting there, staring as if they were both watching a movie together. Finally, Jennifer jumped up.

She looked around frantically for her clothes. After she found them, she hurriedly put them back on her body. Ashley's heart rate was going so fast that she felt like she would have a heart attack if she moved, so she just sat there.

"Ashley!" Jennifer yelled, even though she was only three feet away from her.

Ashley didn't say anything; she just continued to stare.

"Come ride with me!" Jennifer ran to her Mercedes Benz and stood at the door, waiting on Ashley.

After ten minutes of staring, Ashley finally jumped up.

"Hey! Where you going, Jennifer?"

Ashley ran up to the luxury vehicle and stood at the passenger door.

"Would you like to ride with me, Ashley?"

"Yeah, I would! Why didn't you ask me before?"

Jennifer furrowed her forehead, trying to remember why she hadn't asked Ashley before.

"I guess it slipped my mind."

They were experiencing new levels of highs.

To the other customers at the gas station, it was a sight to behold. A luxury vehicle with two of the dirtiest white girls in the city standing beside it. At first, everyone thought that they were trying to beg the owner for some money, but, to everyone's surprise, the white girl with the dirty shirt on opened the door with her keys and let the other dirty white girl inside.

No alarm went off on the Benz. The car started, and the dirty girls drove off.

A working class lady shook her head and tried to erase the disturbing images from her memory. She worked every day and had respect and dignity and had never been able to drive around in a brand new Benz.

Lucky-ass, privileged, disrespectful, ungrateful bitches! She thought as she finished pumping her gas.

$~$~$~$~$

They had been driving around in circles for three hours straight, just enjoying each other's company.

"I don't know what I'm going to do, Ashley. I don't have anywhere to stay, and I lost all of my money when I was at McDonald's earlier this morning."

Ashley gave her a bewildered look. "What? How did you lose all of your money at Micky D's?"

Jennifer turned the steering wheel slightly and switched into the left lane. There was a pickup truck with clouds of blue smoke erupting from the tailpipe, and she was just trying to pass it.

"I got in the thing that the kids play in... the bouncy balls. I had the time of my life at McDonald's. I never knew it was so much fun."

Ashley frowned at Jennifer and said, "But you lost your money? How much money was it?"

Jennifer seemed to be saddened by Ashley's question. A light turned red, and she slowed to a stop, but, somehow, the pickup truck had made it back in front of her even though she was in the left lane.

"I think it was about $49,000."

"Forty-nine thousand?" Ashley was disgusted at the stuff that she was hearing. "How in the world did you leave that much money at a damn McDonald's?"

Jennifer threw her hair back. Ashley realized that Jennifer didn't look like she once had. She now looked like a woman who was past her prime, who was trying hard to hold on.

"One of the little kids said I fell on her… or him, whatever it was. But I wasn't trying to! I was just trying to dive into the soft plastic balls like they were doing. Why can't *I* do it? They're kids; I'm grown! I should be able to do what I want to do!"

Ashley saw that Jennifer had become extremely emotional, so she tried to change the subject.

"You're right, Jen. You should be able to do whatever you want to do."

"And that's what I told the manager, but he still kicked me out! He kicked me out! Ashley, they kicked me out! I left and forgot about the money. I couldn't go back and get it because I had drugs in that bag, too. I only have $200 left to my name!"

The light turned green, and they continued driving in circles for another hour.

Ashley rubbed her crotch. It had been itching all day. "Hey, Jen! I

291

know what you could do."

"What?"

Ashley sat up in her seat and squeezed her thighs together, trying to soothe her vagina from the constant itching.

"I know this dude named Milvy. He went to the federal building and told them he wanted to work for them, and they gave him a job and everything. They took care of him, gave him a car, a house, everything. And I'm told that he doesn't do much."

Jennifer was startled. "Milvy? I know Milvy! The last time I saw him, he was smoking more crack than you and me combined, Ashley! And this was like three weeks ago. No way they'll give a crack head a job, especially not me. What could I do?"

Ashley sat there, not knowing what to say. She didn't know what Milvy did, so there was no way that she could tell Jennifer what she would be able to do. She sat there, feeling stupid for even mentioning such a terrible idea.

$~$~$~$~$

Malcolm was on the recreation yard, waiting on Catfish and Brink to arrive. When they finally came out, he quickly ushered them to a vacant section where no one was within earshot.

"Man, Catfish... we got big problems, homey. Kyla, Sunshine, Rain, and your wife Tricia have been out there on a rampage. Luther said he can't control them. I told Kyla to chill, but she's too far gone. They're all revenge minded, and I can't get through to any of them. The only thing they keep saying is 'we're gonna get y'all out of there'. At this point, they're getting so carried away that I'm willing to take this plea deal in order to end the madness out there. They're digging a bigger and bigger hole for themselves, and I never wanted that for either of them."

Catfish shook his head. "Naw, playboy. We're gon' fight this thing out together. You ain't taking no plea deal."

Brink was usually quiet. Normally, he was lost in thought, worrying about his situation too much to get a sound to come out of his mouth, but, that day, he had some valuable news.

"Did you see the news this evening?" he asked. His tone sounded like there was bad news to follow.

Both Catfish and Malcolm shook their heads.

"They were watching a UFC fight this evening, instead of the news," Malcolm said.

"They were watching the same shit in my unit, too." Catfish said.

Brink put his hand on his forehead and shook his head. "Man... they're saying that they're planning to move our trial up to next week because the witnesses keep coming up dead. They're saying that they refuse to put any more witnesses in danger."

"Next week?" Malcolm and Catfish said in unison.

Malcolm closed his eyes, knowing that he wasn't prepared to go to trial next week, especially when they still hadn't found Pamela Jones. Once they eliminated her, he felt like it would be easier to, at least, beat the thirty year and the mandatory life charges because she was the only witness on those two accusations.

293

"Brink, you saw that on the news *today?*" Catfish asked with worry in his voice.

Brink nodded his head sadly.

Malcolm took a deep breath and finished telling Catfish what he came out there to tell him.

"Man, call your wife and tell her to chill out, Catfish. Tell Tricia to get out of the streets. It's supposed to be—"

Catfish took offense to what Malcolm was saying and interjected. "Why *my* wife gotta get out of the streets? My wife is a street bitch by nature. You think she can't handle herself? She was taught by the muthafuckin' best!"

Malcolm shot Catfish a strange look.

"Why are you getting mad at me? I'm trying to tell you what I heard about in the streets. They say—"

"Man! Fuck the streets, Malcolm!" The streets are what got us into this shit, and the streets is what's going to get us out of this muthafucka! I talked to my wife already. She said that you, Kyla, and Sunshine got all kinds of plans going on, but that you won't tell her *shit!* So, what's really good, Malcolm? You're plotting some shit to help you get out of here, but my wife ain't good enough to plot some shit to get me out of here?"

Malcolm shook his head. "Cat, the stuff that I'm doing is for all of us, man. This shit ain't about me. I'm—"

Catfish interrupted him again, irate.

"Key fuckin' word— *I'm.* I'm doing this! I'm doing that! We're supposed to be a team, Malcolm! Or did you forget that? This discussion about my wife is finished, man, and I don't want to hear another word about her. She's my problem. Anything goes wrong in them streets with her is my muthafuckin' problem. You separated her from Kyla and Sunshine and stuck her with that Rain bitch. Meanwhile, Kyla and Sunshine is handling all of *your* business. Man, keep that bullshit to yourself, Malcolm! Talking about 'you can't get through to them'! Fuck that!"

"That's not what I meant, Cat—"

"Fuck that!"

Brink and Malcolm were both startled to hear Catfish talking like that. Catfish had never raised his voice at Malcolm for any reason, and it created an eerie feeling to hear him talking like that about one of the most delicate situations that they could possibly be in.

Malcolm got quiet, although he was boiling hot inside. He couldn't believe that his best friend had spazzed out on him when he had life or death information that he needed to relay to him, but he loved Catfish too much to not say what he needed to say, so he tried again anyway.

"Man, Rally is mad that you killed Dexter, and he—"

Catfish got even madder. "Who the fuck told him I killed Dexter? I didn't kill no Dexter!"

The whole scenario was confusing Malcolm.

"What? The streets are always talking, man. I don't know how the sun floats in the sky, but it does, man. I—"

295

"Fuck the streets! I done told you once, Malcolm. Fuck the streets! I'm doing what the fuck I gotta do. Me and my fuckin' wife. So let her *be!*"

Catfish stormed off and went back into the unit. Brink and Malcolm both exchanged perplexed looks, but said nothing.

$~$~$~$~$~$

Tricia and Rain brought Luther some chicken from Church's, two changes of clothes, and the porno that he'd requested. Rain figured that he was really flirting with her in a low key type of way, but she figured that she would continue to act like she didn't know what was going on until he came directly at her. She had begun to like Luther over the past few weeks. She liked the way that he was dedicated to getting his business handled.

He was never distracted by the trivial things that most young men his age were distracted by. He didn't smoke or drink, and Rain guessed that this was a trait that he had picked up from Malcolm, who seemed to be his idol.

"Tricia, Rain... I don't think Malcolm wants you two involved in this stuff anymore. He said that everything is under control. I told you three or four days ago that I no longer needed you to do pickups. This is my third time telling you both this. Yet you keep ignoring me."

Tricia rolled her eyes. "Ain't shit under control until my husband is out of that muthafucka! I'm not playing no games and depending on Kyla. And Kyla act like she ain't got the decency to tell me what the fuck is going on! Why won't she?"

Luther wanted to tell her that Kyla and Sunshine had committed fourteen murders over the past two weeks, but he decided against putting their information out there like that.

"Trust me when I say this, Tricia... Kyla is on top of everything. I don't want you to keep coming over here like this. This trap is red hot. I was thinking about moving it in a day or two anyways."

Tricia got silent and grabbed her bag like usual. She started raking the money off of the table and into the bag.

$~$~$~$~$

Tricia sat outside of the trap house in the van and closed her eyes. She was trying to stop the tears from coming, but she was powerless against the force of them.

"What's wrong, Tricia?" Rain asked sympathetically.

Tricia looked at her and spoke through her tears. "I just want my man to come home. I don't want nothing else to do with this bullshit. I don't care about this money. I don't care about nothing but my man. I love Catfish, and I want to make sure that everything is handled the correct way, Rain. I just know what I can do! Kyla and Sunshine won't even tell us what's going on. It's almost like we're two strangers in Kyla and Sunshine's house! What is it with those two?"

Rain caught herself before she blurted out an answer. She was about to expose Sunshine's secret obsession with Kyla, but remembered that Sunshine had made her promise to keep it a secret.

"I don't know, Tricia... I just don't know," she whispered.

$~$~$~$~$

Rally and Diaz had been sitting in an all black Toyota Solara with black tints a half block away from where Tricia and Rain were parked. Catfish had given the Dynasty Cartel a bad reputation when he killed Rally's younger brother Dexter in a drive by at a stop light. He had been reeling ever since he heard the news.

A crack head had been in the area when Catfish shot Dexter and had happily divulged all of the information for an eight ball of cocaine. Diaz and Rally had set out looking for Catfish the very next day, but they had never been able to find him. Finally, the streets let them know that the feds had nabbed him.

But the feds nabbing him had no effect on the Dynasty Cartel's reputation. They had to send a strong message and pay back blood with blood. And, since Catfish was unavailable, they were going to get the next best thing.

The van pulled off and into traffic, and the black Toyota pulled off behind it, trailing it for two blocks. They were already aware of the route that the van was going to take because they had been watching its routine for the past week, but when the van took a right turn, and the Toyota kept going straight. They didn't want to give the appearance that they were following the van.

After a couple more blocks, Diaz and Rally ditched the Toyota and jumped into a black Nissan Maxima and took a shortcut to catch up with the van. It took less than six minutes. They caught up with the van on Antoine, a few blocks away from Gigi's Cabaret. The Maxima zoomed up the street until it was directly beside the van. Then, the driver of the Maxima blew the horn.

The Nissan was in the left lane, and the van was on the right. Tricia looked over at the Maxima and saw nothing but tints. She shook her head because she thought it was just another group of young men flirting with her or something. She ignored it.

Diaz let the window down a little bit, just enough to aim the barrel of the Mossberg pump at the side of Tricia's head. Diaz was going to make sure that he killed Catfish's wife with the same weapon that Catfish had used to make Dexter's funeral closed casket.

Rain looked over at Tricia and yawned. "I'm sleepy. It's taking this light forever to change."

Boom!

Diaz had damn near knocked Tricia's whole head off of her body with the powerful blast from the Mossberg, but he wasn't going to take any chances. He aimed the gun again and shot.

Boom!

In the midst of yawning, Rain caught a mouthful of Tricia's blood in her mouth. Tricia slumped to the floor and her body laid against the gas, forcing the van to jerk forward. Thinking quickly, Rain maneuvered the van through the traffic going sixty miles an hour in a thirty-five mile per hour zone. She didn't really have an option as she ran two red lights and barely avoided collisions with the traffic that had the right of way.

She climbed into the driver's seat and wrestled Tricia's body off of the gas, so she could get control. She slowed down, so she could avoid a wreck. She knew that if she got caught with a dead body, AKs, and $600,000 in cash, she would be locked up just like Malcolm and Catfish, and she was definitely not going for that. She was only four minutes away from Kyla's estate, and she was relieved that the Nissan

Maxima had broken off in the opposite direction.

Her body had shifted into survival mode once the shots rang out, but, now that it was over, her body had approached a dangerous level of panic. She spit the blood out of her mouth and noticed that her entire body was shaking as she kept looking down at the dead body on the floor beneath her.

$~$~$~$~$

Luther made his way over to Kyla's house after Rain called him and told him the news. They were both shocked. Kyla—because it could have been her that had gotten killed, and Luther— because he felt like he could have prevented it if he'd had been more assertive in not allowing the women to get involved.

He had been holding Rain while she cried, while constantly checking his cell phone, waiting on Malcolm to call. Three hours passed before he finally heard from Malcolm. When he told his boss the news, he could feel all hope leave his body. Malcolm was *completely* devastated.

In all of his years of hustling, he had never managed to have so many bad things happen in such quick succession, like they were happening now. His cellmate had given him a few pearls of wisdom, and one of them seemed appropriate for that particular moment.

"God won't put more on us than we can bear."

When he thought about that quote, he knew that everything was still going to be okay.

"Luther... did you take the last of the money out of the trap?"

Luther nodded his head in response, forgetting that Malcolm was unable to see him through the phone.

"Luther?"

"Oh... yeah, we got all of the money here at Kyla's."

"Okay. Good. I don't want you going back to that trap ever again. I—"

"But—"

"No buts, Luther. I want you and Rain to stay at Kyla's until further notice. This thing is almost over with. I promise. This is not the life I wanted for anyone to live. Not me, not Kyla, not Catfish, not Brink, and certainly not you. You have your whole life to live, and I'm going to see to it that you get to live it in luxury. Our plan is in its final stages, and I can't wait to get it over with. This—"

Luther suddenly remembered something. "Oh! Sweetback Fatty came by the trap. He said he could show us where that agent was located at."

Malcolm's forehead furrowed. "What agent, Luther?"

"You know who. Pamela Jones!"

"What the fuck! So, where is the bitch? What's the hold up?"

Luther sat down on a wooden rocking chair and answered, "He said we have to tell him where Tracy is in order for him to tell us where Pam is."

Malcolm, immediately, shook his head as soon as he heard Tracy's name. Tracy had been a dear friend to him during one of the worst

301

times of his life, and there was no way that he could betray her at that moment. There was silence on the phone, while Malcolm sat there and weighed the pros and cons. If Catfish found out that Malcolm could have gotten to Pam and that he had passed on the opportunity, he knew that their friendship would be ruined forever.

If Kyla found out, he knew that anything they could possibly have in the future would, also, be ruined, but, at the same time, Malcolm knew that it was his duty to be loyal. His standard of ethics was beyond comprehension when it came to loyalty. That was the main reason that Kyla was so attracted to him in the first place. The whole time that he was married to his wife, he never cheated on her.

Betrayal was foreign to him.

"Malcolm..."

Luther's voice was gentle. He knew that he was treading across delicate waters, and he didn't want to force any issues.

"What do you want me to—"

"Don't worry about it, Luther. I have another plan. We don't have to knock Pam off to beat this case. And I'm definitely not going to put a friend of mine in harm's way. I'd do my time before I made that decision."

Luther was confused, but he didn't know how to put his confusion into words. Malcolm's best friend had just lost his wife, and it was a definite that Catfish would want to get out, so he could avenge her death. If only Catfish knew what Malcolm had decided...

"Luther... I need you to do me one favor."

"What is it? You know all you have to do is say what, and I got you."

Malcolm rubbed his hand across his face and took a deep breath. "I want you to keep this information between me and you."

Malcolm was like a father figure to him. He had taught him many elements of the game, and, no matter which element he was teaching, it seemed to always be a different variation of loyalty.

"Yes, sir, Malcolm."

Malcolm smiled, but he caught himself once he thought about all of the problems that he would have to deal with in a very short time.

"Aight, kid. I'll talk to you later. The plan is about to take effect. Oh, yeah! I forgot... Happy Birthday, Luther!"

Luther shook his head. He had forgotten that his birthday had arrived. He was nineteen years old.

"We'll celebrate soon, kid. One."

After they hung up, Luther looked across the room and saw Rain curled up on the sofa, crying. She was shaking and crying like a newborn, but Luther hadn't had much experience communicating with women before. He decided to just sit beside her and hold her if she would let him, but, when he made it to the sofa, all of his nerves flew out of the window. He stood there feeling helpless for a few minutes, then he went into the bathroom to wash Tricia's blood off of him.

CHAPTER 10

Three days before the trial was to start, the government sent an order to the federal holding facility to transfer Malcolm, Catfish, and Brink into solitary confinement. Malcolm didn't have access to his cell phone anymore, and he was nervous because he hadn't been able to get in contact with anyone for the past three days. The last conversation he'd had was with Tracy, who thanked him for his realness and started making plans to move out of Houston.

He had known all along that he would never be anything but great friends with her, and she had known the same thing. She promised to keep in contact with him no matter what the circumstances were. That promise was all he wanted from her. In the middle of that conversation, the officers bombarded the unit, and Malcolm had to quickly get rid of the cell phone.

He flushed the sim card down the toilet and stuffed the phone into a roll of socks. It turned out that the officers only wanted to take Malcolm to the hole because they had spent so much money preparing for this trial that they couldn't afford for anything to happen to him.

They put Malcolm in Room 3, Catfish in Room 4, and Brink in Room 5. The single bed in each of their rooms had paper thin mattresses on them, but comfort was the least of their worries. A preacher had delivered the tragic news of Tricia's death to Catfish on the day that it happened, and Catfish had refused to speak to anybody else since that day. Even when his lawyer came by to talk to him about preparations for trial, he refused to even come out of his cell.

When his wife died, a part of him died, and his world had been torn apart. The day before trial, Malcolm had tried to speak through the vents to communicate with Catfish, but he wouldn't respond.

At first, he thought that maybe Catfish couldn't hear him through the vents, until he heard Catfish yell, "Helllllllp! Helllllllp! Helllllllp! Aaaaaaayyee! Ahhhhhhh!"

Malcolm had never heard Catfish sound like that before, so he immediately ran to the door, so he could see what was going on. He watched as two nurses and five officers ran down the hallway. They unlocked the door to see what was going on and stood there for a moment. After a while, they closed Catfish's cell back and walked away, giggling amongst each other.

"That boy sure has went crazy!"

"Yeah. I thought something was wrong with him, but he was in there screaming at the toilet. It's too damn late to act crazy now. The trial starts tomorrow!"

The officers and nurses were all black, yet they still found it amusing that one of their brothers was about to stand trial right after losing his wife.

Pathetic! Malcolm thought as he laid across his steel bed. He listened to Catfish wail for half of the night before sleep finally took them both out of their misery.

305

$~$~$~$~$

The rain pounded against her windshield, and the wipers worked in overdrive, trying to create visibility for her. It was the night before the Bankroll Squad were to go to trial, and she was mad at herself for not being able to help Malcolm. The last time she spoke to him, he'd told her that she needed to hurry up and leave the city because Sweetback Fatty was looking for her.

She told him that she would, but Tracy felt obligated to help Malcolm relieve some of his stress. She knew that she wasn't as aggressive as Kyla was and knew that Kyla had no interest at all in her assistance, so she decided to take things into her own hands. She knew that she wasn't a killer, so the best thing she could think of was to show up at Malcolm's trial for moral support.

She had been in Beaumont since she'd last talked with Malcolm. Tracy wanted to make sure to stay out of her baby daddy's grasp until the trial started. That way, if something happened to her, then, at least, Malcolm would know why. She pumped Keri Hilson's "One Night Stand" through the sound system of her Ford Mustang as she slowly made her way into Houston. She was afraid to go too fast because she had hydroplaned once when she was younger.

As she drove along, the rain started slacking up, but the visibility got worse. She wiped the tears from her eyes as she tried her best to concentrate on the road. When it became unbearable, she pulled over at a Dunkin' Donuts, so she could get a hold of herself. She sat there and thought about everything that was going on in her life. Her mother had been taking care of her child because her whole family thought that it was time for her to move on from Sweetback. He had been a negative influence on her from day one.

Tracy got out of the car and walked into the Dunkin' Donuts to get a coffee and a cream donut for herself. While she sat at a table, she continuously glanced at her phone, hoping that Malcolm would call her to let her know that he was alright, but her phone didn't make a sound. She sighed, then closed her eyes for a moment to suppress her surging emotions.

She bit into the donut, and the smooth, creamy taste relaxed her momentarily. She took a sip of her coffee, and, as she was putting her cup back on the table, she saw a couple arguing right beside the women's bathroom. She generally wouldn't have paid them any attention, but since it was a black lady being scolded by a white man, she had to try to see if she could help her. She hated racism, and just wished that it would come to an end.

She wrapped her donut up and laid it down. She grabbed her purse and phone and started making her way towards the couple. When she got closer, she saw that the lady was crying, so she put a little speed in her steps. When she got within earshot, she slowed down. The conversation caused her to freeze in her tracks.

"Pam! I leave the house for five minutes, and you disappear! I asked you not to leave! The trial is tomorrow!"

"I just came up the street to buy some fuckin' donuts! You don't have nothing to snack on at your house! It's all *health* foods. Granola this! Oatmeal that! I'm sick of that—"

"I should lock you up, Pam, and charge you with—"

"Noooo! I'm sorry. Please don't lock...."

So, that's Pamela Jones? Tracy thought as she briskly turned around

307

to go to her car. Once she got outside of Dunkin' Donuts, the cool air brushed across her face and tickled her ears. She sat in the car, trying to figure out what she could do to prevent her from testifying at Malcolm's trial. Her mind was racing 1,000 miles per hour, but she couldn't seem to come up with a clear enough idea.

If she just went up and asked her not to testify, she would more than likely be arrested. It seemed that the only way to stop her would be to kill her, *but how?*

Tracy had never killed anyone in her life, had never even entertained the idea of being a killer. Yet, here she was, trying to protect one of the greatest friends that she had ever had. She didn't own a gun and certainly didn't have time to go find one. Whatever she decided to do would have to be done immediately. She glanced up and saw Pam and the white man walking out of the donut shop.

The two were walking together at first. Then, they split up and went in separate directions. The white man's car was parked right by the entrance, while Pam's car was parked beside a propane gas tank. Tracy knew that she wasn't strong enough to kill Pam any other way, so she would have to grit her teeth and just go for it.

When Malcolm told her that Sweetback was trying to give him his freedom in exchange for her whereabouts, she was astonished that he didn't accept his deal. Any average man would have happily thrown her into harm's way in order to save his own skin, but it was extremely apparent that Malcolm was beyond the average man. Sweetback wanted her dead, and, in a way, Malcolm had risked his life in order to save hers.

Sitting in that car, watching Pam walk to hers, Tracy finally reached the conclusion that had been lingering in her subconscious for the last few days.

She owed her life to Malcolm.

She started up her Mustang and left the headlights off. She put the car into gear and pressed down on the gas pedal. The car gained acceleration quickly, and, when she was within ten feet from running Pam over, she suddenly remembered something. She had been so caught up in the moment of passion that she had forgotten about the most important thing in her life.

She tried to hit the brakes, but it was too late. The front grill of the Mustang made contact with the back of Pam's body. Since she knew she was going to probably get the death penalty for that crime, she went ahead and tilted her wheel so that she could hit the gas tank and take the easy way out. The car crashed hard into the gas tank, and Tracy closed her eyes as she waited for the explosion to surround her, but nothing happened.

She opened her eyes in a panic and tried to start her car back up, but it wouldn't crank. She opened the door and got out with the intention to run.

She took one step and ran into the white man who had been arguing with Pam. She fell to the ground after colliding with his solid body, and she hurt her wrist when she tried to break her fall. She attempted to get up, but there was a pistol in her face. The white man cocked the gun, and Tracy held her hands up as if her hands could block the bullets.

"Please! Don't shoot me, sir! Please don't! Please!"

Pam's boss stared at Tracy with a scowl on his face.

309

"You just tried to ruin my career, you black nigger bitch! Give me one reason why I shouldn't put a bullet in you right now!"

With tears in her eyes, she stared up at the white man and pleaded, "I-I-I'm pregnant."

$~$~$~$~$

Emotionally and physically, Pam was hurt. She had dedicated her life to the United States government in an effort to help them make the world a safer place. Instead, her superiors had taken advantage of her and put her in one of the most dangerous situations that they could think of. There had been easier jobs than the BRS, but they had given most of those jobs to the field agents with lighter skin.

She laid in her hospital bed and wiped the tears from her eyes while she thought about how badly she had been used. The girl who had tried to kill her was in custody and facing a mandatory life sentence, but that was no consolation. The impact from the vehicle had damaged her leg up so badly that the doctor removed it.

She stared down at the nub where her leg used to be, and the feeling was unreal. It felt like her leg was still attached to her body even though it was gone. She had cried to her boss, trying to get him to convince the doctor not to amputate her leg, but the doctor had adamantly shook his head.

"Your leg cannot be saved. It is barely hanging on to your body. We must remove it."

Pam had never felt worse than at that moment. What was supposed to be an honorable job for her had turned into a complete nightmare. Her boss had only come by once since the trial started. He had come by to ask her if she felt like testifying at trial. Pam had looked at him like he was crazy. She couldn't believe that he could ask such an unrealistic question.

Her boss had smiled at her after that and brushed his fingers across her cheeks.

"That's fine, Pam," he said, "We were already prepared to start the trial without you anyway. You see, we thought the Bankroll Squad would have murdered you a long time ago. The director of the FBI has asked for your resignation."

And he was gone. She had sacrificed her whole life for an organization that cared nothing about her. She laid in the hospital bed and cried herself to sleep.

$~$~$~$~$

By day three of the trial, the prosecution had pulled out trick after trick. Kyla wasn't able to attend, so she and Luther stayed home while Sunshine and Rain relayed the information back to them. Even though Kyla and Sunshine had killed seventeen witnesses, the FBI had still been able to find more witnesses willing to testify against the squad.

Some of the people testifying had never even heard of the Bankroll Squad until they got on TV, but they lied just to be a part of their demise. Even though Pam didn't testify, it was clear that they were still losing the trial. Malcolm had attempted to speak with Catfish, but his mind was gone. He couldn't get through to him.

On day four, the prosecution brought in what was supposed to be their ace in the hole— Jennifer Powers. They were certain that she had the necessary information that would influence the jury to convict her husband and his associates. Malcolm wasn't even surprised when she walked in. So many people had betrayed him that he couldn't even imagine anyone else remaining loyal. He sat there and waited on her to rip his character to shreds, but, midway through her testimony, he came to a new realization.

"Ladies and gentlemen of the jury, if you all don't believe anyone else's testimony, just take this female's word for it. She is the ex-wife of Malcolm Powers, and she knows all the details of his operation."

That was how it started. Brink and Malcolm both shook their heads in disgust.

"Jennifer, how long have you been married to Malcolm Powers?"

"Four years."

"And is it safe to say that you've witnessed a lot in those four years?"

"Yes."

"What are some of the things that you have witnessed?"

"Ummm... murders, drug deals, hundreds of millions of dollars being counted..."

That got a rise out of the jurors. The judge had to bang his gavel and restore order to his courtroom.

"Did you say murders with an 's'?"

"I sure did."

"Did you ever see your husband commit any murders personally?"

"No, I did not."

The prosecutor was thrown off balance for a moment. Then, he regained his footing.

"You didn't?"

"No. I said I did not."

"When you came to us willing to testify, you told us that you had seen him commit murders.

"No, that's what you all told me to say. You told—"

"Wait, Mrs. Powers! Maybe, I'm asking the questions incorrectly. Let me ask you this. Do you still love your husband?"

Without hesitation, Jennifer answered, "No, I do not."

"Do you want to see him go to prison, Jennifer?"

"Yes, I do."

"Which crime do you want to see him go to prison for?"

"For leaving me!"

The courtroom erupted into chatter and noise. The judge furiously banged his gavel again, trying to calm everyone down. The prosecutor's face was red, and he was steaming hot. He walked up to the witness stand and whispered to Jennifer, "What's wrong with you? If you mess up this case, I will throw you under the jail! Did you see him kill people or not?"

"Yes," she answered back.

"Well, when I ask you, you *say* so!"

The prosecutor walked back to the table and pulled out a chart.

"Jennifer, do you remember telling us that you saw Malcolm kill someone last December?"

"Yes, I remember telling you that."

"Who was this person or did you know the person?"

"I didn't know the person."

"How did Malcolm kill that person?"

Jennifer hesitated for a moment. Then, she said, "Look. You told me that if I lied for you on the stand for a few minutes that you would pay me. I can't remember the lies that you told me to say, but can I still get paid for trying?"

$~$~$~$~$

Jennifer's airhead performance had delivered a crushing blow to the case against Malcolm, and, for the first time, he felt optimistic about the outcome. After the prosecution rested, Brink and Malcolm both testified for themselves, even though their lawyers had advised them not to. They ended up lying on the stand with no effort, and the momentum had finally shifted.

Now, the outcome seemed to be favoring the Bankroll Squad. They denied every charge and accusation effortlessly, and the prosecutors couldn't gain any traction from them during the heated cross examinations. The defense lawyers smiled because they were on their way to beating a major federal case.

Then, Catfish took the stand and sealed their fate.

He got on the stand and denied every charge against Malcolm and Brink, but he accepted every accusation that had something to do with him. It was obvious that his mind wasn't there because he sat there and started talking about murders he'd done that no one even knew about. Malcolm and Brink were blown away, but they knew that Catfish hadn't been the same since his wife died.

After Catfish's crushing testimony, the jurors went back to deliberate. The whole time they were discussing the verdict, the prosecutor kept smiling at Malcolm and his defense team. Malcolm glanced over at Catfish and noticed that he was staring off into space. He could see that he didn't care what happened one way or the other. It was like his spirit had left his body when Tricia got killed. Malcolm felt for him. He knew that he wouldn't even be mad if they sent him away for life.

S~S~S~S~S

The jury returned with verdicts of guilty on all counts for Malcolm, Catfish, and Brink. Because they were on trial together, the jury had to assume that, if Catfish had done all that he'd claimed he'd done, then the leader was certainly a responsible party, as well as the pilot. It was unanimous, and it took less than thirty minutes to return with the verdicts.

Sunshine shook her head in disbelief at how Catfish had messed up the whole trial, and Rain was in tears. One of the officers had to bring her a box of tissues.

S~S~S~S~S

315

There were two U.S. Marshals in the front seat of the prisoner transport van, and they had both witnessed the breakdown at trial. They had the radio up loud and were discussing the trial openly. In the back, Brink and Catfish both felt like it was the end of the world. They were going to get life sentences, but, from the beginning to the end, they always stayed true. They never snitched on each other despite the severity of the situation.

The van pulled up to a stop, and the driver watched the traffic pass through the cross street. The marshals had their handguns cocked and ready, and there was a shotgun sitting in the middle of the seat in case a prisoner tried to escape. On the left, there was a camouflage army truck with three soldiers in full uniform, sitting in the transport bed. After noticing that one of them was a decorated officer, the marshal that was driving saluted him.

Immediately, Luther aimed the street sweeper at the driver and pulled the trigger. There were close to eight hundred bullets in a double rotating drum, and Luther shot, at least, one hundred of them before the light turned green. The marshals didn't even have a chance with their little weapons. Luther, Kyla, and Rain jumped out of the back of the truck and tried to open the door to free Malcolm, Catfish, and Brink, but the doors were locked.

They knew they had to hurry up because the van was being tracked by GPS, and the FBI would swarm them in a minute if they realized that there was a problem. Even though the windows were destroyed, they still couldn't get the locks open to free the squad. One of the marshals had hit an emergency button right before they got ambushed that permanently locked the doors in case of a takeover attempt.

Luther ran back to the truck and grabbed the heavy.50 cal. He secured it in a harness because the weapon was so powerful, and it felt like he was riding a mechanical bull with every shot.

Whoooooooom!

Whoooooooom!

The shots sounded like miniature bombs as the bullets knocked the doors off of their hinges. He put the weapon back in the truck and grabbed Brink and pulled him out of the van since he was the closest. Rain and Kyla both teamed up to help Catfish out, and Malcolm had known that it was going to happen anyways, so he was already prepared.

The three men were still handcuffed, but that could be fixed later. Right now, they just needed to get as far away as quickly as possible. Sunshine hit the gas and swerved through traffic as she listened to the sirens in the distance. She drove until they made it to Kyla's estate, where they had Brink's old jet gassed up and waiting, but, when they jumped out of the truck, the officers were right behind them in their vehicles. Luckily, the entrance gate to the runway closed automatically, and that bought them more time.

Kyla climbed into the jet and helped pull Rain in. Then, the two girls helped pull Catfish in. Next, Luther climbed in and helped Brink into the jet. They ran to the cockpit and started the jet up. They looked out of the window and saw that the officers had used their vehicles to ram through the gate. They were now rapidly approaching the jet.

They were about the length of three football fields away. Sunshine climbed into the jet and looked back at Malcolm, standing there with his handcuffs on. There was no way he could climb a ladder with his handcuffs on, and she smiled at her triumph. She had wanted Kyla for herself since she'd first laid eyes on her, and she was certainly not going to blow the opportunity of a lifetime to have the woman of her dreams.

There was no way that she was going to pull Malcolm onto that plane. She loved Kyla too much. It was set in stone. A dream come true. Malcolm frowned as he stood there. Then, he asked, "Are you going to help me?"

Before she could answer, she heard Luther's voice in the distance.

"Sunshine, is everything set? Do you need help? Is Malcolm on board?"

Sunshine grinned as she pulled the ladder up out of Malcolm's reach.

"Everyone's here! Let's go!"

Malcolm wanted to scream to get everybody's attention, but the pistol that Sunshine was holding in his face changed his mind. He stood there in complete dismay as he looked at the treachery in Sunshine's eyes. She was one of the most beautiful women he'd ever laid eyes on, yet her intentions were the ugliest of anyone that had ever betrayed him.

She was a monster in makeup and a mini skirt. Her French tipped fingernails laid against the steel pistol while the agony of the situation set in. For a minute, Malcolm thought that Sunshine was joking with him. Then, she backed out of the entrance and locked the door shut. Malcolm stood there, helpless, as he watched the jet lurch forward, so it could gain the speed necessary to lift off. Behind him, he heard the police sirens getting closer, and he knew that his days of freedom days were over.

He had just lost his trial and had escaped from the transport van on the way back from court, killing two U.S. Marshals in the process. His life, as he knew it, had come to an end. Even in that moment, he still never regretted starting the Bankroll Squad. He had started hustling, so he could stay in college, and the hustle had taken on a life of its own. A life with its own personality and beliefs and with its own set of consequences.

He watched the jet as its momentum rivaled with gravity. In this competition between the jet and gravity, gravity lost as the jet lifted off of the ground, soaring to new heights, while Malcolm's spirit sunk to new lows.

Behind him, he heard doors slamming and guns being cocked.

"Get your ass on the ground! Now! Right now!"

If his ankles hadn't been shackled, he would have taken off running as soon as the jet lurched off. Instead, he was locked in an even worse predicament. He was angry, but he was, also, happy because, even though he was headed to a maximum security prison for the rest of his life, he had managed to get Catfish and Brink free of the government's clutches. He heard the rapid pounding of footsteps as the officers and agents ran towards him.

He felt a nightclub slam against his back, and he smiled through the pain. It wasn't a problem for him to endure this because he knew that he would always have an ace in the hole. As long as Kyla continued to breathe, he knew that it was only a matter of time before he would once again be free.

S~S~S~S~S

Kyla and Rain had popped the champagne and were filling the flute

319

glasses.

"You had a helluva plan, Kyla! It worked out all the way!" Rain said as she downed her glass.

Kyla smiled. "It wasn't my idea at all. It was Sunshine's plan, and me and Malcolm fine-tuned it. I'm so happy!"

Rain couldn't help but smile because Kyla's happiness was infectious. She was beyond glowing. She was illuminated with the gentle color of love. As if on cue, Sunshine walked into the luxurious cabin with a smile on her face.

Still smiling, Kyla looked at her in appreciation.

"Sunshine, tell Malcolm to come get something to drink. Here's your glass."

Sunshine grabbed her glass and downed it. Then, she stood in front of Kyla and Rain with the saddest eyes she could muster up. "Kyla... we need to talk..."

"Talk about what, Sunshine?"

Sunshine sat down because they'd hit a bit of turbulence.

"About us..."

"What about us?"

Sunshine tried to force a smile, but she looked nervous and insincere.

"I-I-I love you, Kyla."

Kyla looked at her curiously.

"Of course! We're family, girl! I love you, too!"

"No, Kyla. I'm *in* love with you, and I want to be with you until the day I die. There's no other woman on this Earth for me. I *need* you!"

As Kyla stared at her, confusion showed on her face.

"What the… where's Malcolm?"

"Kyla, do you love me like I love you? Answer me!"

Kyla glanced down and saw a pistol in Sunshine's trembling hand.

"I said, 'Do you love me, Kyla?' Do you? Stop asking about *him*. We don't need *him!* I'm the only one for you!"

Kyla was seeing the psychotic side of Sunshine for the very first time, and she was mad at herself for having ignored the signs. Not only had she ignored the signs, she had ignored one of Malcolm's very first lessons: *Keep your enemies close and your friends closer.*

No enemy could hurt you as bad as the closest one to you. Kyla felt a tear approaching, but she blinked it away before it could slip. Sunshine had the gun pointed in Kyla's face, while the jet breezed through the clouds effortlessly.

"KYLA! I SAID DO YOU LOVE ME??!"

Keep up with the latest news!
Text TBRS to 22828

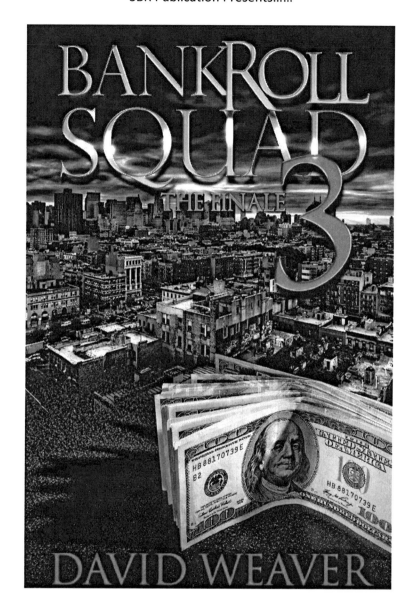

Bankroll Squad 3: The Finale

Definition of Power:

Ability, regarded as put forth or exerted; strength, force, or energy in action; as, the power of steam in moving an engine; the power of truth, or of argument, in producing conviction; the power of enthusiasm.

Capacity of undergoing or suffering; fitness to be acted upon; susceptibility; -- called also passive power; as, great power of endurance.

The exercise of a faculty; the employment of strength; the exercise of any kind of control; influence; dominion; sway; command; government.

The agent exercising an ability to act; an individual invested with authority; an institution, or government, which exercises control; as, the great powers of Europe; hence, often, a superhuman agent; a spirit; a divinity.

A military or naval force; an army or navy; a great host.

A large quantity; a great number; as, a power o/ good things.

The rate at which mechanical energy is exerted or mechanical work performed, as by an engine or other machine, or an animal, working continuously; as, an engine of twenty horse power.

A mechanical agent; that from which useful mechanical energy is derived; as, water power; steam power; hand power, etc.

Applied force; force producing motion or pressure; as, the power applied at one and of a lever to lift a weight at the other end.

CHAPTER 1

"Sweetback. Hey Daddy, what's up?"

"Whassup Ma?" Sweetback Fatty said as he smiled while waiting on the news that he knew he was going to hear eventually.

"They just brought your baby mama, Tracy, up in the federal holding facility."

Sweetback thought about how he'd patiently outworked and slowly outmaneuvered the Bankroll Squad. He was bitter initially when they took over, but he realized that they hadn't quite infiltrated the prison system. So he'd kept in contact with inmates from high security prisons to lows, from federal holding facilities to state correctional facilities.

Doing this enabled him to have a reach longer than anything the Bankroll Squad could muster together. If someone had wronged anyone, tried to snitch on anyone, or killed anyone in his crew, then there was no place on Earth that would shelter that person, there was no cubicle or tent, nor shed or barn that could hide them from the reaches of Sweetback Fatty. There was no prison secure enough to stop him from his payback.

"Are you there Sweetback? Tracy just came in here... She looks lost as hell. You want me to look out for her? You know I'll do anything for you Sweetback."

Sweetback smiled and shook his head. "O.K. Ma… I do want you to do something for me."

"What is it baby? You know I'll do it, please tell me and it's done."

"You see my so-called baby mama right now you said?" Sweetback asked for clarity.

"Yes, I'm looking directly at her."

Without remorse in his tone, and without another thought about the consequences, he spoke. "Kill her."

$~$~$~$~$

"KYLA! I SAID DO YOU LOVE ME?!?"

Kyla was thrown for the biggest loop of her life when she heard those words come out of Sunshine's mouth. She didn't know what to do or how to respond; so she responded to the pistol instead.

"Of course I love you Sunshine!"

"You should never have to ask me anything like that Sunshine. Ever! You know I love you."

Rain was shocked. She'd known all along that Sunshine was infatuated with Kyla, but never thought that it would be on *this* level. She was beyond angry to have done all of that work and for it to go down like *this*.

"Sunshine," Rain spoke up, "put the pistol away baby. Kyla told me herself how bad she wanted to be with you. So I know you both feel the same way about each other. Why would you go through this instead of

327

just asking her outright? She would have told you…"

Sunshine stared at Kyla's face, admiring the beauty and grace that was molded into it. She had never met a woman so magnificent before and knew that she never would again. Now she was standing there feeling foolish for having to pull a pistol out just to get an answer. But now that it was out, she saw no reason to put it up just yet.

"You really love me Kyla?" Sunshine said as her eyes misted.

"Yes Sunshine. I love you. But at the same time, I owe Malcolm everything. I owe him my loyalty because he held it down for me while I was in a coma. Is that ok with you baby?"

Sunshine smiled. Her dream had come true. All of her life she'd simply wanted to be accepted; to be loved and respected, and it had finally happened for her. Kyla *loved* her. She lowered the pistol a bit and went to give Kyla a hug, but stopped abruptly. She stood there and tried to feel the situation out from Kyla's standpoint. She knew how much in love Kyla was with Malcolm, and knew that there was no way she could now just be "in love" with her out of the blue. She felt that something wasn't adding up, so she had to play her cards right in order to keep the upper hand.

"Sunshine," Kyla said in a calm manner, "please tell me what's wrong. Why the pistol and why are you asking me questions that you should already know the answer to?"

Thinking fast, Sunshine responded with trepidation in her voice, "I-I- I made a mistake…"

Kyla was getting angrier by the second. "You made *what* kind of *mistake!?*"

328

"Don't worry Kyla, I can fix it! All I have to do is call Treasure; my homegirl. She runs a gang called The Lipstick Clique. I can fix-"

"Fix what?!?! Sunshine, you better tell me what the *fuck* is going on right this minute!"

Sunshine felt her bladder weaken because she knew she was about to come off sounding like the fool of the century. She knew how hard they had worked on this mission and she felt horrible for ruining it. *What the fuck have I done?* She thought as she stood before Kyla and Rain trembling. She knew she would have to tell a lie.

"I-I-I couldn't pull him up... the-the police shot a taser and I lost my gr-grip! I'm so sorry!! Please let me redeem myself! Please Kyla!"

Kyla felt dizzy and nauseous as the words left Sunshine's lips. After all of the hard work she had put down to get her man back; this *bitch* had just fucked up *everything*. Her immediate thought was that she wanted to *kill* Sunshine. She wanted to gut her from vagina to forehead and let her insides spill out onto a dirt road in the middle of nowhere. She was *pissed.*

But she was smart. Anger didn't mean hit the panic button and being pissed didn't mean stop being rational. Kyla closed her eyes and took a deep breath while she sat waiting to hear what dark lies would leave Sunshine's mouth. She knew that she was going to kill her. But first she was going to make her fix her mistake. *Then* she would be sure to make her blood spill from one end of the map to the other.

Kyla sat in pain and madness as she watched this clown of a bitch Sunshine stand there spewing out more bullshit. She trembled; her lungs rattling against her chest as she took a ragged series of deep breaths. She couldn't believe that she hadn't picked up on the signs.

329

First, Malcolm had gotten thrown for a loop with Pam; and just like him, she had been tricked by Sunshine.

"Kyla! Rain! You two know that I would never do anything to betray the Bankroll Squad right? I mean… just give me another chance. What do I have to do Kyla?"

Kyla was disgusted by the sight of her, but she managed to she swallow her fury. "Sunshine… put the pistol up baby."

Sunshine looked up and smiled. She loved the tone of voice that Kyla was using. It was something that she often fantasized about hearing on a regular basis. She just didn't know that she would get the opportunity so soon.

She slid her pistol back into her purse and smiled an uneasy smile.

While Sunshine was putting her pistol back into her purse, Kyla only had one thought on her mind. It was a quote that she had held dear for as long as she could remember, and she was definitely following it at that moment.

Never interrupt your enemies when they are making a mistake.

She smiled at Sunshine, it was a smile that no one in the world could read except for Malcolm. If Sunshine were able to read that particular smile, there was no doubt in Kyla's mind that she would take the gun back out of her purse and attempt to close the book on Kyla's life.

And there was no way she could allow the book to be closed this early in her life, when she was supposed to be starting a new chapter with Malcolm. She stared at Sunshine and tried to determine her true intentions. For the first time, saw her clearly; the new enemy. She knew that the end would be coming soon for her betrayal.

"I'll tell Brink to land the plane Kyla. I'm telling you, I'm going to make this situation right baby. I promise…"

$~$~$~$~$

Treasure sat back in her chair and relaxed as she saw the news flash across the television screen. The Bankroll Squad had just escaped from the clasp of the federal government, and every person representing the streets was rooting for them. It was truly an exciting moment for Treasure, especially since Malcolm Powers himself helped her out on a few occasions and asked no questions about it.

He had been the main inspiration for her squad, The Lipstick Clique, and she had been living it up ever since. She glanced at the living room floor and saw money stacked up from one end of the room to the next. There were gold bullions, gold chains, gold rings, just about everything of value imaginable, sitting around like unwanted garbage.

For the Lipstick Clique, this was their "bank." It was a place where each member had the key and could go in and get whatever they pleased. There were 4 banks, but only one of them was private. The Lipstick Clique had adopted the free-stunting mantra of the Bankroll Squad, and believed that *everybody* in the crew should be able to ball.

The Lipstick Clique committed a mass assortment of crimes; everything from murder-for-hire to murder-for-profit. They were relentless in their pursuit of the green dollar, and would stop at nothing to stack one on top of the other and keep it that way.

Treasure, Skye, and Milan sat around in a mini circle at the "bank" and watched the news with their legs crossed. Treasure made it mandatory that they watch the news every single morning and evening. She wouldn't be able to operate if she didn't know what her enemies were planning, and so far, it had been working.

At the end of the news segment on Bankroll Squad, a *breaking news* notification appeared and the screen immediately went to another news reporter.

"I am at the scene of *The Manladdin Estate,* an upscale mansion that was owned in secret by one of the members of the Bankroll Squad; a young female woman named Kyla Brent. Just a few moments ago, the Bankroll Squad led the authorities on a high speed chase following a daring escape that resulted in the death of two Federal Marshals. The majority of this ruthless criminal organization was able to escape, but their leader, Malcolm Powers was captured.

Authorities say that the escape, while unexpected is not shocking due to the overwhelming amount of power and resources that the notorious crime family had amassed from their extensive illegal activities. Special Agent Greka of the FBI is addressing the media now. "

"This situation is a classic example of underestimating the strength and power of street gangs.... As students of the law and masters on societal behavior, we assume that street gangs are more reckless than smart. Rest assured that we will not make the same mistake twice and the rest of the Bankroll Squad will be captured and brought to justice."

Pissed, Treasure hit the power button on the remote, which was something she *never* did. Skye looked at her in silence. She knew that whenever Treasure did something out of character, it usually meant that soon, they would *all* be doing things outside of their character.

There was a strict no-talking rule in the "banks," so they sat there in silence and stared at the riches that had been compiled on the floor. The twins, Skye and Milan knew that life was no fairy tale, but they were in their slippers and planned to run as far as possible before the clock struck 12. Cinderella's laws would have to come get them!

$~$~$~$~$

Malcolm's face slammed into the wall and he didn't make a sound. He was in the interrogation room at FBI headquarters with three of the dirtiest agents in the bureau. A knee went into his stomach, causing him to fall over. He couldn't even land properly because the handcuffs were still locked onto his wrists behind his back. Blood leaked from his nose and lips; the left side of his face was swollen from the beating he had received. He felt another agent elbow him in his rib cage as hard as he could. The other agent grabbed him by the neck and slung him into the corner of the room.

"Where the *fuck* did those fucks *go?"*

Malcolm glanced up at the agent and smiled. His white teeth shone through the mixture of fresh and dried blood that had accumulated on his lips. "They went away."

The first agent ran up to him and kicked him in the face as hard as he could, causing one of his side teeth to be loosened.

"Fuck you smart ass! You think you're the smartest man in the world don't you? Well get this! I don't care how smart you are! The only way you learn right from wrong is through experience!"

The other agent stepped in and tried a different approach. "Look, Malcolm… you're pretty much dead. That you can definitely bet on, all we're trying to do is get you to give us the information on the people that kicked you out of the plane and betrayed you. Obviously, it was a betrayal; otherwise you would be on the plane with them right?"

Malcolm grinned at the agents and spit on the floor. He looked the first agent in the eyes before he answered. "I don't feel like I'm smart enough to answer the questions being asked to me."

Both agents looked at each other and took a deep breath. They had been beating that man for hours and he still hadn't cracked or budged in his loyalty. It angered them that he could sit there and be so loyal to people who were obviously so disloyal. They would never be able to understand why he still held true to his beliefs, even when his life was over.

The third agent had an ace in the hole that he had been patiently waiting to use. He walked past the other two agents and stopped about five feet away from Malcolm. He stared down at him with a bit of arrogance; as if he couldn't care less if Malcolm replied to his question or not. The agent reached into his pocket and grabbed a photo. He held the photo to his face, shook his head, and threw it at Malcolm without saying a word.

He stood there as if in triumph, but still not speaking. The picture landed on Malcolm's chest upside down, so he pushed his body sideways so that he would be able to get the picture to flip over. When it landed onto the floor, the visual made Malcolm's eyes bulge. He backed away from the picture while simultaneously wishing that he was closer to it. He was confused. He had no idea what was going on and how that picture came to be.

He stared up at Agent #3 and saw that the man was standing there with a smirk on his face. Not a smirk that says "I won," but a smirk that says "I will always win."

"Sir... Are you telling me that Tracy is dead?"

CHAPTER 2

Jennifer woke up in a hospital bed with tubes attached to her body. She had no idea how she'd ended up in this situation. She glanced down at the hospital gown she was wearing and immediately she was ready to get up out of there. She looked around for her clothes, and didn't see them anywhere. She was furious.

She sighed, and was about to reach out to hit the button for the nurse when she felt a wave of dizziness flood her body. She had it in her mind to just get up and leave the hospital; but she knew that she would need to wait until she was feeling better in order to do so. She was strangely tired for some reason. Just as she was about to go back to sleep, a nurse approached her.

"Hi Jennifer! How are you feeling today?"

Jennifer stared at the lady like she was her worst enemy. Jennifer had never acted like that before, but the way she was feeling at that moment trumped her history.

"How the fuck do you think I feel?"

The nurse pulled out a tablet and read over it briefly, then she quickly put it away. "Well ma'am, you've lost a lot of blood... You had puncture wounds in both buttocks that appeared to have gone unattended for a few days now... What happened there?"

Suddenly Jennifer remembered. That bitch Tracy stabbed her in her butt implants in the parking lot of the prison and in response; the only thing she could think to do was get high.

Damn, she thought as she lay there feeling like the world's dumbest blonde.

"I had an accident." She managed to blurt out before she was overcome with tears. It was as if the dam had finally broken. She'd been told once that she had the strongest wall in the family. She was the one in the family that cried only at life-changing moments. The last time she cried was *at* Malcolm; and here she was again… crying *for* Malcolm.

The magnitude of her mistakes overwhelmed her. She had been selfish instead of willing to learn. She had been a liability instead of an asset, and now she lay there in the bed realizing how she'd thrown her entire world away for no reason. She thought about all of the drugs she'd been doing lately, and knew that it was time for the madness to cease.

"Are you o.k. Jennifer? Here's a tissue. Do you have a headache or anything?"

Jennifer stared up at the lady that she had been so mean to just a couple of minutes ago, and wondered how she could find it in her heart to still be so nice to her. It truly amazed her, and it showed her that everyone in the world wasn't against her. She also realized at that moment, that Malcolm wasn't trying to hurt her either … He was only trying to make a living for them.

"No, thank you nurse. I don't have a headache, I'm fine."

The nurse picked the tablet back up and wrote something down. "O.k. then, I'll bring you your clothes out so that you can leave."

"Wait!" Jennifer said. She knew that the way she blurted it out seemed panicky; but she *was* panicking. She didn't have *anywhere* to go!

"What is it Jennifer?" The nurse said politely.

"I-Can-I just wanted to know... if you could let me stay here a little longer... just overnight at least?"

The nurse looked over her shoulder. "Well... it's not standard policy... but I heard about what happened with the trial and everything, so I'm sure you're trying to avoid going into the public right now anyway. No problem, I'll let the doctor know."

Jennifer lay there with a blank stare as she watched the nurse walk away from her bed. *The fuckin' trial!* Everything came back to her at once. The last thing she remembered was leaving the courtroom in tears and going to get her fix. *Malcolm will never forgive me now!* She thought as she felt the tears stream down her face.

She had gone completely against everything Malcolm had stood for just because she thought that it was going to lead to a quick high. She lay there and thought back to the days when she had codes and rules to her life. When she had standards and goals, principles and character. In those days, she was a dynamic woman. Her personality was in 3-D. It was glowing and full of life back then. It was so strong that it attracted one of the most powerful men in the world and possessed him to marry her. And she had *ruined* it.

She dozed off to sleep thinking about what she would have to endure in order to get her husband back. She didn't care how many women she had to compete with, she had it set in her mind that she was going to change. She felt like this entire scenario all stemmed from her over-reacting about the initial discovery of the cocaine; and she wanted to do everything in her power to restore things to where they were supposed to be.

$~$~$~$~$

"Ughhhh! Ugghhhh! Ugghhhh! Ughhhh!"

The sound was that of a wounded animal.

"Ugghhhh! Ugghhh! Ughhhh! Ughghh!

Jennifer woke up to a semi dark hospital room. Her TV monitor's glow illuminated her cubicle, and Lysol's odor was taking the place of oxygen for that night. She heard the gentle splash of someone mopping the floor in the near distance, but the thing that concerned her most was the sound of the animal crying.

"Ugghhh! Ugghhh! Ugghhh!"

After hearing it again, she knew that it wasn't an animal; it was a human who had been treated like one. She could be placed on any part of the continent and know exactly what pain sounded like when it was being expressed. She started to close her eyes and go back to sleep, but since the only barrier separating her cubicle from the next one was a thin curtain; she decided to speak through it.

"Uhm… Hellloooo?"

"Ugghhh! You there? Who are you? Where are you at?"

339

Jennifer was confused for a moment; it was obvious that her neighbor was having problems, but she didn't know if there was anything that *she* could do to fix it. However, it was still in her nature to at least attempt. "Do you need something over there?"

The voice got silent for a moment, as if it was in deep thought and concentration about the question that she'd asked. Jennifer became more attentive; trying to zone out the sound of the mop splashing in the distance in order to hear what her neighbor had to say. But the silence reigned supreme.

Jennifer laid there for a little while longer with her eyes open, and after not hearing a response from her neighbor for 5 minutes, she found herself dozing back off to sleep.

As soon as her breathing started getting heavy, a sound moved through the curtain like a bullet.

"Fuck them! Fuck them! You hear me? Fuck them!"

Startled, Jennifer tried her best to sit up in her hospital bed so that she could find out what was going on. She looked right and left for a nurse so that her neighbor could get help if it was needed, but saw no one.

"Fuck who? Can you hear me?"

"The FBI! Fuck them! Fuck them! Fuck them! They just took my life from me! Agghhhh!!! Fuck them!"

Jennifer felt a stab of pressure rush through her body as she listened to the pain in the person's voice. It was a deep pain; a pain that she had been feeling herself all along, but just didn't have the nerve to express it. She too, had been wronged by the FBI, and in more ways than one. The first one was when they took her husband away from her, and made it seem like he was never coming home. The second was when they turned her against her husband. But this person in the next cubicle was acting like she was in a worse predicament than her.

"Excuse me... Hey. Can you hear me?" Jennifer asked her while looking around for a clock to see what time it was.

"Yea! I hear you! Can you fuckin hear me? Fuck the FBI! Fuck em! They took my life away from me. My leg is gone! They took my leg! Do you hear me?"

"Excuse me... my name is Jennifer. What's your name?"

Silence again.

Jennifer glanced up at the ceiling while waiting on her neighbor to respond to her question. She couldn't believe that the lady was blaming the FBI for taking her leg away from her. She had been raised to believe that the United States government was strong and was there in order to protect you, not prey on the weak. But then again, she only had to look at her own situation to know that sometimes, prey on the weak is exactly what they did.

Suddenly the voice spoke out again. "Your name is Jennifer... as in Jennifer Powers?"

Jennifer was stunned. "How do you know who I am? Who are you?

"My name is Pamela Jones... You probably don't know me, but I used to be a federal agent. I was once in charge of having your husband sent to prison. But-"

341

Jennifer cut her off. "Bitch I should come over there and strangle you! What the fuck made you think that I was going to be cool with the fact that you wanted to take my husband to prison?"

Pam sighed, but it did nothing to calm the tone of her voice. "Because I was supposed to take you to prison as well Jennifer. Just for living off of the proceeds of illegal money; you were supposed to be a part of the case. But I spared you. I'm really sorry about everything though, if that helps."

Jennifer's heart was racing a mile a second as she absorbed everything that the female had told her. "Why didn't you turn me in then?"

Pam turned the channel on the television to a home shopping network. "I didn't turn you in because I didn't think you'd be alive this long. You see... Jennifer... I know your secrets."

Jennifer was taken aback by this sudden change of conversation. "Hey, I thought something was wrong with you over there. You were just hollering and carrying on. What the hell happened? You just all of a sudden stopped hurting or something?"

Pam giggled, then said "Jen... yes, I am in pain. However, the pain that I'm in could never compare to the pain that you'll be in once I release your secrets. True, I'm missing a fucking leg over here; but you'll be missing a got damned life bitch!"

Jennifer was getting more and more nervous, because she knew that there was only one secret that she could be referring to, and she had gone to great lengths to ensure that it was never discovered. She was confident that there was no way possible for her to hear what she thought she was about to hear. Until she heard it.

"The whole time you were married to Malcolm, I watched you do this shit with disgust. But I never said anything about it until now. Why am I saying it? Because misery loves fucking company bitch! I'm mad and miserable, and you should get what's coming to you. How dare you cheat on your husband throughout your whole fucking marriage; and with his best friend on top of that. You cheated on your husband with Catfish you dumb bitch!"

Jennifer was completely confused. *Wait… I didn't cheat on Malcolm with Catfish!* "You're such a lying bitch! You know I didn't cheat on Malcolm with Catfish!! Where the fuck did you get your information?"

Pam coughed. A horrible cough that sounded like her lungs were covered in phlegm. She couldn't breathe without wheezing and couldn't sleep because of her missing leg. Every time she thought about the way that the doctors removed her leg, she could only scream. "Grrrr!! Fuck!"

Jennifer was sitting up in her bed now. The dizziness that she was experiencing earlier had suddenly vanished. In its place was the deposit of a frightening level of anger. She looked around the room for a weapon she could use, and saw nothing. "I said how did you find this out bitch?"

Pam ignored her once again.

Jennifer continued to look around the room, and eventually spotted something that she could use. It was an ink pen lying in a holder. She looked closer and saw that the actual ink pen holder was stronger than the pen. She climbed out of her bed.

The floor was cold against her bare feet, but she had a goal to accomplish, and she knew that it *must* be done. She grabbed the ink pen

343

holder and walked around to Pam's cubicle. She swallowed hard when she saw the condition that she was in. It hurt her to see a woman so young and in a situation like the one that she was witnessing. However, she couldn't allow her to continue to live while holding on to secrets like the one she knew. Catfish was her *past,* and she hadn't seen him anymore since she met Malcolm. *This Pam bitch was playing with fire! She* had to die.

She walked up to the side of the bed silently. The weight of the ink pen holder felt powerful in her hand. It had a thick wooden base with strong iron accents. She stopped when she got right beside Pam and lifted it over her head. The holder felt like it weighed around six or seven pounds, and she knew that this would do it for her. She took a deep breath and swung it with all of her power.

$~$~$~$~$

Diaz and Rally left the club completely different than the way they entered it. They'd been celebrating and representing the Dynasty Cartel all that night. They'd done the typical major player activities; from buying out the bar, to even making the club admission free. But at the end of the night, they'd felt slighted and disrespected. A group of bitches that called themselves the Lipstick Clique had come over to their table and dumped off twice the amount of money that they had initially spent buying out the bar.

The leader of the three women had an unlit cigar in her hand and a business suit that looked like it could have come out of a man's closet; although it fit her figure like a grown woman. The leader had stood before them and openly spoke out of the side of her neck. "The Bankroll Squad isn't dead negro. The Lipstick Clique is an extension of them. Don't *ever* doubt the words I'm saying, and don't *ever* try to stunt again in a city owned by the Bankroll Squad. Just don't do it. If you do, I'll kill you both."

Rally had been blown away by the scenario at first. Here were three women wearing three different shades of red lipstick and calling themselves the Lipstick Clique. He was amused, and instantly developed a crush. Diaz pointed at the twins and smiled at Rally. "I want both of those!"

Rally grinned. "You can *have* both of those. But you know I want that wanna-be boss ass bitch! Them hoes thought they could come over here and dump a bag full of one dollar bills on us and we'd think they were as major as the Bankroll Squad? Haha! Funny shit!"

It wasn't until they'd gotten into the car and ready to leave that they realized that their assessment of the Lipstick Clique was completely inaccurate. They were sitting in Diaz's Escalade flipping through the bag of money that had been dumped on them while in the club. To both of their surprise, it was nothing but hundreds in the bag.

The two of them instantly scanned the parking lot to see if they could spot them. But they were nowhere in sight. Rally's eyes were wide open and he was fully alert despite all of the bottles of alcohol they'd just downed. "Man, I have to either get that bitch on my team, or kill them hoes. They can't co-exist with the Dynasty Cartel. Fuck them and the Bankroll Squad. It's Dynasty Cartel or nothing."

Diaz sat back in the seat and thought about the words Rally had just spoken. He started his vehicle and turned the music up while he tried to remember if he'd ever seen or heard of the Lipstick Clique before. He sat there in silence; unable to recall anything in his memory relating to them.

345

He exhaled and glanced out at the pavement. It seemed that no matter how close he managed to get to the streets, the further away he always was. No matter how many steps ahead he managed to jump in the streets; he was always 4 steps behind. The streets were forever going to be a mystery to him; and he was forever going to try to solve it. The Lipstick Clique was number one on their list of things to be done. He would get started tomorrow.

$~$~$~$~$~$

Sunshine got up so that she could head to the cockpit, but as soon as she turned, she bumped into Luther. The impact of his solid body caused her to fall to the floor and lose control of her pistol. The pistol slid into Rain's reach, and she quickly grabbed it and trained it on Sunshine.

"Where is Malcolm?" Luther demanded with a psychotic edge in his voice. He had two sets of cuffs in his hand along with the dead Marshall's handcuff key.

Sunshine's heart was beating a hundred miles a minute. "I- I- I made a mistake! I- I-"

"You made a *what?* A *mistake?* Bitch, grown women don't make mistakes; they make decisions! Now where the fuck is Malcolm?"

His first instinct told him to make sure that Malcolm got onto that fuckin' plane. His gut had never led him wrong, and for him to not follow the path that had been proven, made him look like less of a boss. He hated that feeling, and he knew he had to do something about it.

"Malcolm ain't on this fuckin' plane?!"

346

Luther glanced at the sad look on Rain's face and knew the answer immediately. He glanced over at Kyla and almost shed a tear. Here was a woman that had gone above and beyond the call of duty in order to save the love of her life and in a tragic turn of events, it had blown up in her face. Luther felt sick to his stomach, but he was never a man without a plan.

He sighed and suddenly grabbed Sunshine's right arm.

"Stop it muthafucka. Get the fuck off me!" He overpowered her while she was screaming, and even though she was fighting him back; he still managed to cuff her wrists to a steel post.

"Get this shit off of me muthafucka!" She screamed as she tugged and pulled away from the grip of the handcuffs. She still had one arm free, but it was nothing she could do to help her situation.

Luther met Kyla's gaze and wished that he could absorb some of the pain that she was feeling; he knew *that* was impossible. In order to make up for what he couldn't do, he was going to elevate the things that he was *capable* of doing.

"Rain, Kyla, grab those parachutes; we're going to jump... we're not authorized to use anyone's landing pad in this part of Texas, and we *have* to get back to Houston asap to get Malcolm. Let me get Catfish and Brink prepared."

When Luther returned, everyone had their gear on. Catfish was with him and was looking as glossy eyed as ever. It was like his mind had gone completely blank. One look at him and anyone would immediately know that he was a man in desperate need of a psychiatrist.

Catfish and Kyla went to the exit and stood there, staring at each

347

other. Kyla had tears in her eyes that were stubborn to leave. She seemed to be perpetually having bad luck and didn't know why she couldn't catch a break. Her latest betrayal, Sunshine; lay on the floor pleading for her help.

"Kyla! Pleeeeaassee Kyla! Please don't leave me down here like this. You're too *loyal* to do me like this. I was there for you through thick and thin. You have to think about that Kyla. I did everything for you! I love you! I'll help you do anything in the world and you know it! Where else can you find someone as loyal as I am to you?"

Rain walked up to Kyla and whispered to her. "Tune her out Kyla. You know what you want and deserve, and we're all behind you 100%. We're your true family, with no hidden motives. You know that when a person hides their motives, they hide themselves; so ignore that bitch."

Sunshine kicked and screamed as she struggled to pull away from the grasp of the handcuffs. She was angry and couldn't believe she had slipped and lost control by bumping into Luther. She looked into the safety compartment and saw another parachute available, but knew that there was no way possible she would be able to get to it. They were going to see to it that she died on that plane.

When they got over a forest clearing, they decided that it was the best place to allow the plane to crash. Luther walked to the front of the line and tapped Catfish on the shoulder. "You ready Cat?"

For a second, Cat just stared at him in silence; then he abruptly opened the door and leaped. Luther and Kyla instantly looked down and wondered if he was going to actually use his parachute, or leap to his death. They looked at each other briefly; their eye contact speaking the unspoken. Kyla immediately jumped after him.

Luther looked at Rain. "You ready baby?"

Rain smiled at Luther. She liked him genuinely, and she really wanted to have a future with him, but strangely she still felt a certain attachment to Sunshine; even though she had betrayed them all. She hated her but loved her like a sister. In short, Rain was a forgiving soul. She forgave and wanted to move on, but she knew that Sunshine should be punished. "Luther, I'll jump when you jump baby. We'll jump together."

Luther smiled at Rain. He thought she was a beautiful woman, and he was fully interested in the level of excellence that she brought out of him when she was in his presence. She felt like the right match, and that made him feel like a true boss.

A couple of moments later, Brink came out of the cockpit saying briskly. "Let's go!"

He jumped out.

Luther watched, then pulled Rain close behind him. He crouched low and told her to do the same. They looked like one. They were two people in love not wanting to do one thing without the other in tow. She leaned her head against his back sideways, partly so she could be careful about bumping her head; and partly so that she could glance at Sunshine.

Sunshine looked at her with pleading, begging eyes. Rain tried to blink the effect away, but found herself unable to.

"Wait Luther, something's hurting me. What's that?"

Luther reached around and pulled the knife out of the inside of his

349

belt. "I always kept a knife handy. Here." He handed it to her and they began their jump.

But before Rain cleared the door, she'd thrown Sunshine the knife. She knew that there wasn't much that she could do with the knife, and that the plane will have crashed by the time she figured something out. But still, it made her feel good to at least be able to do *something*.

She enjoyed the feeling of the wind against her body, knowing that the only thing separating her from a casket was a parachute string. It felt lovely, and it also felt great to be descending with Luther. They were side by side, looking into each other's eyes through goggles while gravity accepted them into its rulebook.

CHAPTER 3

Malcolm was on his way to Fremont County Colorado to go to ADX Florence. ADX Florence was a super maximum security prison that housed the most dangerous criminals in the United States Prison system. They took him in an envoy of armored vehicles, to ensure that no street crew tried to repeat what had happened previously. He sat there patiently as he thought about the life of an extravagant boss that he'd lived in his young life. He didn't regret one second of it, and wouldn't change a thing if given the opportunity.

He was most proud of Kyla. She was one of those women that only came along once in a lifetime; he was just happy that he was able to experience a love like that. They told him that he would never get out of prison again, and he didn't worry about that either. Things he couldn't control had never been of much interest to him. He looked at the six armed officers in the transport van with all of their weapons and bulletproof vests on. They were overly cautious this time around, but he didn't blame them. Better to be safe than sorry.

He thought about Tracy. A woman who had loved him unconditionally and wanted nothing in return. He thought about the things the agent told him she'd went through to try to save him from prison. The attempted murder on Pam was surprising to him, but her being pregnant with his child was even more surprising.

351

He thought about the picture he had been shown of her with her face swollen. Initially, he thought that she was dead, but the agent explained that she had been beaten while in the women's federal holding facility. He felt so bad for her, but he knew that there was nothing that he could do at this point. He was locked down in every possible way, and didn't know how he would ever see daylight again.

He wanted his best friend, Catfish to be happy. He had gone through so much in the past few months and it saddened him to see the look on his face since he had lost his wife. Luther... He wanted him to become the boss that he was supposed to be, and he just prayed that all of them got out of the country so that they could live their lives with no regret. He even wanted Sunshine to have a great life; even though she had betrayed him.

As far as Kyla went, he had no doubt at all about her figuring out a way to get him out of there. She was his ride or die chick to the end, and he would forever be happy that he had a woman like her in his corner. With her he would always have faith in her loyalty. She had proven it time and time again. He knew that faith could move a mountain, but Kyla could move a volcano.

Malcolm was a true boss. A top tier general and a 5 star minimum. He was the absolute last of a dying breed; and he had no regrets about the way that he went out. He'd made history *again*. Had his crew broken out of federal custody after being convicted on all federal charges. He'd made and controlled so much money in the streets, that when they arrested him; the United States went into a recession.

He looked at the wicked set-up of the maximum security prison and closed his eyes in peace. He didn't get to where he was planning to go in life, but it didn't matter. Mentally he was in harmony, and he would never let anyone break his spirit. The last thing he thought about before they entered the maximum security prison compound was his wife, Jennifer. She'd fallen victim to the exact drug that she wanted to leave him over. Her disloyalty and ignorance had really been the turning point of his life. He knew at one point that she loved him, but maybe it had been the wrong type of love.

He didn't want a woman who would love him as a King, if she couldn't love him as a man first.

$~$~$~$~$

Kyla balled her body into a dive so she could catch up to Catfish, but she soon saw that there was no need; he was preparing to pull the string on his parachute. She moved out of the way and watched as his parachute shot out. She exhaled and pulled her string as well.

The five of them landed in an abandoned campground; and in the distance, they heard the loud crash of the plane that they were just in. When it exploded, Kyla flinched from the closure. She had been too emotionally drained to react properly to the stunt that Sunshine had pulled, so she was happy that Luther had taken charge when he did. She looked at Catfish and saw a gleam in his eyes. She knew that if nothing else could brighten his day, death could.

Brink walked up to Kyla with open arms and they all fell into an emotional group hug. The tears leaked out of each of their eyes as a result of the emotional rollercoaster that they were continuing to ride. But even when standing there, Kyla knew that there was still serious business that had to be handled. She broke the embrace and started walking in the direction of the highway.

When she turned around, she noticed that they were following her, so she stopped them. "Just one second guys, I'll be right back."

Catfish stood there staring at Luther while Kyla made her way to the highway. When Luther looked up and saw Catfish staring at him, it immediately startled him. Catfish was a living legend, and Luther only wanted to be accepted into the upper echelon of street bosses. He immediately got into the defensive. "What's up?"

Catfish stared for a second without saying anything, then grinned at Luther. He hadn't said over a couple of words since they'd broken him out of the inmate transport van, but he felt inclined to speak at that moment. "I like what I see out of you, young buck."

Luther instantly relaxed. Having Catfish think so highly of him meant the world to him, and he just wanted to do right by the Bankroll Squad. His chest puffed out a little, and he stood straighter as he absorbed Catfish's words. He smiled, and right before he was about to tell Catfish how much he looked up to him, Catfish grabbed him in a bear hug.

"But you's still a lil' nigga! You a fuckin' youngster and you don't have no gotdamn experience in this here game. What the fuck are you doing in these streets boy? Don't you got a momma to go home to? You see what I'm doing to you boy? I'm manhandling yo' lil' ass. You can't get out of this grip right here until I'm finished with you. This is what will happen to yo punk ass in prison. Why don't you listen to what the fuck I'm trying to teach you boy! Leave this street shit *alone!*"

Brink and Rain both stared at each other in shock. They didn't know what was going on with Catfish, but what they did know, was that they didn't like it one bit. They knew he had been extremely upset because of his wife dying, but he seemed to be taking things to new heights with his new antics. Catfish threw Luther to the ground and walked off.

A few seconds later, Catfish turned around and looked at Luther while he was getting up off of the ground. "Boy you ain't ready to be no fuckin' *boss*. Stop that shit."

Luther, Brink, and Rain stood and watched Catfish walk off into the clearing. Luther had tears behind his eyes that he refused to let fall. They were tears of rage and anger, and he wanted nothing but to pay back Catfish for disrespecting him like that. He swore in his mind that he would not rest until he handled that issue one day.

He had risked his life and freedom time and time again for the Bankroll Squad; he had even helped pull off the inmate transport attack to get Catfish out of prison, and this was the thanks he got? He was so upset that despite how hard he was trying to stop his tears from falling, one of them still managed to seep out of his eye.

An SUV pulled around to the campground going about 50 miles an hour. For that vehicle to be going so fast in a camping area, Luther immediately thought that the FBI had come for them. He pulled out his pistol and aimed it at the SUV as it got closer and closer to the trio. He was too caught off guard for him to take off running, and Brink and Rain must have felt the same because they put their hands up in the air.

The SUV swerved to a stop right beside them and a window rolled down. "Get in this fuckin whip! Let's roll!"

They smiled when they saw Kyla's work. She seemed to have wonder woman powers. Here was a woman who could do it all from stash millions of dollars to carjack SUVs off of the highway. She was high caliber work, and they smiled as they all climbed into the vehicle.

355

"Where is Catfish?" Kyla asked Luther directly.

Luther looked back towards the clearing and didn't see Catfish. He got back out of the SUV and cuffed his hands around his mouth so that he could shout.

"Catfish! Yo Catfish! We're ready to go!"

Luther stood out there for a second waiting on Catfish to respond to him, but nothing happened. After about 5 minutes or so, he opened the door and explained to Kyla the situation that had happened between him and Catfish.

Kyla looked at him curiously. "Why didn't you tell me in the beginning Luther?"

"Because I knew how much you and Malcolm loved and respected Catfish. That's why I tried to call him back just then."

Kyla shook her head. "Yes Luther; me and Malcolm love and respect Catfish, but that is not the same Catfish that we grew to love and respect. So… until he gets his self together, I'll have to move forward. I just don't have time to waste, there are more pressing matters."

Kyla hit the gas on the SUV and they swerved out of the park. Right before they got on the highway, she turned to Rain and stared. She seemed to be in deep thought for a second, then she spoke.

"Rain. Do you know of any *trustworthy* people we can get on our team? I have no other choice but to put together an army right now. I don't know where they're going to have Malcolm housed at, but I know I'm going to need an entire army to try to break him out. I don't give a fuck about the consequences or the punishment."

Rain thought about Kyla's question. She didn't want to answer the question carelessly, because she knew how important the situation had become. It wasn't just Malcolm who was in trouble anymore; now all of them were wanted by the FBI. She thought back to what Sunshine said on the plane, and knew that she may have been honest when she mentioned her home girl Treasure.

"Kyla," Rain spoke confidently, "I know Sunshine is a stupid bitch, but I think it will be a good idea to combine the Bankroll Squad with the Lipstick Clique. It's only three of them, but those women are ruthless killers. The kind of damage that they will inflict will have you thinking that it's 3,000 of them. Let's go to Houston and speak to them."

Kyla considered Rain's words as she thought back to how Sunshine had betrayed her and Malcolm. She sent a silent prayer asking God to protect her from the things that she was about to do. She sent another prayer so that Malcolm would have a guardian angel around him no matter where they decided to place him. She needed her man healthy, and she would make sure that she got exactly what she needed.

She glanced at herself in the mirror and sighed. She knew that she was the spiritual epitome of a bad bitch. Not a bad bitch because of her stripper's body; and not a bad bitch because of her cover girl's face. She was the ultimate; the Queen of all Boss Bitches. She knew this was true because a bad bitch couldn't be judged by the amount of friends and followers she had; but by the level and the magnitude of her enemies.

She was the baddest.

$~$~$~$~$

Skye grabbed her duffle bag off of the kitchen counter and threw the strap over her shoulder. She had on a black and cream skirt against her bright yellow skin; along with matching black and cream stilettos. She had long flowing hair and plump, suggestive lips. Although her and Milan were identical twins; Skye had done everything in her power to set herself apart from her sister.

She had continuously tried to figure out ways to separate herself, and none of the things had worked. Finally, she came up with a way to fix everything once and for all, and she did it all from the kitchen table.

When she knew she'd already eaten too much food, she ignored it and ate even more. She hated not being unique, so she would have done anything to change her appearance; and this was the most satisfying way for her. She now stood 5'4 and weighed 174 pounds, while her sister was 5'4 and weighed 122 pounds.

She enjoyed the fact that she weighed more; and sometimes it really came in handy. She didn't have to worry about people thinking that they could just over-power and run over her, and she certainly received less yap from other bitches.

The last time she'd been in a confrontation, she'd drug a rail thin chick who thought she was a model from one end of the club to the next. She beat the dog shit out of that lady for talking reckless to the Lipstick Clique. Out of the three, she was the most physically powerful woman in the Lipstick Clique, and had proved it time and time again.

Treasure came downstairs with another duffle bag on her shoulder. "Where's Milan at Skye?"

Skye looked down the hall trying to see if she saw Milan. "Uhm... She should have been out of there by-"

Just as she was finishing her sentence, Milan came sprinting down the hallway. "Hey you guys! Come look at what I just found! You won't believe this shit!"

The three women hurriedly ran back down the hallway, thinking that this could be the score of their lives. They ran by several expensive paintings and sculptures and stopped when they saw the room that Milan had just showed them. Milan smiled and pointed. "Look at all this shit!"

Cocaine. More cocaine than they had ever seen in their lives. White bricks were stacked up on top of each other in columns and were the only things visible in the entire room.

"It's like *thousands* of these shits!" Skye said as she went in and grabbed one. She looked at the inscription in the middle and knew that this was probably their very last shipment. It had *D.C.* stamped directly in the center of the packaging.

She glanced back at Treasure, who was standing there thinking. "Skye... Milan... you know we don't sell no fucking drugs. I mean, sure this is a helluva' come up, but how the hell could this shit benefit us? We may as well let them do all the work, then come back and get the fuckin' money when the shit is sold. That's what we do, get it easy and quick; not struggle and shit."

Milan's shoulder slumped over. "I understand what you're saying Treasure, but I wasn't actually talking about selling the cocaine. I was talking about making a statement. To let the streets know that the Lipstick Clique is here! Fuck everybody! So let's do it!"

Treasure liked Milan, whose personality was the complete opposite of her twin sister; but she knew that sometimes she could get a little

359

irrational with her thoughts. She was always looking to be in the spotlight; while Treasure and Skye were always trying to figure out ways to stay *out* of the spotlight.

"Milan," Treasure said, "that shit won't benefit us at all. Leave it where it stands and let's get the fuck up out of here before the Dynasty Cartel comes back. You didn't find no money?"

Milan took the bag off of her shoulder and set it on the floor in front of Treasure. She unzipped it, exposing what looked like about 10 pounds of weed.

Treasure stepped back for a second and looked at Skye, who could only shake her head. "That's what you found of value Milan?"

Milan's eyebrows squinched up as she glanced up at Treasure. "And just what the fuck is wrong with my find? It's *weed,* the shit I like to smoke. We have money everywhere, didn't think we needed more of that; but this here weed is what the fuck *I* needed in my life."

Treasure couldn't believe how Milan was acting at that moment. She made a mental note to deal with her before things got out of hand, or before she started to make mistakes that could endanger the entire Clique.

"Fuck it, let's go! Them niggas will probably be home soon. We gotta get the fuck out of here!" Treasure said as she turned to exit the room. They had their car parked on the next block so they would have to jog through the trees to reach it. They all ran through the house until they arrived at the back entrance. They turned the lights off and made their exit.

When they got outside and saw that the coast was clear; they all exhaled. "O.K.," Skye said, "I'm a big girl, so I know if I'm ready to start running through the trees, ya'll asses better be ready as well!"

Each of them removed their stilettos and replaced them with a pair of running shoes out of their bags. Treasure laughed, and started sprinting through the trees. Skye was a big girl, but she could run! She was keeping up with Treasure with ease, duffle bags and all. They finally arrived at their car and exhaled. But when they looked behind them, Milan wasn't there.

"What the fuck just happened!" Skye said as she stared at Treasure. She looked back again for her twin sister and didn't see her coming. She was pissed that Milan had decided to go back for that fuckin cocaine when it was time to go. "Ugh! I'm sick of this bitch! Let's just go Treasure, let this ho learn her lesson!"

Treasure stared at Skye in shock. She would never leave another member of her clique behind no matter what the situation was. That was a rule, and one that she thought each of them had also considered a rule. "Skye, you know I would never do nothing like that. If you want to leave, you can; but I'm going to wait on your *sister* as if she was my own."

Skye smiled at her. "That's what I love about you Treasure. You're always so damn loyal. I never see a moment that disloyalty enters your thoughts. That's amazing. No, I don't want to leave my sister; I just want her to get herself together. Let's go get her."

When Treasure and Skye turned to head back, Milan ran through the trees like a bat out of hell. "Whooooo! Hahahaha!"

"What the fuck is wrong with you sis?" Skye screamed at her sister in confusion.

Milan ignored her and ran straight to the car. She opened the door and climbed into the backseat. Treasure and Skye stood there staring at each other, lost about the situation. Treasure shrugged her shoulders and climbed into the driver's seat. She knew that she shouldn't be driving because she was a woman who was wanted by federal and state authorities all over the United States. She was blazing hot. Ever since her escape from prison with her best friend at the time, she had been on the wanted list; and becoming more and more of a priority as the days went by.

"Sis!" Skye screamed with her strong, booming voice. "What the fuck took yo' ass so long? We were about to head back over there to get you. What were you doing?"

Milan giggled and reached into her duffle bag. "This!"

Treasure and Skye both glanced back to see what she was holding in her hand. It was a tube of lipstick.

"Lipstick?" Skye asked her sister.

"Yea Milan! On their door, I put *Lipstick Clique you fucks!*"

Treasure was appalled. "You did *what?* Why the *fuck* would you do something as stupid as that? They had no idea that we knew where they stayed at, and now you just *tell* them that it was us? That's *dumb*. I gotta go erase that shit immediately!"

Treasure opened the door, but Milan stopped her. "No Treasure, they were just pulling up to the street when I took off running, so let's just get the fuck up out of here."

Treasure sat there not believing that Milan had put them all in some deep shit. The only thing they were supposed to be doing, was getting four times the amount of money that they dumped on the Dynasty Cartel. They stunted, loved stunting; and loved sending messages to other crews, but they were no fools.

They had managed to give away $40,000 in cash at the club to Diaz and Rally; and had robbed them of almost $200,000 in cash immediately afterwards, not counting the pounds of *weed* that Milan seemed to feel was so important. Treasure shook her head and spit out of her window in disgust. She started the vehicle up and left the block.

The more she listened to the laughter in Milan's voice coming from the backseat, the more it brightened her spirit. Initially, she was upset that Milan had dared to autograph a fuckin crime scene; but she knew that Milan and Skye were good women and would stand by any consequence that would arise from it. Treasure glanced at Milan in the rearview mirror and saw the laughter and joy on her face, and smiled. She glanced at Skye, who was also smiling; shr felt a strong level of pride in these two women. She sighed, and took advantage of the silence by summing up the actions of the night.

"This is life, and sometimes you lose some and win some. But fuck it though, as long as the outcome is income."

CHAPTER 4

Clack! The ink pen holder broke into two different sections when Jennifer hit Pam with it. It was far weaker than Jen expected it to be, and it angered her that it didn't kill her like it was supposed to. As soon as it made contact, Pam started screaming.

"Ahhhhhhhh! Help! Nurse! Helllp!"

Realizing that she was about to be in some serious shit, she tried to hurry and run back over to her bed when she slipped on a piece of the broken pen holder and fell to the floor. She tried her best to get up and back to the bed unnoticed, but was frozen in place when she saw the shoes from three nurses and a doctor. She knew she was finished and that there was nothing she could do about it. She was caught red-handed.

"That bitch just tried to kill a federal agent!" Pam screamed. "Contact the authorities now! Either she gets turned in or I sue this hospital for everything from the fucking alcohol pads to the vending machines!"

$~$~$~$~$

Jennifer Powers was amazed at how fast they had taken her to jail. She had been in this same situation before, and she hated every second of it. They took her through the entrance and began the process of entering her back into the database. When it was time for her to give up her fingerprints again, the lady doing the prints recognized her from the last time.

"Hey Mrs. Powers. I thought you told me that you were going to stay out of trouble this time sweetie?"

Jennifer closed her eyes and turned her head, attempting to avoid the eye contact from the older lady that she respected and admired. She felt horrible that she'd had to go back against her word with this woman who'd clearly believed in her the first time. She knew that no matter what she said, nothing would change the fact that she was back in jail with the same lady doing the same fingerprints.

"Ms. Sukis, I know I told you I was going to change; and I've been working on that. I honestly didn't mean to come back in here, but once again; I've made a mistake. I swear on everything that this is truly the last time of me ever, *ever* coming back to jail."

Ms. Sukis smiled at her as she continued booking her into the fingerprint processing station. Ms. Sukis didn't really care for any particular criminal's story; she just cared for the overall good of the women that came through there, and wanted them to do so much better for themselves. She processed the last fingerprint and led Jennifer to a holding cell.

Jennifer stepped in and looked through the bars at Ms. Sukis. Her eyes were pleading for help, but Ms. Sukis was in no position to help her in any way. "Ms. Sukis," Jennifer said, "I don't want you to feel sorry for me or anything… But could you please place me in a nice jail unit? Like you did last time? Send me to one where no one is fighting or angry."

365

Ms. Sukis laughed involuntarily. She knew it was more pitiful than it was funny; but she didn't quite know how to express pity in a sound. She locked the cell door and placed the keys back inside her pocket. She looked Jennifer in the eyes before she answered.

"Jennifer… here is what I can tell you about your situation… For one, you won't have to worry about going to jail." Jennifer smiled the brightest smile she could muster. "Wait one second though… I haven't told you the bad news yet… The reason you won't have to worry about me separating you from the normal jail house people is because you've separated yourself. Your offense is federal, so you'll only be around federal inmates."

Ms. Sukis locked the cell and turned to leave. Jennifer stood at the cell flabbergasted as she watched her walk down the hall and turn the corner. Just as Jennifer was about to sit down, she heard a loud commotion in the hallway.

"Get the fuck off of me! Get the fuck off of me you bastards! Leave me the fuck alone!! Nooooo!" The lady was in obvious stress and seemed to be raging mad. "Get the fuck of of me!" Jennifer glanced away, but refocused in on the situation when she heard them bringing the lady in her direction. "Get offff of meeeee!" The lady was fighting, pulling, squirming and kicking. The officers were struggling to contain her like she was a wild bull running loose. "Get awaaaaaayyyyy! Get awwwaaaaaaaay!" The lady continued screaming in desperation.

The officers got in front of Jennifer's cell and pulled out a key. Jennifer felt bad for the lady because of the way that they were handling her. It hurt her, but she tried to ignore the situation. She started fidgeting with a string that was hanging off the side of her pants while she tried to calm herself down. Anytime she saw negative physical activity going on, it always seemed to make her nervous. She took a deep breath and looked up to see what the lady was doing who they'd just thrown in there.

When she looked up, she saw a swollen face; as if the lady had just been on the receiving end of one of the worst beat downs ever. Her face was swollen on both sides, and her eyes… looked familiar.

"Yea bitch! What's that shit you was talking in the visitation room that day? Yea, you thought I forgot it didn't you? Coming in front of me and Malcolm talking about how good your *ass* looked. I *stabbed* that shit in the parking lot, but I'm not finished with you yet!"

Jennifer's heart dropped through the floor as she watched Tracy's fist cock back and swing.

$~$~$~$~$

When they arrived in Houston, reality set in. True, they wanted to get Malcolm out of federal prison; but how would it be this time? Kyla drove a little slower as she attempted to formulate a plan that made sense and was still fair for the Bankroll Squad, who had already sacrificed so much. She pulled over at a *Fiesta* grocery store and into a vacant parking space.

"O.K. guys, here's the deal. We have money that is being wired to BPI; The Bank of the Philippine Islands, as we speak. This was set up that way because there is no extradition treaty between the US and the Philippines. We also have extended Bankroll Squad family ties over there. I have a lot of good girls over in Boracay. And let me tell you this… Boracay has the whitest sand on a beach that you will ever see, as well as the clearest waters. It is a truly amazing work of beauty."

367

Kyla took a deep breath before continuing "I told you all of that to say this… I want you all to walk down by the bus stop and stand there for a moment while you think about these statements:

I can either meet you in Boracay, or you can accompany me on a suicide mission to try to break Malcolm out of whatever situation he's in. You have to think realistically about this. Don't do it just because you think you're being loyal. It's not about loyalty anymore. Now it's about being loyal to your own life. If we try this, all of us could pretty much die. I'm doing it because I love Malcolm just about more than I love myself. None of you are me, so you couldn't possibly feel what I feel.

There are no hard feelings regardless of which decision you make. But I'm asking you all to think and choose carefully.

There are accounts for each of you in Boracay, and I will see you when I arrive; if I arrive. Please remember that this is entirely a life decision that you will need to make on your own. Do not let anyone influence you, and please realize that if your heart isn't in it; you will only make matters worse for me. Do yourselves a favor and go to Boracay and wait on Malcolm and me. Take that walk now; I'll wait here for 15 minutes."

Kyla unlocked the doors on the vehicle and looked away as the members of the Bankroll Squad got out. When all of the doors were closed, she locked them back and stared at her surroundings carefully. She knew that she was a wanted woman, and so were the members that had just gotten out of the vehicle. Their faces had surely been plastered all over the news by now, and she hoped that they each possessed the perceptiveness to be aware that they were no longer just common citizens.

She glanced at her watch and saw that she had 12 minutes left to see if she would be going solo or not. She knew that what she was doing was necessary. There was no way that she was going to risk trying to rescue Malcolm again with people who had interests in the wrong area. She closed her eyes and reflected on the activities that had just taken place. She knew that she would need to get to a television soon so that she could see how out of proportion the Feds had blown the scenario. For the time being, she could only imagine.

$~$~$~$~$

Rain, Luther, and Brink stood there at the transit bus stop and tried to blend in with the crowd. They watched the cars and trucks ride up and down the street, living the free life. Luther put his hands on his head and stretched while he thought about the importance of the decision he was about to make. He knew how long he'd patiently waited to become a boss, and deep inside, that's exactly what he wanted to be. But at the same time, he wondered whether voluntarily putting himself in harm's way would be justified as a boss decision or an amateur mistake. He understood how Kyla felt about Malcolm, because they were lovers. He on the other hand wasn't in love, so his emotions couldn't speak for him like hers did.

Rain stared at the pavement while she thought about the powerful words that Kyla had just spoken. She loved Kyla wholeheartedly, but after the situation with Sunshine and after seeing Catfish's wife's brains blown out; living that lifestyle was hardly something that interested her at that moment. She'd worked hard and had done what was asked of her for the Bankroll Squad; she wouldn't feel bad at all about leaving and going to the Philippines. She had initially been contacted by Kyla to work in a strip club and take a few clients; so pulling incredible stunts wasn't exactly in her job description. White sand and blue waters sounded exactly like something that she could use in her life. That, along with a mani/pedi.

Brink stood alone and reminisced about all of the great times he'd shared with Kyla. He had known her for so long, and she was one of the greatest people that he had ever run across. However, he felt like she was doing too much. She had already risked her life to rescue them the first time, and for that, he was grateful; but to do it a second time sounded like madness. But... he still loved her more than any of the other two people that stood there at that bus stop with him. He had been flying her overseas for Malcolm for years, and he would never be able to live with himself if he saw something bad happen to Kyla. So he made up his mind right there at that moment.

The three of them looked at each other in silence. The silence, along with their hesitant movements told the entire story. You had winners and losers in life. Then you had people that won, who wanted to play the game again just to see what a loss would feel like. And none of them was that person. They wanted to continue winning.

Brink walked first. He took about 5 steps towards Kyla's direction, and stood by a trash can for a second. At the next break in traffic, he sprinted straight across the street away from Kyla. When he arrived on the other side of the street, he stood there and stared back at Kyla with sadness in his eyes. Kyla stared back at Brink, and shed one tear. No matter how strong a person is, it was impossible to not feel some sort of emotion when a person who you thought had your back, did not.

It was a sad moment for Kyla. Her and Brink had done so much; had become such good friends, that there was no way she would have guessed that it would have been him that wanted to distance himself from her cause. She'd always known him as a ride or die fighter, and refused to think of him as anything else or less. True, she'd told them that there would be no hard feelings, but once reality hit; she was a little disturbed. She sucked it up quickly though, because the whole plan had been her call. After wiping the lone tear, she decided that if that's what makes Brink happy, then he fully deserved it.

She watched as he walked off into the distance, on his way to freedom and happiness and wondered how long it would be before it was her and Malcolm's turn. She exhaled.

Luther and Rain stood there staring at each other. The move by Brink to walk off and abandon Kyla for this mission when he had been one of the original members of the Bankroll Squad certainly had Rain shook. She looked at Luther for help and guidance, and saw love in his eyes, and ambition in his smile.

"Rain, tell me this... Are you with me or not?"

Rain stood there for a moment, not responding. She stared at the sharp glossed sheen in his eyes, and knew that he was destined to shine brighter than bright. "Yes Luther, I am with you baby."

Luther turned his body to face hers and continued. "You're with me no matter which decision I make?"

Rain smiled at him. "Yes I am. You know I can't leave you Luther. I think I'm really falling for you."

Luther leaned in to kiss her. It was a passionate kiss that seemed to carry nervous energy with it.

Luther stood there and thought about how Brink had just walked off without saying another word. From that, he gathered that Brink had lots of love for Kyla, but he had more love for his own life; and wasn't willing to give up one for the other. He felt like Brink had contributed enough to the Bankroll Squad, and was now ready to enjoy the fruits of his labor. Then he thought about how much money was awaiting him in the Philippines.

Millions of dollars that they had all collectively grinded and took chances for was all sitting in an account in his name, and by damn he was about to go get it. He had a beautiful woman willing to ride with him all the way to the end of the earth, and he was going to go spend his damn money and live his damn life however he chose. He put his hand around Rain's and walked to the same trash can that Brink walked to and stopped. He glanced at Rain to see the expression on her face, and saw that she was all smiles.

"Are you ready to go to the Philippines Rain?"

"Of course I am baby."

Away from Kyla, they crossed the street in the same manner as Brink. They stood on the other side of the road and looked at Kyla as she got out of the car and stood there with her hands on the sides of her hip. The expression on Kyla's face was one of a five star general. One who didn't mind losing a few soldiers if it meant that she could win the war. But her facial expression didn't reflect the sadness and disappointment that was heavy in her heart.

Luther and Rain stared back at Kyla and then turned their backs. "Rain, I'm so happy that we started talking. It's the greatest thing that has ever happened to me."

Rain stopped in her tracks and smiled. "I'm happy that I started talking to you as well; if I hadn't, I would have never known how fake and *lame* you were. Kick rocks to the Philippines you weak ass nigga." She turned her back to Luther and jogged back across the street to a surprised Kyla.

"Wh-Wh-What hap- happened?" Kyla hadn't meant to stutter, but it was nothing that she could do about it. Her blood was pumping at twice its normal pace, and she was trying to calm down a bit.

"What happened is only what was supposed to happen. You convinced everything fake to go be fake together. You know I'm down with you no matter what girl! I'm just a real ass bitch. I don't need any special titles… I don't need to be labeled a boss… I don't even need a dollar to my name, but I will *always* be a *real bitch*."

Kyla told herself that she wouldn't cry again, but at that moment it couldn't be helped. When she saw the passion start leaking out of Rain's eyes, tears started flowing down her face as well. They stood in the parking lot of the grocery store and hugged each other while onlookers drove by and admired their beautiful physiques. After a while, they became aware that they were being watched and got back into the vehicle.

"Rain… I know you're a real ass bitch, but I don't want you to do this just to prove that you're real. You'll always be that…"

Rain didn't respond. She just leaned back in her seat and put her seatbelt on. "I have an idea Kyla!" She said, ignoring Kyla's last statement.

Kyla smiled at her. "O.K. What's your idea?"

"Let's ride to the southside of Houston. If we're planning on getting information about Malcolm Powers and rescuing him, there is only one

373

set of people that can help us at this point."

Kyla looked at her curiously. "Who? The FBI?"

"No silly, The Lipstick Clique."

CHAPTER 5

Rally and Diaz were jubilant when they arrived home. It was hard to have been given thousands of dollars in cash at once for nothing and be sad about it. They were all smiles. In order for them to celebrate, they paid two prostitutes to come back to the mansion with them. They parked in their usual parking place and locked the doors. Rally lit a Newport and held the smoke as long as possible. When he couldn't hold it anymore, he blew it into the face of one of the prostitutes and burst out laughing.

Diaz saw it and started laughing as well. He took his own cigarette out and tried to do the same thing when the other girl took her hand and smashed the cigarette into his face. Everyone started laughing except for Diaz.

"Fuckin' bitch! I oughta' punch you in your fuckin' lip! I would do it if I weren't planning on sticking my dick in it."

They walked around the paved walkway and approached the mansion's entrance. When they got close, they realized immediately that something was wrong. On the ground, they saw a clear plastic top, and knew that it hadn't been there when they left. Rally squinted his eyes, trying to figure out what it was, when one of the girls finally picked it up.

"A lipstick top." The brunette said as she handed it over to Rally.

375

"You sure your wife or girlfriend isn't going to burst in here? I don't want any trouble, I can't afford it; I'm already on probation."

"Shush your fuckin' trap slut!" Rally said as he snatched the top and looked at it.

How the fuck did a lipstick top get on my walkway? Maybe it blew in from the street.

Diaz was still wiping the ashes off of his nose and lips when they turned the corner. Standing at the entrance of the mansion, their jaws dropped to the floor. *Lipstick Clique you fucks* was written in bright pink lipstick across the dark steel door. Rally immediately pulled out his pistol and pointed it at the two girls. "Who the fuck did you tell, bitches?!"

The girls looked at each other in confusion while they held their palms up facing Rally. "We didn't tell anyone anything sir." The brunette said in absolute terror.

"You liar!" Diaz said as he grabbed the girl by the neck and started choking her. "You definitely told someone in the club that you were coming with us. That's why you asked for our address and went off to the back bitch!"

The blonde haired girl started hitting Diaz on the arm. "No! No! No! You bastard, get off of her!" She kept tugging, but his grip was too tight; so in desperation, she pulled out her mace and sprayed him in the face.

"Arrgghhh! Arrrghhh! Stupid bitch, this shit burns!"

Rally was about to pull the trigger, but the brunette started explaining. "Th- th- th-… The o- only re- reason that I g- g- go to th- th- the b- b- back, is when I… have a- a- client. I- I have to.. write d- d- down th- th- address…" She couldn't even finish her statement because her tears drowned her out. She was upset that Rally had a pistol in her face, and even more pissed that Diaz had just tried to kill her.

The blonde wrapped her arms around her friend and spoke up for her. "What she's trying to say is that we don't have anyone to look after us. We don't have pimps or anyone that even knows where to start if anything were to happen to us. That's why she goes to the back and adds our new clients' addresses to the Big Diary that me and her keep at the strip club. We keep it locked, but if something were to happen, they have instructions to open it in whichever way works."

A chill ran through Rally's body as he thought about the mistake that he almost made. If he would have killed those women a few moments earlier, he would surely be headed off to prison for the rest of his life since his name was in their diary. He closed his eyes and took a deep breath, and while he was releasing it; he suddenly remembered.

The Lipstick Clique. Those were the chicks that had given him and Diaz that bag full of money at the club. His hustler's instincts kicked into overdrive, and he sprinted into the house and up the stairs. He went to the room where he kept his safe, turned on the light, and saw a big smiley face on the wall next to an open and empty safe. Pistol in hand, he hurried down the stairs, almost knocking Diaz over along the way. He ran down the hall to his converted game room.

He had a backup safe in there with the cash that he owed his cocaine connect for the next shipment, but when he turned the light on, he knew he was in trouble. This safe was located in the floor and was supposed to be hidden from plain view. There was supposed to be no way that anyone would know which part of the floor came up and revealed a safe. But that night, it was wide open.

He walked up to it slowly, thinking that there would be no money remaining inside of his safe. Surely they would have wiped that one out if they wiped the other one out. But when he stopped at it, he realized that he was wrong. There *was* some money in there.

Two one hundred dollar bills with smiley faces drawn in lipstick.

He was about to have a panic attack. Rally hadn't been robbed in so long, that he didn't even recognize the feelings that this robbery was bringing to him. He staggered, and caught his balance as he backed away from the safe without looking.

"Ouch Rally, watch it!" Diaz said as he rubbed his shoulder from the minor collision. "What's going on in here?"

But Rally was gone. He ran down the hall and through the kitchen at full speed. Being robbed of his money was one thing, but if he lost that shipment of cocaine that he had just purchased; it could mean *death*. He couldn't remember running that fast in all the days of his life. He was a cheetah about his money, and he didn't stop until he made it to his office.

He kicked the door in and closed his eyes, fully expecting the worst. When he opened them again, he could breathe a fulfilling sigh of relief. His shipment of cocaine was still intact. Nothing had been disturbed in that room it seemed, except for one minor problem.

There was a huge smiley face drawn across his white wall, and the words underneath the smiley face absolutely made his stomach turn. *Lipstick Clique you fuck!* He couldn't believe that a small ass group of women had just taunted him by breaking into his home! He took a mental photo of the wall and left the room. He ran down the hall with his pistol still in his hand. "Is everything alright Rally?" Diaz asked him, concerned; although he could tell from the look on Rally's face that something had gone haywire.

Rally looked at the two prostitutes and sighed. "Let's drop these bitches off. It is going to be a very red day."

$~$~$~$~$

Catfish was in a stupor. He was disappointed and confused, and didn't know which of the emotions were stronger than the other. He was hurt. Not because of what Sunshine had done, not because of Luther's young ass; but he was hurt because of what happened to his wife while he was locked up. He would have never imagined in his wildest dreams that he would have to lose his wife for the Bankroll Squad. If that would have been clear to him in the beginning, there was no way he would have joined.

The night he got into an argument with Luther and stormed off, he went and made a place for himself to sleep on top of a pile of raked straw. He laid there throughout the night, ignoring the bugs and sounds of the night while he thought about his life and what had become of it. He had time to focus on everything during those hours, and among the things that were the most important was his betrayal of Malcolm. He'd betrayed him in court, allowed his emotions to get in the way of his decision making; and one thing led to another.

He said a small prayer and apologized as if Malcolm could hear him. "Yo… I'm sorry about everything bro. Me and you have been friends for years now; and you know how much respect I have always had for

379

you. I just want you to know, that in case you thought anything different, that it's wrong. I was going through a tough time bro. A real tough time. Even to this moment I still haven't gained my footing back, but that's still no excuse for me to cause you to fall too. I'm sorry bro… I'm sorry…"

Catfish had killed and injured many people in life without remorse. He had done all the dirt that the government had accused him of, and more. He was ruthless. A person who would kill the world to protect his family, and kill himself as well if he thought he was a threat. He was the perfect right hand man to Malcolm; the absolute best when it came to pistol play. He had been killing people for so long, that out of boredom he would do something random like sew a person's mouth shut. His reputation was deep and strong, and his presence and stature was his reputation's shadow. Until lately…

Lately he had made a variety of flawed decisions and that's what was eating at his heart. In his entire existence, he had never made worse decisions. He laid there staring into the darkness for a couple more minutes, and then, before daylight hit, he started walking. He didn't have a particular destination in mind, but he wanted to fix himself. He wanted to get himself together. He wanted to…

He thought about Jennifer and a sudden pain gripped his entire torso. He had met Jennifer before she met Malcolm, but had kept it a secret because he didn't know how his family and friends would take it. He knew he would be judged, and his temper wouldn't allow him to tolerate that. He ended up letting her go, and coincidentally; she met Malcolm. Malcolm was a man who wanted what he wanted and didn't care what anyone else thought. He admired him for having the strength that he could never muster up, and he was sorry that he had never told Malcolm about him and Jennifer. His only goal was to stay as far away from Jen and Malcolm as remotely possible. She didn't even need to know that him and Malcolm were friends. And it had worked out that way.

Had she been his wife, he would have been killed her.

He kept walking until he saw an exit that claimed to have everything from the Waffle House to Wal-Mart. He knew he wasn't too far away from the city of Houston, but no matter how close he was, he wouldn't be effective with his mind all over the place.

He walked past Starbucks and McDonalds and kept walking until he saw an independent restaurant. It was a small place that served food and coffee and had a friendly waitress. That was the type of setting that he would forever be familiar with. He went in and sat down. There was a long line waiting to order food, and he didn't feel like standing in it. He looked around the shop and caught his reflection in the mirror. It scared him.

Hair was all over his face and neck growing wildly. His lips were chapped and there were pieces of straw all over his body. He looked a hot mess and he knew it. He glanced around and saw that people were staring at him, so he tried to go to a more private table. He went to the back and found that it was the same amount of people back there, except they were preoccupied with something. They weren't staring at him, so he went and sat down.

When he looked up, he saw what they *were* staring at, and it made him sick to his stomach.

"Authorities tell us that the leader of the dangerous street gang, the Bankroll Squad, has been transported to a super maximum security prison. He will be placed on immediate lockdown and his visitation

381

rights are revoked for the beginning of his stay except for his lawyer. This all stems from the double murder prison break-out by suspected members of the Bankroll Squad after the gang leader lost at federal trial. Two more convicted felons are loose and on the run right now, here are their mugshots. The first one…"

Catfish panicked. He didn't have a gun on him and he knew shit was about to get crazy. All the sadness he had in his heart instantly flew out of the window when he thought about what the hell was going on. He watched as his face flashed across the news, but he stayed calm because in the mugshot; he didn't have a bit of hair on his face. There was still a chance that no one would recognize him.

"There he is right there!" An older white lady pointed him out, less than two minutes after the telecast went off.

The older white lady's young son went and held her hand. "Sit down Mama, that's not him. You know all of them look alike."

Catfish looked outside and saw a redneck's pickup truck parked right outside of the diner. There was a hunting rifle in the storage glass right behind the driver's seat, and he knew that he had to have it. He got up and walked out the door, as he went out, a few people started whispering and pointing. He made a mental note to see what the pointing was about when he got back in the restaurant.

He forcefully opened the door on the stranger's truck and grabbed the rifle off of the display. There were two boxes of shells in the seat, so he grabbed them all and took them with him back inside of the diner. He went back to his table and loaded, and cocked his stolen rifle.

"Everyone put the phones on the fuckin' table!" He bellowed across the diner. Seeing what Malcolm was going through on the news inspired him all over again. In that brief amount of time, he had gone straight back to being the old Catfish; the old thirst for violence and danger was back. He was already convicted and headed to prison for life, so he felt like he might as well break as many laws as he could while he had the opportunity.

"Bitch, get your hands out the air, this aint no robbery or no concert. This right here is a massacre."

He estimated that there was about 16 people in there, and he was about to let them all have it. He had a new motto in life. *Fuck everybody.*

He started off with the white lady that was doing all the talking. He took his rifle and aimed it at her head with arrogance dripping off of his shadow. Without further thought, he pulled the trigger and blew her brains out of the other side of her head. After he did it, he glanced down at her brain matter and burst out laughing like a mad man as he kept shooting. He had murder on his mind, and nothing short of his wife coming back to life would stop him from laying people out. It was about to go down. He didn't need guidance when it came to this line of work. It was what he did.

He thought about the money that he had been blessed to receive from Malcolm and realized that he no longer had it. He hadn't worried about money in so long, that he had forgotten how to get ahold of it. And he knew he would need a few dollars to get a few things done in Houston. He thought about Kyla, and felt horrible about how he'd been acting. He hoped she was making the right choices by herself; and if she wasn't it would be fine because he was on his way to track her and the rest of the Bankroll Squad down.

383

He went behind the counter, grabbed a bag, filled it with money and snatched 2 glazed donuts. He filled up a cup with black coffee and walked out of the diner. He sat in the pickup truck and enjoyed his breakfast while he watched the police roll up the street. He doubted that they had any idea of what was going on, so he calmly pulled off as they pulled in. They would have to examine the scene, and by the time they realized that they needed to search for that pickup truck, he would be in another stolen vehicle. *Fuck it, I'm on one.*

CHAPTER 6

"O.K. muthafuckas! This is a regular routine for us, so please don't try nothing stupid. We will blow your head off of your neck round this bitch!" Treasure commanded as she walked around one of the Dynasty Cartel's main trap houses with a chopper in her hand. She was not through with Diaz and Rally's arrogant asses, and she was going to make sure that she made her statement to them.

"What the fuck you looking at nigga?" Skye bellowed at one of the guys who was sitting back and groping himself while he was watching her. She couldn't believe that a guy had gotten low enough to play with himself during a robbery, but if he liked it; she loved it.

Wham! The high-powered rifle sounded off as she put a bullet through his hand and smiled at the horrified expression on his face. Blood was leaking into a small puddle, and he was squirming in it like a fish out of water. It was a beautiful masterpiece in Skye's eyes, and she had almost completely tuned out her surroundings to admire the effects of the bullet from her rifle.

Milan walked over and slapped Skye on the shoulder. "Come on bitch with all this foolishness!"

Skye glared at her like the maniac that she was. "What the fuck you mean *foolishness?* After all the dumb ass shit you did, and now you got the nerve to call what *I* do foolish? Bitch please, go hang yourself."

385

Treasure spotted the sibling rivalry and tension between Milan and Skye, and knew that she would have to be a mediator; as well as push to proceed with the robbery. Skye and Milan argued a lot with each other, but this was the first time that they'd done such a thing in the midst of a robbery. It was terrifying, because not only were they putting each other's lives in danger; they were endangering hers as well. She did not like that.

"Ya'll bring ya'll asses on! Let's get this money!"

Skye and Milan rolled their eyes at each other and went back to business. They pulled small folded bags out of their pockets and went straight to the tables. There were piles on top of piles of dope money and they were helping themselves to it. Treasure went to another table in the back and saw even more dope money. Only this pile was more organized and had larger bill denominations. There were stacks of hundreds everywhere.

"You two! Come here!" Treasure screamed. Skye and Milan stopped bagging up the money and ran to the back table. Along the way, Milan spotted a guy reaching for his pistol all the way across the room. She wasted no time and took no chances. *Tat-ta-tat-ta-ta-t-at-a-at-at-a-t-at-at-at-tat.*

She was only aiming for the person who was the most dangerous, but she ended up clearing the whole wall off. She had killed 4 people in less than a minute, and had done them all just so that she could get one person. Skye and Treasure both looked at their family member and shook their head. They loved that she was real and ride or die 'til the end, but they knew that she sometimes got a little carried away when it wasn't necessary.

Milan ignored the looks that Skye and Treasure were giving her, and stopped in front of the table with them. Her jaw dropped when she saw the amount of money that was just sitting on the table. It wasn't that the Lipstick Clique didn't already have money stacked up for months; it was the fact that this was looking like their *biggest score,* and that had them all in a daze. They had been grinding and stacking millions in robbery results, but they had never grabbed a million or two at once. This was sure to be it.

Treasure thought about how they could do that particular job and give it a break for a minute, but Milan was thinking about how much her name would be ringing in the streets once they handled a job like this. Surely it would solidify her as one of the realest bitches in the streets handling those pistols. She knew no one would compare to her in any manner.

She would lay down the whole hospital just to knock off a nurse who had wronged her. She was deeply vindictive and had revenge on her mind even as she slept. Milan was very spiteful, and was always doing things to try to touch that very last nerve. When she had touched that nerve; only then was she happy.

Skye and Milan started sliding the money off of the table and into the bags while Treasure continued to scour the trap house. She could tell that it wasn't just any ordinary trap house by the way that it was set up. There was expensive furniture and flat screens; flat top stoves and black steel refrigerators. Most places of crime were as grimy as possible, so when the police came to kick the door in; whatever they seized wouldn't be a big loss in terms of value.

But this spot had PlayStation 3s, computers, smooth glass tables and beautiful, bright chandeliers. It didn't add up to her that this would be a house that a person sold dope out of. She decided to go find out. She looked for the guy in charge, and saw him sitting on the floor by a table with his eyes closed. She knew that he had to be in charge by the way that everyone looked at him when they initially kicked the door in. It was like he was their leader and even in a moment of distress, he kept a cool expression on his face.

Treasure nudged him with the rifle and motioned for him to get up. She pointed to the wall and held the rifle out as he made his way over to it. The man looked at Treasure with a smile in his eyes; looked at her as if he knew something that she didn't; as if the robbery that was taking place was irrelevant and a waste of his time.

Treasure found herself getting angry very quickly at the guy's arrogant expression. "What the fuck is your issue? What do ya'll sell out of this house?"

The guy didn't respond, he only looked at her as if she was the worst thing that God had ever invented in the history of life. Irritated, Skye walked up to where Treasure was standing and shook her head. She grabbed her pistol, held it at the guy's penis and started smiling. The guy got immediately nervous when he saw Skye walk up.

He'd seen the work she'd put in earlier when she shot a hole in a man's dick and stood there admiring that shit. He would rather lose his life than to keep his life without his manhood; Skye didn't seem to be giving out options. Instinctively, he put both of his hands over his dick, mentally shielding it from all forces and outside intruders. He glanced up and saw the look on Skye's face, and knew that he would have to just give up the goods.

"It's a storage house. We don't sell shit. Money comes here and goes straight out. Dope comes here as a receiving point, then it's gone in the next hour. Nothing is here long. That money from the table was on its way out. The money on the other table just came in."

Skye and Treasure looked at each other, then Milan came sprinting over with the heavy bag full of money in her hand. "Girls, let's get the fuck outta here. We've been here too long already."

Treasure and Skye looked at Milan like she had lost her mind. "Bitch," Skye said, "this nigga just said this was a storage house. So it's some more money in this bitch!"

The guy frowned. "Hey, I didn't say that! That money right there on the table was-"

"Shut up nigga!" Treasure said as she kicked him in the throat with her white and red stiletto.

He coughed frantically, trying to catch his breath and regain his composure. He was the man responsible for storing the Dynasty Cartel's money, and he was failing greatly. He had never experienced any problems in the past, so he was hoping that Diaz and Rally wouldn't go too hard on him. He thought that telling them it was a storage spot was enough of an explanation for all the money on the table; boy was he wrong.

Skye positioned herself in front of him, and looked him in the eyes. "Ho nigga, you got 5 seconds to tell us where the fuckin' money is or I'm blowing your dick off. That's on everything! 5… 4…"

"There is no more money. The money on the tables is all of the money that is on the entire premises. There is-"

389

"3... 2.."

"O.K. o.k.! Fuck! I'll tell you. Shit!" The guy rubbed his hand across his head as he tried to figure out a way out of this predicament. There were no ideas coming to him, and he was beginning to get irritated. He told Rally earlier that he need additional protection to help out at the storage house, and Rally had told him to fuck off. So now, Rally would get what he deserved, he reasoned as he tried to make his decision right in his mind before he told them.

"That whole wall opens up over there. You have to put the temperature on 68 degrees, turn the microwave on 49 minutes, and release 3 cups of ice out of the refrigerator dispenser. Then it opens..."

Treasure stared at him carefully while Milan went and followed the instructions. By the time she'd released the third set of ice, the wall popped open exactly how he said it would. Skye jogged off to the wall opening, her pistol out and about, daring anyone to jump wrong. "Holy shit!" Skye said as she stood in the door way staring at what was inside.

Treasure couldn't maintain her excitement. "What is it girl? What is it? Tell me!"

"Girl, you will not be able to believe this shit! It's money in here from one corner to the next, it's over 5 million dollars in here *easily*! All this muthafuckin' dope money. Bitch what you wanna do?"

Treasure looked down, saw tears in the guy's eyes and felt no emotion; only triumph. She had been done so bad in life that she was going to make sure that every person she ran across who wasn't on the same team as her *felt it*. There was no more reasoning with her. There was no more innocence and naivety. There was only a cold well inside of her that continued to pump nothing but the iciest fluid through her body. After Benji and her best friends had messed over her, she knew that she would never again be the same.

Cla-cla-cla-cla-cla-cla-cla. She dumped bullets into the man's head with no remorse. Blood splattered against her white and red heels and seemed to give them a neat new design. She glanced around the room at the other six people in there and saw fear etched in their faces. She instructed them all to get in one corner and stood there holding her chopper while she watched Milan and Skye empty the wall of every dollar that was inside.

They were going into the wall and back out to the SUV, dumping money into the trunk, filling up the backseats and floor, and eventually there was no room in the backseats for anyone to sit. The SUV would only hold a driver and a passenger at that point, and the plan would need to be discussed quickly, because they were sure that a house like that would have constant contact going on with it. And for the past 10 minutes, no one had been able to contact anyone.

Sick of babysitting the 6 men, Treasure pulled the trigger on the chopper and blew blood and bone fragments across the floor and against the white wall in the corner. One guy's blood became another guy's; and it seemed to be so much bloodshed going on in that one section, that no one could tell who's blood was who's. It would look like a horror movie for the old Treasure, but it looked like a Disney movie to the calculated, updated and betrayed version of her. She spit on the pile of dead bodies and started walking out of the door with Skye and Milan.

$~$~$~$~$

Wham! When Tracy's fist connected with the side of Jennifer's face, it was just like she'd hit copy and paste on her computer. Jennifer's face immediately swelled to the size of Tracy's, and Tracy wasn't finished there. "You *stupid, stupid, stupid* ass bitch! Why the *fuck* would you fuck over a good man like Malcolm?"

Wham! Wham! Tracy was giving Jennifer back to back blows to the face and head. She had just gotten jumped by some women courtesy of her baby's father, Sweetback Fatty; and she had to take it out on somebody. Jennifer was going to be the perfect punching bag.

Wham! Wham! "You stupid, stupid, dumb ass bitch! I done beat your ass one time, now I'm remixing that shit!" *Wham! Wham!* Tracy was going crazy. It was almost as if another person had taken over her body and sent her into an erratic frenzy. "Who- told- you- to- try- to- flex- in-the- prison- visitation- room- bitch! I'ma beat that asssssss bitch!" *Wham! Wham!*

Jennifer's mouth was bleeding, and her eyes were swollen shut. She knew her nose had to be broken; and her spirit was crushed. She was on the ground helpless while Tracy kept on swinging and kicking her. She watched as Tracy's closed fist continued to connect with her face. She felt each cut and bruise at the exact moment that it happened to her body. She was hurting bad, both physically and emotionally; she didn't know what to do.

Wham! Wham! But it was the last straw for Jennifer. She couldn't take it anymore. True, she had betrayed her husband and done the wrong thing by him. Yes, she had made many mistakes in life, and there was a lot more to be made as long as she lived. But no, she didn't deserve all of the abuse that she was getting. A mixture of tears and blood rolled down her face and dripped off onto the nasty cement floor.

Tracy cocked her foot back one last time, and when she swung her leg, Jennifer caught it and lifted it off of the ground. That one motion carried enough momentum for Tracy to slip and fall. Tracy landed with a thud. She hit the ground so hard that Jennifer thought that she'd gone unconscious. Jennifer got up and stepped away from Tracy, trying to get a better look see if she was o.k.

She walked around her still body; but when she saw the look in Tracy's face, she instantly felt miserable for what she'd done. Tracy laid there silent, with tears streaming down her face at a rapid pace. Her mouth was wide open, but no sound was coming out. Jennifer looked down and saw Tracy gripping her stomach with both hands. She looked at her jail issued jumpsuit, and saw a growing blood stain between her legs.

The look on Tracy's face was that of pure misery. She looked like she was a woman who had been robbed of her entire life and still allowed to live. She was hurt, and the level of hurt that she was on held no enemies. She was hurting at the deepest level that a woman could hurt. She had lost life.

Jennifer shook her head and took a deep breath. She was about to go get some help for Tracy, but first she needed answers. "Tracy... I'm sorry."

Tracy's body continued to tremble, and her crying seemed to have no end. She was crying in silent convulsions, and the hurt from her spirit was being absorbed by Jennifer.

"Tracy... That was Malcolm's baby wasn't it?" Jennifer said in a knowing manner.

Tracy glanced up at Jennifer and couldn't do anything but cry
393

harder. Jennifer sat down beside Tracy and held her head in her lap. She had never given Malcolm any kids, even though he had always talked about how bad he wanted one and how many he was going to have. It wasn't that she wasn't trying, it just wasn't happening. And after all of her betrayal, it seemed the least she could do is preserve his child; she couldn't even do that right.

The fact that Malcolm had gotten another woman pregnant didn't even affect her, it was the least of her worries. She knew that she had absolutely no room to speak when it came to betrayal. Had she known that this woman was pregnant, she would have just laid there on the ground and accepted her punishment. She knew that it stemmed from bitterness because of the way she'd been acting.

She had done wrong by so many people... Her tears leaked out of her eyes and dropped onto her forearm. She was sad, not just for her and Tracy, but for Malcolm and the future. She didn't know what was to become of her, and it seemed as if she was just now taking the time to realize it.

She felt Tracy's hurt as she listened to her scream out in agony. She felt her frustration and absorbed her anger into her own body. Physically, she was beat up, but she deserved that and more for what she'd done to Malcolm, and now Malcolm's first born child. She knew that there had to be some way for her to make the whole thing right. There was no way in the world that she was going to continue to be a failure for the rest of her life. She would do something right if it was the last thing she did.

The two women sat there crying and embracing each other as the officers ran down the hall to find out what the all the screaming was about.

$~$~$~$~$

Rain and Kyla had ditched the stolen vehicle and taken the Metro bus to the Southside of Houston. They'd heard the announcement about Malcolm being in Super Max and the reward for their capture on the radio right before they ditched the car. What made them get on the bus was the fact that the news reporter was announcing to the public to stay on the lookout at the airports. So if everyone was watching the airports, surely they didn't care about two women getting on the bus. It was risky, but it worked.

They were standing outside of a two story house on the opposite side of the street, and were scouring the scene for any activity. "Rain, are you sure this is a good idea?"

Kyla had heard about the Lipstick Clique before, but the things that were being said about them were all negative. Sure, the Bankroll Squad was negative at times; but only when it *came* to that. The Lipstick Clique was just negative for no apparent reason. With so many things on her mind, it had literally not even occurred to her that the Lipstick Clique was "L.C.," which was the way she'd heard the stories being told about them in the streets. Rain had vouched that they were official; that's all she really had to go on.

She remembered that one of the women had been cool with Malcolm; that didn't really say much about her character because Jennifer Powers had also been cool with Malcolm. What she did know, was that if those chicks got out of line…

"Rain, I'm trusting your judgment on this particular decision. My main objective is to get Malcolm out of the fuckin' Super Max they say he was in on the radio. I don't give a fuck if you turn your back and walk away right now; I'll go die in front of that prison with a machine gun in my hand if I have to. I don't-"

"Zip it. This is where Treasure lives; but I'm not sure if she's home or not. I'm about to go knock."

"Wait Rain!" Kyla said impatiently. "Who the fuck is Treasure, and how do you know her? Mannnn I don't trust all these bitches these days. You saw what Sunshine did. I heard of L.C., but I never heard of nobody named Treasure. Are you sure this shit is legit? Are you-"

"Zip it Kyla. It's time for you to let the burden roll off of you and onto someone else. I'm volunteering to be that person. Stay right here, I got you."

Kyla listened to her words and dismissed them immediately. "Rain you cool and everything... You're a rider or whatever, but *fuck that.* I can't take any more chances with Malcolm. I need my man *home* and I need him home in the most desperate way."

There was a momentary silence while Kyla and Rain stood there staring at each other. Kyla knew that maybe she was tripping a little too hard on the only girl that elected to roll with her, but after all of the bullshit that she'd been through, she just couldn't afford any more fuckups.

"Rain, I don't need this shit right now. Either I'm about to go see what the bitch is about too, or I'm fuckin *gone!* Do you *not* hear the frustration in my gotdamn voice right now? I'm sick of this shit! I'm pissed and I don't even have my fuckin' *pistol!*"

"But I have mines though." Treasure said as she walked up behind Kyla and Rain with pistols pointed to the back of her heads."

CHAPTER 7

Yo Rally, we just been robbed man! Three fuckin' bitches came in here with all kind of choppers and machine guns and shit and robbed-"

"Wait muthafucka!" Rally screamed into the phone as he hurriedly threw on his t-shirt and jeans. He had been trying to catch a quick nap before he went after the Lipstick Clique, when his worker called him with the nonsense. He had gone to sleep with them on his mind, and now he was being woken up by them. "Robbed!!!? What the fuck you talking about?!!" Rally screamed into the phone like a madman.

His heart started to beat franticly as he stood there realizing that his worst fears had come true. He'd held a secured location for transporting illegal money for years and had never had any problems. It was customary for him to do so because the amount of money he was moving was equivalent to what a Fortune 500 company would receive. And there would never be a way for him to explain to the authorities that he was getting Fortune 500 money with four soul food restaurants. He was heated.

Who the fuck is telling these bitches this info? He thought as he stood there shaking uncontrollably.

"Rally? Rally? Can you hear me?"

The voice on the other end sounded like a foreign language to Rally.

397

He couldn't comprehend another word his guy was telling him after he heard the word *robbed.* He was sick to his stomach, and knew that he would need to sit down and attempt to focus before he made any rash decisions. He knew what was required of him, but he wanted to make sure that his requirement fixed *everything,* otherwise it would need an upgrade.

He'd heard about the Bankroll Squad's plane crash on the news, so he knew some of the major members were still hanging around on the low. He wondered if they were behind some of the Lipstick Clique's recent robberies. His guy was still on the phone talking.

"Rally, I said one of our workers had just pulled up when he saw the Lipstick Clique loading the money into the vehicle. He followed them all the way back… So how do you want to proceed with this?"

When Rally heard that info, all he could see was blood. He couldn't imagine anything less than a bloody massacre from a barrage of bullets. It was either that, or torture. If he could corner them while they're defenseless, he would make them pay rest of the week for the shit that they'd done to the Dynasty Cartel.

He walked down the hall and to the guest room where Diaz was and saw the door halfway open. Instead of knocking, he decided to glance inside of it to let him know the new information. What he saw shocked him.

The same two prostitutes that he'd sent away from his house earlier were *back.* One of them was positioned behind Diaz with a dildo strapped-on penetrating him. The other girl was underneath both of them alternating between licking his balls and licking the dildo girl's vagina.

So that's why I was seeing blood! He thought as he pulled out his gold plated Desert Eagle and went into the room. He didn't know how long Diaz had been a bi-sexual funny boy, but he knew when the end of it was. He stood over the bed with the most disgusted look that he had ever had to give his right hand man. The three-way orgy festival continued without any of them paying attention to their surroundings, and it saddened Rally that Diaz had been this way.

He had given off many signs that something was wrong, but Rally had assumed that it was always because of the stress of the high-powered decisions he had to make every day. *But to let a woman fuck a grown man in the ass?* That was completely uncalled for. A misdemeanor of flesh.

Diaz saw something move out of the corner of his eye and dived forward like he was going into a pool. But he was not. He turned around and gave Rally the most pitiful look that Rally had ever seen. "Hey Rally… I meant to come and wake you up to let you know that you got next. When I was about to drop them off, I decided to go ahead and let them be a stress reliever for both of-"

"Are you gay?" Rally's powerful voice interrupted whatever it was Diaz was trying to lie about.

Diaz sat there in silence, with only a frown on his face. He knew he'd messed up by not locking that door when he started to. He listened to the prostitutes tell him it'll be o.k. instead of doing what he was supposed to. And now he was exposed. He thought about saying something, but couldn't; he was speechless. He dropped his head and stared at the crisp white sheets that he was sitting on.

Pccccckkkkk! The sound of the Desert Eagle echoed through the house when it was fired. The bullet was so hot, that when it entered Diaz's body, he could see the smoke lift off of his flesh right before the bullet threw him against the headboard. He grabbed at his wound and stared up at Rally with sorrow in his eyes. He couldn't believe that his partner in crime would kill him for his personal tastes, when he had done everything right by him and never betrayed him, but he didn't have enough time to dwell on it. The next bullet created a clear path directly through the middle of Diaz's forehead.

The prostitutes were screaming throughout the whole ordeal, because they knew what was going to happen. They both had been ordered to get the fuck on and they were back anyway, due to their greed for money. Rally shot both of them and laid the three of them in the bed together and covered them with a blanket. He made sure they were all dead, and left the room. As a boss, he would never overlook the unexpected when it happened; he would always *do* the unexpected as a response.

And that was what had taken him so far in the dope game.

$~$~$~$~$

In the time of darkest defeat, victory may be nearest.

Malcolm stared at the cell that he was being housed in, and felt no emotion. It was a concrete bed with a matching concrete table. There were steel doors and a small window that he couldn't see out of. There was a camera; and the thought of him never having privacy again didn't affect him either. He thought about how strong his faith and confidence was in the people that loved him, and didn't worry about being in that cell for 23 hours out of a day; his heart was free as long as they had it with them.

What *did* bother him, was the caliber of the people he was locked up with. He had seen nothing but terrorists in the place. He couldn't believe that the United States government considered a young black male from the slums a terrorist because he wanted to be as rich as possible, as quick as possible. Money moved the world; it opened and closed doors, and not having it was frowned upon. Half of the things that the U.S. considered legal, was illegal at some point anyways… and the owners of the companies processing such things, still continued to rake in cash.

Alcohol was being sold by the tons; and numbers houses had turned into organized lottery tickets. Yes, he'd committed major crimes. Crimes no more hideous than what a serial killer would, but he didn't even see any serial killers in the prison when he was coming through. That was only on his mind momentarily. He knew not to focus energy on things that he couldn't control, so he relaxed his mind.

At this point, he could do nothing but wait and pray. If it came down to it, he would learn how to find enjoyment all alone. One of the things he learned throughout the years was that a person had to learn how to be happy with himself, just himself in order for other people to genuinely be happy with that person as well. And if anyone was pleased with himself; it would surely Malcolm Powers.

$~$~$~$~$

"Hey Pam. Wake up sleepy-head."

Pamela's boss was sitting in the visitor's chair in her hospital room with a big shit eating grin on his face. She thought she was seeing things at first, but eventually; she realized that it really *was* his trifling ass. After everything that she had been through for the FBI, the way that they were planning on paying her back was by *firing* her…

She burst into tears.

"Calm down Pammy Pam. I came to see how you were holding up in here. I'm sorry about what happened with your leg and the harsh words that came about during the Bankroll Squad trial. It was only because we wanted you to not think about anything else besides getting better. We didn't want you worrying about doing your job because we know how precise you are when it comes to handling your business." Mr. Berlin said as he sat in the chair with his legs crossed like a bitch.

Pam wiped some matter out of the corner of her eye and stared at him intensely. She couldn't believe that he'd had the nerve to say the shit he had just said. She lay there in the hospital bed feeling even more insulted than she would have felt had he not come. She stared into his blue eyes and knew that he was trying to squeeze the last few drops of self-worth out of her body. She hated him at that moment. Tears rolled down her cheeks while she lay there thinking of all of the rude and hurtful things that had been said to her before the Bankroll Squad case. She had done it all for the FBI, and they had turned around and squatted on her in a manner that the Bankroll Squad would never have done.

"Don't cry Pammy Pam. I came with a peace offering… and before you say *no,* just please hear me out-"

"Helllllllll no! Get the fuck out of my hospital room! Nurse!"

"Wait Pam, please listen to me, I really need your help! If you help me, I promise you that you will get a promotion!"

Pam frowned at Mr. Berlin.

"Pam, I know you have no reason whatsoever to trust me right now… but please understand that I have always meant and wanted the best for you. I never wanted to see you in a predicament like the one that you're in; I want to make it right."

Pam exhaled and turned her head to the opposite direction. Mr. Berlin saw it, but he continued his pitch.

"I basically came to ask you if you will accept a promotion… You will be *my* boss, if you accept and carry through with this assignment. I have the contract in my pocket if you care to take a look."

Still no response.

"O.K. Pam… I'm going to leave the contract right here on the table. So when you wake up, I want you to really look into it to see if it's something that you're interested in handling…"

Nothing.

Mr. Berlin uncrossed his legs and stood up. He stretched and put his hands in his pockets. He yawned before he spoke.

"The reason I selected you was because I know that you're the most qualified for this assignment. The Bankroll Squad members have escaped, and you have the most intel on them. If anyone can find them, it would be *you* Pam. I'm also giving you a chance to finish what you started… You started the prosecution against Malcolm, and I'm going to let you finish it. They're supposed to be shipping Malcolm Powers to a local holding facility right here in Texas soon. He has to face the murder and continuing criminal enterprise charges that stem from his prison break that he constructed, planned, and executed."

403

Pam's eyes widened to the max. *A second chance?! Yes!* She immediately turned around and saw her boss smiling at her. She smiled back. "You're giving me a second chance Mr. Berlin!? I can't believe it!"

Mr. Berlin opened his arms and walked over to her bed. They embraced while Pam thought about how it would feel to be in a position where she would be able to boss Mr. Berlin around. It was a dream come true for her.

"It's not really a second chance Pam… You were never fired to begin with of course. We had to say that to you in order to get you to sit down and relax. You'll always be with us. You've invested too much into the federal bureau to just be expendable. You are amazing."

Pam hung on to Mr. Berlin's every word as she lay there wide eyed staring at the person who had just came into the room and given her life. "But… uhm… what about my leg?" She said as she pointed to her nub with a sad face.

"Oh yea, if you check out page one of the contract; you'll see that you'll be receiving a prosthetic leg this evening after you sign the contract. All of your medical expenses will be covered with the signing of this contract, and we have room for any three special requests that you may have. Do you know of any requests you may have at this point Pamela?"

Pam wanted to scream. Wanted to shout and smile and pout and cry. She didn't know what to do or how to express herself. She felt joyful and sad, but happy and mad simultaneously. She don't know what it was that drove her to want to be a part of the FBI so bad, but here she was; about to go head over heels into it again.

"Yes… I do have a request… I want to accompany the U.S. Marshal when he transports Malcolm Powers to the holding facility."

Mr. Berlin was relieved. "Is that it? Wow. I thought you actually had a request. We already had you scheduled for that; you don't have to request that, unless you really want to use up a request of course, haha."

"Oh… why am *I* the one scheduled instead of someone else Mr. Berlin?" She was starting to feel skeptical about the situation.

Mr. Berlin never paused or hesitated with his answers. He always came correct and the words were fluid. "Because this is a top secret transfer. The media will not know about this, and neither will any of the other agents at the bureau. This is very serious; and we can't afford to have this information leaked. The media will blow it out of proportion, and I trust that you will keep it confidential like you've always done Pamela."

Pam stared back at him without smiling. "O.K… well I'll have to think on it then Mr. Berlin."

"Pam…" Mr. Berlin asked, suddenly nervous again, "Do you know if you're going to end up signing the contract or not? Do you need a lawyer to look over it for you?"

Pam sighed, then reached over and grabbed the contract off of the table. By the time she leaned back against her pillow, Mr. Berlin had extended a gold- plated ink pen and was holding it in her face. She looked at his silly smirk and felt comfortable that she could do the job. She knew that they were going to need her one day, and she was just happy that she didn't have to wait too long for them to admit it.

She grabbed the ink pen from Mr. Berlin and scribbled her name

405

along the dotted line. She didn't have to question the contract because she *knew* that this was the correct thing for her to do. She passed the contract back to her smiling boss and laid back into her pillow. *I knew they would need me. They can't do anything without me! Even with one leg, I still stand tall in presence!*

"Special Agent Jones, we'll also need your help in trying to find the rest of the street gang… Do we have your word on that as well?"

Pam grabbed the remote and turned the television on. "Of course you'll have my help with that. That's one of the easiest things in the world when you know their backgrounds and movement patterns. And let me guess… I'm the only person in the bureau that knows this information correct? Is that why you want me back?"

Mr. Berlin just stood there, he was speechless.

"Don't worry Mr. Berlin… no need to explain. I'm fully on board, so when can I start?"

$~$~$~$~$

Catfish ditched the vehicle, and made the 12 block walk over to TrapQuarters. In all of the drama and confusion, the Feds have never been able to link TrapQuarters to the Bankroll Squad. He was proud of that, because he knew that if there was one place in the world where the members of the squad could link up; it would be here.

He went inside and searched to see if there were any weapons left inside of the kitchen cabinet. He didn't see anything there, so he went to the master bedroom in the back. He slid the bed out of the way to uncover a locked door. He located the hole in the mattress and reached in it, feeling around until he located the key that was required to open the door to the basement.

He climbed down the ladder and went to check for weapons. Finally, he found a small stash of guns, none of which he preferred dealing with; but guns nevertheless. He grabbed a 9 millimeter and tucked it into his waistband. He also grabbed 4 full cartridges and stuffed them all into his front pockets. He started climbing the ladder. Throughout his climb, he started thinking about Malcolm's situation. He knew he would need more than a 9 millimeter to rescue him, but he would have to wait to get to Colorado in order to get the heavy artillery. For now, he just needed a "stay-a-way" announcement.

And nothing announced "stay-a-way" better than a pistol.

When he climbed out of the basement, he paused for a second because he thought he heard something moving. But when he stopped, the movement also stopped. He took the 9 millimeter out of his waistband, and rounded the corner; bumping into someone.

"Hey! Luther, can I get a nickel bag?"

Catfish gave the man a withering look. "Do I look like my name is muthafuckin' Luther?"

The man was an obvious crack head. He wore dirty shoes and his clothes looked as if they hadn't been washed in over 2 weeks. There were chocolate stains on his shirt and oil stains on his pants. His hair was nappy and had grass inside of it as if he'd just woken up off of the ground. His lips were crusty and his skin was ashy. His body was skinny and frail; he looked as if it were going to fly away with the next breeze.

The man shook his head. "I'm sorry big dog. If you running the spot now, lemme get a nick bag if you straight."

Catfish stood there thinking for a minute. "Sit down."

The man started looking around the room with nervousness showing in his actions and demeanor. He was paranoid and it showed in his every breath. Catfish sat on the sofa and stared at him for a second, absorbing the visual side effects of the drug that they had been killing for and selling to make a living. He stared at the effects of the drug that he had lost his wife over. The drug that he had lost his own life and best friend over.

Cocaine.

It had destroyed many families with the premise of helping. It had created many poor people with the premise of riches and the illusion of grand accumulation. It had done what the lottery had failed to achieve and brought what Santa had failed to bring. It was a horrible drug, yet such a great product. It sold without a seller. Without a marketing scheme, a person could get rich in a month if they bought the right amount.

But it had consequences. Consequences that dug deeper than the deepest root of the oldest tree. It had side effects that were stronger than platinum and more valuable than life. Cocaine had an entire life of its own. It had happiness, joy, pain, death, betrayal and friendship. It had confusion, jealousy, hurt, unpredictability, and sadness.

The junkie's face reflected every element that the drug contained. Catfish looked into his face and saw the contribution that he had made in life and was embarrassed. He thought about all of the lives he'd taken and the faces he'd crushed, as well as all of the lives that he would have to take to put closure on the whole situation. His number one goal was to get Malcolm out by all means, he hadn't figured out the rest yet.

"Look. You tell me what I want to know and I'll think about helping you." Catfish said in his blunt and straightforward style.

The man fidgeted in his seat as he sat there trying to figure out if the deal was fair or not. He didn't have much time to think about it though.

"What's the word on the street about the Bankroll Squad?"

The man looked confused for a second, as if Catfish was telling a joke. He smiled, showing a mouth full of orange yellowish teeth. "What's the word on them? Hahaha! The word is that they're fucked up! I thought I saw Luther come in this here house, and that's the only reason I came over here. I'm tryna get my *fix!* Oh, you know what? I do know a few things. This dude, Sweetback Fatty had some information that they said could probably help them out with some shit, but that young kid, Luther told him to fuck off! Hahahaha! Now *that's* funny."

Catfish sat there stunned. He couldn't believe the words that were coming out of the man's mouth. "What kind of help would it be dude?"

Finally realizing that Catfish wasn't laughing, the fiend straightened his face up. "Oh, oh… uhmm… he had his peoples keep track of that undercover lady who told on everybody, and that boy Luther told him to fuck off. Look… I need some dope! If you ain't got no dope, then I gotta go get to where some is."

Catfish gave the man a paralyzing look. "Sit yo muthafuckin' ass down boy."

The crackhead was much slimmer than Catfish, and felt like he would be able to get up and take off without consequence. There was no way a dude that big was going to catch him. Besides, he didn't feel like sitting around having a conversation with some lonely ass muthafucka' anyways. He got up and took off. He ran three steps before he felt his life being yanked out of him from behind.

Catfish had gotten up immediately and clotheslined him from reverse by sticking his arm in front of the man's neck. The man flipped backwards and onto the floor. All the remorse that Catfish had just felt about the side effects of cocaine went completely out of the window. He stood above the crack head and felt the way he had always felt throughout his life. Like God.

His pistol let loose and he blew the man's brains through the wooden floor with no remorse. He hated that he felt that way, but this was who he was. There wasn't a revelation in life that was going to be powerful enough to restrain him from his pistol addiction. He knew Sweetback's information, so he didn't need further help. And what he *didn't* need was some random crackhead running around in the streets telling people where he was posted up at. If he hadn't killed that man, he would've been on his way back to prison in less than 3 hours.

Standing above the junkie, he briefly thought back to his childhood. He was raised by his father, a tough ex-Marine who didn't take any shit around the house. His mother had left his abusive father when he was 3 years old, so his father had been unable to re-enlist. Instead, his father took all of his government training out on him. They would kill puppies and cats in cold-blood just for fun. He thought back to the first human they'd killed together back when he was 13. A person had just climbed onto his dad's private property, and without warning; his dad put the shot gun in his young hands and instructed him to just *shoot.*

He shook his head and exhaled the hell, and continued trying his hardest to inhale heaven. Catfish had been trying all of his life, to no avail.

CHAPTER 8

Tracy and Jennifer had grown closer since the fight that led to Tracy's miscarriage. Tracy needed a familiar face for emotional support, and being that Jennifer was right there in the same cell with her; she couldn't ignore her forever. They'd come to terms about the fight, and the driving forces behind it. They'd discussed each other's love and respect for Malcolm Powers, and the impact that he'd had on their lives.

Jennifer admitted that she'd committed too many errors against their marriage for it to be respectfully salvaged, so her plan was just to help him in any way that she possibly could. Tracy admitted that she had fallen in love with him through the strangest of ways; she also discussed the fact that she was wrong as well for having sex with a married man. They had stayed up many late nights discussing the situation and finding out that they had more in common than they would've ever thought.

They'd laughed about the fight they had outside of the visitation room when Tracy stabbed Jennifer. Then they turned around and laughed about the way Tracy was beating her ass when she came into the cell. The only sad part about everything between them was the miscarriage that Tracy had experienced.

They'd discussed Sweetback Fatty; Tracy's baby's father, and talked about the aggressive nature of his character. They discussed the Coward; and the conversation started to grow cold. Tracy felt very bad hearing that Jen had stooped so low that she was out there on crack cocaine and just doing random shit for no apparent reason. As far as she could tell, she still seemed like an addict in waiting.

On their day in court, the judge had granted them both bail amounts of $100,000 each. Back in the cell, Jennifer had been elated that she had been granted bail; the lawyer had told her that she probably wouldn't be able to get bond. Tracy's lawyer had told her the same thing, but the judge felt otherwise. Judge Shilf felt like the crimes were both smaller than they appeared to be; he knew that he needed to clear some federal cells for the bigger crimes. So if they could afford to make bail, they could leave.

Jennifer had been walking back and forth in the cell with a huge grin on her face. "We are sooo freaking lucky Tracy! We're finally getting out of here! That's so freaking awesome!"

But Tracy was paying no attention. She was lying in the bunk staring at the ceiling. She was in deep thought about her situation. Her baby's father had tried to have her killed in jail on her first day in there. Then Jennifer had managed to make her fall and miscarry her baby. Malcolm Power's young prince had been taken away from the world before he could make an appearance. She lay there hurting, sulking, and feeling as if she wasn't deserving enough of a person to get out of jail.

"What's wrong Tracy? You're not speaking to me today?"

Tracy ignored her and turned over so that she could face the wall. In that small jail cell, Jennifer had become a friend. But when the jail cell doors opened up, she had to ask herself what would prevent her from

413

killing Jennifer for killing her unborn child. She had to pray and ask God for direction and understanding. She stared at the wall until her vision clouded with tears. She wiped her face and exhaled.

She knew that she had to become stronger than how she was acting, and she'd have to do it as quickly as possible. She took a few moments to get herself together, and then sat up in the bunk. She slid her newspaper to the side and took out a pen and a sheet of paper. On that sheet, she wrote: O.

She wrote that zero as big as she possibly could, and just sat there staring at it. Jennifer had become tired of walking back and forth, and ended up sitting down on a steel stool. She looked at Tracy, who was staring at her paper. "Tracy... tell me what the problem is. What's up with that piece of paper you just wrote on? Clue me in please; you've been silent ever since we received the good news!"

Tracy threw the paper at Jennifer. "What good fuckin' news?! Huh? Ooooh, we can bail out of jail for $100,000 each! Wow! I don't have a hundred muthafuckin' thousand dollars bitch! How the fuck is that good news? I don't have anybody out there who cares about me. Malcolm was the last person I had who would go to bat for me. I have no family. My baby daddy wants me dead. Fuck a good news! I don't have it!"

Jennifer's heartbeat sped up when she listened to Tracy express herself. She felt the emotion that she was trying to convey and the message reached her loud and in high definition. She closed her eyes while she thought about the differences in the two scenarios. She could rely on her parents at all times; someone like Tracy had no one. She was just out in the world trying to make a path for herself.

"My daddy will bail you out with me Tracy! Calm down, I got you."

Tracy's heart dropped to the floor. She had just *known* that she was not going to get out of jail anytime soon. She thought about what she would be able to accomplish once she made bond, and felt as if she had just been sent a guardian angel. After watching the news, she'd realized that the Bankroll Squad was still in the Houston area; and she had a great idea of where they might be laying low at.

"Thank you Jennifer. If you can really do that, it would mean the world to me!" Tracy said as she smiled. When she looked at Jennifer, she saw that there were tears sliding down her face. That was strange because she had only looked away for a few seconds; before she looked away; she had the happiest look on her face that anyone could possibly have.

"Of course I can Tracy. I got you. After I get out of here, I'm going to give my life to the Lord. I've been thinking about that a lot. He kept me safe through the darkest of nights and kept me sane through the craziest of times. I love Him. I was raised to love Him, but then money took root and an evil tree sprouted. That tree uprooted my foundation, and my base was forever misplaced. *I* may not be perfect as a person, but God is perfect… and if I roll with Him, He will help me become more like Him until it's my time to go."

$~$~$~$~$

They were both in Florida with two different plans in mind. Brink wanted to take a boat to Cuba, and then fly out to the Philippines from there; but Luther wanted Brink to contact some of his old friends so that he could borrow some aircraft and just fly over there.

"Look young buck, it's bad enough that you followed me all the way

415

down here to Florida, now you wanna try to dictate the way that I travel? That's some crazy shit boy. I thought you were smarter than that. You certainly look it!"

Luther huffed and shook his head at Brink. His plan had been to convince Brink to use his talents to get them where they needed to be, but his persuasion skills weren't working. "Brink... there are hundreds of miscellaneous aircraft down here in Miami. We would blend right in, I tell you. Actually, I'm so convinced that they're not paying attention to us, that we could literally go board a commercial flight to wherever we want to go."

Brink rolled his eyes as they stood outside of the Starbucks café. He was listening to Luther's amateur reasoning and knowing that he hadn't fully matured to having a true boss's instinct. There was nothing in the world that could convince him to take a flight out of the United States while on the FBI's most wanted list. Nothing except for Malcolm Powers.

Malcolm Power's mind was so strong and intense, that if he suggested they take the flight, he would have been on it. Malcolm thought 5 moves ahead of the world at all times; he would definitely have had all possibilities covered. He just didn't see the same thing when it came to young Luther. He didn't even see the same amount of loyalty in his eyes.

"Luther, your young ass is crazy as shit. We're involved in some pretty serious shit for you to stand here beside me and tell me we'll be o.k. at the airport. How could you try me like that and still feel safe? I really feel the need to reach over and slap the dog shit out of you. Yo... do me a favor and get the fuck away from me lil dude before I snap."

Luther stood there for a moment, taking in everything that Brink had told him. He registered his statements, and still came up with the same conclusions… That someone had once again underestimated him. Luther had studied Malcolm's decision making techniques for so long, that he was starting to see out of his idol's eyes. He understood Brink not trusting him because he hadn't actually proven himself, but it was going to be just fine. He took a deep breath and shook his head. "You know… it's old heads like you who prevent the game from becoming more advanced. You're stuck in your ways and beliefs, so you reject anything that comes from a fresh perspective. That's why the Feds keep on nabbing the big dogs of your caliber. Because you're hard headed. I'm telling you right now that I know what I'm talking about Brink. Let's go holla' at my dude and get us both the proper credentials to take that flight."

Brink stood there for a second, as if he was actually considering Luther's statement. He stood there trying to figure out what was going on mentally with that kid, and couldn't place it. He knew that being a gangster and a crime boss had become one of the "in" things to do, but in no way was he prepared to take orders from a child.

Brink took his right hand and rubbed it across his face slowly. He thought about Malcolm and the effortless power he had when it came down to the art of persuasion. Malcolm could convince a flower to duck sunlight and a dopeboy to run red lights. He didn't have to argue about it or worry about someone sharing in his beliefs. He didn't worry because if no one else believed in it, *he* did. Brink looked to the sky briefly, then looked Luther directly in the eye.

With a grimace on his face and anger in his voice, he told Luther exactly how he felt.

417

"Lil man... kick rocks! Fuck off! You go in your direction and I'ma go in mine!"

$~$~$~$~$

Shit! Kyla thought as she stood there with a cold barrel laying against the back of her head. She felt sick to her stomach for listening to Rain and carrying on with such an unplanned event. She was standing in someone else's yard, on someone else's property *with a barrel laying against her head.*

"Excuse me," Kyla said, not wanting to go through the bullshit at all. "I'm Kyla from the Bankroll Squad, and I was trying to get in touch with the Lipstick Clique. I don't want any trouble at all. I come in peace ma'am. If you don't know who I'm talking about, please disregard my request and let me go."

Treasure was instantly curious. To that very day, she'd owed the Bankroll Squad a favor and had never been in a position big enough to pay them back. "Turn around ma."

Kyla turned around and stared at Treasure. Treasure was floored immediately. It wasn't the beauty that she was floored with, but the aura. Her Real Bitch meter went off and sounded like a broken fire alarm. She knew automatically that this was the realest bitch that she had ever met in her life. She stood there speechless as she added up the reasons that Kyla was the baddest.

She knew about how strong of a role she played in the Bankroll Squad, and subsequently the Bankroll Squad's prison escape. She knew that she was fuckin' with a winner. Anyone that had ever seen Kyla would have put their money on her being a stuck-up pretty girl. But her abandoning her pretty girl looks and getting out in the field like a grown man had struck musical chords with Treasure. Nothing but admiration spread across her face as she smiled.

"Treasure, where the fuck you at?" Skye's booming voice approached from around the corner.

"Both ya'll hoes out here playing hide and seek and shit." Milan's voice floated from behind Skye's. She jogged and caught up with Skye. "Where the fuck *is* Treasure?" She said as she reached to pull out her set of keys.

When Skye and Milan rounded the corner, they both froze in their tracks. Milan reached for her weapon first and ran up to Kyla and Rain with the pistol out. "What the fuck ya'll want! Huh! Who the fuck told ya'll to trespass? I'm about to blow your shit out."

"Milan!" Treasure said.

But Milan was uncontrollable. "Do you hear me you stupid bitches? I will blow your muthafuckin shit *out.* This ain't no gotdamn spring chicken you fuckin with over here, this is the real gotdamn deal! You thought you was about to run us didn't you?! Ain't no robbing the robbers bitch!"

"Milan!" Both Treasure and Skye said simultaneously.

But Milan was far from trying to hear them talk. She walked up to Kyla and pointed her finger in her face. "Bitch who you think you is ho?"

Kyla stood there for a moment, not even believing that that young ass girl had dared to try to disrespect her like that.

"Bitch you hear me talking to you! Speak when spoken to!" Milan
419

took her index finger and nudged Kyla in the middle of the forehead. "What you wanna do bitch?"

In a flash, Kyla was on her.

She wrapped her arms around Milan's neck like a wrestler and pulled her towards the ground with her. But before Kyla could hit the ground, she spun her body and slammed Milan against it *hard*. She grabbed Milan's hair with her left hand and balled her right fist up. Milan was stunned. She had no idea that she was going to end up on the ground so quick, and was trying her hardest to blink off her surprise attack. By the time she blinked out of her blurry vision, Kyla's right fist was coming in a rapid succession.

Kyla punched her in the nose, lip, eye, cheek and throat, then took her nails and dug into her skin. Kyla was a pretty girl, and during her childhood, she'd had to fight many jealous girls because of it. She was the total package. Strong, mentally powerful, beautiful and could whip a bitch's ass if it came down to it. And it had certainly come down to it.

Wham! Wham! Wham! Kyla was putting on a show that no one would ever be able to forget. Treasure stepped back and admired the young veteran's work. She was glad that someone was finally teaching Milan a lesson on life. Milan was trying to fight back, but Kyla was much too fast for her. She pummeled her into a stupor and kept on punching.

Skye was happy also that Milan was getting what she deserved, but she felt as if it had gone on a little too long. "O.K.-" She attempted to say, but Treasure held her hand out for her to be silent.

After a few more punches, Kyla finally backed off on her own. She had literally beat Milan until she started snoring.

Kyla stepped back and looked at the woman's sleeping body. Then she ran towards her like a field goal kicker, but Rain was able to grab her and prevent her from kicking the poor girl. "Let me go Rain!"

Rain held on to her and looked back at Treasure at Skye for help. She kept holding on until she could feel some of the angry energy dissipate from Kyla's body. After a minute or so, Kyla had finally calmed down. She stood there with a light sweat on her forehead, and breathing heavily. All three of the girls were shocked that Kyla had such a nice hand game. They thought for sure that loud mouth Milan was about to beat that ass.

Treasure reached her hand out to shake Kyla's. "My name is Treasure… and us three… are the Lipstick Clique."

$S{\sim}S{\sim}S{\sim}S{\sim}S$

Kyla and Rain were in the great room discussing the situation at hand. "I'm not feeling this shit Rain. Them hoes can't fuckin help us! It's only three bitches, and I already beat one ho's ass in the opening minutes. Ain't no got damn way that they can help us with this high-powered shit that we need to pull off! This is not the clique I heard about, Rain."

Rain sat back in her chair thinking about Kyla's remarks. She compared Kyla's remarks to the facts that she already knew about the Lipstick Clique and came up with her own point of view. "I think you should give them a chance Kyla. If it's anyone that can help Malcolm get out of prison, it'll be Treasure… She broke out of prison, and is still out on the run doing good for herself. She's a vet, Ky."

Kyla stopped pacing back and forth long enough to let Rain's words sink in. She took a seat and thought about the endless combinations of

421

outcomes, and knew that she could only be happy with two of them. Either it was her, Malcolm, and their child, or the world would pay severely for ruining her happiness. She would not take substitutes or stand-ins. She was an official chick and she required official possessions.

She took a deep breath and tried to relax a bit. As soon as she was starting to relax, Treasure, Skye, and Milan came walking down the hallway. Milan's demeanor had changed completely and her appearance had the matching beat up glow to match. She was downtrodden and sad, but still managed to give Kyla a slight smile when she walked past her. Milan sat down and didn't say a word. Skye sat down and stared at Kyla. She was astonished that Kyla had managed to beat her twin sister into submission. That had never happened before, not even by their parents. Milan had always had an indestructible personality.

Treasure walked in and quickly grabbed the remote control. She turned the television on to the news and turned the volume down. She absolutely *had* to make sure that the FBI was nowhere close to her trail. There was no way she was going back to prison, and under worse circumstances than she was in before. She thought about that bitch who'd betrayed her, and wished death upon her entire family.

"Kyla, first I want to say that it is an honor for you to have trusted and sought us in a time of need. I was desperate and lost at one time in my life; and your man Malcolm Powers reached his powerful arm across the United States and helped me out of my situation. To this day I have never been able to repay him for his favor. If there is anything I, or *we* can do; please let us know."

Kyla remained silent for a moment. She'd heard about Malcolm being on 1-dial in the past, but had never met anyone who'd received 1-

dial's effects. The 1-dial was when he gave his number to a single person in the streets whom he trusted and told them to pass it to the one person they trust once every year. When the person called that number, the person on the other end of the phone would help them out of whichever type of jam that they're in. It was Malcolm's version of philanthropy.

Kyla got straight to the point with her request. She didn't have any time to waste. "Look, I need Malcolm out of prison. I need help with a prison break."

Butterflies shot through Treasure's body when she heard those words come out of Kyla's mouth. She didn't expect for the return favor to be *that* expensive. Treasure pulled up a folded party chair and unfolded it. She sat down in front of Kyla and bit one of her fingernails. "A *prison* break?" She spoke without masking her confusion and disbelief. Treasure was sick. She couldn't believe what she was hearing.

Of all of the things that she'd expected to hear, she had to get a grip on herself because that wasn't even an *option.* Malcolm Powers and the Bankroll Squad had *certainly not* helped her to escape prison, so she didn't logically see a reason why she should put her life and her clique's lives in danger like that. Skye looked and Milan and then at Treasure, who was just staring straight ahead.

"I'm down if you're down Treasure," Skye said. "Me too." Milan said.

Treasure looked at them both and shook her head. "Fuck no. I'm sorry Kyla. As leader of this clique, I can't allow us to get involved with this. The only way I would help you is if you'd have come to me with a plan that you'd been working on for quite some time, *and* if that plan made sense to me. But you come to me with no plan, with strictly emotions pouring out of you. I do understand the love you have for this man, and to that I wish you nothing but the best. However, as a boss; I know you understand me when I say I can't afford to get involved in your emotional pursuit Kyla. I'm so sorry."

Rain stared at the floor in defeat. She felt bad for recommending the Lipstick Clique to Kyla now that they couldn't help. She was sick of seeing Kyla being thrown through the emotional rollercoaster that she had been on lately; she wished that she could do something about it. But she couldn't, she was only one person.

Kyla stood up and extended her hand to Treasure, surprising everyone, including Treasure. "Thank you Treasure, for being a real ass bitch; and not faking out on me at the last minute. I can respect it when a bitch is up front about something I don't like, as opposed to when a bitch waits until the end to jeopardize everything I love."

Kyla looked at Milan and Skye and smiled. "This is a true leader you two have over here in Treasure. You should learn from her and her actions. They will enhance your character, and if you ever find yourself in a situation where you don't have her with you; you will always have the qualities that she shared. She is correct however, about me acting on emotion and not planning. I am not going to lie to you… I'm running on pure love right now. This isn't adrenaline or planning. It isn't strategic thinking or sly side-stepping. All of those things I've done already. At this point, I have only love… and with ya'll's blessings… Hopefully I'll have a pistol when I leave."

Treasure took her hand in hers and gave her a hug. Milan, Skye, and Rain all joined in with the hug; it was indeed a heartfelt moment. Treasure backed away and looked Kyla up and down. "*You* can act on love and it will work for *you,* but it won't work for me because *my* love isn't in it; therefore *my* love isn't going to carry me as far as yours will carry you. I would suffer. But besides that; Skye, bring the girl some pistols!"

CHAPTER 9

Rally was *pissed!* There was nothing in the world that could compare to the betrayal that was done to him by his right hand man Diaz. He had four double barreled shotguns in the truck, and was on his way hunting. He was going to make sure he gave the Lipstick Clique everything he could give them. He no longer cared about sending one of his professional killers at them; he wanted to make a statement in the streets once and for all.

He felt as if he'd lived a beautiful life off of drug money; he was 44 years old and had been selling dope since he was 18. He had known nothing else but dope money and street love. His crew, the Dynasty Cartel would live on forever; with him or without him, and he was content with the contribution that he had made to the world. He felt that his crew would forever be stronger than the Bankroll Squad on any day of the week.

The truck swerved around one pothole and still ended up hitting another one as it zipped through the cold crooked streets of Houston Texas. He was so mad that he could barely think straight. He had been tolerating a lot of shit since the Bankroll Squad started their little empire; and he had taken it and backed away. There had been no reason for him to argue with a bunch of wild children when he was a grown ass millionaire.

But this group of young women had been causing him too many problems lately. He wouldn't even try to imagine what the streets would say. Picturing the streets finding out that he had gotten robbed by a group of young women without payback seemed like a joke. His Avalanche provided a smooth ride all the way to the other side of Houston.

"Hey. I'm almost at the address you gave me."

The guy on the other end of the phone cleared his throat. "Rally, I've been calling you for 15 minutes now. I've been trying to tell you that my guy has followed them back over to the Northside."

"Shut the fuck up! Stupid muthafucka!!" Rally was getting even more pissed off, and he thought that his own worker was either lying, playing games, or in on the robbery himself. "I'm bout sick of your stupid muthafuckin' ass! Let me find out that you're in on the got damn robbery too! The earth will not be big enough for you to fuckin' hide! Grrrrrr!"

Rally slapped the display on his cell phone, shutting it off. He couldn't believe how the game had changed from when he was just starting. The loyalty and respect level had decreased to the point that newbie women crews were trying to stand up to legends. Briefly, he remembered what his father had told him before he died. "There are no legends in the drug game; only fools." He dismissed it then, and dismissed it today.

His father knew nothing! He had slaved on top of houses with hammers in his hand all of his life. Rally was a slave to million dollar deals, and he loved it. He glanced at his watch and figured that he had about 20 minutes to get to where he was headed. He reached over and

427

grabbed his shotgun with his right hand; pulling it against his right thigh as if he had to protect it. Of all of the things that had ever let him down in life, there was still one thing in the world that had never betrayed him. His shotgun.

$~$~$~$~$

Ms. Linda Gray drove the van to Pam's mother's house in silence. She was the designated nurse, personal trainer, and conditioner for Pam's rehabilitation and she intended to do her job well. She went around to the passenger's side door and reached to open it when it slid out of her grasp. She looked up and saw Pam's face, and the irritated expression that accompanied it.

"Ma'am, you don't have to do that." Ms. Linda Gray told her while trying to relax her.

"Fuck outta here. I don't need your damn help." Pam grabbed her set of crutches and swung them to the ground, causing Linda to quickly move out of the way. She shifted her weight up out of the van and onto one of the crutches. That crutch would have to help her balance since she only had one leg.

"Better yet… Ms. Linda, you wanna help me? If you do, could you please put that prosthetic leg on me so that I can get the fuck on about my business?"

Ms. Linda shook her head. "I'm afraid you have it all wrong Pam. You can't just put on a prosthetic leg and expect to be 100%. You will be off-balance. You will be lost. My whole purpose is to help you rehabilitate Pam. You need extreme physical therapy and training. I think you'll be ready to roll in about two or three months."

"Two or three months?!?" Pam shouted. "There is no got damn way I'm about to sit around and wait 2 or 3 months to go out and get my job handled. You need to get on top of this shit immediately!"

"I'll work as fast as I can, but it will still take two-"

"Get the fuck away from this house then. Take your fuckin' fake leg packages with you. I don't need but one leg and a set of crutches to do what the fuck I need to do." Pam climbed out of the van and landed face first into the grass. Using all of the upper body strength she had, she managed to balance herself upright. Ms. Linda tried to reach over and help her straighten her shirt, but Pam swiped at her hand immediately. "Don't fuckin' touch me."

Ms. Linda nodded her head and stood there watching as Pam limped herself into her Mom's house. She had been told that Pam was going to be difficult; and if she hadn't have seen it with her own eyes, she would have never believed that a girl who seemed so sweet could be so bitter.

$~$~$~$~$

"Mom! Mommmmm! Mooooom!" Pam screamed as she stumbled into the house. She went to the couch and sat down as best she could. Not having a leg there was a very strange experience for Pam. The weirdest thing about it was that she kept looking down because it seemed as if it was still attached. She looked on the table and saw a piece of white construction paper with handwriting on it. She reached towards it, and lost her balance.

She flipped off of the sofa and sat on the ground sideways feeling angrier and angrier about her situation. She reached up and snatched the note off of the table and read it.

Pam...

I'm sorry I betrayed you. I really am. I didn't mean to, but I know you wouldn't understand me right now, so I decided to leave you in the house on your own. Some of this was my own idea, and some of it was Mr. Berlin's, so thank both of us

Pam didn't even finish reading it. She balled the letter up and slammed it against the floor repeatedly in order to express her frustration. But it wasn't working. The floor wasn't enough to show how frustrated she was, and the paper was too weak of a messenger. She looked around the house and tried to imagine herself sitting around for months trying to rehabilitate herself.

She grabbed the phone off of the table and called Mr. Berlin. He picked up on the first ring. "Hi Pam. How's Ms. Linda working out for you?"

"Fuck the bullshit. What the fuck happened to our agreement? You said I would be able to transport the fucking inmate to the fucking county with the-"

"Wait... hold on one second... Relax Pam. You can't do anything in your current situation but help us locate the Bankroll Squad. It takes months of intense physical therapy to get a prosthetic leg working properly. It's not something you do overnight. Just help us with-"

"Fuck that! Either you follow through with what I asked you, or I don't help you with shit!"

"Pam... you know I will lock you up for going against orders."

Pam was heated. She was sick of being threatened every time she tried to do the right thing in life. "Well lock me up! Bring your monkey ass on!"

Mr. Berlin was silent for a second. He wanted to calm the mood down so that he could think properly. It would be easy to just mouth off in response to her statement, but that would get no one anywhere. He thought about how big of a promotion he would get for the *recapture* of the Bankroll Squad, and just knew, without a shadow of doubt, that he *had* to have that. He would be dubbed the most brilliant agent who ever lived.

He also knew that Pam would be expecting a promotion as per her contract. But the contract was ripped up as soon as he left her hospital room. She wasn't registered with the FBI anymore, so the work she did, had to be done under his name. He simply wanted to reap the benefits of her knowledge, so he told her what she wanted to hear.

"O.K. Pam. No need for name calling. If you really want to transport Malcolm to the Federal pre-trial facility, then I need you on the first thing smoking to Colorado. I'm about to drop by your Mom's and bring you a credential packet and a new weapon. I'll see you then."

Pam sat there with her eyes closed and her mind open. She was trying to picture all of the possible scenarios and situations. She tried to put herself into Mr. Berlin's mind so she could spot the flaw. She tried to put herself into her Mom's mind to identify the cause of her betrayal; but she couldn't spot anything with either of them. A tear rolled down her face as she looked at her set of crutches and thought about her predicament.

One day I'm going to make everybody pay! She thought as sizzling anger ran through her body like oxygen. In all of her life, she could only identify one moment where she had been angry on this level; and it was when Malcolm made her feel like a failure for not bringing the cocaine back from overseas. She hated the feeling. That feeling alone seemed to always cause her to make a decision that she would later regret.

$~$~$~$~$

Catfish found about $2,300 in the dresser. Luther had either overlooked it, or completely forgotten that it was there. He grabbed the cash and walked out of Trapquarters. He needed a vehicle ASAP. Catfish walked down the block and stood at the gas station. He saw a few cars with For Sale signs on the windows, but they wanted too much for them.

A few people gave him suspicious looks, and he gave them suspicious looks right back. He had a pistol in his pocket and that was all that mattered in those situations. He kept scouring the scene until he saw exactly what he needed. It was a broken down pickup truck that couldn't be worth more than $1,000. He walked up to the vehicle with the intent to bargain with the owner.

"Hello sir, how are you?" Catfish said to the driver.

The driver glanced up briefly, then continued pumping gas into the truck. He didn't even speak to Catfish or acknowledge him at first. When he finally spoke, it was acid. "I don't got a dollar for your junkie ass to go buy drugs with. Get away."

Catfish was insulted, but he wasn't going to let it rattle him. Instead of lashing out, he smiled. "Excuse me sir… I'm willing to pay you $2,000 for your truck if you wish to sell it."

The man looked back at Catfish and looked down at his shoes. He nodded his head. "I am trying to sell it, but I want my baby in the hands of someone who's going to take care of it. You can't even take care of your shoes son. Get away from me."

Another fleeting moment of anger rushed through Catfish. He took a deep breath and turned to walk away. After taking 3 steps, he realized that taking the high road would never work correctly for him. He put his hand on his pistol, but quickly released his grip on it. He would only use that if it came to it. Instead he walked back up to the man.

"Excuse me sir. I promise you right now that I'm going to take good care of your truck."

The man finished paying for his gas with his credit card and grabbed his receipt. He walked to the passenger's side of the truck and opened the door. "O.K. son, well drive me home. Depending on how well you drive, I'll let you know if you can buy my baby from me. She was my first vehicle."

Catfish got in the truck and drove the man to his address. The destination was a broken down three bedroom house that didn't look much better than his pickup truck. When they got in the yard, the man reached across with his hand out. "Yea… see… give me those keys there son. You don't know how to handle a vehicle like this. I'll let my son take you home."

Catfish pulled his pistol out without any further questions or statements. With an astonished expression, the man hurriedly tried to grab the door handle, but Catfish instantly put an iron grip around his neck; preventing him from going *anywhere*. The man was scared out of his mind. He had been talking shit his whole life without anyone doing anything about it; he had finally run into his first problem.

Ca-Blam!

The gunshot blew the man's brains across the passenger's side window. He grabbed a towel off of the floor, cleaned the window and folded the dirty towel up inside of the man's shirt. He opened the door and pushed the man out onto the ground. He had been trying to come at him like a respectable business man, but it seemed that the only thing that niggaz respected sometimes were bullets; hell, they didn't even respect them unless they were receiving one. He shut the passenger side door and backed out of the driveway.

The more mature Catfish had never arrived. It seemed that every day of life brought more lessons out about why he should remain the young trigger happy dude he was back in the days. The closest he had ever gotten to being mature was when he sewed that guy's mouth shut. Even that move had been a mistake according to Malcolm. What Malcolm had failed to understand back then was that Catfish *needed* to do that. He needed to do the mouth sewing for his mental health. But all of that was out of the window at this point. He was on a mission, as the muffler from the pickup truck screamed and coughed down the expressway.

He needed information from Sweetback Fatty, and he was going to see that he got it. If he didn't, he was going to kill everything in his path until he was satisfied.

$~$~$~$~$

"Thank you so much Jennifer, I don't know how I'll ever be able to repay you." Tracy said once they had been processed out of the federal pre-trial facility. "If it wasn't for you and your family, I would have been stuck in here for a mighty long time. I don't have anyone that has

434

my back like that. All I want to do right now is get my kids, sit down and raise them the correct way. I don't want to have to work shady jobs because my baby's father instructed me to. I don't want to have to watch my back because my baby's father has beef. I just want peace."

Jennifer smiled at Tracy. She was like her in so many ways. A person who had gone through so much and deserved the happiness that was on the other side of the pain. They were standing outside of the facility waiting on Jennifer's parents to come, and there was no one out there except for them. Jennifer's plan was to move to Oklahoma so she could get away from the fast paced life that Houston, Texas continued to bring to her. She wanted better for her life. She wanted to give herself to the Lord.

"Tracy baby, no matter what problems you're having, I can help you. If you need a place so that you can get yourself together, you're so welcome to join us out in Oklahoma. I'm not going to try to force religion on you; but just know that it's something that I've been thinking about for quite some time now. It's a very peaceful environment out there and I'm going to go study and get my life together."

"Thank you Jennifer." Tracy said as she smiled at the new glow on Jennifer's face. It was like an angel had come to her and finally awakened her. It was amazing. "But… I'm not sure I want to intrude like that right now. I appreciate everything that you've done for me, and I appreciate the gesture; just let me think on it and I'll call you, O.K.?"

Just as Jennifer was about to answer, a grey SUV came swerving into the parking lot. The passenger's side door unlocked and Sweetback Fatty hopped out with a pistol in his hand. "Get in the muthafuckin' truck bitch!"

Tracy could feel her heart as it sank along with her dreams of living drama free. It just was not going to happen. Still, despite all of the fear that Sweetback was bringing to her at that moment, she still decided to try to stand up for herself. There was no way she could just let this man handle her any type of way anytime he felt like it. There *had* to be a threshold.

"No Sweetback. Please leave me alone! Please just let me live my life." She pleaded.

Sweetback walked up to her with a smirk on his face. "And your life includes going to federal prison when you have kids out here that need their mom? Fuck no! get your dumb ass in the truck bitch."

"Noooo! Get your hands off of me!" Tracy screamed as Sweetback grabbed her left wrist. She tried to pull her wrist away from his grip, but he was just too strong for her. She pulled and struggled, but to no avail. "Pleeeaaasseee Sweetback! Pleeeeasee leave me alone!" She begged him with tears flowing down her face.

"Shut up bitch!" He said as he started pulling her towards the SUV. But the closer he got to the SUV, the more she started to fight him. It was like she knew that if she got inside of that SUV, it would mean death for her, and she was doing everything that she possibly could to prevent it. She started swinging her other fist at his face, and that's when he had to wrap her up so that he wouldn't have to kill her in public.

As soon as he wrapped her up, Jennifer had run over to try to help Tracy. "Get off of herrrrr! Get offff of her!!! Get offff of her stupid!! Get the fuck off!" She was hitting him on the head with her shoe, irritating him with a passion. He took his hand and blocked one of the shoes, then took a good look at who was hitting him.

A random white bitch?

He didn't know her from anywhere, and definitely couldn't understand what the fuck she had to do with why he was taking his baby mama to the house. "Look, you stupid ass white bitch! Get the fuck away from me and go mind your own business. Never step in black folks business when one of them has a pistol. What the fuck is wrong with you?"

Jennifer continued to swing her shoe at him regardless of the words he spoke and threats he made. When he continued to ignore her and kept dragging Tracy to the SUV, Jennifer went to drastic measures. "In the name of the Lord, I rebuke the devil! Help us down here Lord. Help us to save this woman. Punish and teach this man a lesson Lord. Punish him God. Teach him he can't put his hands on women like this."

Sweetback grabbed Jennifer's throat and slammed her against the window of the SUV. He pointed the barrel at her head while staring into her eyes. "Bitch, you can't ask God to punish me! What the fuck was *you* thinking!? You obviously don't know much about what you're talking about, but I'm gonna teach you! You wish punishment upon me, and I wish death upon you. You can't curse me to the Heavens above! But I *can* curse you to the Hell *below! Ca-clam! Ca-clam!"*

He shot Jennifer once in the chest and once in the head while he held on to her throat like a madman. Sweetback's driver rolled the window down and screamed at him. "Nigga you can't be out here killing white bitches in *public!* You about to get us *all* the muthafuckin death penalty!"

Sweetback looked back at his driver with a crazed look on his face.

437

"Yo, I *had* to kill her for what she said to me! If you'd had this same stuff said to you while you were minding your own business, you would have done the same muthafuckin thing!"

Tracy was in a mental stupor. She was in shock as she stood there staring at Jennifer Power's dead body. Tears were streaming down her face so fast that she didn't even feel like they were hers. She was hurt. In all of her years, it had taken sooo much to find a genuine friend who wanted nothing for payment. Jennifer hadn't had ulterior motives, didn't want to be introduced to millionaire street dudes, didn't need an occasional ride to the club or the mall in a nice car; didn't want anything but to give her life over to the Lord.

Tracy didn't even realize it when Sweetback had picked her up and sat her in the backseat. To Tracy, she still felt like she was standing still and watching Jennifer's dead body. "Ahhhhhh! Ahhhhhh! Ahhhhh! Ahhhhhh!" Tracy released a series of screams in a delayed pattern once the SUV had pulled off. "You just killed Jennifer Powers! You just killed her! Whyyyy! Why you kill her!!! Whyyyyy!"

The driver caught Sweetback's eye as he glanced over at him. Neither of them knew that the white lady was Jennifer Powers, but they were glad that she was. The Bankroll Squad always acted like they were the greatest things that had ever walked the planet. They had always acted as if they were untouchable, even when they were in the midst of defeat. Sweetback was happy to be able to teach them a lesson, no matter how they had to receive it.

He turned around with the pistol pointed at Tracy. "Bitch, shut up! As soon as we get in the yard, I swear on everything I'ma beat your fuckin ass!"

Tracy kept screaming for her friend. She didn't hear anything that Sweetback was saying because it was irrelevant. As soon as Jennifer had attempted to turn a new leaf, she'd had her life taken away from her. It was so sad of a situation that Tracy's soul refused to accept it as truth. She closed her eyes and started shaking from the sorrow that she felt for Jennifer and Jennifer's family. Her heart went out to Malcolm, who had no idea that his wife had been murdered. She put her hands over her face and continued to cry.

CHAPTER 10

Brink was in Miami outside of a StarBucks in a meeting with a guy by the name of Roraf. He'd met Roraf in a bar right after he got through arguing with Luther about which way to go about leaving the country. Luther was swearing up and down that simply taking a commercial flight was going to work out fine; but Brink had known better. There was way too much security at the airport, and they were on the FBI's wanted list. It made absolutely no sense.

In any normal circumstance, Brink would never have approached Roraf; but when he saw him snorting cocaine and getting drunk, he figured Roraf had to be a guy in the know. And it turned out that he was.

Roraf had a brother named Ralph who was the captain of a ship. As a side hustle, he worked with criminals trying to flee the country, people trying to take things out of the country; and people trying to bring things back into the country. "Yea, my man, I told my bro about you, and he should be here any minute homes." Roraf said as he put fire to a freshly rolled, *long* ass blunt. The strong stench of the weed sent a tingling wave through Brink's head.

He coughed and stood up to avoid the smell of it. "How long has your brother been a captain Roraf?"

Roraf inhaled his blunt and held it for a second. Then he released it like an album. "He's been a captain for 8 years now Brink. My brother is the shit man, you'll see. When you meet him, you're going to be like "damn this dude is cool." Watch what I tell you my man. You wanna hit this shit? I'm smoking *loud!* Hahaha! I'm smoking that 2 Chainz! Hahahaha! It's an extension cord! I love this shit! You understand this extension cord thing? I rolled two long ass blunts together and made an even longer one! This shit is amazing!"

Brink shook his head at Roraf's antics. Roraf had him at ease, and he was glad that he had chosen to take his route to fleeing the country as opposed to Luther's. He stretched while he was standing up, and decided that he would need to get on that ship as soon as possible so that he could get some sleep.

"Roraf, when-"

"Yo Brink! There go my brother right there in that Bentley!"

Brink looked in the direction that Roraf was pointing and saw an older model, 1999 Bentley pull up to the Starbucks. He took the last parking spot available and didn't pay the parking toll. He opened the door and got out wearing a shiny gray business suit and carrying a black brief case. He looked like he could pass for a mobster instead of a captain.

"Yea, don't let the suit and the suitcase fool ya Brink! People with briefcases can steal more than people with guns can. Heyyyyy Ralphy!" Roraf stood up and greeted his brother. He hugged him and they both sat down.

"How you doing Roraf? Is everything well?"

"Yea, everything is indeed well babeee! You know I'm doing well.

Hey, this is my new friend Brink; he's trying to make it up out of here. You feel me?"

Ralph nodded his head knowingly. "Yea, I feel ya; I can dig it." He reached his head towards Brink and they shook. "Nice to meet you Brink."

Brink sat there with so many questions that he didn't know where to begin. He didn't have much time, so he just started randomly. "So… when can I leave?"

"Hahaha! Relax Brink baby," Ralph said. "Relax… First, tell me where you're trying to get to."

Without hesitation, Brink answered. "Cuba. Immediately."

Ralph shook his head. "I'm sorry, I can't do Cuba; but I can do Haiti. From there you can more than likely get to wherever it is you're trying to get to by taking a flight. But Cuba is off-limits for me. Will you need to drop something off and come back, or will you need to pick something up and come back?"

Brink shook his head. "Neither. I just want out of here."

Ralph and Roraf shook their heads in mutual understanding. "Ohhh, I get it. You need to get out of the U.S. for good. That can be done. How much money do you have?" Ralph asked him.

Brink was baffled by that question. "How much do I need? Let me know the price and I'll see if I can cover it."

Ralph smiled for a second while he thought about the various numbers he could throw at him. "O.K., well I need $10,000 for that trip. You can pay me a $5,000 deposit right at this moment and I'll have a spot ready for you for tomorrow night. You'll be in Haiti and two and a half days. Is that fine?"

Brink looked disturbed. "Roraf, you told me that your brother was only going to charge me $2,500. I told you that that was all I had until I got over to my destination. Once I get there, I can send you whatever you want; I'm far from being a broke nigga. I just don't have any cash on me. Hook me up Roraf. Please man, you promised me."

Roraf took a toke of the extension cord he was smoking and released it in Brink's face. He winked at Ralph while Brink coughed and wiped the tears out of his face. Ralph took a deep breath of the second hand smoke that his brother had just exhaled. "O.K. O.K. Alright. Brink, I'll help you out for the $2,500. But I'll need that right now. Plus I'm going to have to put you on my friend's ship and it leaves out *tonight.* So meet me back here at 5PM and I'll introduce you and get you ready to roll."

Brink took a deep breath of appreciation. Being able to leave that night was even better than the offer that he had. *Awesome!* He thought as he hurriedly paid Ralph the $2,500. Ralph got up and shook Ralph's hand. "O.K., I'll be back here at 5PM. Be here, don't be late Brink." He walked to his Bentley, started the engine; and left.

"Alright Brink, I'm about to go get some of my own business handled, so I'll talk to you later man." Roraf said.

The two men stood up and shook each other's hand. Roraf put the extension cord out and took a deep breath of fresh air. "Brink, if I never see you again; I wish you the best aight?" They gave each other a hug and Roraf walked off. Brink was so anxious to leave the country, he decided he wasn't going to leave the Starbucks until 5PM came. He had no time to play or wait around. Time was of the essence for him.

$~$~$~$~$

Luther walked into the Miami airport with confidence on his face but fear in his heart. Normally he wouldn't be afraid of anything, but Brink had him second guessing his own decision making skills. He'd had to ditch his pistol in order to walk into the airport and go through the necessary procedures, and that had him pissed off more than anything. Now, if anything were to jump off, he'd just be a sitting target at the mercy of the government. He hated that.

However, he'd done all of the necessary requirements to ensure that he didn't appear on their radar. He'd met up with a guy from Venezuela named Prirec who had sold him legitimate credentials. He had a passport and 2 forms of identification. The IDs had real people's names on them and his picture. He was hoping that Prirec was keeping it real with him, but all he had to go on was the recommendation from the streets.

He walked up to the counter and could have sworn that he saw a guy staring him down from his right side. He shifted his body weight and stance to the opposite direction as he stood at the counter. "Hey, I would like a one-way flight to Boracay, Philippines."

The lady behind the desk hit a few buttons and stood there smiling. "O.K. The best we can do is a flight from Miami to Kalibo, Phillippines. The exact route will be Miami to Los Angeles, the Los Angeles flight will take you to Manila, Phillippines; and then you will fly from Manila, to Kalibo, Phillippines. So… from Kalibo, you'll have to find transportation to Boracay… is this a ticket you're interested in purchasing?"

Luther hurriedly paid for his ticket and turned to go through the check in process. As he made his way to the metal detector, he could have sworn that he saw the same exact guy from the beginning staring at him. He was wearing black shades and a black suit, and seemed to be talking through a radio to someone. *Shit!* Luther thought as he went through the metal detector.

Ancccckkkk! The metal detector went off, bringing even more attention to him. At that point, he just knew that it was over for him. He should have listened to Brink when he'd tried to warn him. The man started walking over to his direction, and that sent beads of sweat going down his face. He reached in his pocket and pulled the coins out that had set the metal detector's alarm off. He placed them into the basket and walked on through the detector.

The man had gone and consulted with another person wearing the same style suit and glasses. They were pointing, staring, and nodding their heads. Luther's heart dropped to the floor as he tried to suck it up and take his lick like a man. He would never be mad at a decision that he made, regardless of the outcome; he did what *he* wanted to do, and not what anyone else wanted of him. So if he erred, then his error was self-made; he could never be angry at that. All men were entitled to errors and corrections.

When he got on the other side of the metal detector, he continued to walk down to the section that was located on his ticket. The two men had turned to four men now and were following him the whole way. He said a prayer for Kyla, a prayer for Rain, a person whom he had a lot of love for; and a prayer for Malcolm. He said a prayer for the whole Bankroll Squad, and wished them nothing but the best. As for him, he knew they were about to send him to prison and he was just ready to get the shit over with.

445

Abruptly, he stopped and turned to face the four men who had been following him down the walk-way. "What the fuck do you want from me?" Luther screamed with irritation in his voice.

The first man that he saw when he first entered the airport spoke up. "Hey, my name is Tony Riller. I'm an agent. Do you have time to come speak with me?"

Agent? What the fuck?! "An *agent?* What the fuck do you want from me?" Luther asked with panic in his voice. If he'd had a pistol, he would have shot his way out of the situation. But he didn't have one. He felt like the biggest idiot as the guy pulled out his wallet and showed his credentials.

"I'm from Acme Motion Pictures. I'm a casting agent. When I saw you, I knew that you had the look that we needed for this new movie. You'd be perfect for the role. It could be worth as much as $1.5 million for you. What do you say?"

Luther was so caught off guard that he didn't know how to respond. He stood there with a blank expression on his face. The man had confused him so much that it seemed as if the room was swirling around him at a rapid pace. Luther took full deep breaths and tried to relax himself. There was no time for a panic attack at that moment.

"O.K. Tony. Just give me your information and I'll be sure to get back to you. I have to take a trip right now, but I'll certainly give you a call when I get back. Is that alright?"

The casting agent smiled. "Sure! Filming for the movie won't start until a year from now, so take your time. Even if you're not back from your trip, we can come to wherever you are and film it. Here's my card. And thanks!"

One of the other 3 guys looked at the man as if he was being a nuisance. "Are you finally finished sir? You're lucky we haven't reported you to the authorities by now, as long as you've been in here harassing people about this movie."

"But it's very important! I…."

The four men walked off into the distance, leaving Luther standing there with his heartbeat going triple the normal speed. The only thing he would have to do is clear customs, and he'd be fine. There was still a bit of doubt about him being able to make it. There was no way the FBI was going to slip that bad and let him fly across the United States and *then* fly out of the country. There was just no possible way.

But a couple of hours later, he was in Los Angeles.

And a day after that, landed in Manila, Philippines with millions of dollars deposited at the bank in his name.

There was no extradition treaty. There was no going back to the United States. He had made it. He was officially a muthafuckin' boss.

$~$~$~$~$

Kyla and Rain stood in the parking lot of Trapquarters while talking to Treasure. She was learning as much as possible from Treasure, who was a veteran when it came to breaking out of prison.

"And Kyla… last thing but not least; in fact I should have told you this first… Make *sure* that you watch the news *every* night and *every* morning! The news will tell you where you stand in life. You're a public figure; which means that the public figures that you need to be arrested. In order to protect your interests, you will need to know where

447

they're looking for you at. The news will allow that. It will expose their hands and show you the latest developments. Based on that, you can find out how and where to move. But you have to be smart about it."

Kyla and Rain were nodding their heads while listening to the knowledge that Treasure was kicking. It was truly a work of beauty, the amount of criminal intelligence that she had accumulated throughout the years. Kyla felt as if she had found a kindred spirit, and wanted to remain in contact with her. She'd listened to her story about how Benji had set her up for life in prison and wished that she had been able to help her before she became a federal fugitive... But as long as she was free, it didn't matter how it happened.

"So... yea Kyla... You need to go to Yahoo and Google and search for the latest news related to your situation. Then you need to turn the news on in the next 10 minutes so that you can see what's going on in real-time as well. I gotta run, I have to go turn the news on too. God Bless you Kyla and I pray that we can meet again one day."

Kyla smiled at her. "Yea, I think we'll be able to arrange that... boss to boss."

Treasure nodded her head. "Hell muthafuckin' yea... boss to muthafuckin' boss."

$~$~$~$~$

Treasure got into the car with Skye and Milan and started it up. She was revitalized after having such a power conversation with Kyla and knew that if she could do it big, then the door was open for her to do it as well. She turned her radio up and drove to the gas station a few blocks away. She was a huge fan of the Bankroll Squad, and an even bigger fan of the work that Kyla had put in. The stuff that Kyla had

448

already done in her young life was enough to solidify her as one of the realest criminals in the history of the game.

Treasure got out of the car at the gas pump. She checked her surroundings and saw nothing out of the ordinary, so she felt confident that she could handle her business and get out of the way as soon as possible. "Treasure," Skye said in her exaggerated husky voice, "do you want me to pump the gas babe?"

Treasure threw on her sunglasses and smirked at Skye through them. Skye smiled at her arrogance and threw her hand at her. Milan leaned from the back seat into the front and turned the music up until their trunk was rattling from the bass that the subs were pumping out. She had been trying to outdo the vehicle that had just pulled up on the other side of the gas pump. Its sound system was beating so loud that the girls could hardly focus on their own thoughts.

After realizing that their system was no competition, Skye reached forward and shut theirs off. "It's no need for acting like monkeys out here Milan. This is no competition; we'll just have to come harder next time."

"What the fuck you mean?" Milan remarked, her hot-headed nature starting to raise her blood pressure.

Skye exhaled and shook her head. She was in no mood to argue with Milan at that moment. She was exhausted. "I don't mean a thing Milan... I'm sorry. I just have a headache."

Milan didn't respond well to neutral demeanors unless they were committing a robbery. She sat there silently staring at her sister and shaking her head in disbelief.

449

Her sister caught her staring and cracked a sly smile in return.

"You guys get down! Get down!!" Treasure screamed. Her scream sounded raw and far from the natural voice that she normally used. It put Milan and Skye's nerves on edge and they didn't know what to do except follow the instructions given to them by their leader.

Their instinct told them to get their guns and shoot whoever the culprit was, but their bodies wouldn't allow them. Their mentality told them to take whatever the culprit was going to dish out, as long as they dished out bullets in return; but an invisible shield held them back.

Treasure couldn't believe it when she saw Rally from the Dynasty Cartel block her car in and jump out with that shotgun. Her mouth dropped open and his smirk turned into a smile.

$~$~$~$~$

"My name is Sanow."

"Nice to meet you Sanow." Pam said as she hobbled her way out of the hotel room. She had been struggling the entire flight to Colorado, but there was no way she was going to let her boss know. She had waited too long for this to turn back now. Sanow attempted to help her make it to the government van, but he only caused her more grief.

She fell and hit her shin against the pavement. "Fuck! You clumsy muthafucka! This is my only good got damn leg man, what the fuck is your problem!"

"I'm sorry, I was only trying to help you Pamela. I'm sorry, let me help-"

"Get your fuckin' paws off of me you bastard!" Pam screamed, as she struggled to lift herself up using her crutches and her one good leg. She was pissed, and she hated that she had to live life like she was living it; but it was either that, or die.

She hobbled and hopped her way to the van and stood there. She figured that she would have to be creative in order to make her situation more bearable. She clasped two crutches together and used it almost like a pogo stick to climb into the truck. The sight looked pathetic to Sanow, but he was only following the instructions given to him by his superiors.

He got in the van after making sure that she was in and secured. As he drove down the street, he fixed his mirror and turned the air conditioner on low. "Yea… I don't know why they wouldn't send a backup or a monitor van to accompany us. This is truly some crazy shit Pamela. The government wants his transfer top secret so that they can try to convince him to cooperate one more time. So they're jeopardizing *our* safety for this shit."

Pam listened to what Sanow was saying, occasionally nodding and saying *yea* in agreement. "It's easy to give directions for something in which you are not physically responsible for the results of. That's just like George Bush…"

Pam had to tune him out. He was just running his mouth constantly without letting up or stating any facts that she could agree with. She just wanted to get this show on the road; she had better things to do. She tuned him completely out and dozed off to sleep in the van.

$-$-$-$-$

"Wake up Pamela. We're here."

Pam opened her eyes and looked at the outside of the prison. It was the most secure place she had ever seen in her life. It was state of the art in every possible dimension.

"This is how the schedule goes Pam… We only get one brief stop; just a gas station and rest stop, and then we'll have to get on the road asap. This van is tracked by three different GPS locators, so any stop for any reason that isn't mandatory will have us surrounded by local, state, and federal authorities. That's the only comforting thing about this situation."

But Pamela wasn't comforted at all. She had asked to accompany Malcolm to the facility, but she would have never guessed that they weren't going to send backup along with them. To her it seemed as if the FBI was forever placing her in dangerous situations. She hated that part of her career. If people would stop trying to get over on her, she was sure that she would never have a complaint as long as she was a federal agent.

Six armed guards came out of the front door and walked up to the van. They triple checked Pam and Sanow's credentials before the guy who was in charge spoke up. "So… it's only you two right?"

Sanow understood what he was saying, but at the same time, he was insulted. "Sir, no disrespect, but this is a federal operation and you have no right to question or interfere with it in any manner. You're only a correctional officer. Do your job."

Pam was shocked that Sanow had such a sharp mouth. She had only thought of him as a geek when she first met him.

"Very well then sir… we'll be bringing him out shortly."

"I don't know what's wrong with those idiots." Sanow said. "They just think…"

Pam sat there and ignored Sanow as he went on and on about nothing. Her mind was all over the place as she thought about the sweet payback that she was going to get by watching Malcolm suffer in the backseat of the van. She wanted him to see that *she was* valuable to a team. *She was* a leader. *She was* someone that could go to a new place and get things done.

She wanted Malcolm Powers to see that just because she couldn't get a dope deal done, didn't mean that she wasn't important. And at the end of the day, that's the only thing that was eating at her when she was with the Bankroll Squad. She'd told her therapist that she indeed was in love with Malcolm Powers and her therapist had made her swear to never repeat it ever again.

She sat in the front seat staring down at the nub on her body, feeling like she was *outside* of her body. She didn't feel like her old self at all. The only thing that she felt from her former self was her thoughts on Malcolm.

And those thoughts became that much deeper when the guards brought him out of the prison in handcuffs.

She was mesmerized by his presence. Here was a fine chocolate man who gave off the energy of a King, and carried the charming smile of a prince. Multiple emotions ran through her body as she stared at the man that she'd set up. She felt a pain ripple in the center of her heart and vibrate to the outer depths of her soul. She was hurt.

Sanow got out and made sure that Malcolm was secured with the help of the guards. He signed a few clipboards, gave a few fingerprints

453

and left the premises.

Pam looked in the rear view mirror at Malcolm. She studied his appearance, realizing that he hadn't changed even slightly. Prison couldn't break or alter a person like him. Even the prospect of spending forever in a Super Max facility didn't even add an extra week on to his appearance. He was still well groomed and composed.

His demeanor was still that of royalty and his teeth were still perfect and as white as-

"Pam, did you hear what I said? I asked you if you thought we should stop at the first gas station or if we should wait until we're halfway there to stop."

Pam had lost herself in the mirror, and hadn't realized that Sanow had been speaking to her the whole time. She opened her mouth to speak, but before a word could escape, Malcolm's eyes met hers, and she became breathless. His eyes were magnets; when hers met his, it felt as if she couldn't pull hers apart. Her thought pattern went from fluid to scattered, and she couldn't seem to pick an organized thought to save her life.

She glanced at his lips. Glanced at the structure of his face and the depth of his skin pigments, and knew that in another lifetime; that could have been hers all to herself. When he initially looked at her, she expected the hurt to pour out.

She thought that her hurting him was going to reflect in his eyes and his demeanor. Maybe that he would just completely ignore her and hate her guts for still existing… but that was not the case. She had committed the lowest of lows when it came to dishonesty, and he still didn't scowl at her or roll his eyes at her. She was impressed.

"Pam, is there a problem?"

"Oh… No Sanow. There is no problem… I think we'd better stop at the very first gas station since we're on three quarters of a tank. Let's fill it up and keep moving."

Sanow nodded. "Just understand this Pam… If I stop this vehicle once, I can *not* stop it again for any reason whatsoever. If I end up stopping this van a second time, the authorities will be on me immediately. They have *shoot to kill* greenlight instructions, and I'm trying my best not to become a part of that!"

"I know that's right. Me either!" Pam said as she re-focused her attention back on Malcolm in the mirror. She was in love with that man more than anyone could ever imagine. But there was nothing that she could do about it.

CHAPTER 11

"Bitch! You had the audacity to try me for Malcolm Powers? Huh?" *Wham!* "You thought you was gonna' get away from this shit ho? *Wham!* Sweetback Fatty was using Tracy like a punching bag. He was cocking his fist back and literally slamming it into her feminine stomach.

"Plleeeeeeeeaaaassee!" Tracy was getting beaten so bad that she couldn't even get a tear to come out. She had just recently had a miscarriage *and* lost a good friend; it had become entirely too much to carry. "Pleeeasseee! Sweeeetbacccckkk!"

Wham! Sweetback Fatty was beating her like she was the devil herself. He took his fist and slammed it into the top of her head. *Wham!*

The impact from the punch sent her face first into the dirt. There was a deep gash on the top of her head that was caused from one of the rings on Sweetback's fingers. The gash was open and blood was leaking all over the place.

Tracy had become so dizzy that she had went into complete loss of awareness. She was laying there with the ground spinning beneath her and the sky spinning the opposite direction. When she opened her eyes to try to focus, it was as if she was staring inside of a hurricane. *Wham!*

The next blow wasn't as hard as the previous ones. *Wham!* When

Sweetback Fatty hit her that time, it wasn't as difficult to accept anymore. His blows had become comforting to her. She had become used to him hitting her. Used to the weight of his fist smashing through the structure of her face and head; had become used to the domestic abuse. She had once told herself that she would never again be a victim of this artificial hell; but it was starting to seem as if *never* was an artificial word.

She had lost focus so much that she didn't even know which side of her he was on. Then, as soon as she had come to expect his punches and body blows, they stopped coming.

She heard a gun cock back, and felt instant panic. She absolutely *knew* that this was going to be the end. It had to be, there was no other option.

Ka-blam! Ka-blam! Blood was all over her face. It was all over her throat and all in her hair. Then she heard the weapon cock again. *Ka-blam!*

She didn't hear anything else.

$~$~$~$~$

Brink was still at the Starbucks café when 5PM came around. He was anxious to get on the ship so that he could get the hell up out of America. Brink paced back and forth while he waited on Roraf and his brother's friend to come. He checked his watch and sighed. They were already 8 minutes late and the clock was still running. He had been sitting there all day and he was beyond frustrated.

He looked inside of the café and saw that the manager was staring at him. Attention was something that he didn't need at that time in his life.

457

He grabbed the bottle of water that he had been drinking, and started to walk away. But as soon as he took a few steps, he saw Ralph and Roraf pull up in a Lincoln Town Car.

But something was wrong.

On one end of the street, there were men approaching him with the word FBI on their shirt. He turned to go in the opposite direction, but more men were coming from around the corner with guns drawn. He stood there looking back and forth at the men who were approaching him rapidly. He felt sick to his stomach.

He glanced at Roraf, who had no expression on his face, and who also had an FBI lettered jacket. Roraf and Ralph had guns in their hands as well, so they wouldn't be yielding to him at all if he tried to buck against them. He knew that he really wanted to run; he also knew that he would be caught or shot dead on the spot.

He thought about Luther and the words and logic that Luther had explained to him, and felt stupid for not believing him. In that moment, Brink realized what it was that Luther had. It was a trait reminiscent of the one that Malcolm contained. Luther was a leader.

Luther had been a person who could plan multiple steps ahead of the most difficult of situations and come up with a crystal clear execution plan. Brink closed his eyes as he stood there listening to the agent's boots stomping against the pavement in a rapid succession. Thinking about the people who get killed by accidents, he hurriedly threw his hands in the air so that they wouldn't think he had a gun.

He didn't realize that it was the wrong move until the first bullet entered his flesh and knocked him off of his feet.

He fell back against the Starbucks' table that he was sitting at, causing it to crack. It didn't break, it still held his weight up, although anyone could tell that it was *about* to break. He looked in the direction that the bullet came from, and couldn't focus at first. He forced his body to balance itself on the table until he could focus on the person who shot him. He did not want to die at the hands of another man without at least taking his face to Hell with him.

Finally he got a clear view... He passed out completely and fell through the table with a huge thud. While lying on the ground squirming and convulsing, he was only able to get one word out. His last word was the name of his killer.

Roorrraaaff."

$~$~$~$~$

Pam sat in the passenger seat of the government van while she waited on Sanow to finish pumping the gas. She had many things running through her mind simultaneously. Many questions that she'd wanted to ask Malcolm, but at that moment, she couldn't figure out what to ask him first. She looked inside of the store and saw that Sanow was picking up some snacks in the back of the store. There was a long line inside of the store as well, so it would be a few minutes before he got back. She decided that either she would speak or forever hold her peace.

When she turned around, Malcolm was smiling at her; her question flew out of the window. Instead, he asked the question. "Pam... I understand now that you were only doing your job when you betrayed me... But didn't you think that you also had a job with me? A very important job at that. You didn't like the opportunities that I had created for you?"

His silky voice drilled straight into her conscious; her guilt came off as panic and worry. She was supposed to be composed under duress, but she had *never* been composed when it came to matters dealing with Malcolm. "I… Yes Malcolm. I loved what you did for—"

"Then why hurt me?"

Pam heard the question and couldn't think of a legitimate enough answer, so she became silent. She searched her mind for an answer, but realized that the answers would not be there. They were in her heart.

"Because I love you Malcolm."

The words ripped through the van's silence and sent chills down both of their spines. "It's true Malcolm. I love you. I love you more than any of those other bitches *ever* could! You know why? Because I cared enough about you to want to see you *off* the streets breaking the law. *I* did that! And I'm *sorry* that I had to hurt you in the process."

Malcolm shook his head and broke his eye contact.

"Malcolm… will you please look at me?"

Malcolm continued to look away without responding.

"Look at me Malcolm! Damnit look!"

Malcolm took a deep breath and gave her one of the most menacing looks that she had ever seen. But she felt like she deserved that. She needed *something* from him so she could feel some of the hurt she'd done him. She sat there and absorbed the hatred in his eyes for as long as it glowed. When the lights of hatred dimmed, the love shined back through.

Malcolm was a loving person, through and through. He was a man who was too much for a woman who didn't think she was enough mentally. He was tough. And she wished that things had been different.

"Pam… so you're telling me that if I'd have had sex with you, that you wouldn't have turned me in? That still doesn't change the fact that you were an undercover. Neither does it change the fact that you *did* turn me in."

Pam shook her head. "I disagree… Malcolm I was the reason that your run lasted as long as it did. I continued to slack when it was time to turn the material in on you. I loved you! And no, it wasn't only about sex… if you had *chosen* me, I would have chosen you in return. So, no, you wouldn't be here."

Malcolm frowned. "That's the most selfish shit I've ever heard. Does everything have to be about you? Why couldn't you just be happy for me?"

"Selfish? How? Why couldn't I be happy? Why? Am I a woman who doesn't deserve it? And if that's the case, show me one who does and explain the difference!"

Malcolm nodded his head at Pam. He'd always been fond of her strong attitude. It brought a smile to his face.

"Are we smiling now?" Pam asked while putting on a smile of her own.

Malcolm was about to respond when Sanow came to the van. He opened the driver's side door with his hand clutching his stomach.

461

"What's wrong with you Sanow?" Pam asked with concern in her voice. She was also hoping that he didn't see her smiling at the inmate; that would ruin her career.

"It must have been something I ate. I'm- *blouggg.*" Sanow threw up all over the pavement, and when he lifted his head up, he had tears in his eyes. "Pam… I know your situation and all… but I was wondering if you are able to drive?"

She looked at the pedal and looked at her leg. She thought about it for a second, then stretched her leg out and flexed it a couple of times. "Sure… I can drive the van. No problem."

"Thanks so much Pam… I'm sick. I'll just ride shotgun."

Malcolm watched as Pam slid over into the driver's seat with her one good leg. He shook his head at the hoops that the feds were making her crawl through. He surmised that this was a woman who'd only wanted acceptance in life, and he'd failed to accept her the way she wanted to be accepted. He sat back as he watched Sanow get in the passenger's seat and put his seat belt on.

Pam glanced in the mirror as she started up the van. Her mind was set.

"Pam, we must go now." Sanow said as he checked his watch."

"O.K. Sanow." She said as she backed away from the gas station to turn around. When she had backed up away from the store, she reached down and grabbed her service pistol.

"Do you want me to hold it for you while you drive Pam?" Sanow asked as he studied how bad she looked in her situation.

Pam glanced at Sanow without speaking.

She then turned to Malcolm and smiled. "Malcolm. A true friend is one who has the same enemies that you have. I remember when you first told me that."

She pointed the pistol at Sanow's neck and blew him a kiss in the rear view mirror. "This is for you." *BLOUW!*

Malcom panicked when he saw her kill the federal agent. *If she was killing agents, then surely he was next*, but he was wrong…

She hit the gas and rode the feeder road up onto the expressway. She was coasting along at 65 miles per hour. Malcolm had no idea what the fuck was going on, but he *did* know that he was tired of taking charges for people he hadn't killed.

When they were 20 miles away from the federal pre-trial facility, Pam looked in the rear view with a smirk on her face. "Malcolm, I've been thinking… I was disloyal to you, but it wasn't how I really felt. That's not the way I intended for it to be. I wanted you to *love* me and *need* me. I know that you're in a tough position right now, but I also know that I've finally gotten my wish Malcolm. If you don't love me right now, you sure as hell *need* me right now."

Pam opened a safety slot on the protective window and slipped him the handcuff key. "Malcolm, I wish you nothing but the best. You're going to have to jump out as soon as I slow down… I can't stop this vehicle or they will kill us."

Malcolm picked up the key and stared at her. "But what will happen to you, Pam?"

Pam smiled her brightest smile. "Oh, I'm gonna be just fine! I'll see you some other time Malcolm… I love you."

He was shocked. Malcolm Powers had seen and done a lot in his short life span, but he could have *never* imagined the turn of events that had jeopardized his freedom. And now he was a free man. He looked at Pam one last time, saw the tears streaming down her face, and said a silent prayer for both of them before he jumped out of the van.

$~$~$~$~$

Pam glanced into the rearview mirror and watched as Malcolm hit the ground. He was a man who had great upper body strength, so he was able to support his weight without rolling through the grass that he'd landed in. Tears continued streaming down her face as she sped away from her past. She was going 70 miles an hour, but it seemed as if she still couldn't escape it fast enough.

Without thinking about it, Pam continued to drive. She looked at her watch and figured that she'd given Malcolm plenty of time to make a getaway. She had at least 15 miles to go before she reached the facility. But those 15 miles seemed to have went by in 15 seconds; and before she knew it, she was nearing panic mode.

She thought about what the consequences would be once she made it to the pre-trial facility without the Bureau of Prison's most prized inmate and a dead body in the van. She shook her head when she saw the sign in front of her. It read: FEDERAL CORRECTIONS PRE-TRIAL 3 MILES.

At the speed that she was going, she had about 3 minutes total to figure out the greatest excuse in the world. She also knew that if she pulled into the parking lot in 3 minutes, that there was also a great possibility that they would easily be able to catch up with Malcolm. She didn't want to have done all of these things for him and it not help. She *needed* it to work in order for her conscious to be freed. She cried as she saw the exit approaching for her required destination.

She ventured off to the exit, and at the last second; she jerked the wheel back onto the expressway. She pressed down on the gas harder, pushing the van to 90 miles an hour on the open road. She drove and cried; the whole while praying and hoping that Malcolm had made it to a safe place. She missed Malcolm, and would forever miss him, but she knew that he deserved better as a person. He had done more for her than the FBI had ever done, and she felt that it was to him that her loyalty was owed.

She looked above her and saw a helicopter tracking the van.

She looked in the rear view and saw a stream of police cars following her every move.

Despite what the odds were, she continued to drive. She pushed it harder, making her way to 110 miles an hour on the expressway. She had lost a leg for the FBI, but had gained soul from the experience.

The needle on the dash reflected the speed of the van and the rate of her heartbeat. It was truly an exciting time for Pam. At that moment, there was no question that she *was* valuable. There was no question that she was *needed.* She had always wanted to feel as if she was a part of something big, and by the people on the outside not knowing what was going on inside of the van; she *owned* the moment.

She thought about how much of a hero she must look on CNN Live. She thought also about her double-crossing mom, and sighed.

She kept driving. Speeding. Running from her past with only one leg remaining.

50 minutes into her chase, she looked ahead and saw her future. Finally.

She slowed down to a stop as she stared at the 60 or so police cars all assembled into a barricade. She looked behind her and saw that there was no turning back. She looked above; and even if she could fly… she couldn't. Finally she sat there and took a deep breath. She prayed for Malcolm's well-being, and rolled down her window just enough for the cameras to catch what she was about to do.

Off to the side angles were police officers standing around with guns drawn, ready to kill who they *thought* was driving the vehicle.

But when they got a load of who was really in charge, they would shit their clothes.

Pam shot a bird out of the window and pointed it at the sky as she stomped on the gas pedal. The van charged forward like a running back; although it had no blockers, no protection.

Bullets spiraled from all directions. There were so many bullets entering the van, that they had almost made it transparent.

As the bullets entered Pam's body, she thought about how it would have ended up if the inmate *had* hi-jacked the van. She realized that if that were the case, that they would have killed her anyway. That last thought made her feel better about betraying the FBI.

Her last thought was that she'd rather betray the world than let the world betray her.

CHAPTER 12

She woke up to a household full of confusion and a man with a warm damp towel repeatedly patting the top of her head. She was dizzy at first, and tried desperately to regain her focus. She blinked rapidly, and opened her eyes as wide as possible; as if that was going to make a difference. After a while, the room stopped spinning and she was overcome with a strong feeling of déjà vu.

She saw Catfish and was instantly reminded of the time when she'd been kidnapped by that same person along with a few of his other cronies. In a panic, she looked around the room; but only saw two other women.

"Where- where am I?" Tracy asked as Catfish continued cleaning the blood off her face. "And what happened? I thought I was dead."

Before Catfish could answer, she burst into tears while mentally reliving the horrible beating that she had just endured. Catfish felt sorry for her and her situation. He had witnessed the terrible beating and had been inspired to step in and help her. Although he'd went to Sweetback's house for information on Pam, his natural protective instincts had kicked in and he'd been forced to kill Sweetback.

The size of the bullet holes that he left in Sweetback's body were the size of a child's fist. He had a natural passion for always wanting to protect a woman; his woman or otherwise. He dipped the towel in the

467

water and squeezed it out while she sat there staring at the wall.

"You passed out Tracy. Sweetback was well on his way to killing you. I *stopped* him."

"How did you-"

"I *killed* him, Tracy."

Tracy's tears came out even faster when she realized the depths of the situation. She remembered thinking to herself while getting beat, that surely death will rescue her.

It did.

Tracy got up off the sofa, but without a destination. She stood there, unaware of who she was with or where she was. She recognized the guy, but had no idea who the women were. She looked at them, and looked back at the guy who'd rescued her. "You killed Sweetback!!"

She sat back down and cupped her hands around her face, allowing her tears to flow freely. She was happy that she'd finally gotten Sweetback off of her back, but she didn't know if she wanted that over having her kids grow up without a *father*. She made a mental note to go pick her kids up from her mother's house. They had been staying with her since all of the Bankroll Squad beef kicked off and it was time that she went and got them.

She looked up at Catfish, her face wet with remorse; his face shining with satisfaction. She glanced from his face to the two women sitting at the table staring at her. She got up and walked over there with her hand extended.

"Tracy. What's your name?"

"Hey Tracy, my name is Rain."

"Nice to meet you…" Tracy said as she stood there awkwardly. She looked at the other woman, and was taken aback by the strength of her beauty. She was amazing. "I- I'm Tracy…"

"I know who you are."

Tracy swallowed. She didn't know where the icy tone was coming from, and didn't have the energy to delve into it. She had seen so much death in the past few days that she didn't know whether she was going or coming. She knew that she would have to get herself together soon though so that she could move on with her life.

"So… what's your name?"

"Kyla."

"Nice to meet you, Kyla."

"Yep."

Yep? I know this bitch didn't just tell me yep! I oughta-

"Look Tracy. Wipe that fuckin' mean mug off your face. Don't be staring at me like you want to *do* something when you know you *don't.* You already pissed me off with the rumors of you and Malcolm, but that's so petty to me right now that it's irrelevant. So we automatically will start off on the wrong foot. And don't roll your got damn eyes at me either. You know what? Listen here… for lack of a better phrase, *bitch* I'll beat that ass!"

Tracy stood there knowing that she didn't feel like fighting, nor did she have any fight left in her spirit. She was tired of it, and wanted to really let go… but she knew that the only way to let go was to let God. Just when she was about to speak, Catfish interrupted her.

"Guys! Turn the television up! Hurry!"

Kyla grabbed the remote and turned the volume up almost to the max as they all stared at the screen with wide eyes.

"I'm Donavan Smiff with Fox 29 breaking news. We are live on the scene of a complete disaster! The young leader of the notorious criminal enterprise known as the Bankroll Squad has escaped from a Super Maximum security federal prison here in Colorado. Authorities say that the entire situation was a breach of required protocol, and that there will be severe punishments and infractions handed down to multiple federal employees.

This comes after Malcolm Powers, leader of the infamous Bankroll Squad had been sentenced to serve his entire natural life in federal prison for an assortment of crimes, including murder and international drug trafficking. He had recently been indicted on a host of new charges stemming from his daring escape attempt from federal custody. The FBI was attempting to transport him to a federal pre-trial facility in Denver when he escaped. He was to be formally charged for organizing the escape that left two federal marshals dead. Retired federal defense attorney, Billy Powell was open in his criticism of the feds:

"This is a pathetic example of how our justice system can sometimes fail. It comes off as a ridiculous attempt by the FBI to try to milk every second of a big case; even when the case is over and the people have been sentenced. I feel as though they should have just let the man be. He was already sentenced to life in prison! He was never getting out! He was in a super maximum security prison, and they had the nerve to

try to add charges to him? I am appalled by the way that the protocol was breached to allow for this madness.

Officials everywhere went on high alert for the escaped convict when the government transport van shot straight past the facility, leading authorities on a high speed chase. Helicopters and all levels of local and state law enforcement pursued the vehicle for close to an hour, going at speeds upwards of 110 miles an hour at times.

Eventually, they laid down a barricade in order to stop the vehicle. The vehicle paused for a second, then took off straight towards the police. They opened fire on the vehicle, killing all of the passengers that were inside. Among those that were killed, were Special Agent Pamela Jones and U.S. Marshal Wilson Sanow.

Convicted crime family leader, Malcolm Powers is currently still at large. I am Donavan Smiff, Fox 29."

"Whooaaaaaa shit!!" Kyla, Catfish, and Rain said simultaneously.

They were overjoyed at the prospect of having their leader, their friend, lover, and family member back into the warm folds of their presence. Catfish clenched his fist up and closed his eyes. "That's my muthafuckin' nigga to the end! I knew he was gonna make something happen. He's always been a cut above the rest. He got out on his *own*! Ha!"

Tracy smiled. She was truly happy for them all, but she knew that this particular crowd was no longer for her. She had learned a lot from Jennifer in the small amount of time that she'd been around her. Tracy thought about her nervous laughter and the beautiful presence that she had become towards the end of her life. She was sad that Jennifer's life was cut short, but she also knew that when it was your time to go, you just could not stay. She said a silent prayer for everyone in the room and walked out of the house.

She looked back at Trapquarters one final time, feeling confident that Malcolm was going to be in good hands with the people inside of that house. Tracy had personal and spiritual things to do. She was going to give her life to the Lord the same way that Jennifer had planned to. She was going to walk in the footsteps that Jennifer had planned. She was going to allow Jen to live through her; and she was going to provide closure on the situation with Jen's family. Praise God.

Rain thought about the journey that she had taken along with Kyla, and was happy that she was finally going to get her man without any more interruptions.

Kyla was on her knees in prayer. "Lord, only *you* know the ordeal that I've just been through. I say only *you* because *you* understand the mental and emotional rollercoaster that I've been on. I also know that *you* love me unconditionally, and that the love you have for me, helps me to love others the same. Only *you* could teach me the things that I needed to know instead of what I wanted to know. Only *you* could bring me what I need exactly when I needed it. There is no such thing as *my* plans. I only plan around what you have already put onto my schedule. You are everything to me. Thank you, lord. Amen."

Kyla got up off of the floor with tears in her eyes and a half smile on her face. "So do we have to go pick up Malcolm now?"

Catfish laughed at her, then shook his head. "So you mean to tell me… that me and you had the mindset to come to Trapquarters, yet *Malcolm* won't have the mind to come here? You know better Kyla. I say we lay low and wait. He'll be here… He knows this is the only place that isn't hot."

Kyla started laughing while she wiped the tears from her eyes. She looked at Rain and Catfish, and was happy that she was surrounded by these two people instead of the others. These two people represented everything that she stood for, the loyalty and royalty. She went and pulled her chair up to the window and sat there while she daydreamed about how life was going to be in the Philippines with Malcolm and her family. She looked down and rubbed her stomach. She didn't even know how many months along she was because of all of the things that she'd been through. She couldn't wait to tell Malcolm that she was carrying his child. Kyla giggled to herself as she thought about the infinite happiness that she was about to receive.

$$S\sim S\sim S\sim S\sim S$$

Malcolm had done so much for so many people, that it was easy for him to get the favors returned. His first favor returned was the one that took him out of Colorado in the trunk of a black Cadillac DHS. His Mexican friend took him from Colorado to Dallas, where he called upon another favor.

His Dominican friend took him from Dallas to Houston in a white Yukon. His Dominican friend had so many guns in the SUV, that if the police pulled them over; they would be the last people they would ever pull over.

His Cuban friend, Astillo picked him up when he got to Houston and took him to the street where Trapquarters was located. They rode over there in a Cadillac Escalade with dark tints on it. When Malcolm saw the street, his heart dropped to the floor.

Police were everywhere.

473

"Yo… what the fuck is going on over here? You haven't heard anything?" Malcolm asked his friend.

"Oh yea… They was saying something about the Lipstick Clique and the Dynasty Cartel having a shootout or something. They said some girl got shot or some shit, I don't know…"

It made sense to him then. He'd seen police officers piled up at the gas station and thought that maybe they had stationed over there waiting on his return. But he knew that couldn't be the case when he saw the coroner's van. The entire crime scene was stripped off, and he instantly started to worry that maybe it was Treasure who'd gotten killed. He hoped not.

They parked the vehicle adjacent to the Trapquarters location, and Malcolm jumped out. "Just relax, I'll be right back playa. If you need money to convince you to stay, put a price in your mind and release the price when I return. I *am* Bankroll Squad, so you never have to worry about that when it comes to me."

Astillo shook his head. "Already too much for me you've done." He spoke in his ragged accent. "I here. I wait, you go. My word you got."

Malcolm went across the street and raised his hand to knock on the door, but before it could even connect, Catfish pulled the door open. Malcolm went in and hugged his best friend. He was happy that the Catfish that he'd known had overcome everything and was back. It was an wonderful time for the both of them.

Malcolm walked into the living room and saw Rain laying on the sofa with her legs hanging across on a wooden table. She was sleeping peacefully. He looked around and saw a woman sleeping in a chair facing the window.

Kyla.

To Malcolm Powers, Kyla was the most beautiful person in existence. Even while asleep, she looked awake and lively with emotion. She was a woman who couldn't be described in skin type, hair type, weight, or height. She was a woman that could never be described in words. In his eyes, she was Kyla Powers; a woman that could barely be described in pictures.

His mental picture of her couldn't be taken with any cameras in existence. The image was so big and detailed, that it would take at least 26 years to upload.

Her smile was the brightest thing he had ever known. He'd once thought that his future was bright, but when he couldn't see her smile anymore; the brightness turned dim.

Her hands were delicate and refined; her eyes were beautiful moons that lit up his night.

Malcolm turned to Catfish. "Get Rain, it's time for us to roll, asap."

Malcolm picked Kyla up while she was sleeping. He moved carefully so he wouldn't wake her, but after taking three steps, she leaned in towards him and gave him the most passionate French kiss that he had ever received. Her eyes were closed, but her soul was wide awake. She opened them briefly and shook her head. "Damn Malcolm... even in my dreams you get the job done. Mmmm." She was tired.

They got into the car and Astillo took off.

"Where to Mal?" Astillo said, as he rolled through traffic.

475

He thought about it for a second before he answered. "Astillo, can you make us legit fake passports and IDs? How long will it take you?"

Astillo laughed. "I have the stuff in my trunk right now as we speak. I actually have that stuff already made for you, Kyla, and Catfish; I just didn't know about... What's your name baby?"

"Rain."

"O.K. Rain. When we stop, I can take the picture; and I can put it all together in five or six minutes."

Malcolm nodded his head. "Well in that case, I think our best bet is to take a commercial flight straight out of this bitch. They'll never expect any one of us to be bold enough to take a flight, and that's why it'll work. Let's roll."

And when Malcolm said it, no one questioned it or even thought twice about it. They took it for what it was, a boss decision from the most talented of all bosses. Malcolm's IQ was beyond that of an average man, and his street IQ was supreme to all. To question him would be like questioning the color of the sky.

Kyla woke up and knew she was in heaven. She wanted to scream, but she held it. Wanted to jump, but she controlled it. She wanted to run, but she relaxed. Her heart beat fast and she inhaled quicker. Her brain was tingling. Her *body* was tingling. She knew that no matter what happened in their lives, that there was no way that she could be without her man ever again.

Malcolm looked into her eyes and saw the surface of his existence. Kyla was so inspirational to him, so motivating and beautiful; that he knew she would forever be the one for him.

Malcolm sat back in the seat and stared at the scenery as they rode through the city. He thought about everything that they had done and everything that they were planning to do; he knew that there was only one phrase available to describe their success.

Bankroll Squad isn't a gang, it's a lifestyle.

$~$~$~$~$

Boracay, Phillippines was beautiful. The texture of the sand and the color of the water… It made for an extremely effective backdrop of Happily Ever After. It was amazing. Kyla and Malcolm were millionaires. They were set for life. Catfish was rich. Luther and Rain had gotten together, and they too were rich.

Everything the Bankroll Squad stood for, they were *standing for*.

Kyla, Malcolm, and the newest addition to the Powers family; Majalla Powers. Their daughter was gorgeous. Powerful. She was the genetics of two legends combined inside of a compact one year old child. She was exuberant, happy, and always smiling. But she was indeed bossy. She wanted what she wanted; *when* she wanted it. There was nothing getting past her, even at one year.

Majalla was their first born. She was the picture that could describe what their lives meant. She was their heaven. The only complaint that Kyla had about her daughter was that she was soooo possessive over her daddy. Whenever Kyla laid against him, her daughter would take her little hand and try to move her out of the way. She was always running to Malcolm whenever he stood up. Majalla didn't want to do anything without her father.

But she couldn't be mad. Majalla had gotten that trait honest. She'd received it directly from Kyla. In Majalla she saw where she'd gotten her dedication, loyalty, and her obedience; from Malcolm she'd received his skin tone, lips, and command that he had over people. Majalla was such a doll.

Kyla, Majalla, and Malcolm had just pulled up to the market in their new white convertible. They were considered royalty in the Philippines. Every time they went out, they gave away stuff and never expected anything in return. People were always saluting them. Always admiring the Powers couple. Malcolm and Kyla embodied what it meant to be official street legends. Legends that defied all odds in order to obey their love.

"Kyla, you wanna get out?" Malcolm asked when they parked.

She shook her head. "No... I don't feel like dealing with Majalla right now. She's sleep, so I need to let her stay that way as long as I can."

Malcolm looked into the backseat and saw Majalla's eyes closed. His baby was sleeping peacefully. Her face had love etched in the texture of her skin; her eyes, when open, radiated happiness. He smiled at her and Kyla and went inside the market to pick up a case of drinks. Catfish, Luther, Rain, and Kyla were going to have a celebration party that evening, and drinks were the only thing that Kyla had forgotten to pick up earlier.

He paid for the drinks and walked outside of the supermarket with this biggest smile on his face.

Then his smile dropped.

Kyla was sitting in the driver's seat with her head turned, facing

Majalla. She was paying no attention to her surroundings. But in the near distance, there was a girl walking towards her with a pistol in her hand. The funny thing about the woman was…

She only had one hand.

He dropped his drinks and took off running. The girl with the pistol wasn't paying attention to her surroundings either, she was completely zoned in on Kyla. She started walking faster.

Malcolm was sprinting towards the car, moving the small crowd out of his way. The closer he got to the girl, the more he started to realize who it was.

Sunshine. She had one hand cut off and a pistol in the other one. She was the same chick who Kyla said they'd left on the plane to die in the crash. And most importantly, she was the same chick who'd left him to die at the hands of the authorities when it was time for him to be helped onto the plane.

She walked up to Kyla and pointed the pistol at her. Right before she was about to shoot, Malcolm came from the side and lifted the pistol towards the sky. *Ka-blam!* The pistol went off. Malcolm twisted the pistol towards himself by mistake, trying to get it out of her hand. *Ka-blam!* A bullet lightly grazed his shoulder. He twisted it once more and the gun fell on the ground; out of their grasp.

Kyla immediately went into protection mode. But when she saw the face of the bitch that had fired the shot, she snapped.

She jumped out of the convertible without opening the door. As soon as Sunshine tried to run, Kyla grabbed her by the hair; causing her to fall backwards to the ground. But Kyla didn't let her land, her hand was still gripped and entangled in her hair. Sunshine took her one arm and tried to force Kyla's two strong hands off of her head.

To no avail. Kyla sat on top of Sunshine and mushed her face into the nasty concrete. Sunshine tried to move her body, but by her having only one hand; it was impossible under Kyla's weight. *Whap! Whap! Whap!* Kyla gave her a quick three piece to the face, each blow causing more damage to her nose. *Whap!* The last blow broke her nose, causing blood to flow freely.

"Kyla! Kyla! I love you! Please listen to me! I cut my hand off to be with you! I love-"

Whap! Whap! Whap! Kyla wasn't trying to hear *shit*! The only thing on her mind; the only thing she could focus on was beating Sunshine's ass. She thought that the bitch had died in the plane crash, not survived the muthafucka with one hand remaining. *Fuck this shit! Whap! Whap! Whap!* There was no greater feeling in the world besides being in love than beating an enemy's ass.

Kyla took both of her hands and gripped it around the front of Sunshine's neck.

"Please Ky-"

Kyla lifted Sunshine's head in the air as high as she could lift it, and sent it cascading to the pavement. But Malcolm caught Sunshine's head before it could hit the ground. "Kyla. I got you babe. I got you... You get in the car with Majalla, I'll handle this."

Kyla was seething with anger as she climbed into the car to her crying daughter. "Shhh baby, I'm here; everything's o.k. baby. Shhhh…"

480

Malcolm grabbed the pistol that Sunshine had with one hand while he grabbed her head with the other. There was a crowd of people standing around watching him with wide eyes. This was a totally different place with different rules and procedures; however the rules to loyalty were always the same no matter where a person was. He didn't even hesitate; he put the pistol to her forehead, prayed and pulled the trigger.

Ka-blam!

$~$~$~$~$

Peaches. Flowers. Strawberries. Two fruits and one plant adorned the table.

Heat. Moist. Heat. Two bodies and one thing separating them.

Malcolm's arms wrapped around Kyla's upper body like he was doing a pull-up.

He laid her down gently. Softly.

Kyla's eyes closed, mouth opened; asking for his tongue, *demanding* his tongue. *Needing* his tongue. His tongue was the greatest thing in the world, and she possessed it. Caged and controlled it.

She sucked it. Tasted it. Wanted her man in the most primal way... wanted her man in nature's rawest form.

Malcolm kissed her neck. Avoided her demanding appetite, and commanded her hunger. He controlled her body like a steering wheel, manipulated her sensitivity like a soap opera, had her open like a supermarket.

481

He was shopping. Delicacies.

He tasted what she had to offer. Tasted her structure and passion. Mouthed off at her breasts and placed the weight of them on his warm tongue.

Tongue. Breasts. Moans. Moans. Moans. Kyla was in love.

Malcolm's mouth danced around the most sensitive areas of Kyla's upper body.

One breast, two at the same time; whatever he had to do, he *did*.

He did not slack when it came to his wife. His love. His *everything*.

He tasted her waist. Her belly button. Her hip bone. Her complete midsection. He sucked it, licked it. Slurped it. Sneak previewed what was to come. He was enthralled with the taste of her. Excited about the nectar that she contained.

He'd had sex with her before. He'd even made love to her before. But tonight he was making love to his *wife* officially. The one who had been there in the beginning. The one who had his back through hell and back.

Love pushed his head down below with his tongue extended. Love pressed his tongue against Kyla's clit. Passion rotated his tongue in a circular motion. Love made him slurp the nectar that his passion was seeking. He pressed his thick lips against her clit gently and massaged it with his warmth.

"Uhhh…" Kyla expressed how she felt without thinking about it. She expressed herself never in words, but always in sounds. "Uhhhh…. Uhhhh… Uhhhh…"

Malcolm lifted her legs up to the ceiling and slurped from Kyla's clit to her spine.

"Uhhhh… Uhhhhh…. Uhhhh…. Uhhhh…. Uhhhh."

The sounds of ecstasy filled his ears and longing filled his loins. Her passionate and feminine cries made him feel like the King that he was. No woman could make him feel like a king unless she was his queen, and she had successfully gotten everything correct.

Malcolm turned her sideways and softly sucked one vagina lip at a time.

He pleasured her without restriction. He was a porn star in the making when it came down to his wife. He took his tongue and probed her anus with it, causing her nerve endings to shatter with desire.

Before he knew what was happening, she had grabbed his neck and was pulling him up towards her. She kissed Malcolm softly, her kiss becoming frozen in place when she felt his manhood rub against her opening. That was the first time that she'd felt Malcolm grow that big. Usually he'd grow big, but not *that* big.

She had aroused him on another level. She had him on the erotic expressway, driving them both down the path to an orgasmic landing.

Her vagina throbbed, pulsed; had its own heartbeat as it begged for Malcolm to fill it to capacity.

Her vagina leaked with excitement; begging for his thick penis to separate her walls with its thickness and length. Her pussy *begged* for his dick.

And it received it. In slow. Slow. Slow. Slow strokes.

He took his time and filled up every element and angle that her vagina possessed.

"Uhhhhhmmmmm…" Her head tossed back with sensation and pleasure. Her body shook in reply to the call of his strokes. And they were long strokes…

He started to speed up, but 10 strokes into his faster speed; she came in an explosion.

"Ohhh! Uhhhh! Uhhhh! Uhhhhh! Ugghhhhh! Uggggggg! Uggghhhh!"

She came twice at once.

Malcolm had taken his time and expressed how he felt about her through orgasmic calculations. And her body understood it. He had her body feeling so good, that every time she came, it felt like she was having orgasms in *sets*.

He pleasured her in deep strokes. Strokes so deep that they touched the depths of her soul.

Strokes so deep that they gave orgasms to her conscious *and* her sub-conscious mind.

She came so hard that she refused to think of it as "coming" anymore. She had long since arrived on the very first stroke. So every release from that point on, was referred to as "returning."

And no matter how much she tried to compose and pace herself; no matter what she tried to rename her sexual releases, no matter how she tried to think of it as "returning," Kyla Powers came

SBR Publication Presents......

Available now for Pre-Order

Order your copy today!

Author Commentary

I was a fresh federal inmate when I started writing Bankroll Squad 1. Initially I'd been inspired to write urban fiction after reading some of Triple Crown Publications' material. I think my stance was like… if these people can write a book, then I should be able to write one also… especially since I had all of that time on my hands.

Another part of me was doubtful though. I didn't know how long to make my books, so I had to count up the words of a novel I had recently read so that I would know where to stop at. I was doubtful because I felt like… a lot of these writers have been writing books or stories all of their lives, and that a newcomer like me would have to take many college courses in order to get on their levels. Despite my doubts, I started writing.

Midway through my story, a few of the inmates read my work and were amazed by it. They were literally sitting at my table as I wrote the book, literally awaiting me to finish another page so that they could grab it and pass it around the table. Those inmates inspired me to finish that book, and in turn; I attempted to inspire them to write them a book also. I was wondering why they were just sitting around when they could be doing something as fun as writing a book.

They heard me, but most of them didn't want to take advice from a guy as young as myself. I was 25 years old at the time, and most of the federal inmates who were reading my material were ranging from 35 and up.

I didn't know what the hell to write about when I first started writing the book… I only knew that I wanted the main character to drive a lime-green Lamborghini. I guess I wanted that so bad because that was the dream car that I wanted to get before I made it to prison. And my goal was accomplished… my character drives a Lambo!

Many people often ask me how to start their books or projects, and it's usually a hard question to answer… But now that I think about it, it's simple… To start your book, all you have to do is start with action, drama, sex, or all three. You have to catch the reader's attention because you have too much competition out here to fail. I started my career driving like a maniac- which was a sign of things to come.

When I first released Bankroll Squad, in 2010; I was in Louisiana's Oakdale federal prison, and I was miserable as hell. The book was my only bright spot in life, and I felt as if I could change my life if I could sell some books. If I couldn't sell any books, I didn't know what the hell I was going to do once I made it out of there.

I'd just read some articles that said there were a lot of self-published authors making money using Amazon's Kindle platform, so I wanted to try it out to see if I could make some money too. The first month Bankroll Squad went on sale, I only sold 7 damn copies and my revenue was $21.

How the hell was I going to make a living if I was only going to be making $21 a got damn month!?

So from that moment forth, I had it in my mind that I wasn't ever going to write another book again. My $21 a month pattern continued. I gained momentum one month and made like $33, but what the hell!? $33 was not enough money to inspire me to write a part 2 to Bankroll

Squad.

10 months after I put Bankroll Squad 1 on sale, I ran across an article on a self published author by the name of Amanda Hocking. The article said that Ms. Hocking had sold over a half million books in one month! I was immediately blown away! I read more into the article about her, and it said that many of her books were only $1.

I sat in the prison and thought about it… $1 wasn't a whole lot of money, but it damn sure beat out zero dollars, which I was currently getting! I wrote another book so that I could make it $1. The book was called "A Love Story," and it was an erotica…

Being caged up for almost 5 years had left me with some very deep sexual frustration, which I easily released onto the pages using an ink pen. I released that book at the price of $1, and it took straight off. After that, my checks went from $21 to $140 to $680--- and at this point I was inspired to write another Bankroll Squad book.

A few months before I was released, I wrote Bankroll Squad 2; and released it at $2.99. The profit from that month was $3,400; a check that was waiting on me when I came home from prison. My persistence with writing book after book built my check up to a point that allowed me to help others. It was an extreme difference from being in prison and getting $21 a month. I was then at a point to where all I had to do was work and I'd get $21,000 a month.

In the beginning I set out to change my life, and in the process I ended up changing lots of lives. I'm thankful for my journey, no matter how many obstacles I had to hit before arriving here. I'm thankful for each and every person who has inspired each and every character in the Bankroll Squad books.

I'm truly thankful for the women of TBRS (Team Bankroll Squad) who represent #TBRS in a major way and in a daily way. I decided to re-release all three of these books as one trilogy so that I could prepare people for the books that are about to be released... most notably "Bankroll Squad 4" which is set to be released on October 29th, 2013. If you haven't read "Lipstick Clique," and "The Power Family," make sure you check those out as well.

Our company, SBR Publications; is thriving. The SBR letters stand for Smart, bold, and rich. Originally it stood for smart, black, and rich; but when I realized that our supporters were multi-cultured, that name switched immediately.

I am David Weaver, the 29 year old CEO/Owner of SBR Publications, and this is the story about the beginning of my career. To stay in the loop on all the upcoming SBR Publications releases, pick up your phone and text: TBRS to 22828 and join our exclusive mailing list.

Sincerely yours, the 2013 AAMBC Author of the Year, David Weaver.

Follow me on Twitter: @bankrollsquad

And follow me on Instagram: bankrollsquad

CPSIA information can be obtained
at www.ICGtesting.com
Printed in the USA
LVOW10s1130160617
538384LV00009B/259/P

9 781489 502025